Blood Awakening
Woven in Blood – Book one

By
Ian Woodhead

Also by Ian Woodhead

Parasite
Shades of Green
Rags and Bones
The Mirrored Blade
Spores
Third Sight
Woven in Blood
Kingdoms of the Dead
Fungal Tide
The Bone Architect
Chemical Flowers (with Suzanne Reeves)

The Zombie Armageddon Series

The Unwashed Dead
Walking with Zombies
Infected Bodies
Dead Veil
Dead Reaping
Human Filth
Harvest of the Dead (with Christine Sutton)

Blood Awakening
Woven in Blood Book one
by
Ian Woodhead

This book is a work of fiction. Names, characters, places and incidents are products of the author's imagination. Any resemblance to actual events or locales or persons, living or dead, is entirely coincidental.

Second Edition

Please visit me here -
https://www.facebook.com/Ian.Woodhead.Author

Prologue

The light from the pale moon made the puddle of oil-coated water shimmer like liquid silver. Cade McCrae took a deep breath and felt his heartbeat increase when he detected the faint scent of her perfume beneath the multiple layers of industrial stench. She had turned up; The girl had actually made true on her promise to meet him here. Cade wandered between the rusted shelves, gazing from left to right, desperate to catch a glimpse of Katy Barnes through the gaps.

He slowed down his breathing, not wanting her to sense his presence, then frowned, still not convinced Katy hadn't brought along company in the shape of her older brother. Cade checked his watch. He had a few more minutes before he was due to meet her, just enough time to finish scouting the area.

Her scent now filled the air, overpowering the stink of ancient grease and oil. Cade caught sight of a cascade of primary colours blasting through the dull greys and browns. He dropped to the ground, keeping hold of the metal shelving—he had no wish to touch the floor and cover his fingers in the muck under his feet. He still expected to help the girl out of her clothes. The whole sexy ambience would fly through one of the many smashed windows if he covered her pretty clothes in black grease.

There she was. Katy had indeed arrived without an escort. He watched her look at her phone and sigh. Was she just checking the time or perhaps thinking of giving Cade a quick call? There were only a couple of minutes left before their appointed rendezvous time. Cade glanced towards the huge open hanger door to her right, assuring himself that there was nobody skulking outside. Even if her brother had decided to hide outside, Cade knew he'd still be able to lose him in this abandoned industrial labyrinth. He knew this area like the back of his hand.

"Are you there?" she hissed.

He saw no one about, and his instincts told him this really was the genuine article and the gorgeous blonde girl standing just a few metres from him really did want to see him.

The girl wrapped her arms around her chest and shivered.

"Come on, I'm not mucking about. You're supposed to be waiting for me!"

Despite his self-taught calming routine, Cade could not stop his heart from trying to beat through his ribs when he detected a tinge of annoyance and fear in her dulcet tones. He ran his tongue over his lips, tasting minty toothpaste, before he stood up.

"Over here."

The girl spun around, fist raised, lips trembling, and eyes as large as saucers as she screamed, "You bastard! Do you get off from creeping up on people?"

Cade stepped over a chunk of decaying machinery and walked over to her, keeping his eyes on her bright blue eyes, which were full of indignation and fury but still beautiful. He knew he'd never be able to stop looking into those delightful orbs, even if they were demanding an apology.

"Didn't you hear me approach? I was making enough noise to wake the dead."

He knew her game: Katy expected him to come over all meek, to not stop apologising, to let her walk all over him. Cade wasn't going to let that happen. She was the most desirable girl in college and could have her pick of any boy. Yet, Katy chose Cade? It didn't make sense to him, not at all, unless it was some bizarre tactic to get her own back for embarrassing her in front of the class this morning.

He checked his fingernails, making sure no stray piece of dirt had decided to take up residence since he'd last scrubbed them clean before leaving the house. He stared up at the black sky showing through the rafters high above their heads. "You know, I wasn't sure that you'd come." Cade ate up the last few steps and stopped directly in front of her, drinking in her delightful scent. He noticed the delicate touch of makeup and her gloss red lipstick. Was all this really for him? Or did Katy intend to meet another lad once she'd finished making him feel as worthless as something she had just stood on?

She placed her hands on his side. "You're shivering." Katy looked up into his eyes. "How can you be shivering when you're so hot?"

Cade jumped when she moved both her hands slowly down the front of his body and cupped his crotch.

"What do you mean?" he stammered, feeling her probing fingers caress his balls. Cade moaned when Katy began to pull his zip down.

"You know exactly what I mean," she replied. "You are going to be my little secret." Katy wrapped her fingers around his hardening shaft and groaned herself. "Oh my, I never expected that, Cade. You're more than a handful." The girl giggled, then unfastened his trousers, hooked her fingers under his boxers, and jerked them down to his ankles. "Oh yes. I'm going to take my time with you."

"What do you mean by that?" He felt the summer breeze on his bare flesh and watched the girl ease herself out of her blouse. The sight of that black lacy bra struggling to hold in her full breasts helped to take away a large portion of his deep suspicion, but enough of it remained for him to still believe this was a trick.

"I mean that we are not going to tell anyone about our meetings, silly." Katy returned her fingers to his now erect penis and pulled back the skin. "You do know that I have a boyfriend." She pulled him closer and drew the tip of his penis up her bare thighs. "We can stop right now if this bothers you, Cade." She ran her tongue over his lips. "I mean, we can just turn around and walk away. I won't be hurt, and we'll never speak of this again. What do you want to do?"

Katy rolled her forefinger over his tip and brought it up to her mouth. "It's your decision, Cade." She licked her finger clean and gazed down at his solid shaft. "Made up your mind yet?"

Cade nodded, then bent down and pulled up his boxers and trousers.

"You bastard!" she snapped. "What! Don't you like girls or something?"

He zipped up his trousers and grabbed her wrist. "I thought you said you wouldn't be hurt?" Cade saw a single tear roll down her cheek. He leaned over and kissed it off her warm flesh. "Katy, you misunderstand. I have made up my mind all right, and I want to take you somewhere that isn't so grimy." He scraped the sole of his boot on the lump of metal beside him, watching the black slime slip back down to the floor. "Unless you want your pretty clothes covered in this shit."

"But, but I thought …"

He brushed his lips against hers. He didn't really care if Katy considered him to be her rough bit on the side, as long as she was not taking him for a ride. He didn't believe that was the case, not anymore. There was no older brother waiting to kick the crap out of him and no vengeful boyfriend wanting to kill him. Cade ran his fingers down her spine, smiling when he felt her shiver. He intended to show this girl just what he could do with his equipment.

"Oh my," she gasped, pulling away from his lips. "You sure know how to kiss a girl. Where did you learn that?"

Cade took her hand, covering her long fingers with his own. "I'm very good with my tongue, Katy." He pointed towards a set of metal stairs leading up to the next level. "There's an office up there. It's dry, warm, and best of all, there's a clean mattress in the middle of the floor." Cade pulled the girl towards the stairs."

"You're kidding me?"

"No, I'm not kidding you, Katy. I used to play here when I was younger. I started coming back here a few months ago to get away from the shit going down with my family. Hell, I've even stayed the night a few times, going to sleep on that mattress after getting stoned or drunk." He wished he hadn't thought about his mum and dad. That last thing he needed right now was to have those two idiots in his head while he was about to bang this gorgeous girl.

"How the hell did you find this place? I didn't even know it existed until you told me about it." She stopped and wrapped her hands around his waist. "Wait, just how many girls have you brought here?"

"You are the first one," he answered. It was true; he had never told anyone about this place, not even his best mate, Damien Myers. He traced the edge of her bra with his forefinger, then pushed his hand inside to cup her breast. "Why me?" Cade asked, feeling his penis push against the fabric of his trousers and hearing her gasp when he caught her hard nipple between his fingers.

Katy pulled his hand out. "Oh my, Cade, are you really that naive? I have fancied you for years. Good God, half the girls in our class drool over you." She pushed her fingers through his long black hair. "You're kind, very hunky, and unlike the rest of the morons our age in Willmouth, you don't try to fit in. Admit it, Cade, you are unique."

She reached behind and unhooked her bra strap, pulling it off and holding the material with her blouse. Katy giggled when he reached for her breasts, slapped his hands away, then ran over to the stairs. "Enough chatter. I need to feel you inside me." She wrapped her fingers around the black metal railing, then looked over her shoulder. "Catch me if you can?" She winked. "Or stay there looking like a big dumb bear." She grinned and rushed up towards the open door at the top of the balcony.

Once at the top, Katy leaned over the balcony. "I've never been this wet, Cade!"

He raced up the stairs and dragged the girl towards the office, trying his best to keep his hands away from those wonderful breasts.

"What are you grinning at, sweetheart?"

"I still can't believe this is happening," he muttered to himself. Was this really happening? This girl had literally thrown herself into his embrace. Cade tried to imagine the look on Katy's face if she could have seen him two hours ago, locked in the bathroom, furiously masturbating. At the time he was still convinced this was all a wind up, but just in case it wasn't, Cade did not intend to disappoint the girl by exploding as soon as she touched him.

Katy squeezed his behind. "Believe it, my lover." She turned her head, chuckling at the sight of the mattress through the office window. "Oh, this is very cosy, Cade. Why am I not surprised that you have a secret den? Am I seriously the only person to see this? I mean, what about your buddy?"

"I'm not gay, you know."

"I didn't mean it like that. I know you two are best friends. Have you two never just hung out in here?"

"No, this is all mine."

She did have a point there. It had never crossed his mind to tell anyone about this place, not even Damien. She was right, they were close, more like brothers than best mates. Hell, they even shared a birthmark. They both had a sickle shaped brown mark on their forearms. Damien had told him that his mum had one on her arm too. Cade didn't really believe that though; his mate did have an annoying tendency to exaggerate on occasion.

Katy pulled him over to the mattress. "Lie down." She straddled his chest, grinning down at his beautiful face. "Take me now!"

Cade reached up and placed his hand on her full breasts, ready to pull them down to his mouth. He stopped and shivered, suddenly feeling as though he'd been pushed into a deep freezer. Cade pushed the girl off his body and sat up, yelping at the sight of a girl's face staring back at him from outside the office.

"What the hell are you looking at?" Katy shouted. She spun around, scooped up her blouse, dropped it over Cade's hips, and then crossing her arms over her breasts. "Go on, get out of here!" She glared at Cade. "I thought you said nobody came here!"

He climbed off the mattress and pulled his up his trousers. "Nobody ever does come here," he said, zipping himself up. Cade ran over to the door and looked out but saw no sign of the girl.

"That's the first time I've seen anyone in here." Cade hurried over to the balcony and looked down at the ground floor. *Where did she come from?* He ran back over to the office, feeling annoyed and disappointed to see Katy had dressed herself.

"You might as well take me home," she muttered. "I'm never going to live this down. That kid will tell everyone. I can't believe that I was dumb enough to meet you here." She collapsed onto the mattress. "That's it, my life is over. Everyone is going to find out now."

Cade looked down at this girl, trying to come to grips with his tremulous emotions. He felt like those sheets of toilet paper that he had used to wipe himself clean after his bathroom session. In Katy's eyes, he really had been nothing but a bit on the side. Cade felt like a complete fool.

"Where are you going?" Katy cried as he spun around and marched out of the office.

He ignored her shouting and walked along the gantry, trying to see where the little girl had gone. He put aside Katy's shallow emotions and concentrated on the fact that this place was no longer his sanctuary. If that little girl knew about this place, who else knew? Cade had to find out. He'd no longer feel safe until then.

"Wait for me!"

He reluctantly slowed down and turned around, waiting until Katy was by his side before setting off again.

"I'm sorry," she whispered, sobbing. "I didn't mean it to sound like that." She pushed her fingers into his hand. "Cade, I was as randy as hell." She squeezed his hand. "I'm still randy, Cade. Look, let's go back. I still want you."

He shook his head. "You don't understand. I've been coming here for fifteen years. In all that time, I've never seen evidence of a single person setting foot in here. I've even laid traps for when I wasn't around."

Cade pulled the girl into his embrace. "I need to find out who she is." He gazed into her eyes; he saw disappointment in them and nothing else. It then hit him that the girl was only using him as a vibrator replacement. He was only useful as long as he performed. Cade released her, went to the end of the gantry, and looked down towards the front entrance. Was she still in here? Crouched behind one of the many rusted relics, covering the concrete floor, silently watching them like he did with Katy?

"Come on, the brat's obviously gone. She had probably just lost her doggy or something." Katy spun him around. "Look, if she does blab, I want to at least make sure that it's something worth losing my social position over."

"You're not helping my confidence here, Katy."

She giggled. "Stop being so silly, I don't mean it like it's a bad thing. My life is really complicated. There are things that I'm not supposed to do. Letting some long-haired hunk fuck my brains out is probably right at the top of the list."

Katy wrapped her arms tight around his neck. "Come on, Cade, I do need you. Don't leave me like this. You have to sort me out as well." She tried to pull him back over to the office. "Cade, are you even listening to me?"

Cade shrugged her hands off his arm and spun around. Katy just didn't understand his anxiety. He wasn't too sure that he understood it either. These deserted buildings were obviously owned by somebody, they didn't belong to him, and yet, Cade felt that this was his territory, his own personal province.

"What's gotten into you?"

Cade ignored her; she didn't interest him anymore. All his desire for Katy had vanished. The urge to find that little girl overwhelmed every other emotion. He hurried back towards the gantry, trying to list in his head all the obvious hiding places in this one factory. There were loads of good spots to remain unseen, but that didn't faze Cade. He had all day.

"I mean it, Cade," she cried. "If you don't come back right now, I'm leaving."

He shrugged. So be it.

Right now, he no longer felt comfortable in this building. Simply the thought of two strangers trespassing on what he considered to be his personal space made him break out into a sweat. "I shouldn't have brought Katy here," he muttered, jumping down the last few steps. He would check the floor first. Cade didn't really think the little girl would dare venture down into the network of tunnels beneath their feet. He hoped not anyway. Even after fifteen years, Cade still got lost down there. He was sure he still hadn't mapped that area fully.

It didn't take long to check through the more obvious hiding places, but there were still another three buildings to search through. Cade wouldn't be happy until he found out where she had gone.

Katy hadn't gone through with her threat to leave him. She was still on the gantry, leaning over the handrail, watching him search. Could she have been right about her looking for a dog? No, of course not. Who in their right mind would allow a pre-teen kid take their dog out for a walk in the middle of the night?

The sound of a door slamming shut reached his ears. It came from below. Cade's heartbeat sped up, he felt an ice-cold finger run up his spine, and for the first time in fifteen years, Cade wanted to leave this place and never come back. His body and mind screamed at him to follow his instincts.

"Cade?"

He turned to see Katy slowly make her way down the steps, her gaze fixed on the open doorway at the other end of the factory floor. She had heard the noise as well.

Katy hooked her arm into his. "Where does that door lead to, Cade?"

He looked into her eyes, then dropped his gaze to the floor. "There's a labyrinth of tunnels under our feet." He pulled her towards the opening.

"Wait, we can't leave her down there!"

He stopped and looked over at the doorway, allowing her words to sink in. Of course, he couldn't leave some innocent girl down there. What was he playing at? Cade didn't understand what came over him. *This is just stupid. What is the matter with me?* He nodded and pulled out his mobile phone."

"Are you ringing for the police?"

"No," he replied, selecting the flashlight icon from the menu. "I'm going to get the silly girl out of there." He turned on the light and played the beam along the floor. "Are you still thinking of going, Katy?"

Katy didn't reply to his question, so he took the silence as acknowledgement that the girl wasn't going to leave him after all and pulled her across the dusty floor toward the doorway.

The stone steps beyond the wooden doorway lead down into inky blackness. Cade squinted into the darkness beyond and found himself shivering. Somebody else had been here all right. He had no idea how he knew this. It just seemed right.

He shone the torch along the surface of the first few steps, and the light picked out a few discarded sweet and crisp wrappers.

Cade was right. There was the evidence. It appeared he had acquired a lodger. Was she a runaway? That made sense, although why anybody would wish to runaway to this shitty town was beyond him. There had been a few kids leaving Welbourgh to seek a future in the larger cities, but to his knowledge, nobody had come here before.

He made his way slowly down the stairs, feeling his anxiety lessen the further he walked. The sense of belonging strengthened; in fact, Cade felt as though he never wanted to leave this place.

"What are you doing, Cade?" hissed Katy. "What's wrong with your arm?"

He saw that he'd been scratching the area around his birthmark. "That's weird," he muttered. Cade bent down, picked up one of the crisp packet wrappers, and held the plastic under his nose. He could still smell the cheese flavouring. That kid must have dropped this. How long had she been living down here? More importantly, why hadn't he realised that someone else was using his private retreat as a dosshouse?

He ventured further along the stone corridor, feeling the cold damp air settle in his lungs. He needed to get the girl out of here. Cade then stopped, looking in disbelief at a missing section of wall.

"What's wrong?" Katy asked.

Cade shone the light along the wall, shaking his head. "That wasn't there the last time I came down here." The harsh white light clearly made out where the wall had swung back to reveal another corridor. He took one more step and ran his hand along the damp wall, allowing the tips of his fingers to explore the gaps in the stonework.

"Oh my god, Cade, just look at all that stuff!"

He cast his eyes across the accumulated piles of decaying weaponry stacked up against both walls. *This stuff must have been here for generations,* he thought. He could make out the remains of large curved swords, numerous axe heads, and a couple of large metal balls covered in spikes. He turned around and examined the corridor walls before turning back to look at this uncovered section.

"It looks like the remains of an ancient castle." Cade ventured inside, noting that another smell replaced the faint odour of mildew. It reminded him of meat close to turning. He walked between the two piles of decaying metal and headed towards a large metal door set into the stones a few metres from them.

"Look at that," Katy whispered. She bent down and picked up another sweet wrapper. "Let's go back. I have a bad feeling about this, Cade."

He mentally sighed in pleasure, gripping her hand tight and feeling her trepidation. Cade had no idea how he was doing it, but he could actually taste Katy's fear. The sweet emotion seemed to flow from every pore of her body. He turned around and held her at arm's length. What an incredible sight. He could even see it: a thin cloud of dark green mist surrounded the girl, obscuring her features. The stuff reacted when he opened his mouth by rushing towards him. Cade groaned in pleasure as it enveloped his head, then entered his waiting mouth.

"What are you doing?"

He blinked, seeing her staring at him, her eyes displaying confusion and fear. There was no mist around the girl, and he felt no different. He blinked again, not sure at all what had just happened to him. Cade looked behind them, almost expecting to see a large cylinder pissing out gas.

"I'm fine. I just came over all funny, that's all." He stopped in front of the door, placed his hand against the metal, and wondered if he dared open it. That decision was taken out of his hands when the door slowly opened of its own accord.

Katy pulled him through the door. "Come on, don't dawdle," she said. "I want to find this kid." She stopped and took a deep breath. "God, I don't half feel weird."

Cade, didn't answer her. His emotions had not been right ever since they had walked through that doorway. That vague feeling of belonging here had increased tenfold, along with the resentment of knowing that he wasn't the first one down here. This should have been his discovery; it wasn't fair that he should find this place by accident.

"Are you okay?" she whispered. "You're shivering." Katy squeezed his hand tight. "Look at that!"

Just above their heads, carved into the smooth grey rock, were the detailed etchings of two designs. The one on the left was unfamiliar, but Cade recognised the design on the right. He had been wearing the exact pattern on his arm since birth. Cade stood under the etchings, listening to his heart beating. It was so loud. His eyes dropped to his feet, and he noticed the patterns were duplicated on the floor as well.

"Someone's coming," whispered Katy. She pulled him over to the far wall and ducked behind a stone outcropping.

Cade bobbed down next to her, his mind in turmoil. None of this made any sense to him, but he couldn't shift the feeling that this hidden chamber had been waiting for him for over a decade, had been what convinced him to keep coming here.

He caught his breath at the sight of a shadow climbing the wall. The elusive girl had finally made an appearance. He couldn't understand why he felt the sudden urge to jump out of their hiding place, run over to her, and carry the little bitch away from this chamber before she had chance to …

Cade frowned, that last piece of information refused to make an appearance. He had no idea what the little girl intended to do.

Katy's foot slipped, causing a pile of tiny stones to tumble down the slope. Katy gasped, but the girl didn't even register the noise. She just crouched down, traced her fingers along one of the patterns, and let out a loud sigh. It was a sad, mournful sound, almost heart wrenching. She then shrugged off her tattered green dress and sat down cross-legged on the floor.

None of this made any sense to Cade. He gazed in confusion at this pretty little girl wearing only panties, white socks, and shoes, slowly rocking back and forth. He then saw something that made him start; the girl had a large birthmark on her left shoulder. It wasn't like his though, the pattern was different.

"Oh no," Cade whispered. He realised it matched the pattern on the floor and above the girl. He shook off Katy and stood up, suddenly aware of where they were and what this place was. Those patterns gouged into the stone floor all led to the lip of that well. They were there for only one reason.

Then he saw a flash of metal in her hands. The girl held one of those ancient weapons. Cade screamed out, but the girl didn't even flinch. She lifted the blade above her head and savagely slammed it down, burying the blade deep into her chest.

His limbs unfroze, and he found his body lunging forward of its own accord.

The girl see-sawed the knife down her chest, opening herself up, and the two sections split apart like a huge set of bloodied lips. The girl's robotic motions stopped. She dropped to her knees and slumped forward, her forehead cracking against the lip of the hole before she fell into the dark abyss.

Cade stopped by the hole, unable to take his eyes off the sight of her thick blood flowing along deep gullies cut into the stone and dripping into the hole.

"Why the hell did she go do that?" Katy ran over to the rock, leaned over, and emptied her stomach. "Oh God," she blurted. "We have to get out of here, right now." She stumbled over to the entrance, looking behind her and seeing he had not budged an inch. "Cade!"

"That should have been me," he murmured, feeling his birthmark itching. It felt alive, biting into his skin, like a thousand fleas all needing to drink from that one area. Somewhere in the distance, at what sounded like a thousand miles away, he could hear the other girl screaming his name. She didn't matter; this had nothing to do with her. He crouched down and traced his finger along one of the furrows, feeling the remainder of the girl's blood coat his flesh. It wasn't an unpleasant sensation. In fact, the action woke up a memory that he knew wasn't his.

Cade closed his eyes and felt himself fall backwards.

***

The sound of the others screaming through the clan's defenses chilled his already cold blood. He didn't have long to finish the preparations. The Swarmer clan was going to rip him to pieces and feast on his flesh. He already knew of his fate, he would be their final meal, no matter what happened next. He could not fail his own masters though. The ceremony simply had to be completed.

The girl in the corner had stopped her quiet sobbing. Had she, like him, resigned herself to her fate? He shrugged, it mattered not. Her life was unimportant. The Swarmers had reached the final barricade. Even from down here, he could hear their screams of frustration at finding their way to salvation blocked. Despite his master's hastily built fortifications, it would not take them long to break through. There were hundreds of those evil things now; they would make short work of the wooden barriers.

As he summoned the shivering girl over to the well, he could hear the guards' low muttering; they were getting ready for the final assault. Like the barrier before them, their weapons would only stop the Swarmers for a few minutes, just enough time for him to complete the task. The girl jumped at the sound of the wood splintering.

"It is none of your concern," he hissed, forcing the naked girl into the kneeling position. "Put your head down, you stupid child! Hurry up, they're nearly here."

He held his dagger up, seeing his emblem stamped into the blade—they all carried the mark of the clan. It was in their blood to serve their masters from birth to death. He gazed down at the trembling girl, counted to three, and hoped her body would contain enough blood to keep his masters alive until their next awakening.

He dropped to his knees, listening to the others giving their lives to stop the Swarmers from entering the temple before he had completed his task. Soon it would be his turn. He slammed the blade down, feeling the razor-sharp metal bite into the girl's flesh and pierce her heart through her ribs. For the girl, death was quick and painless. He looked into the well, gazing down at the five undead pale faces looking up at him, their long, yellowed fangs gnashing together, waiting for him to throw the girl in. He glanced towards the entrance, sensing the final guard fighting like a wild bear protecting her cubs, then pushed the body down, watching it tumble, the long, serrated knives jutting out from the stone slicing through her flesh.

He sighed and stood up. His task was now complete. The other clan would no doubt perform the same ceremony, but he now knew that they were the first. No matter what happened. Their clan would survive the big sleep.

***

Cade snapped his eyes open, feeling somebody tug at his shoulder. He sat up with the vision still vivid in his memory.

He had failed his master. Because of his lack of vision, the enemy, the Swarmer clan, had received their sacrifice first. Those bastards would now awaken and destroy them all. Cade pushed the girl away and crawled over to the hole. Maybe he wasn't too late. Sure, the Swarmers would awaken, but they'd be slow, weak, and defenseless. If his master awakened at the same time, both clans would stand a chance of surviving.

The jagged blades were still there, long strings of wet flesh dripping from the metal shards. All he needed to do was to cut himself and then drop down. He scooped up the ancient weapon and sliced the blade down his lower arm.

"What the hell are you doing?"

Cade shook his head, trying to clear that hurtful voice ringing in his mind. He had no time for imaginary voices. He had to finish this before it was too late. Cade watched his own blood drip into the well, then stepped up to the edge.

He cried out in agony and shock when something heavy slammed into his legs. He stumbled and fell back, landing on the girl's body.

"What the fuck has got into you, Cade?"

The voice was not imaginary. The mention of his name cleared his vision, and a young woman's face swam into view. She looked so familiar, but he couldn't yet place her. Cade's heart skipped a beat when a mournful noise rose from deep beneath the well.

"They are coming!" He sobbed. "I didn't stop them." Cade then looked deep into the girl's eyes. His mind, like his vision, began to clear. "We are so fucked." Cade hissed in pain, looking at the gash in his arm. "He wanted me down there." He shuddered at the thought of those blades biting into his screaming body before those things down there tore him into confetti-sized, bloodied meat.

The noise from the well grew louder as more of them awoke.

"I don't know what's happening!"

He looked at the few spots of blood left from the girl. Just how far had she travelled to get here, and how had she been able to find a way into this chamber so easily? Was the other clan that strong? He realised he was actually jealous of her. "Fuck me," he muttered. "I really am going insane." He grabbed Katy's wrist and pulled her out of the chamber. "Come on," he hissed, "if we don't move now, we'll never get out of here."

Chapter One

Darlene Myers clamped her hand tight against her lips, trying not to burst out laughing. Her son had kept that one quiet. She approached his unmade bed, unable to take her eyes from Damian's newest poster. Clad in a skin-tight black leather outfit, complete with a random collection of satanic trinkets hanging from her wrists and neck, the long-haired, blonde young woman cut an impressive figure. She wielded her long handled, double-edged axe with dexterity and expertise, if the pile of decapitated mythical animals lying around her feet was anything to go by. The only detriment to the whole panorama was the female's impossibly huge breasts.

Even with good support, she would have trouble walking, never mind fighting. Darlene leaned forward and attempted to read the band logo splattered across the woman's legs in a mixture of black and red ink. It looked like House of the Unholy, but she wasn't willing to put money on her guess.

If it was House of the Unholy, the band had some serious misconceptions about how sexy women were supposed to look. Then again, what did she know? Darlene was only a mother, and according to her seventeen-year-old son, she was way past it.

She giggled. "If only you really knew, Damian." Darlene turned, walked over to Damien's dressing table, and gazed into the long mirror, pleased at the trim thirty-six-year-old woman smiling back at her. Darlene shrugged off her white t-shirt and pushed her hands up under her black bra. "Give me an axe, and I'd show you how well a proper woman could handle herself," she said giggling, imagining the look on her son's face if he happened to walk in right now. Darlene picked her t-shirt up off the carpet and quickly dressed herself, looking at his poster one more time.

Her mood darkened ever so slightly at the thought of how her husband, Geoff, would react to the sight of what Damien had blu-tacked above his bedpost. He would not find the image so amusing, which was ironic considering he was just like Damien when she first met him all those years ago.

Okay, so all of this modern extreme metal horrified Geoff, but when he'd been Damien's age, his taste in music wasn't exactly mainstream. Hell, her husband-to-be even sported hair as long as Damien's and a rather cute beard. Darlene so missed that gorgeous mane. When did he start to look and act so old?

"More to the point, sweetheart, how come you never noticed it?" She shook her head, vowing, one more time, never to grow old gracefully.

Why wasn't her husband comfortable with Damian's musical taste? Geoff preached to her on more than one occasion that he believed anyone listening to metal just had to have something wrong with them. Geoff said the only reason he had tolerated Damian's current passion was because he thought it was just another one of Damian's silly phases. According to him, Damien went through a lot of silly phases. She didn't find it all that surprising that he never used those remarks on their daughter, Elsie. In Geoff's eyes, Damien's twin sister couldn't put a foot wrong and butter wouldn't melt in her mouth. Then again, what did he know? The man hardly ever saw his kids nowadays. Even when he was at home, he was too involved with work to pay attention to anyone else.

Darlene pulled her son's quilt cover up to his pillow, making note that she ought to get this lot in the wash at the weekend. She walked over to the door, taking one last glance at Damian's walls. Over the last few months, he'd covered three walls with posters depicting scenes similar to the one she'd giggled at. Geoff would not find it funny, that much she did know.

"He'd go mental." Darlene nodded to herself. Oh yeah, he really would go spare if he saw that poster all right. Considering she was trying to keep the equilibrium, it might be a better idea to have a quiet word with Damian. He'd understand.

"He'd better," she muttered. That last thing she needed right now was for anything to upset the apple cart. Darlene turned off the light and closed the door, wondering for the tenth time today why she didn't have the guts to admit that her marriage was dead.

"Honey, are you up there?"

"No, I'm stood in the kitchen, you silly man," she whispered. Darlene rushed along the landing and saw Geoff at the bottom of the stairs swapping his car keys from hand to hand. "Is it that time already?" she asked, smiling down into his distracted face. Even from up here, she saw his mind was elsewhere. It certainly wasn't where it should be, staring up at his beautiful wife wearing a very tight t-shirt and sexy black shorts. Darlene was proud of her toned legs. By the looks of it, though, she was the only one.

He nodded. "Yeah, it's time for me to get the hell out of Dodge."

At thirty-eight, her husband retained the looks that Darlene had fallen for eighteen years ago. Granted, a few grey hairs had made an unwanted appearance on that thick head of short brown hair, and more than a few pub lunches and lack of any serious exercise had given Geoff a noticeable paunch, but he was still a gorgeous hunk. At six foot five, he towered over Darlene by a full foot.

"Come on then," he said, impatiently tapping his watch with his right forefinger. "Where is my kiss? I don't want to be late."

Darlene inwardly sighed and walked down the steps, still keeping the smile fixed upon her face. "Of course not, sweetheart, we wouldn't want that, now would we?" Did the bitterness show in her voice? Darlene threw her arms around Geoff's neck and brushed her lips on his. "Take me upstairs, Geoff," she said. "I need you. I need you right now." She dragged her hand down his spine and squeezed his arse. "Take me upstairs, sweetheart. I need to feel you inside me. Come on, I want you to fuck me raw."

He untangled her arms and gently pushed her away. "Darlene, for crying out loud. Don't do this to me, my little flower pot. You know I've got a presentation to prepare for tonight."

She closed her eyes and nodded, desperately trying not to allow his rejection to get to her. This was so unfair. Did she honestly expect him to choose between work and his wife?

"I'm sorry," she whispered. Darlene gave the man the accustomed kiss on his cheek before opening the door for him. "You try to have a good time at work, Geoff."

He returned the kiss then gave Darlene an unexpected hug. "If I have enough energy left when I finish work, I'll see if I can do something about your urges."

Darlene kissed him back and grinned, wanting to punch the bastard in the nuts. He made it sound like she had something wrong with her, that wanting sex was somehow dirty. "That's great. I'll be waiting for you, my little peanut."

Geoff slowly walked up the garden path, stopping before he reached the gate to wave to Darlene one last time. She looked into the starlit sky trying to work out just when everything in her life turned to complete shit. Darlene gave him the customary wave and watched him climb into their family car.

"It's time for fun now, girl," she said, watching him turn the car, reverse, and drive out of the cul-de-sac. "You ought to be grinning, feeling all sexy, your heart all aflutter." She felt none of that. All Darlene wanted to do now was go to bed and stay there for the next fifty years.

As she whispered goodbye to the car's headlights, the door to number twenty-eight opened. Darlene watched as Paul Spencer made his way through his own garden and crossed the road, heading towards her house.

Her affair with the young man who lived across from her was getting as tired as her marriage to Geoff. The danger of getting caught had worn off months ago. She tried to compete with Paul's eager grin and found that she really couldn't be bothered.

"He's definitely not coming back tonight, is he?"

Darlene shook her head, even their conversations followed the same nightly pattern. *Yes, Paul. He's coming back tonight, and when he finds you in our marital bed, he's going to smash a hammer into your face.* "No, Paul, you have me until the morning."

Paul slyly looked both ways before placing his warm hands on her side and sliding them over her t-shirt to her breasts. "That's good, 'cos I want to have you." He groaned and rubbed his thumbs across her nipples.

She pulled him into the house and kicked the door shut. "Not out in the street!" she snapped, although she had to admit to herself the thought of some nosy neighbour peering through their window and catching this young man caressing her tits did turn her on. "I'm not wearing any knickers, Paul." Darlene saw his hand automatically heading towards her thigh and slapped it away. "No, not yet, not here. You know the bloody rules." She ran up the stairs, stopped in front of her son's bedroom, and turned to watch this eager young stallion race after her.

"You want to go play in there, Darlene? But, I thought you said that room was forbidden."

"It was," she whispered, pushing open the door. "But I need a change of scenery." She wrapped her arms around his strong body and walked him into the previously prohibited area of the house. "Tonight has got to be different, Paul."

The boy briskly nodded and chuckled, "Oh yes. I can do that, my darling. You bet I can do that."

Darlene fell back onto her son's bed, trying not to sigh. She looked up at the poster. Bloody hell, the lad was only a few years older that Damian. She hadn't stepped foot into Paul's house, but she still thought his bedroom was probably just like this one.

She'd just have to tell him tonight that the fun would have to end. It wasn't even fun anymore. Despite her gentle teaching,

Paul still couldn't satisfy her needs. She received better and more rewarding climaxes from her hidden collection of secret toys. The boy's equipment was definitely impressive, but he lacked the skills to use it correctly. She closed her eyes. She'd give him this one chance tonight to prove her wrong. She sighed, knowing for a fact that the poor boy wouldn't have a clue on how to try something different. Within a few seconds, the big oaf would be all over her, fumbling around, trying to rip off her clothes as quickly as he could whilst telling Darlene just how lucky he was.

"Undress!" Paul commanded.

Darlene snapped open her eyes and stared at the imposing looking young man glaring back down at her. Now, she was seriously confused. Where did her shaky, nervous man bugger off to? Gone were those eager-to-please puppy dog eyes. Paul's trembles had vanished. He stood there as if carved from marble. Darlene didn't know who this man was, not that she was complaining. Bloody hell, this was exciting.

"Sit up, Darlene," he said. "Start to undress. Don't make me tell you again."

She did as the man ordered, trying her best to suppress a smirk. "Of course, Paul," she replied, putting a slight quiver into her voice. If he could put on such a magnificent performance, then so would she. This was so unreal; Darlene couldn't stop trembling.

She threw her top to the floor, daring to not tear her gaze away from Paul's icy-blue eyes. Darlene reached behind her back and undid her bra strap, expecting him to jump on her at any moment. He didn't move a muscle. She saw no excitement, no desire; there was nothing in his stare. It was like looking into a pair of doll's eyes.

Her lacy bra landed on top of her blouse. Oh god, she hoped he wouldn't slip out of character. This was such a fucking turn on.

Paul treated her to a quick smile before he slowly slid his index finger into his mouth. She pushed her thighs together and clenched every muscle in her legs in a vain attempt to stop the shaking. He dropped to his knees, pulled his finger out of his mouth, and examined it before slowly drawing it down her cleavage. Darlene let out a guttural moan, reached up, and wrapped her fingers around Paul's wrist, wanting, needing him to grab and massage her breasts.

Paul ripped her hand off his wrist. "Did I say you could do that?" He placed his hand on her knees and pushed them apart. "Keep still!"

She nodded, biting her lip. For the first time, Darlene wasn't completely certain she liked this game anymore. The realisation that this man currently pulling her body towards his hips could do anything to her and there was very little she could do to stop him took up residence in her head and refused to leave.

Paul placed his hands around her neck and forced her forwards.

She yelped.

"Come here, you little bitch," he snarled. "You've upset me, and now I think it's time for you to learn your place."

Darlene went cold inside. The game was getting out of hand. Something was seriously fucking wrong with this picture. Paul shouldn't be acting like this. What the fuck was going on?"

He scraped his stubbled chin against her ear. "Is this too much? I'm not overdoing this am I? I've never done this sort of thing before." He glided his hand up her thigh. "I can be more gentle, Darlene." Paul brushed his fingers against her clitoris and pushed two deep inside her. "Do you want me to be gentler, Darlene?"

She cried out and thrust her hips forward, grabbing the top of his jogging pants and yanking them down. She wrapped her legs around Paul's thighs. "I want you to remove your fingers, Paul, and fuck me." She gasped. This was just incredible. He was taking way too long to comply.

Darlene snapped open her eyes. "Honey, what's wrong?"

He jerked his head towards the open door. "I'm sorry," he replied, trembling. "I thought I heard something!" Paul jumped back, almost tripping up over his trousers.

Darlene huffed in frustration. "Yeah, my fucking passion flying out of the window."

"I'm serious, Darlene. I think there's somebody else in the house."

She stood up and marched over to the open door, glaring at Paul. He hadn't moved one inch, and it didn't please her to notice that the trembling boy had returned with a vengeance. Fucking hell, and to think, even if it was for a moment, she'd actually been scared of this big oaf.

Darlene gazed along the hallway. There was nobody there, and the only sound she heard was Paul's panting.

He sounded like a hot mongrel dog.

She placed both hands on her hips. "Well?"

Paul shook his head, "I did hear something, Darlene. Please believe me. I swear down, I did."

Did he really just say that? God, Paul sounded like her son just then. "Well, go and look. You're the big hard man, Paul."

Darlene wanted to grab hold of the boy's throat and throttle him for making her feel like a mother again. Paul was terrified. She honestly thought he was about to start weeping.

"It's not my house, Darlene. What if it's your husband, or your two kids?"

She turned away from him, took a deep breath, and held it while counting to five. Paul wasn't the only one in the room who was now on the verge of crying.

"I'm sorry," he whispered, placing his hands on her shoulders. "I'll go down to check, if you like, darling. I'm so sorry. I didn't mean it to come out like that. It's probably nothing anyway. I mean, aren't Damien and Elsie staying over at Jenny's house for the weekend?"

Darlene didn't bother to reply. Paul already knew he wouldn't be stood here in her son's bedroom if they were due back.

"Look, Paul," she said, not turning around. "I want you to …"

"You want me to go?"

She almost nodded. His slip back into his old self had ruined everything. It would be better if he did go home. All Darlene needed to do right now was to finish herself off and get wasted on red wine.

"Darlene, I'm talking to you," he snarled. "Don't you dare fucking ignore me, you whore."

She jumped, feeling the beginnings of a smile appearing on her lips. Perhaps this evening still had some promise. "Get those clothes off, Paul," she whispered. "Then climb into bed and wait for me." Darlene picked up her son's red dressing gown, wrapped it around her body, and hurried over to the bedroom door. "I'll bring us back a bottle of wine," she said, turning her head. "We'll drink it together, after we have both satisfied each other. You are old enough to drink?" She giggled and dodged the thrown pillow.

"Don't keep me waiting!" he shouted after her.

Like that was going to happen. She wanted to forget all about checking out the house for Paul's imaginary noises, go back in there, and dive onto his body. Darlene reached the top of the stairs, turned around, and sighed. He wouldn't be able to relax if she did that though.

Darlene placed her hand upon the banister and made her way down. "Just how confused are you?" she whispered. Experiencing Paul dominating her had seriously turned her on. She grew wet just thinking about what other surprises that boy had for her. Where did that hidden desire come from? How the hell did Paul know what buttons to press?

She reached the bottom of the stairs and checked the front door. It was locked, just like she had left it. Why was she even doing this, for crying out loud? She should just run back up those stairs, tell him there's nobody here, and get that big boy to fuck her brains out.

"He'd want to know why I didn't bring the bloody wine." She might as well check the other rooms while she was here. Besides, she still needed to get wasted, but not before that virile young man had finished abusing her.

Darlene wandered into the living room, running her fingers along the spines of her husband's many books. She found it a little strange that Geoff had never suggested any bedroom role-play. Darlene stopped and pulled a book out at random. The cover showed a large-breasted blonde girl dressed in tight leather and standing over a semi-naked muscular young man. "And I wonder where Damian gets his odd ideas about women from." Was it too much of a coincidence that the man on the cover bore a slight resemblance to Paul? Darlene threw the book on the sofa and headed towards the kitchen. She needed wine, and she needed that boy to climb back inside her. "Perhaps I ought to buy a whip?"

"You have several already, my princess."

Darlene's shriek stuck in her throat at the sight of the huge dark-haired man leaning against the refrigerator. No matter how hard she tried, Darlene could not find the will to tear her eyes from his deep, hypnotic gaze.

"I thought I'd truly lost you, that those filthy fucking animals had found you first." The man held out his hand and blinked.

The movement was just enough to break her paralysis. She turned around, trying to remember where she'd dropped her mobile phone. *Oh Jesus, what am I going to do now?*

"Don't make me tell you again."

She spun around. "Paul?"

The man shook his head, his arm was still outstretched. "No, my princess. It was me on both occasions. The soft human beast currently lying on your son's bed had no idea I was inside him. Then again, how could he?"

"Who are you?" Darlene then saw the bottle of wine he held in his other hand. "How did you know I wanted that?" Her initial terror passed, leaving behind only confusion and curiosity.

"Come here, my princess. Allow me to embrace you, and I promise that I will tell you everything."

Despite her trepidation, she crossed the few tiles between them and placed her hand into his. The man yawned, revealing his oversized canine teeth. Darlene panicked and desperately tried to break from his grasp as he leaned closer to her neck.

"Don't fret," he said. He wrapped his other arm around her trembling body and pulled Darlene tight against him. "I'd never hurt you, my princess. I love and adore you. I always have, and I always will."

"But I don't even know who you are!" she wailed.

He tilted her head up and sighed. "I hid you amongst the beasts many years ago, my princess. I am sorry, but there was no other way." He leaned forward and gently kissed her on the lips.

Darlene closed her eyes, feeling her passion rise when his other hand released hers, slipped under her dressing gown, and cupped her breast. A raging fire detonated between her legs when he ran his other hand up her smooth thigh.

He drew away and wiped his bloodied lips.

"Don't stop!" she cried. "Oh my, please do that again!"

He cast his gaze at her ankles and traced her smooth form up to her soft thighs. "Do you not think I desire this as well, my beautiful wife? We will, that I promise, but not just yet."

She leaned back against the counter and gripped the edge, waiting until her jellied legs were strong enough to take her weight. "Wait," she muttered, running her tongue along her lips and tasting blood. "Did you just bite me?"

The man pushed his own tongue out and licked his thin lips. He gave her the wine bottle. "Yes, I did bite you, but it was just a nip, my princess. Go take your bottle up to the beast. By the time you reach the bed, you will remember who you really are. You will remember I am your real husband, and you will remember what we do to those human beasts."

She found her eyes closing. After what seemed like hours, Darlene was able to open them. There was no sign of the handsome stranger. Darlene gazed at the wine bottle in her hands. Had she imagined him? She ran her tongue across her lips and tasted blood. No, he'd been here all right.

The sweet taste of her blood awakened a memory hidden from her for many years.

***

She stood in the middle of a blood-drenched field, surrounded by churned mud and scattered pieces of human flesh. The stench of decay lay heavy in the air. This was not a fresh battle. The smell invaded her nostrils, yet did not sicken her. She embraced the aroma, breathing it in like a fine wine.

Darlene opened her eyes and found that she'd already climbed halfway up the stairs, the bottle held tight against her breasts. Paul stood at the top of the steps, gazing down with concern and worry etched into his young face.

"You've been ages, my darling."

"So troubled that you almost came down to make sure that I was okay?" Darlene slowly licked her lips, disappointed not to taste any more of her blood. Her tongue did find something of interest as it explored her mouth: Darlene's own canines had grown, ever so slightly.

"I was just about to check on you," he replied.

Just seven steps stood between her and the beast. The beast? It felt so natural to think of Paul as food. The memory of that battlefield rushed back into her mind. She watched herself stride over the many dismembered corpses, towards her husband, towards Amulius.

Her beautiful husband stood a few feet away from her, holding a long-handled, curved sword covered in congealed blood. "It's not here, Freya. The bastards have lied to us." He spun around. "We need to move quickly, my princess. The Swarmers and their foul constructs are closing in. They'll be here any moment."

In the distance, she saw the vast cloud of approaching enemy vampires. The Swarmers had indeed brought their flesh dragons. Freya felt her weak human heart race at the sight of the monstrous winged amalgamations: huge, almost unstoppable warriors, created out of vampirised flesh.

Her husband swept her into his embrace. "We will meet again, my princess," he growled, exposing his large teeth.

"You told me that I would be spared, Amulius. That you wouldn't change me until the war was over."

He nodded. "And I will keep my promise." He looked over her shoulder. "The Swarmers have changed the balance. They have accessed the dark arts forbidden to every clan. For the Deathgazer clan to survive, we must do the same. It could be decades before we see the outcome. By then you will be an old woman." He bent forward.

Freya felt his teeth pierce her flesh, and then she felt no more.

***

She opened her eyes and found she now stood at the top of the stairs. Paul's arms were resting on her shoulders.

"Darlene? God, what's wrong with you?"

She smiled, enjoying watching his face change to terror when he saw the size of her teeth. The bottle fell from her hands and rolled down the stairs. "My name, food, is Freya." She knocked his arms away and shoved him back, giggling as his back slammed into the wall behind him.

"Well, isn't that a bit of a surprise, Paul? It appears I'm a lot stronger than I thought." She watched him slide down the wall, revealing cracked plaster and a couple of blood spots. "Oh dear, did that hurt?"

She crouched down in front of Paul and lifted his head up, relieved to see that he was only dazed. She'd never forgive herself if she'd already killed the boy. "I've been living a lie for over a thousand years; all that unaccountable time involved in so many banal relationships without knowing about my true destiny. He removed the veil from my eyes, Paul. Have you any idea of the misery I've suffered?"

The boy didn't answer. She looked through his eyes and skimmed across the surface of his thoughts. All she could pick out were confusion and terror; this was a waste of time. He had no idea what she was talking about. Even so, Freya had to continue. She needed an audience, if not for him, for her to put the forgotten pieces back into their correct slots.

"The Swarmer clan had destroyed all the other clans. Only the Deathgazers survived the cull, and they were down to their last few numbers. Those things wouldn't stop until they'd exterminated every last one of the remaining vampires. Why should we humans have cared about monsters slaughtering themselves? We cared because our clan had looked after us and kept the towns prosperous. Allowing the Deathgazers to take their pick from the strongest men and desirable females was a small price to pay. If it wasn't for the Deathgazers, we would be crawling in the dirt, looking for scraps of food like the rest of the humans."

She tilted his head to one side and stared in fascination at the huge artery pumping sweet blood up to his brain. "I was one of the chosen few, Paul. It was my destiny to become the wife of the First Father. If it wasn't for the filthy Swarmers destroying the land, I would have helped to rule a dynasty that would still be feeding on you pathetic animals."

Freya sank her teeth into his flesh and drank deep, gasping in pleasure as his hot blood filled her mouth. She would still take her place beside him. Freya would relish her role as loving wife

33

and adviser. Amulius needed to understand that the world had moved on.

Chapter Two

She was going to launch into yet another bitching session. Damien Myers didn't need to even look at his sister to gleam that nugget of information. It was like sensing the onset of a major storm. As soon as Elsie's mood took a dive and swung into the red, the hairs on his back stood at attention, and more often than not, Damien found himself burdened with a deep grinding headache.

It was pointless trying to stop the inevitable. Instead, Damien drained the beer from his can and laid back down, feeling the damp grass pressing against his shirt. He stared up at the star-lit sky for a few seconds before closing his eyes.

"What the hell is he playing at, Damien?" His sister poked his side. "I swear that damn Ben is so going to pay for this, you know. I'm not an idiot. It's obvious that he just can't be bothered to drive all the way up here. I tell you, I'm so going to smash his face in for this."

Even with his eyelids shut, Damien could still picture the vast sea of stars blitzing the night sky. There weren't many delights left from being stuck at his Aunt May's on a weekend, but he had to admit this was one of them. The advantage of being away from the town centre was that the view was awesome, even with his eyes closed.

"Will you just cool down your jets, sis? Will you at least give the man some time to get up here? It's not exactly next door, is it? Hell, even dad still makes the occasional wrong turn, and he used to live here."

"That's 'cos dad is an idiot," she muttered.

He smiled. "Just give him a few more minutes."

The irony of the situation did not fail to amuse him. Damien cracked opened his eyes to see if his imagined star map matched the original and recalled how excited he had been when Ben casually informed the pair of them that he'd be bringing up a friend. By the smirk plastered all over Elsie's boyfriend's face, Damien knew the lad was going to bring up a female companion—a date for Damien so he wouldn't have to play gooseberry.

No matter how many times Damien had asked, Ben refused to reveal any information. He kept his mouth firmly shut, only telling Damien that he didn't want to spoil the surprise. Ben would not even reveal her name to him.

All those pent-up hormonal feelings only invaded Damien's psyche during daylight hours. When the sun went to bed and the moon and stars came out to play, he found that his daylight worry and stress simply faded away. Both he and his sister preferred the night and had since they were small. The darkness was their friend.

He turned his head to face Elsie and frowned. Her normal night time placid self was absent tonight. This problem with Ben not showing his face was really getting to her. Come to think of it, she had been acting a little odd for the past couple of hours.

"Are you going to tell me what's really wrong with you?" He lifted his body, turned to look at her, and rested his elbows on the grass. "You're not usually this weird."

She shrugged. "There's something in the air, Damien. Can't you feel it?" she whispered. "It's like there's a storm coming." Elsie sighed, then quickly shook her head. "Oh, just ignore me. I'm being daft."

He wasn't too sure how to respond to that outburst. He knew his sister was more sensitive than he was, and she was susceptive to unexplained events. Either that or she was just in a really bad mood and was looking for some excuse to explain away her feelings. Elsie had fallen deeply in love with this Ben. Damien decided to ignore her last comment and slip into his usual brother routine. It seemed to be the best course of action.

"He will get here, sis. You know that. Think about it: you know for a fact that your Ben has been looking forward to climbing inside your panties for the last few days. Wild horses won't stop him from getting up here." He ran his eyes up and down her well-proportioned body, trying his hardest not to leer and look like a perverted old man. Damien then ran his tongue over his lips and dramatically groaned. "Oh, he is such a lucky young man!"

"Jesus, Damien, will you please stop doing that? Have you any idea how weird and creepy that is?" she said, tutting in disgust.

He nodded and giggled. "Ain't my fault that I have a hot sister."

"God you can be such a dirty fucker sometimes."

The deep, grinding pain drilling through the back of his skull subsided just a tad when he saw the beginnings of a smirk appear on her face. Even after seventeen years of living together, it still felt weird staring into his sister's face. It was just like looking into a distorted mirror. His twin sister was the spit of him, apart from the fact that his dyed black hair hung past his shoulders and Elsie preferred her blonde hair cropped short.

"I don't know what Ben even sees in you. Let's be truthful here; we both know that I received all the best bits from our parents."

"You're such a cheeky twat," she retorted. "I thought you said I was hot?"

Damien laughed. "You are hot, at least on the surface. But you know that I'm right, sis. If you looked under the bonnet, anyone would see that you were just cobbled together from all the leftover bits."

"I seriously am going to punch you, Damien."

"Don't kid yourself," he replied, shaking his head and happy to see that Elsie's face now exhibited full-on grin mode. Damien grabbed two cans of beer from the carrier bag next to his hips and passed her one. "You're too weak to hit anything. It's taking all of your strength just to hold that can. Hit me and you'd break apart into your constituent pieces. There'd be bits of stale spunk and fragments of rotting placenta scattered all over the grass."

Elsie giggled. "You're getting fucking worse, Damien."

He nodded, happily. "I'll take that as a compliment. Besides, I make you happy so stop being such a prude." Damien spotted a new light, low in the sky, and sighed with relief when that new light doubled up. "You see. I told you to stop worrying," he said, watching the headlights grow as the car approached the house. "You were getting your knickers in a twist over nothing."

Damien shivered, then looked at Elsie and saw the car had transfixed her. He blinked in surprise when she shivered as well.

"It won't be long now before your Ben will have his tiny penis deep inside you. Admit it, lass, that's the only reason why you were getting stressed out."

His sister surprised him by refusing to bite. Was he losing his touch? Damien then found himself gazing at the approaching car as well. He couldn't see if it was Ben's car, but that didn't matter; although not many vehicles passed this way, even in the day, he knew Elsie's current boyfriend, Ben White, was in the driving seat.

His sister wrapped her fingers around his hand. "Admit it, Damien. Despite all your piss taking and your constant crude remarks, you don't really think that Ben's a bad lad, do you?"

"You have been fucked by worse," he replied, smiling when she viciously pinched the thin web of skin between his fingers.

"For crying out loud, Damien, will you please just give me a straight answer?" Elsie sighed loudly. "You know that I value your opinion above everyone else's. Although I do sometimes wonder why I bother."

How could he tell her the truth? Damien knew deep down that Ben was a decent enough lad—he was just a year older than the pair of them, had his own car, a decent job that gave him plenty of disposable income—and Damien knew Ben doted on Elsie. He didn't doubt the lad would take care of his sister.

His reluctance stemmed from the fact that he didn't want to see anyone turn her into a pet housewife, didn't want to watch her priorities change to housework and doing the weekly shopping. Deep down, Damien didn't want to lose her.

"You've gone very quiet, Damien. Come on, tell me, what do you honestly think of Ben?"

Damien shrugged and turned around to stare at the house. Who was he trying to kid? He tried to pretend they were both a pair of rebels—what a load of crap that was. How many other seventeen-year-old kids stayed at their auntie's on a weekend? He already knew the answer to that question: precisely none of them. They'd all be in the town centre, drinking their way through the pubs or having the time of their lives at house parties.

He used to look forward to visiting his aunt May; they both did. The woman hadn't been able to have kids of her own, so she always went out of her way to spoil them both stupid with sweets, unlimited television, and lots of toys to play with. It used to be great coming to visit when they were kids because Aunt May would give them anything they wanted. It wasn't just the fact that she treated them like surrogate children, Damien was under the impression that spoiling them was her own way of apologising for her brother's behaviour. Aunt May knew how much of a bastard their dad was to them at times.

They were getting older though, and their needs had altered. The prospect of unlimited sweets and staying up until past midnight no longer had the same appeal.

"She'll be sleeping for a while yet."

Damien sighed. "She'll never accept the fact that we're not kids anymore, you know."

"She will. It'll just take time." Elsie followed his gaze and smirked, "Right now, she won't be bothering us tonight. I've made sure that she'll sleep to at least morning."

His stomach lurched. "Oh shit, what have you done?"

"Well, I didn't want her to find me and Ben in her bed."

He jerked up, aware that the car had stopped. "What the fuck have you done?" he hissed.

"I think you should cool your jets now, Damien. I just added some of her crushed-up sleeping tablets to her mashed potatoes at our supper."

"Are you out of your mind? You don't know how that'll affect her. That was so fucking stupid."

"Oh, hush your lips, you big girl's blouse. Of course I know what they'll do. It'll keep her asleep. Don't worry, I've done this before. I know what dose to give the woman." Elsie got to her feet and waved at the two figures climbing the stairs and heading for their auntie's huge back garden. "Ben might not have told you what he was bringing for you, but he sure as hell told me all about her." She sighed. "He's not himself for the past few days, Damien, and I did start to get some very odd ideas floating around my head." She elbowed him in the ribs. "Looks like I was wrong after all. I'm going to make sure that Ben doesn't get any odd ideas."

Were his eyes actually functioning correctly? Damien stared open-mouthed at the young woman accompanying Ben up the stairs.

"You're starting to drool," his sister whispered. "Now you see why I wanted to make sure that aunt May stayed asleep."

His first thought, once he had got past the black leather jacket straining to hold in her large breasts, was he had no idea who she was.

"Ben has found your poster girl. You make sure to thank Ben for bringing you a hottie."

They were now close enough for Damien to see her face in detail. She was just gorgeous, and he was right, he had never seen her before. Their town wasn't that small, but he was sure he would have spotted a pretty young thing like her swanning around the area.

"Have fun with her, Damien," she whispered, then ran down the grassy slope, towards Ben. "The bed is still ours!" shouted Elsie.

Damien leaned against a tree and watched his sister grab Ben's hand and pull the lad over to the front door. He noticed that she didn't even bother introducing herself to the new girl. His legs felt like jelly, and the shaking increased as the girl neared. She really was a fucking stunner.

Her raven hair was even longer that his, and he longed to brush his fingers through it. Beneath the leather jacket, her black latex trousers clung to her shapely legs like they were painted on her.

Elsie had her initial description perfect. The girl really did look as though she had just peeled herself off his wall. "I'd so like to peel that clothing off her," he murmured. Damien wondered who he was kidding.

She won't be interested in me.

As soon as that notion lodged in the back of his head, Damien's bulge softened.

"Er, I'm sorry about my sister," he stammered.

The girl slowed down, then stopped a couple of paces in front of him. He felt his heart start to beat a little faster when her face softened into a smile.

"Elsie isn't normally that rude."

He wanted to slap himself. *Why the fuck did I have to go and spurt out with a stupid comment like that? It wasn't the best of chat up lines.*

Damien had never been so tongue-tied before. He'd never had any problem with charming members of the opposite sex, no matter how desirable. His mouth felt like the bottom of a budgie cage.

"Well, isn't this a bit of a surprise?" she murmured, chuckling. "Ben did tell me that you were good looking, but I thought he was having me on, you know? You really are a bit of a cutie-pie."

The girl covered the last few strides, and Damien blinked, not sure how she had done it. He could swear he hadn't seen her move.

"You smell so different." She leaned a little closer and breathed in. "Yeah, there is something about you." She wrapped her arms around his waist. "I'm called Eleanor Slinta, and you have confused me. That has not happened for a long time. Oh, don't you worry, it's not a bad thing."

He fought the desire to push her away as he felt goose bumps spread under where she held him. The girl was freezing cold. "Would you like a drink or something, Eleanor?" Damien gazed down at the carrier bag. "Or perhaps a cup of tea or something. You seem to be a bit chilly."

Damien's awakened raging hormones drowned out the sensation of wrongness about this strange girl. Something deep inside his body was telling him to get away from her, to run as fast as he could. Damien suppressed that urge and tried not to gasp as Eleanor dragged her long fingernail down the front of his shirt. He couldn't help but yelp when she glided her long nails up the inside of his thigh.

"I think I'm going to enjoy the rest of this night." Eleanor licked his earlobe and exhaled seductively. "I so need to find out why you are different. Would you like me to taste you?"

"Oh yes please!" he gasped.

As soon as the girl released him and took a step back, he grabbed her jacket zipper and tugged it down, releasing Eleanor's heavy breasts. Damien gasped again. She was perfect. Her contours were plainly visible through the gossamer veil of her black blouse.

She shrugged off her jacket, then grabbed his wrists and placed his hands on her breasts.

"Oh fuck," he murmured. He rubbed his thumbs over her hard, pointed nipples." I must be dreaming this."

Eleanor chuckled. "You are so sweet." The girl leaned forward and brushed her cold lips against his.

Damien stiffened.

"Sorry," she said, giggling. "I know that I am not very warm. The heater in Ben's car did not work." Eleanor wrapped her arms around his chest. "Do not worry. I'm sure you will be able to warm me up. Hmm, perhaps we could go find a quiet place to lie down?"

He nodded eagerly. "Oh yes please. You are so incredible."

"The others have no concept of the pleasure I get from milking the animals," she said. "All those heightened emotions and volatile chemicals riding your body before you spit your germ vitalises the experience.

Damien's body shuddered as her fingers travelled down his spine. He cried out even louder when he felt her teeth sink into the side of his neck.

The sharp pain was gone in an instant. Damien was sleepy. The girl hadn't moved away from his neck, but that was okay, it didn't really hurt too much as long as he didn't move. He felt his eyelids grown heavy. Everything was slowing down, and Damien's conscious thoughts were slipping away. The pleasant harmony of drifting into oblivion came to an abrupt end when Damien felt two heavy weights lands on his shoulders. He snapped open his eyes and saw two huge men stood beside him and Eleanor. They were both dressed in identical tattered leather trousers and tunics.

He couldn't move his body. He then realised there was another man stood behind him, digging his hard, bony nails into Damien's flesh. His mental apathy collapsed the instant the two men ripped the girl from his neck. She fell back onto the grass and smiled up at Damien. Thick red blood dribbled down her chin.

"Thank you," she said. "That was just exquisite."

He watched her tongue escape from between her lips and lick the bottom of her face clean like a ravenous worm.

"What the fuck are you?" Damien slapped his fingers against his throat, moaning when they came away soaked in blood. "You're a fucking vampire? You've got to be shitting me!"

He noticed the two men's hungry eyes followed his hand until he wiped his palm against his trousers. "This is just so much bullshit."

Damien felt the figure behind him lift his hands, and when he turned his head, he saw the man had simply vanished. Damien yelped when he turned back and saw there were now three men facing him. The middle one smirked while the two others stood with their arms folded.

"Get out of here before I call the police!"

The man in the middle chuckled. "I think it is way too late to cry for help now, boy." He glared at Eleanor. "You were told to just taste the beast, you spoilt little brat. You were not supposed to fill your greedy little face." He then stared down at her exposed breasts. "We all watched how you allowed the food to maul your body, Eleanor. Does Desmonus know of your perversions? Maybe even he isn't able to satisfy you?"

The girl growled. "You cannot tell me what to do, Caldis." She got to her feet and snatched her jacket off the grass. "Desmonus is our First Father, you will treat him with the respect he deserves." She shrugged into her jacket and zipped it up.

Damien felt a sigh of regret leave his lips.

Caldis spun around and broke into a deep laugh. "Look at what you have done. Your new pet is now enthralled!" He took a deep breath then turned and tapped his two companions. They both nodded before sliding back, heading towards a slump of trees on the other side of the garden.

Damien tried to keep them in his vision, but their serpentine movement threatened to give him a headache as he kept seeing them shimmer and then appear to jump forward. He had never seen anything move that way before in his life. Damien blinked and found that they were no longer to be seen.

"Were you too busy enjoying yourself with this beast to extract the required information?"

Eleanor sidled up to Damien. When she gave him a slight smile and a wink, he thought his heart was about to burst.

"Don't you dare question my judgment," she hissed. "Desmonus put me in charge of this expedition. Just remember that. You and your two quarter-breed cast offs take orders from me. Of course I got what I wanted. He is just a stupid beast. They are not that hard to read. Even you, with some practice, might eventually be able to pick out the occasional word from inside their animal minds."

Caldis grunted. "Desmonus won't shield you forever, you mouthy little bitch. You remember that. He'll soon find another fine piece of firm flesh to change. You need to keep that in mind. You might have been his independent wife before the long sleep, but now?" He cast his arm aside. "We have all seen that the beasts are a plague in this land. He can have whichever piece of young flesh his lustful gaze lands upon."

"You are so wrong, Caldis."

He laughed again. "No, I am not wrong. You are a spiteful, devious hag. The First Father will not put up with your tricks for much longer."

Eleanor smiled. "Perhaps you do raise some good points. None of us are indispensable. Does that include your good self as well? I'd wager Desmonus has already made plans to remove you from the clan." She leaned towards Damien. "They are in the trees, my new lover," she whispered. **Fall, roll, and flee when they drop. I shall keep them occupied.**

She hadn't opened her mouth to tell Damien the last part. He watched her turn around and place her body between him and the other one. Damien's mind was in turmoil, unable to grasp the situation. There was something else too. Damien could feel his body reacting to the woman's bite. The sensation of cold needles perforating his flesh speared out from the two puncture wounds. It wasn't an unpleasant feeling.

"There are only four beasts, including this one, in the vicinity, and you were correct about this place being isolated. There are no other dwellings close by, and the road is seldom travelled. I believe it will serve our needs well."

"For tonight, perhaps."

She slammed her hands against her hips.

Damien had managed to fasten his trousers, and while he gazed at the girl's firm behind, he felt the changes within his body accelerate. His strength returned, and his muscles lost their ache. As his mind cleared, Damien realised that a hidden emotion had moved from dormancy. Behind his female shield, he suppressed a smirk, the girl was right about him being different, and that disparity sought dominance. Damien welcomed it with open arms, now thankful that Eleanor had opened his gate.

"Should I be all that surprised to see that you have not changed, Caldis Autick? I must be a fool for believing that our long sleep might have distilled in you just a fraction of respect for our First Father. We would have all died if he had not saved us. Why do you continue to defy him?"

"I am the Swarmer Clan commander. It is my role to seek an alternative answer to his instructions." Caldis drew himself up to his full height. "It is not my role to take orders from some ancient fishwife who is more devious than a snake with four heads."

The girl sighed. "And once again, I waste my precious breath talking to you. Even after all these centuries, we still bicker like young children arguing over a tasty treat. Although, I will admit you have become worse since waking. Could that be because the mighty Clan commander has now only five warriors left to instruct?" She giggled. "Wait, my mistake. Desmonus has even taken three of them to explore that settlement. Oh, you poor, sad vampire. He has only allowed you to play with these two slug-brained fools. I pity you, Caldis."

"You have no idea just how close you are to the truth there!" he cried. "Look at how these animals have spread across the land. It is not natural for them to breed like flies. We are Swarmers, Eleanor. Why are we not with him in that settlement and feasting on all that bountiful flesh? Desmonus has forgotten why we exist. It is built into all of us to feed and infect until the surviving beasts are back to hiding in their filthy caves."

Caldis's two companions were now positioned in the tree above Damian's head. Not only could he hear them moving about, he also sensed their excitable thoughts. They couldn't contain their eagerness to drop on him and drain the rest of his life-fluid. Like the other male vampire, those two fools still believed he was just a walking food container.

None of the males attempted to shield their thoughts. Oh, they still kept their personal mental static in place to prevent the others from worming into their heads, but not from Damien. Then again, why should they guard against meat on the bone, an animal awaiting slaughter?

That beautiful woman stood before him had a clue of his linage, at least she did when his blood hit the back of her throat. Even if Damien was connected to their enemy, he still had the taint of the species running through his veins. He and his sister had always known something set them apart from everyone else, and now he knew they were just like the four creatures around him. They were night hunters.

Damien felt his passion ignite at the sight of her well-defined body. They weren't just hunters either. He shook away the thoughts of sex when he caught the thoughts of the ones above him. They were ready to jump and only awaiting the signal to kill him from Caldis. The man had more important subjects on his mind though. Caldis was too busy scowling at Eleanor.

He found dipping into the other vampire's mind was becoming much easier. Caldis craved control of their tiny clan, thought of eating Desmonus and then forcing himself on the luscious female currently making him feel so unimportant.

"You can fuck off," growled Damien. "She's mine."

Eleanor spun around. "You just had to go and open your big, stupid mouth!"

He gazed in horror at her crimson eyes, set deep in her bestial face. The sweet looking girl was nowhere to be seen. Damien refused to believe this nightmarish construct could be the same creature.

"Stop staring and run!" she screamed, looking up into the tree.

He didn't need to follow the vampire's terrifying eyes to know they were about to drop on him. Damien jumped back and twisted his body while sensing the two blood-crazed minds snap. He streaked across the grass, heading towards the house, knowing they were all right behind him and gaining.

They were all chasing him now. Caldis's mind, boiled over with fury, drowning out all other thoughts. Damien reached the front door and glanced behind him to see the four monstrous creatures racing across the grass. He wrenched open the door and ran inside. Damien knew it was a futile gesture as he slammed home the two bolts, but he figured it would give him a few precious moments to save his sister.

Damien ran past the open living room door and spotted his aunt sprawled out along the sofa. He realized her life now meant nothing to him. All he desired was to get his sister away from this isolated house, find somewhere safe, and work out exactly what they were going to do now.

Why was he not horrified at the plain fact that he, like those fiends outside, now considered that sleeping woman as food? There were no emotional attachments left; she was just livestock to him now. If that sense of indifference applied to his aunt, why was he so concerned with saving his sister?

The heavy wooden door shuddered in its frame, shattering the silence in the house. Damien sensed no change in his aunt's sleeping pattern. His sister was right about her not waking until the morning.

Damien took his eyes off her exposed thighs, knowing the males outside would not be able to resist the sight of all that flesh. Her sleeping body would give him enough time to get his sister out of this house.

He raced up the stairs and stopped at the top. The door finally gave in to their assault, and just as he predicted, they all ran into the living room. Except for the female. She walked over to the foot of the stairs and gazed up, seeking out his face.

This woman will not keep their lust quiet for long. Search for me, my new lover. We have unfinished business.

She turned around and disappeared into the living room. Damien hurried along the bedroom, knowing that the female had a point: he didn't have much time to get his sister out of the house. He stopped in front of his aunt's bedroom door, sensing the three vampires below pulling, ripping, and tearing off the remainder of his Aunt's clothing.

The woman's instinct for self-preservation finally rose to the surface, and the burst of adrenalin flushed the drowsiness out of her body. Through her eyes, Damien saw two of them spread her legs wide as Caldis started to unfasten his trousers.

The last piece of Damien's humanity screamed out, begging him to intervene and stop them from continuing their vile act. He pushed that thought away and left the woman's mind, cringing when she screamed. Her noise came to an abrupt end, and he guessed that one of them had pushed something into her mouth.

"She's just meat," he murmured, grabbing the door handle.

Damien pushed open the door and looked with confusion at the empty bed stood in the middle of the floor. There was no sign of them. The couple had been here, that was obvious from the dishevelled bed covers.

"Where are you?" he hissed.

This didn't make sense. Damien could even hear their thoughts.

"Elsie!

He dropped to the floor and checked under the bed, then ran over to the large wardrobe stood at the far end of the room and pulled open the doors.

"What the fuck has happened to you?" screamed his sister. "Get away from me."

They were both huddled at the base of the wardrobe, shaking like leaves. It took a moment for him to spot that they were both naked.

Damien caught his reflection in the small mirror bolted to the inside of the door and looked at the crimson eyes staring back at him

"You need to come with me," he said.

Elsie shrank back into the wardrobe.

"I don't have time for this nonsense." Damien reached inside and effortlessly pulled them both out.

You need to change her right now, my lover. She'll only want to take the food. Bite your sister. You need to turn her into one of us. It is the only way you'll both get out of here in one piece.

Damien nodded. He wrapped his hand around Ben's wrist and dragged him over to the door, fighting off his sister's futile attempts to stop him.

"What are you doing? Leave Ben alone!"

He could feel the others now slowly making their way up the stairs. Damien pulled open the door, threw Ben out into the hall, and slammed the door shut. He leaned against the wood, ignoring the man's frantic beating against the door. Damien growled, feeling his blood lust rise. The sight of his naked sister was making him hard again. He violently pulled her over to him, sank his enlarged canines into her throat, and drank deep.

Her warm blood re-energised him, giving him strength and vitality. He sensed the others reach Ben and drag his screaming body down the hallway.

Damien suppressed a quiet chuckle and threw his sister's naked body over his shoulder. He glanced at the window on the other side of the bedroom, knowing time was running out. If he didn't make use of it, those things would soon be tearing into their flesh, but he couldn't stop himself from opening the door just a crack. He needed to watch them.

The blood from Ben's shattered body coloured Aunt May's carpet crimson. The four vampires had pulled him apart, fighting over his meat like jackals scrabbling over a carcass. Damien watched Eleanor backhand one of the larger vampires when he pawed at her breasts. His emotions flared up, and a low growl left his throat. Eleanor jerked her head up, and he quickly pulled his head away and clicked the door shut. He ran for the window, feeling like a fool for staying so long.

It was time to return home, and time for their mother to explain exactly why she had kept this knowledge hidden from the pair of them.

Chapter Three

Darlene twisted her hands into rigid claws and jerked both arms hard against the wall, screaming in frustration as her fingers just pushed through the tissue-thin membrane. The thick, gelatinous material beneath the skin coated her flesh and dribbled down her bare arms.

The crimson light below her body grew brighter as she continued to fall down the well.

"Help me!" she cried, feeling the freezing cold jellied material slide past her elbows.

Darlene clamped her mouth shut and forced her gaze away from the light under her feet. She frowned, watching the stuff around her arms thicken up. She now found herself immobile, unable to move her limbs as the translucent jelly began to harden like resin. Darlene's velocity stopped, and she hung in mid-air, feeling like a fly caught in a web.

"I must be dreaming this," she gasped, desperately trying to hold back panic.

Darlene stared at the curved, red wall in front of her face. It looked like the inside of somebody's throat. It rippled out like a stone dropped in water, and the flesh blistered, the skin expanding and growing towards her. Her struggling only caused the stuff around her arms to tighten more. The bubble continued to increase in size, getting closer to her flesh. She choked back a sob as the bubble detonated, covering her face in dark red blood.

Darlene jerked, arched her back, and shrieked out in orgasmic pleasure as her skin pores opened up and greedily absorbed the fluid running across her body. The influx of alien fluid rushed through her system, pooling at the base of her skull. She jerked again when the stuff stripped off the outer skin of amnesia protecting her newest mental incarnation. The dozens of her layered past lives unravelled and filled her screaming mind with a thousand fragmented memories.

The dried fibrous material webbing her limbs lost cohesion, and Darlene dropped to the floor. The intense crimson light filled her vision, blocking out every other detail. She shrieked out all her past names, each one triggering more recollections from her hidden existence.

Darlene shot up in bed, opened her eyes, then leaned over the side and vomited foul smelling, runny blood over her carpet. When the heaving passed, she stayed still, allowing her delicate stomach to stop churning before she flopped back onto the cold sheets.

She fixed her eyes on the light shade, and even in the low light, she had no problem seeing the decorative dome surrounding the bulb. The fact that she could see better than a cat in the dark didn't surprise her. Why should it? Darlene now knew her true nature, her linage, and her future role.

She frowned. She still felt as weak as a human. "This is not right. I'm still not complete." She couldn't believe she still felt this fragile.

She coughed, tensing her muscles when another slight spasm rippled through her guts. This wasn't how it was supposed to be. She was reborn. She'd shed all her previous lives and was ready to take her place alongside her true husband. *So why the fuck do I still feel so weak? Am I not yet complete?*

"You left me down there for too long, you bastard!" She growled, feeling her fury rising. His second bite must not be enough to complete her. She'd spent too many lives living amongst the flock. She still needed more of his blood.

Darlene growled again and jumped out of the bed, "You should have finished it all those years ago!" she shouted, storming over to the door. "Where are you hiding? You can't leave me half finished!"

"I know where he'll be," she said aloud. "He'll be downstairs, waiting for me in the kitchen and expecting his faithful wife to go and run into his welcoming arms." Darlene strongly desired to do just that. But there was still a small part of her old self that was a little pissed off and annoyed to find that her husband wasn't in the bedroom, waiting for her to waken.

"He promised to embrace me," she muttered, reaching for the gown she had left on the floor. Darlene stopped and stood back up. No, she wasn't going to cover her body with that thing. She knew exactly what to wear.

If her real husband expected her to go looking for him then he could think again, nor would she cower down and beg him to complete the process. She looked over at the window, smiling at the gorgeous sight of the fat, pale moon hanging over the rooftops. There were lakes of rich blood pumping through the veins of uncountable people just beyond these walls. All that unsuspecting food running around the land, actually believing they were lords and masters of all they surveyed. Of course they believed that nonsense. Their true masters only existed in legends and locked away in a deep area of their feeble minds. She'd have the pick of the crop. Darlene would be like a ravenous fox let loose in a huge chicken coop.

That, though, could wait until she had found some suitable attire. Their new queen desired to meet her subjects in good-looking clothing, preferably items that would not stain easily. Darlene reached her wardrobe and pulled it open, gazing at her clothes collection and wondering what possessed her to even contemplate wearing any of this foul, shabby, and offensive fabric. She gazed down at her beautiful body, admiring her full contours and grew wet at the delicious thought of that huge creature downstairs using her body in many unimaginable ways.

"No," she muttered, trying to calm down. "If my husband really was that needy, he would be here already." Darlene slowly dragged her fingers down her breasts, lingering on her nipples, imagining his rough hands taking hold and squeezing. Her body responded to her touch by sending sharp needles of pain through her guts.

"Oh, that hurts." Darlene reached out and grabbed the door handles, gripping them tight, trying not to fall. She craned her head towards the closed bedroom door, certain she heard footsteps outside in the hallway.

"Help me?"

Darlene's tear-blurred eyes found the door, and she shifted her gaze down to the handle, praying to see it swing down. "Please, I'm so sorry. I didn't mean to ..." An intense wave of solid agony slammed into her guts. She arched her back as the hot pain shot up her spine. then lost her grip on the wardrobe and crashed to the soft carpet.

The pain washed through her body and left her feeling as weak as a new-born kitten. "What is wrong with me?" She rolled onto her front and pushed her body up, slowly crawling over to the end of the bed. Darlene felt her hot tears drip from her skin and fall into the carpet weave, not surprised to see her expelled liquid was the colour of deep red roses.

"I am a little shocked to see my new talent works on you as well. I thought it only immobilised the humans. What a sad, pathetic creature you are."

She slammed her jaws together, unaware of her enlarged canines slicing into her gums. The hot pain had returned. She cried out, not allowing it to beat her again. The ache from her complaining muscles drowned out every other pain as she moved her head, but she just had to see who had entered the room.

Darlene followed the large shadow that fell across her shivering body and saw a familiar figure framed in the doorway. She blinked in confusion, not sure if her eyes were lying to her. "Is that really you, Paul?" she whispered, unable to look away from the huge man blocking the light from the hallway.

He took a single step into the bedroom and chuckled.

She caught her breath at the sight of her ex-lover staring down at her. His eyes had lost their innocence; all she saw in there now was cruelty and a tinge of pity. It came as a huge shock to sense only disgust oozing from him.

Darlene slowly crawled away from Paul, every movement a struggle as pain cut into her like shards of broken glass.

"You don't look very happy to see me, my dirty little rabbit." He opened his mouth wide, laughing at her quiet gasp. "You thought you had killed me, that I was your first meal? Oh dear."

"You, you mean, you're like me?"

She gazed up at her ex-lover. The man was massive: he'd gained another foot in height and had filled out.

Paul shrugged. "You still haven't got it, my dear. Oh yes, it's true I have grown." He winked. "Yeah, I did snatch that from your open mind, Darlene. But, I'm not like you, my sweet." Paul ran over to her and flung Darlene onto the bed. "I'm much more than you though, you selfish bitch," he snarled. "You're looking at the finished product. You fucked up, Darlene. You're pathetic. Neither human nor vampire."

He sat on the side of the bed, and the springs complained under his extra weight. "I suppose should thank you. You see, for the first time in my life, I will no longer have to cower before my father or hide from him in my bedroom while he takes out his frustration on my mother."

He leaned forward and stroked her cheek with the back of his hand. "Did it feel good when you bit into the side of my neck and drank deep?" He smirked. "I can see from your eyes that it did feel good, it was better than anything else you have ever experienced, like a hundred orgasms combined with a thousand light bulbs exploding inside your mind. I know, because it's how I felt after I drained my father." He giggled. "I'll let you in on a little secret: the first one is always the sweetest. I've drunk from another four necks since I killed that old bastard, and none have come close to how he made me feel."

The pain in her body vanished, leaving her feeling washed out and ravenous, but she still believed she had enough energy to at least escape. Darlene felt his powerful mind slicing through hers like an unstoppable tornado, ripping away her memories layer by layer. She was unable to fight back, but did find ways to block him from sections of her thoughts. The desire to escape was pushed into her secret fortress.

"Unlike me, my victims will not be coming back. You see, I ripped them into tiny little bits once I had drunk my fill. I can't tell you how much fun that was. I once had a friend at school who used to get off by pulling legs and wings off insects. He's in a home now. The freak moved up to doing the same to cats and dogs. I always thought people like that should be put down." He laughed. "And now *I'm* just like that, only far worse." False concern flickered in his eyes. "How are you feeling, honey? You don't look so pathetic anymore. Some of your strength is flowing back into your tired body, yes?"

Paul's mental probes battered down the locked doors in Darlene's mind, eagerly drinking down the wall of her locked-up knowledge. He moaned softly and she moaned with him. "Shall we both find out what our new bodies are capable of?"

He grinned. "Oh yes."

His mental probes left her as he fought to climb out of his clothes. She waited until his lust had taken full control before leaping onto him, her long teeth fastening onto his throat.

He roared out in pain and surprise, trying to dislodge her, but she held on tight, digging her nails deep into his flesh as his hot blood flooded her mouth. He spun around and slammed her into the wall. Darlene cried out as he thrust his head back and his hard skull crashed into her nose.

She fell off him, slid down the wall, and screamed out in frustration when she felt his long fingers encircle her ankle.

"I'm going to rip off your head for tricking me like that, you fucking cow!" he shouted.

Darlene managed to throw her hands under her to stop her head from smashing against the floor. She kicked out with her free leg, snarling when Paul caught that one as well. He pinned them down, then crawled up her body. When she tried to push him off, he swung his fist and punched her hard in the stomach. His blow just bounced off her hard flesh.

Darlene glared into his crimson eyes, sensing uncertainty. "Fuck you," she spat. "It looks like you aren't as strong as you thought."

She bucked, giggling when Paul bounced off her body, then jumped to her feet and raced after the vampire as he tried to crawl under her bed.

"I can feel your slimy fingers trying to find an entrance into my head." She stopped and watched him pull his body further under her bed. The temptation to remove the rest of his precious blood would have to wait until she had found something to wear. Darlene wanted the pain to last a little longer, but had no wish to feel his eyes crawling across every contour of her body.

She resisted the urge to shiver, walked over to her wardrobe, and put the door between her and him. Now that she had beaten him into submission and gained the upper hand, some of the intense heat inside her cooled a little, allowing her to get her thoughts in order.

As she looked through her clothing, Darlene ran her tongue across her teeth, searching for any pieces of flesh she might have missed. "This outfit is just perfect," Darlene said, giggling when her probing tongue found a segment of his flesh lodged between her teeth.

Feeling more confident dressed, Darlene walked back to Paul, smiling as he drew his legs further under the bed. She crouched down and caught sight of his hooded eyes. The sight of his hot blood leaking out of him made her mouth water. It annoyed her to see it go to waste, soaking into the carpet.

"I've always loved you," he whispered, licking his cracked lips. "I still do, you know. Despite the weird filth that your fangs put into me when you first bit into my neck, I'll always love you. The alien poison might paint over my humanity, but it will never be able to take that from me."

"You're lying. You just tried to kill me!" she screamed.

Paul shook his head. "The vampire in me craved vengeance, and I hurt you, Darlene, but I would never kill you though."

She thrust her mind into his, surprised at the ease of her entry. The dying vampire's mind showed her whatever she desired to know. Through his eyes, Darlene watched him stumble out of her house, heard his confused thoughts, felt him struggling to come to terms with the rapid and vicious change spreading through his shivering body at lightning speed.

Paul headed for home, his mind focused on his bedroom, his only sanctuary. Every other coherent thought was unable to find purchase.

Both of his parents jumped out of their chairs when he burst into the living room. Their reactions to his grand entrance were Paul's first anchor to base reality, a familiar situation his swirling thoughts could hold on to.

His mother flinched, her terrified features crunching up in confusion. It was only the reassuring glance from her husband that stopped her shaking. She finally settled back down in her chair and turned her attention back to the glowing television.

Paul watched his father act in his usual fashion by raising his voice and his fists.

Darlene blinked, and the image of Paul's living room faded away, leaving the faint scent of stale tobacco and cheap air freshener. "What just happened to me?" She saw that his eyes were still closed. Without glancing at his large canines and ignoring his extra body mass, Paul could almost pass for that beautiful strong boy who once helped her get through the dark days when she turned to the lure of prescription drugs.

"Instead, you'll now become addicted to human blood." Paul's eyes opened just a crack.

"You were able to read that?"

He nodded. "The thought was too strong to ignore." He chuckled softly, then stopped as his laughter turned into coughing. "We did have some good times though, Darlene." He groaned, spat out a gobbet of deep red-stained phlegm, then turned his eyes and stared at her. "He's here, you know. Right now. Waiting for you in the kitchen. You haven't sensed him yet, but I did. The bastard entered the house just as I caught your ankle."

He coughed again. "Darlene, you have to finish me. It's what he expects you to do."

"What do you mean?" she cried. "I don't understand."

"Yes you do, Darlene. Your first husband is waiting for you downstairs. That fucker just knew that I'd come back to you. Can't you see? I'm supposed to be your first full meal. You'll only attain your full status after you have turned my body into a dried husk."

Darlene watched in fascination as he rolled out from under the bed, painfully lifted his body, and sat cross-legged in front of her. Paul really did want her to drink him dry.

"I can feel your cold touch in my head, Darlene. That is such a powerful gift." He rested his hands on her arms. "My new talent only incapacitated the animals and the lesser developed vampires. You need to keep your talent hidden, my sweet. You can't let him know that you have the power to steal thoughts from his mind."

Paul's whole body shivered as he slammed a clawed hand against the side of his blood-soaked neck. He pinched the flesh between his fingers and yanked his hand back. The skin stretched like tight elastic before finally tearing. His thick blood burst from the jagged wound. Paul fell forward against her chest. "You have to drink from me," he moaned.

Darlene couldn't help herself. The sight of so much blood sent her into a frenzy. She pushed her face against the torn flesh, opened her mouth wide, and guzzled down the hot crimson liquid. Spasms of ecstasy ripped through her body as the last of Paul's life fluid flowed down her throat.

Her gratification was ripped away when she felt her prize pulled from her teeth. Darlene blinked at the re-emergence of light in her eyes, then whimpered at the sight of someone dumping Paul's body onto the bed.

"Amulius, is that you?"

Her vampire husband slowly turned, bent down, and wrapped his fingers around her waist. He then lifted Darlene off the floor. "You are not meant to play with your food, my wife." The vampire threw her.

Darlene cried out as her back slammed into the wall. She opened her eyes, trying not to move while she watched the First Father grab Paul's body by an arm and leg and carry it towards the bedroom window.

"Please no," she moaned. "Don't do that."

Amulius dropped Paul's leg and punched his fist through the glass, then picked up the limp body and pushed it through the window. "I do not understand your concern, my wife. It is just forgotten meat." He shook his head, then walked past her and sat down on the edge of the bed. "You are experiencing the shock of the first bite. There is much alien blood running through your body right now, my wife. Your mouth knows not what it vomits out. Be thankful I know of your experience."

"I'm going to force my fingers through your stomach and pull out your insides, you fucking bastard freak," she gasped.

The First Father growled softly. "Anyone else saying that would be dead by now." He stood up and approached her. "Be thankful I know those words are just the result of the alien blood coursing through your body." He dropped to his knees, grabbed her ankles, and violently jerked her towards him. "Do not fret, my wife. There is a way to cure this." Amulus flipped Darlene onto her back, wrapped his fingers around her throat, then backhanded her.

The sudden pain of his blow breaking her jaw ripped through her face. The agony blocked out every other thought.

"Do not move," he growled, moving up Darlene's body and pinning her to the floor. "All that excess energy is needed elsewhere now."

She couldn't have moved if she wanted to. Darlene closed her eyes, trying to think of ways to kill the bastard who had just damaged her. Try as she might, her brain just wouldn't show her any pleasing images. Darlene then found that the pain had lessened, but it hadn't gone away, not completely. Without the discomfort, she now could actually feel her broken jawbone knitting together.

"All of the excess energy overwhelming your frail body now has a specific task. Instead of lashing out at your husband, it is healing you." Amulius climbed off her body and strode back over to the broken window.

"The most important lesson to remember here is abstinence is the way of the Deathgazer Clan. If you allow your passion to run rampant, your vampire essence will control your fate." He went back to Darlene, picked her up off the floor, and held her in his arms. "The vampire inside you only craves one thing and that is a constant supply of fresh blood. If you go the way of the Swarmer, the candle will burn twice as bright, but your life will be measured in just weeks and months. You are a pure breed now. You are my queen. As soon as we rid this new world of the filth, you and I will make this world our own, and we shall reign together."

Darlene smiled back. Most of her fears had gone, but one fear still remained and grew stronger. She had not yet told him she had two kids. How would her children fit into his scheme? How would Elsie and Damien fit into her new life now?

The First Father released her and walked over to the doorway. "I believe you should collect a few of your cherished items. I will meet you on the floor below." He smiled again. "Our new life will be so sweet."

She watched him go, then ran over to the window and gazed outside. There was no sign of Paul's body.

Chapter Four

Even with his eyes shut tight, Cade could not escape the agony and fear twisted into their desiccated faces. An unpleasant amalgamation of the five victims that they had found so far etched their mark into his psyche.

"Oh God!" hissed Katy. "Get back over here, they've found us again."

Cade snapped opened his eyes, grimacing at the dried-up corpse staring back at him. He glanced to the side and saw three figures framed at the end of the alleyway. This was so unfair. He honestly believed they had given those bastards the slip this time. Cade took a step back, catching the back of his foot on a brick. He stumbled and thrust his arms forward to stop himself from falling backwards. Cade's fingers clutched one of the bin bags beneath the corpse, and he pulled it out from under it. Its head fell backwards, the heavy skull slamming against his wounded arm. Cade gritted his teeth in pain, watching the bandage soak with fresh blood.

As he pulled his arm back, the bandage slipped off, coating the thing's head with his blood. A violent shiver travelled through the corpse.

"No fucking way," he uttered, watching his blood disappear into the leather-like flesh stretched over its skull.

Cade jumped away from the thing, gazing in utter shock as the corpse attempted to sit up. Katy scrambled out from her hiding place and pulled him behind pair of green wheelie bins. He watched their pursuers walk into the alleyway and resisted the overwhelming urge to grab Katy and run in the opposite direction. He daren't move. Those fuckers would see them and be on them in seconds.

"Is it really them, Cade?"

He nodded, knowing she was hoping their visitors would turn out to be tramps looking for a place to bed down for the night. Cade didn't take his eyes off their progress. "Yeah, I can smell them." He heard her next words catch in the back of her throat. Katy didn't question his confirmation, not anymore. After over an hour of playing hide and seek in the town with these resurrected monsters, Katy had come to rely on his unnerving ability to recognise their enemy.

"Please tell me they haven't spotted us," she whispered.

Cade shrugged. He didn't think so. They seemed to be more concerned about the corpse that was now trying to raise its arms. He looked down at the large kitchen knife tucked into his belt and swallowed hard. Even with the blade, he knew the chances of taking down just one of those things were slim. The corpse had now managed to get to its feet and was slowly standing up. It turned towards the three approaching figures.

Cade gripped the knife handle, feeling Katy wrap some clean cloth around his other arm. The lead figure reached the corpse, ducked under its arms, and pushed it back onto the bin bags. Cade held his breath, not wanting that figure to detect either of them. He watched it turn its head and gaze directly at their hiding position, then lift its chin and sniff the air like a hungry mongrel dog. He felt Katy tense up and caught her reaching for her own knife. If those things did walk over to investigate, Cade would ensure that he got at least one knife thrust into its chest before it ripped him apart.

"What are you doing?"

"Have you two not cleaned the shit out of your nostrils? There's the sweet scent of fresh blood in the air."

"Of course there is, Cranus, you docile fool. It is coming from us."

"Healiod, both you and your slow brother have horse dung inside your heads." Cranus reached out, wrapped his long fingers around the corpse's neck, and then lifted it up and flung it viciously against the wall. When its body slammed into the bricks, it fell apart like a large lump of dried clay. "Something caused that dried up dead thing to wake up, unless you were stupid enough to leave some blood in the vessel."

This was the first time Cade had been close enough to see their pursuers clearly. He couldn't get over their size—all three of them were built like American wrestlers and none of them were less than six feet tall.

It was the size of their wolf-like canines that made Cade's blood run cold. He tried not to imagine the terrible agony of feeling those dagger teeth slicing into his flesh and ripping into him as if he was just a piece of tender steak on somebody's plate. Despite all his earlier denials, he had no doubt these things were vampires. Cade thought back to that terrible vision he'd experienced inside that cavern and allowed the images to finally sink in. There was no doubt left inside him at all anymore.

Cade watched the three vampires turn their backs on him, still arguing. All three carried the same emblem branded into their naked backs. The same mark stamped into that little girl's arm and the same one on those invading vampires who had torn that man apart. Cade pushed the knife back into his belt and rolled up his sleeve, looking at his own mark.

"I belong to their enemy," he murmured. "I'm just a fucking branded farm animal."

"This is a bad dream, and I can't wake from it!" Katy whispered as she peered over the top of the wheelie bin. "Oh my God, they are a bunch of blood-drinking fucking vampires." She glared down at Cade. "Please tell me you saw their teeth?" The girl rubbed her eyes. "This really is too much to take in."

He nodded. "Would you kick me if I said *I told you so*?"

Instead of lashing out, her face just collapsed. "What are we going to do now?"

He pulled the girl into his embrace. He could smell her fear, and he held her hot body tight against his, feeling her shivers against his chest. He hoped some part of the old scornful and strong-minded Katy was still inside her somewhere.

This new and vulnerable Katy had been in this dangerous condition ever since they had managed to flee from the girl's own garden just minutes before entering this alleyway.

The cat and mouse game they had played with the pursuing creatures had almost ended with their capture. Cade didn't doubt they'd both be dead if it hadn't been for his strange ability to sense when any of them were close by.

After fleeing across half the town with those silent creatures close on their trail, Katy had just stopped dead right in the middle of the road and begged Cade to take her home, insisting it was only a few streets from where they were. He'd taken her hand and pulled her out of the street, glancing nervously behind them. They hadn't spotted their pursuers for some time now and hoped maybe they'd given them the slip.

Cade had allowed the girl to lead him along the pavements, keeping close to the hedges and not allowing his attention to wander. Katy looked ready to collapse, and he knew he wasn't that far behind. Both physical and mental exhaustion wanted to claim him. Their unknown trackers had run them into the ground.

He had watched her push open a gate and had to find the energy to chase after her and stop her from running up the path. Once again, his senses had gone into overdrive as soon as they reached the house, and he watched multiple shadows converge around a parked car in the driveway of a neighbour's house.

They had been lucky to escape with their lives on that occasion.

"Katy, listen to me. I still think we shouldn't deviate from my original idea," he replied. "We ought to go back to my house. My mum has got some serious explaining to do." Cade closed his eyes and took a deep breath, trying not to think of what he'd do if she couldn't explain why a bunch of vampires were now running around town.

"I don't understand why they are chasing us, Cade." She grabbed his shoulders and shook him. "Are you listening to me?"

He snapped open his eyes and pulled her hands away. "Of course I'm listening to you. While we're on that subject, there's something else that's been troubling me. Why haven't they caught us by now?"

Her shakes came back with vengeance, and Katy wrapped her arms around his body. "Please don't say things like that."

Cade pushed the thought out of his mind and hoped it was just because they had been very lucky and not that these things were just playing with them. "I bet you any amount of money that my mum has one of these birthmarks somewhere on her body as well."

"You don't know?"

He shook his head. "No, I haven't a clue. I mean I've seen most of my mum's body, but not all of it." Cade chuckled. "Bloody hell, just how pervy did that sound? Look, we'll find out soon, we're not that far from home."

He rolled down his sleeve and looked over at the entrance. "I wish they could have stayed a few moments longer," he said, as the last of them left the alley. "Don't look at me like that, we might have found out what they were doing."

"It's fucking obvious, they're hunting us down and killing everybody. Shit, this is dumb. Why aren't we going to the police?"

He sighed, then slowly stood up. "If you recall, sweetheart, that was your idea?" Cade walked over to the pile of dust and bent down to examine it. Going through the snatches of conversation he'd managed to overhear, he'd already worked out that those things were feeding from the locals. Cade guessed that after being stuck down a well for God knows how many years, they were bound to be a bit hungry.

"We should go."

"You still want to go to the police?"

Katy shook her head. "No, you're right, they wouldn't believe anything we told them." She stood behind him. "Do you think my mum and dad will be all right?"

Cade stood up. "Sure they will. You already told me that they're in bed asleep. I don't think those monsters are breaking into people's houses, they're just picking off people in the streets."

"I still think we need to warn somebody," she said. Katy dug out her phone and looked around. "Oh Christ, I still can't wrap my head around the fact that they are vampires."

"Nobody will believe it, Katy. Just remember that." He watched her features change from hope to disappointment.

She thrust her phone into her back pocket and sighed.

"I take it there's still no answer?"

The girl didn't reply. She just looked back at the mess on the floor before marching away from Cade. "Are you coming or what?" she asked. "I thought we were going to your mum's?"

It pleased Cade to see some of her fire return. He suspected they were both going to need the resilience to help get them through the rest of this night. He caught up to her, trying to think back to anything in his past that might have given him some clue to how he could be linked to these terrifying events. Perhaps he was just reading too much into this and his vision had nothing to do was some kind of racial memory handed down through the generations.

Cade felt his birthmark itch again. He grabbed Katy and threw her to the floor, then covered her with his body and hastily pulled some crumpled newspaper over his head. Through the gaps in the sheets, Cade watched a group of vampires run past the opening. They were close enough for him to smell them. All four of the things stunk of the grave.

Cade counted to five before he climbed off her body. The vampires had been in too much of a rush to sense them. Even so, just how many chances did they have left before one of those things did catch them? He gently picked Katy up, then stooped back down and scooped her phone from the ground. "It must have fallen out of your pocket," he said, smiling.

Katy flung her arms around his neck. "Oh my God, they almost caught us! Please tell me we're safe now?"

He pulled the girl back and shrugged. "Sweetheart, you know I can't answer that." Cade took her hand. "Come on, we're safe for the moment. It's not far from here." His birthmark had warned him of their presence. As far as he was concerned, that just sealed the deal. His mother had some serious explaining to do.

Cade saw no sign of any of those things when he pulled Katy out of the alleyway and onto the main high street. They ran over the empty road, keeping watch for any sign of the vampires returning. He stopped at a tall wooden gate and reached his hand over the top, trying to find the bolt. It had been over a decade since he had used this route to get back home. When he was nine years old, it seemed perfectly acceptable for him to cut through other people's gardens in order to get back to his house. Back then, though, he would have made short work of scaling a six-foot fence. He sighed in relief when his probing fingers caught hold of the bolt. After a moment of cursing, he managed to pull it back. Cade slowly pushed open the gate and looked inside before leading Katy into the garden, then he closed the gate and slammed the bolt home.

"Please tell me that your neighbour isn't a dog owner," whispered Katy.

"No, don't worry," he whispered back. "The old guy who lives here has a …" Cade suddenly stopped talking. His mouth dried up.

"Oh please, don't tell me it's those things again," she moaned. "Cade, what's wrong?"

He shook his head, wishing she'd be quiet, then peered through one of the gaps in the gate. "I can hear a car," he replied, trying to calm his racing heart. Everyone knew there were only two types of cars that cruised through the deserted streets of Welbourgh at this stupid time. He just hoped to God this wasn't a taxi.

Cade saw the blue lights on the roof and almost cried out with relief. "Oh, thank you, God," he said, grinning like a loon. All their troubles would be over now. The authorities would sort these things out. Hell, he could now just step back and watch the police marksmen take them out with a minimum of ease. He didn't care what powers these monsters had or how strong they were, those things were just flesh and bone. Hell, they'd been inert for a thousand years, they'd have no idea of the damage that modern weapons would have on their bodies.

"What the bloody hell are you playing at?" hissed Katy, slapping Cade's hand away from the latch on the gate.

Cade couldn't believe she'd just done that. "Are you insane?" he growled. "The police need to know about what's out there. I bet they'll have shotguns in their car. They'll easily take them out."

The girl looked at him as if he had suddenly grown a new head. "Cade, what planet do you live on? This is Welbourgh. It isn't New York!"

The police car slowly rolled past their hiding place. Cade clearly saw the occupants, the driver looked asleep and his passenger was sipping from a thermos. The girl's words whirled around his head; he had no idea where he got that idea from. Welbourgh wasn't exactly the crime capital of the world. The closest these clowns ever got to a major crime would be the same as Cade: watching it on television.

Cade's stomach gracefully did a pirouette when he saw a shadow on the other side of the street grow. Oh hell, those things hadn't gone anywhere. The bastards must have been watching them the whole time, peering out from their own hiding place, alert for any movement.

"We are so dead," he cried, watching the figures leap over a low brick wall and silently run in single file across the street. Cade paused, seeing that they weren't heading for their position. Their target was the police car. For some stupid reason, he hoped their primitive vampire minds would process the police car as some kind of angry magical metal animal and run off in terror. That idea slipped away when two of them leaped onto the car bonnet and peered through the windscreen.

They knew exactly what they had found. To them, this was just a big can of cold meat. All they needed to do was to find a way inside.

Cade prayed the police would slam their foot down and get the fuck out of here. Instead, just like he feared, the car screeched to a halt. As soon as the doors opened, the vampires leaned inside and dragged the men out of the vehicle.

The girl pulled him away from the gate. "Come on!"

Cade nodded, swallowing down bile and feeling like a complete coward for not going over to help those poor men. He ran through the overgrown grass, heading towards the house. He still expected to hear the sound of at least one of those killers leaping over the tall gate.

The only sound that reached his ears was the wet noise of chewing as the monsters ate through their victim's bodies. The poor bastards hadn't even had time to scream out.

Katy pushed past him and quickly glanced behind her. "You're slowing down!" she gasped. "Hurry up. I don't want to be next." Katy vaulted over the front garden fence, then turned around and pulled Cade over the fence. "I almost got us both killed," she cried, collapsing into his arms. "Oh fuck, those coppers are dead because of me! If those vampires hadn't chased us, they would still be alive."

"How did you work that out?" he asked, trying to calm the girl by running his fingers through her hair. "You wanted to check on your parents. It's okay, anyone would have done the same."

"No it isn't. They're not even there. I lied, Cade. They are both on holiday."

Cade wiped the tears from her face. "Wait, I don't understand.

"Shit, you really don't get it, do you?" Katy pressed her lips against his, then pulled away. "It doesn't matter. Look, can we just get to your house? I'll feel better once we're inside."

"Don't you mean safer?"

She shook her head. "I only feel safe with you, Cade."

He took her hand, returned the kiss, then pulled the girl over the road. "That's my house, the third from the left. Can you see the white door?" Cade jerked to a halt when he saw his front door was wide open. "Oh no, please, not here as well!" He let go of her hand. "I need you to wait here, Katy. If I'm not back out in the next few minutes, just get the fuck out of here. Go lose yourself in a big crowd of people or something."

Katy grabbed him. "No way," she hissed. "There's no way I can leave you, Cade."

"Vampires don't just kill. We both know that. They change people as well. If there is one in my house and it does alter me, I don't want to come after you." Cade shrugged out of her hold, pushed her away from him, and ran towards the house. He jumped over the gate and raced along the path. Cade knew that he should have listened to his own plan and just ran home as soon as they were clear of the industrial complex.

He reached the front door and looked back, grateful that the girl had actually listened to him and gone on her way. He knew she'd be okay, that girl could look after herself. He had no doubts on that score.

His arm wasn't itching. He took that as a good sign. Perhaps he had been too over-cautious. It could be something simple, like his mum had just forgotten to close it. He pushed the door open a little wider and stepped into the kitchen. Nothing looked out of place, apart from two bottles of wine standing on the kitchen top next to the kettle. Cade walked over and picked up each one, shaking the bottles and finding them both empty. He frowned. His mum had never been a heavy drinker, unless they had a visitor while Cade was out.

If she had drunk both these bottles alone, no bloody wonder she had left the door unlocked and wide open. Dare he actually walk into the living room? The last thing Cade wanted to see was his pissed up mum sprawled across the sofa snoring her head off.

Cade looked over at the open front door and sighed, now wishing that Katy hadn't taken his advice. He so needed her right now. "What is wrong with me?" he muttered, grabbing the door handle. "You don't even know the girl. My emotions are up and down like a prossie's knickers."

He yelped in surprise when a huge grey hand flew through the gap in the door, the long fingers wrapping around his wrist and dragging him into the room. He blinked a dozen times, not believing what his eyes were showing him. The huge creature gripping him looked down and grinned. Cade's bowels loosened when he saw the oversized canines pressing against the creature's colourless, thin lips.

"How fortuitous to meet you at last, my son." The monster bent his back and pressed his nose hard against Cade's forearm. "All that fine fluid flowing through your young body. It sends me dizzy with anticipation at the thought of consuming you, Cade."

Cade's attempts at getting the thing off him met with failure. The vampire's vice-like grip didn't budge. "Get the fuck off me," Cade growled and jerked his head around the room. "Where's my mum?"

"You have so many demands," tutted the vampire. "You are so strong, Cade, and although you are technically family, if you do not cease your obstinate and insolent behaviour, I will gut you here and now. Your agony will be exquisite, and it will you take many hours to die."

Cade looked up into the vivid red eyes and felt all resistance flow from his body. He could not fight this monster. This was it. His existence was at an end. This thing was going to turn him into one of his kind.

The vampire laughed. "No, my son. You have no future, except for provisioning. You were my waking meal, and even though I am awake, I still intend to finish you off." He pulled up Cade's sleeve and slammed his fingernails deep into the tender flesh of his arm.

Cade screamed out in agony, feeling the vampire's chitin-like nails scrape against his bone. The vampire then slipped them out of Cade's flesh and pushed his bloodied fingers into his mouth. "You are so sweet, my son. I shall regret being unable to consume all of you, but I need my army. I need to wake the others. You might be sweet, but you're not very bright. It pained me to feel you so close to me for all those years."

He was almost ready to pass out, and the vampire's remaining words were lost to him as he came close to falling into oblivion. Through his limited vision, Cade felt the presence of another figure enter the room. Although the pain hadn't let up and the promise of unconsciousness was just seconds away, some part of his brain told him the figure must be his mother. The vampire had already changed her, and she would help the monster holding him to drain him dry.

He heard a deep bellow before feeling the grip on him loosen. Cade felt the top of his shirt tighten against his skin before something hard and heavy cracked against the back of his head.

"Cade, we need to move!"

Another bellow shot through his brain, and Cade felt some of his wits return. He opened his eyes a crack and saw the vampire on the other side of the living room. The monster screamed with rage before flinging himself against the living room window. The glass shattered, and the vampire disappeared into the night as cold air came through the window. Cade lifted his head and looked into the face of Katy.

"I thought you had gone," he mumbled. He then saw another figure lying in front of the bookcase at the back of the room. "Mum?" he groaned. "Oh no, please, not you as well!"

Katy helped him to his feet. "Come on, we need to get out of here."

"I can't leave her!" he said, running over to her prone body. Cade placed his hands on her arm, flinching at how cold she was. He caught his breath, then slowly pulled her onto her back, trying not to cry at the sight of her face crunched into a bestial mask of pure malice.

Katy ran over to Cade, pulled him to his feet, and led him towards the door. "Yes, you can. I'm sorry, but she isn't your mum anymore. That bitch almost had me when I came in here."

He swallowed hard, grinding his teeth at the dull pain that now ran though both of his arms. None of this made sense. "Wait, I don't understand. How did you stop her? Come to think of it, how the fuck did you manage to stop that thing from eating me?"

Katy smiled and kissed him, then dropped something into his hand. "I went through your kitchen cupboards first, and look what I found."

Cade looked down at the now half empty tube of concentrated garlic paste in the palm of his hand. It took a great deal of restraint not to break out in hysterical laughter. He folded his fingers over the tube. "Sweetheart, you're a fucking genius."

She pointed to the torch thrown on the sofa. "I didn't try the garlic on him, Cade, I shone that straight into his face. It appears that he's not keen on bright light." She looked at the woman on the floor. "Your mum got the paste after she snatched the torch out of my hands." She frowned. "We really need to go before he comes back, Cade."

He looked across at his mother, watching her body twitch. His mum now felt like a stranger to him. Something had severed his emotional bond with the woman. He gazed at the wounds on his arms, wondering if that freak had infected him with something. Cade frowned. Why did he need to do that? According to him, Cade was born infected.

Cade walked back over and stared down at her face. There was no snarl now, all he saw was a peaceful looking woman who looked at rest. He then noticed the ugly red welt of blistered skin running across the underside of her arm. Cade guessed that was where the garlic paste hit her. He took one pace back when he saw her whole body shudder again.

"I'm so sorry, mum," he whispered. "I don't know what else to do. Please find some way to forgive me." Cade kneeled down, grabbed her jaw and pulled down, grimacing at the size of her canine teeth.

"What are you doing?" hissed the girl.

"I can't let her continue now," he whispered. Cade held the half-full tube of paste directly over her open mouth, counted to three, then quickly squeezed the last of the contents into her mouth, jumping back when her eyes shot open. She sat up and screeched out in agony as hundreds of blisters bubbled up across her skin and burst apart, filling the air around her with a foul red mist. Cade ran over to Katy, sobbing, not believing what he had just done. He allowed the girl to grab his wrist and pull him towards the front door.

Chapter Five

His own euphoria had long since left him, leaving Jalim Pyga desperate to fill his cavernous mouth to the brim with the sweet blood of some wandering beast. Like the others who were able to feast upon the offered flesh, he only managed to consume a pathetic morsel.

"Do you remember advising me to veil my desires, Jalim?" His companion nervously coughed. "Well, should I not ask you to do the same?"

"I also told you that I would rip out your insides if I caught you sniffing around the inside of my head."

"Jalim, please, I meant no disrespect. I did not intrude. Your craving for the blood is very strong. I suspect even the moles beneath our feet would have picked up your thoughts."

He stopped his descent down the overgrown wooded slope and slowly turned his head, watching with amusement as his fellow scout appeared more akin to a frightened bunny rabbit than a ferocious vampire. Jalim reluctantly softened his features and bit back his harsh retort at the look of genuine concern etched upon the young vampire's face.

It took a few moments for his sluggish thoughts to make the right connections. In relative terms, Dylar Sallis wasn't long changed. A thousand years might have passed them by, and from what he had seen so far, their world had become an alien place. But, Dylar had only joined the Swarmer's clan a few weeks before their ultimate plan had gone disastrously wrong.

Dylar would, in due time, change his whole outlook and allow his recessive vampire blood to rise like oil in water. The inexperienced vampire would need to feast many times upon the blood of beasts for his true form to gain prominence. Until that moment, Jalim would just have to tolerate this sallow excuse for a predator still thinking and acting like human food.

"I will take your words under advisement, Dylar," he replied sardonically, struggling not to visibly sigh when his colleague beamed. Unlike him, the young vampire had yet to come down from his initial first tasting. When he did, the vampire would hit the ground with a tremendous crash. The after-effects of the first taste after the long sleep could even equate to the ecstasy rushing through their veins just after drinking from their first neck.

He swung his head back and gazed up into the tree canopy, watching the night creatures flit from branch to branch. Jalim listened to their minute hearts, imagining their minuscule amounts of hot blood running through their tiny bodies.

Dylar's nervous quip regarding the moles struck a chord. Jalim could sense very little activity under the earth. In fact, there seemed to be very little life inhabiting this forest. He knew why. That much had been obvious as soon as their clan had emerged into the open and gazed in confusion and fury at the impossible number of human-built structures stretched across the horizon. The beasts had bred out of control, and as they advanced, the lesser animals had obviously decreased in numbers.

It made him sick to the stomach to find their food now dominated the planet. How could that have happened? Their kind had not allowed that many breeders to flourish.

It would take them many decades to bring the population under control, if it was even possible. These things were a plague.

He ground his teeth in frustration; there would be no chance of them regaining their dominance if their clan leader would not allow his vampires off the strangling leash.

"It is so good to feel the wind upon my face, Jalim. The scent of the animals and of the surrounding plants makes my blood sing." The young vampire jumped up and snatched something out of the air. "This is just glorious."

Jalim saw a piece of leathery wing poking through Dylar's fingers and listened to the bat's bones crush when Dylar squeezed his fist tight. Dylar raised his hand and allowed the few drops of blood to land on his tongue.

"We should be running down the beasts, Dylar. This is not glorious at all. He has reduced us to the stage of mere parasites." Jalim watched, disgusted, as his companion frantically licked off the animal's blood from the palm of his hand. "Just look at you! That is vile. Have you no respect?"

The other vampire just grinned. To Jalim, the fool looked like some drunken youth who has just had his first taste of a virgin's wet hole.

"He asked us all for just a few hours of patience, my friend." Dylar threw the corpse into the undergrowth and took in another lungful of air. "No, it really is glorious. He will make us all kings of this strange world, Jalim. The food will never end." He ran over, his eyes shining. "Oh, how I wish I could have gone with one of the other two scout groups."

"Are you not enjoying my company? Are you suggesting that I displease you in some way?" he growled, watching the vampire regress to that frightened rabbit. "Your stupidity and blind faith is the reason why we are stuck in the middle of nowhere while the others enjoy the taste of meat."

Dylar shook his head. "Jalim," he said, "he promised t we would all taste together."

"You really are so naïve, Dylar. When he said those words, our courageous leader was not looking at us." Jalim spotted a tree stump and made his way towards it. "Go collect some wood and ensure it is dry."

"Why, are you cold?"

"Of course I'm not cold, you foolish boy," he snapped. Jalim picked up a broken branch and threw it at his head. "It is not just moths that flames will attract." He sat down and waited for the boy to disappear into the foliage, then ran over to the spot where Dylar had dropped the bat, picked up its shattered body, and attempted to squeeze out some more of its bodily fluids. A few drops hit his tongue, and the quantity paled in comparison to what he intended to catch tonight, but the taste did help his own blood cool down a couple of degrees.

"Why are you still allowing that fool to treat you like a whipped dog?" he muttered. The words felt alien to him. Even the thought of being responsible for the loss of cohesion within the clan was unheard of. The clan's strength lay in numbers, even if he could count that number upon toes and fingers.

The last time a clan split, it caused the Great War, a conflict that almost annihilated every vampire in the land. Jalim sat back down and thought back to the last night before their leader and a few survivors all felt the urge to take the long sleep.

The few Swarmers remaining had all congregated behind the burning remains of their last fortification. He, Healiod, and Cranus were watching their last flesh dragon tear into the enemy clan's regiment of beast fighters.

The huge soldiers were an amalgamation of assorted animal parts, sewed together and given pseudo-animation with pure vampire blood. A steel exoskeleton, part cage and part support, ensured no Swarmer could take them down with brute force or human supplied weapons.

Jalim's strength, like his companions', had left him, his broken body covered with countless bites, blade wounds, and shattered bones. His blood could no longer heal him. The unthinkable was taking place—he was going to die here. His last flesh dragon disappeared under the bodies of the beast fighters. It shredded at least half a dozen before the three remaining fighters ripped open the monster with their bladed weapons.

He wanted to close his eyes. The moment of reckoning had finally come to pass. The fact that he had prophesied this moment even as the new leader had announced his scheme to rid them of the clan menace now felt like a bitter victory. Nobody could win this.

Jalim had lifted his head and watched their last Swarmer army attack the three beast soldiers. It was like watching three wolves dive into a herd of goats. Their vampires didn't stand a chance. Despite the beast soldiers' extensive wounds, their armour kept them on their feet.

It did not surprise him to see their glorious leader stagger out of the massacre and stumble over the piles of dismembered corpses as he made his way to their position. "His actions have killed our clan. He is unfit to rule."

Both Cranus and Healiod had growled at Jalim and warned him to still his traitorous mouth.

Jalim opened his eyes. The stench of death from that ancient battle left him. Desmonus had destroyed their clan and was responsible for allowing the enemy to tear apart his beautiful creations. He glanced through the trees and watched Dylar make his way back to where he sat. The young vampire had escaped the worst of the battles. It seemed ironic to think that before the ultimate plan, before their number was cut from thousands to just a handful, not even a desperate First Father would have contemplated changing such a weak willed and soft bodied child into one of their kind. Even with the vampire blood surging through his veins, Dylar was a pathetic specimen.

"I think I have enough to start to good fire," he said. "Do you really think this will work? I mean, it won't attract him as well?"

Their leader had forced him into a corner. Jalim could not allow that fiend to ground him into the dirt. The Swarmer clan was his by birthright. He could trace his lineage all the way back to the time before the clans split in two, whereas that mongrel son of a diseased pig currently making a fool of him was already set on the path to destruction.

Jalim refused to accept that at least one of their enemies had awoken as well. He had dismissed the thought of an enemy clan soldier walking through the landscape of this strange world, regardless of what their leader had informed everyone of this not being so. The others took his confident words as truth.

It did not surprise Jalim to find that the young vampire had already set about building the fire. He worked with quiet efficiency, and Jalim guessed the boy intended to impress him with at least one skill that he had retained from his human life.

Would he be able to convince Dylar to throw off the clan shackles? After all, the leader had recruited him. His vampire blood ran through Dylar's system. Convincing this timid worm to climb from under the leader's wing would be a difficult task.

Even so, Jalim would have to attempt it, and if he could not turn him, then he would have to dine on him. His lips dripped with drool at that thought—killing their own kind was another sacred vow that they were all supposed to uphold. He turned his head, watching the moon shine through the leafless branches.

He was not as foolish as his leader thought. This wasn't a scouting mission, it was banishment. Their leader expected them to just wither and die like old berries on the branch. Desmonus had no need for his skill, not anymore. He had always been jealous of Jalim's ancient skill of manipulating the flesh. Desmonus believed the dark art belonged in the past.

There was nothing out here to scout.

The boy sat back and gazed up at him. "There, as requested." He turned back around and threw a couple of twigs into the small fire. "I was told never to speak of this, Jalim but, there are occasions when I do miss my human existence. I am sure these thoughts are alien to you now. I know you have been a vampire for countless human lifetimes."

Jalim watched the flames dance over the twigs, keeping silent, waiting for Dylar to apologise. His proposition would gain weight if Jalim could drive a wedge between the young vampire and the one that turned him.

"Have I offended you?"

"How were you caught, Dylar?"

"It was my stupid compassion that snared me. We all knew how dangerous it was to venture out of the house after dark. New rumours of Swarmer bands penetrating clan territory spread through the town every day. I was, still am, a stupid youth. I considered these talks to be just gasps of bad air expelled from the mouth of the market fishwives. We were under the protection of the clan, we gave in blood and livestock, we were quite safe."

There were not many protected human towns that had not been hit by the Swarmers. Only the ones in the two inner domains could still boast full protection. The clans had just about given up on the outer domains and left the beasts to fend for themselves. Jalim had personally stripped three human towns for manufacture.

At the time, he had not been aware that their leader had risked everything to raid the inner domain towns. Then again, they kept Jalim out of all major operations. They did not trust him.

"We all knew the war was getting closer, even the elders believed we should prepare to relocate closer to the castles, despite it meaning we would lose everything. But, even slowly starving was far better than getting drained or ending up as part of the Swarmer flesh dragon." Dylar added some more twigs to the fire. He turned his head to stare at Jalim. "I don't understand why I am feeling hesitant to continue. He told me these attached feelings to my past would leave me."

"I'm guessing he told you many stories, Dylar." Jalim leaned forward and ran a clawed finger along the top of the young vampire's ear. "The passing of the night will not stop still, Dylar. Continue with your recollection."

The young vampire pushed the last twig into the fire. "It was my goat that got me caught. She was due to give birth at any time, and because she was my first one, I wanted to be with her. Both my parents had heard the nightwatchers sound the warning bugle. I had no idea though. Both me and my sister were in the shed, alone with the goat, waiting and watching."

Jalim felt a forgotten part of his anatomy stir at the mention of a female. "Why do you hesitate?"

"Two of them smashed through the solid wood door with ease. I didn't even have enough time to move out of the way before I was grabbed and thrown across the barn. The vampires might have been able to destroy the wood with their fists, but my tender body slammed into the far wall, and I felt something crack. It wasn't the wood, though, the sound came from within me."

Dylar moaned softly. "The pain that rushed through me was unlike anything I had experienced. Darkness swept over me, and I urged oblivion to take the agony away. Before I did close my eyes, my last image was of the two vampires tearing off my sister's rough clothing."

Jalim nodded to himself; he would have liked to have been there. "Wait, was she pretty?"

Dylar nodded. "Yes, most boys and some of the men wanted her." He shook his head and sighed. "I awoke, some time later. I felt no pain. I knew they had fed on my blood while I slept. This fact did not bother me, nor did the sight of my sister's mutilated body lying sprawled in the bloodstained straw. Can you believe the sight of my headless goat lying by her feet caused me to break down and weep? The ones who had done this deed thought me weeping over some animal's corpse was very amusing." Dylar sighed. "I never saw anyone from my town again. The last I heard was that a few days after they had escorted me out, the Deathgazer clan broke their decades old promise to protect the town and butchered every inhabitant."

"He should not have turned you into one of our kind. You were too young. If I had been there, I would have slaughtered you, Dylar. Your blood would have given me such strength. Once I had finished, I would have enjoyed your sister before drinking from her too."

Dylar frowned. "I find no comfort in your words, Jalim."

"Did you expect to find any? I am not a wet nurse. You can take comfort in the fact that I would have allowed your goat to live. You need to come to terms with this one solid truth, Dylar. It troubled you to recall your final moments. This is because you are not made of the correct material. I look at you and I see a dreamer and a thinker. Your heart was full of compassion. Those faults are still inside you."

The boy just stared at him. Jalim's brutal words had left their mark. For once, Dylar had left his thoughts uncovered. His mind boiled with many violent and conflicting ideas. Jalim had given the simple boy too much to contemplate. That suited him just fine. He kept his own thoughts shut and locked. It would not be good for Dylar to uncover that his human emotions would, in time, fade like old smoke.

"I do not understand this. We are Swarmers. It is the other clan who adheres to such conservative ideals. At least, that is what he preaches."

"He had distorted the original ideal to suit his own purpose, Dylar. The other clan corralled the humans, turned them into passive livestock, and kept them as pet animals. They believe in restricting our natural urge to kill. How can that be normal? We live for the hunt and for the kill. Of course, we Swarmers still attempted to keep the line pure, but we knew the occasional throwback would join our ranks, such a thing could not be helped. The human should not be caged up and fattened for the eventual kill."

The young vampire's mind moved like leaves caught up in a blizzard. Had he tried to be too clever with this simpleton? "Dylar, tell me why we are here, in this wood."

His companion shrugged, then looked at Jalim as if it was he who was the foolish one. "You know why. We are scouting the area."

"No, stop repeating his words and think for yourself. I have already explained this to you. There is nothing here to scout. He has banished us. He does not care about our wellbeing. All he is concerned with is that we do not poison the others with our thoughts. Can you not see that?"

Dylar slowly shook his head. "I have done no wrong."

The vampire grabbed the youth's tunic and shook him. "What is my purpose?"

"I do not understand," stammered the youth.

Jalim released Dylar. "My purpose, you fool. What is my role within the clan?"

"You are the greatest of all wizards! Your skill and vision in creating flesh dragons is legendary."

"Exactly, Dylar. And where would the clan be without my ancient ability to manipulate changed flesh?"

"They would be nothing."

"They would be nothing," agreed Jalim. "My presence serves as a constant reminder that without me, he would not be clan leader."

"What about me?"

"He does not want you near the others because he does not consider you to be a true vampire."

It pleased Jalim to see his words finally make their indelible mark upon the young vampire.

"Then, we are doomed?"

Jalim shook his head. "No, this is an opportunity. The humans have forgotten their true place, the beasts really do believe they are masters of all they survey. Just recall our journey from the well to where we stand now. Their taint is everywhere. Even these woods were created by them; the trees are too regular for natural growth. They have cultivated the land just as the other clan cultivated them all those years ago. The beasts have bred like flies on a week-old battlefield. Dylar, you still think as one of the beasts. I believe we can use that to our advantage."

"But ..."

"Strike the reticence from your mind," Jalim hissed. He opened his mouth, then slammed it shut again, his words drying up when he felt the vibrations of something very familiar and most welcome. He stood up and scanned the tree line, smiling when he caught sight of furtive movement beside the large trunk of an oak tree in the distance. The fire had indeed attracted attention.

"Listen to me, Dylar. He severed our allegiance to the Swarmer clan when he banished us." Jalim grabbed the vampire's shoulders and spun him around. "Can you see him?" he whispered. "Tell me what you can take from that approaching meal."

Dylar chuckled, "I can read his mind like an open book. Many of his thoughts are of concepts I cannot grasp. I do know he has already seen us. He is curious but not afraid. A strong streak of annoyance runs through his thoughts. The man believes he is a hunter. He thinks we are sleeping in the woods and our presence will disturb the local wildlife."

Jalim smiled. "Wait until he crosses the fallen tree, Dylar."

"Then what?"

"Then, I want you to kill him. There is enough blood in that bloated body to keep us sated until we can find somewhere to roost. He will be our first kill. The first kill for our new clan."

He drew back from the young vampire, surprised at how quickly his thoughts changed from confusion and panic to lust for hot, sweet blood. Dylar's immature vampire senses had finally awoken, casting out his old soft human feelings.

Jalim silently chuckled. "Welcome to the family," he whispered.

The human had not noticed the subtle change in Dylar's posture. Had this supposed hunter never seen a carnivore tense before the kill? He should allow this dumb beast to continue walking towards his death, but no, where was the fun in that?

He drew up to his full height and glared at the human, willing his own vampire senses to full ascendancy. Jalim felt his canines burst through his bloodied gums, filling his mouth with his freezing blood. He growled and clenched both his fists tight to stop himself from ripping into Dylar's back.

The man finally stopped walking towards them. He must be close enough to realise that it wasn't reflection of the fire that he saw in the two strangers' eyes. They were the colour of molten metal. Like a rabbit catching scent of a wolf, the human spun around and shot through the undergrowth. Dylar did not need Jalim's counsel on what to do now. The young vampire emitted a single excited screech before chasing after the terrified human.

It took enormous willpower not to join in with the hunt. The chemicals flowing from the fleeing human smacked into Jalim, setting his nerves alight for the first time in over a thousand years. He staggered back and wrapped his long arms around the nearest tree and slammed his head forward, biting into the rough bark, hoping the fool would hurry up and make the kill. Jalim would share the blood, but only after Dylar had brought down the beast.

The young vampire needed to remember this gift; this would be the bond that forged the allegiance of his new clan. This new world needed vampires that understood this strange land. The old ways belonged in that pit. This would be his world, and anyone who got in his way would suffer the fate of that human hunter. Jalim pulled his teeth out of the hard wood, jerked back his head, and looked at the full moon, exhaling in delight at the sound of his companion bringing down his first kill. Jalim turned and ran out of the clearing when he heard the abrupt end to the man's scream.

His clan would rise, made strong from the blood of the beast. He would not rest until the other two clans bowed down to him. "Before I crush them all under my boot," he growled.

Jalim saw his companion ripping the flesh from the dead man's neck and burying his huge mouth in the open wound. He smiled at the young vampire's inexperience. He still had much to learn, but not just yet. Jalim needed to regain his former strength; he needed to drink until he was bloated. His vampire senses demanded it. This would be the first of many tonight. After they had finished with this one, he intended to take Dylar out of this desolate woodland and find a settlement. They needed to work quickly to stand any chance of bettering their enemies. Jalim ran over to where his companion fed and dropped to his knees, the hot metallic scent of blood forcing out every other thought. All that mattered to him now was sating his overpowering thirst.

Chapter Six

Nothing in their postures indicated to Damien that his arrival had unnerved the strangers. Perhaps, in their eyes, it was perfectly acceptable to wander around the town centre carrying a naked female in your arms. Or perhaps they were just very drunk and hadn't noticed the irregularity.

Damien didn't recognise any of them, and that *did* surprise him. Welbourgh's metallers weren't that large, and Damien knew them all. He had no idea who these were though. The sour smell of cheap lager irritated his nostrils as he neared their makeshift encampment. Three large men, all dressed in similar long black leather coats, were rolling about the grass verge in hysterical laughter. Another scent caught Damien's nose. These idiots were stoned out of their heads.

"Is it that time already?" he whispered. Damien felt like a complete moron. Of course it was; the festival posters were all over town. The sudden invasion of the metal bands and their thousands of fans in the several fields a couple of miles from the town had been the only subject on his dad's lips for the past two weeks. He had even attempted to organise a protest, asking all the local shops to ban anyone wearing any kind of black leather clothing from their premises. His dad's request had gone down like a mug of iced vomit. The town made a bloody fortune from the sudden influx of Goth kids eager to spend their money on food and alcohol.

It appeared that this advance guard had already started to enjoy the town's hospitality. Damien slipped into a passage between two buildings and gently laid his sister down on a bed of cardboard. He wrinkled his nose at the stench of sour sweat and stale urine emanating from the collapsed boxes under her body. It looked like he'd stumbled upon some vagrant's home. This foul place was no place for his beautiful sister. He comforted his feelings by telling himself it would only be for a few minutes, only until those clowns out there had given up their clothes. "And possibly, some of their blood," he whispered aloud, running his hand down her perfect body. Elsie looked so vulnerable, so desirable. He snatched his hand from her cold skin and stood up, trying to control the hot emotions rushing through his body.

Damien cut off the frustrated growl building up within him and turned away, hoping he might be able to shut off this confusing lust if she wasn't visible. He hurried over to the corner of the building and watched his potential three victims continue their task of getting seriously fucked out of their heads.

"I need to get that girl some clothes before I really do something I'll regret." Before he left the alleyway, Damien glanced back, wondering if he really would regret it. He shook the thought away; he needed to focus on his task.

Damien stopped dead when he spotted another figure further down the embankment, away from the others. His whole body flushed with blood at the sight of that firm body encased in tight red leather clinging to every contour. Her position indicated sleep, either that or she had fallen into a drunken stupor—a state her companions were eager to reach.

This couldn't have fallen better for him. The girl's general shape wasn't much different from his sister's. Her clothes would fit Elsie like a glove. "And that dark-haired beauty will fit me like a glove as well," he murmured, chuckling. Damien watched one of the men stagger onto his feet and head towards his location. He smiled. *This will make my job a little easier.*

"Where the fuck are you going, Trev?"

The small built youth, turned around, almost tripping up over his own feet. "I need to go piss," he slurred. "Don't smoke all that shit, while I'm gone."

He heard the others giggling to themselves as their companion stumbled towards the alley. He pressed his back against the wall, listening to the drunken idiot attempting to whistle. The boy walked straight past Damien and stopped to unzip.

I don't believe this. Is this clown that blind? His naked sister was right in front of the guy, and he hadn't even noticed.

Damien sidled up close to the boy, feeling his young heart pump all that sweet blood through his body. His proximity was driving Damien wild. "Hello, Trev," he whispered, clamping his hand tight over the boy's mouth. "No, you're not going to cry out." Damien dragged his fingernails along the boy's hot flesh. "You have no idea what you are doing to me," he whispered. It was no good, all his intentions to extract information regarding their female companion completely vanished as the blood lust overpowered Damien's rationality.

The boy's thin film of flesh melted away as Damien pushed his sharp teeth through the meat. He dropped onto the filthy floor, taking his food with him, wrapping his arm around the boy's head, ensuring that the grip stayed secure.

As Damien feasted upon the boy's blood, his emotions cooled enough for him to realise that like the artery in his neck, the boy's thoughts were also open and accessible. The vampire saw the female wrapping her arms around Trevor and kissing him on the cheek. At first, Damien believed he was drinking from the girl's boyfriend, but then the memory solidified, and Damien saw the girl pull back and smile at Trevor before handing him a framed picture.

Trevor had just passed his driving test, and his sister, Sandra, had framed a copy of his certificate to give to their parents. Damien discarded that thought and ploughed through the dying boy's brain, looking for any other snippets of information that he could exploit.

Damien's mouth slipped from the boy's neck when he found one dominant memory that rose to the top of Trevor's mind. Damien saw himself standing in a hallway lined in pale floral wallpaper. Once more, he saw through Trevor's eyes. This time Damien watched a hand push against a dark blue panelled door, which opened a crack to reveal a green tiled bathroom. The sound of splashing indicated that the room had an occupant. He moved to the side and stopped when the magnificent sight of Sandra's shampoo covered hair and smooth back swam into view. Damien watched the hand push open the door a little more, and he now saw the girl's small breasts, dripping in soap, bounce up and down as she vigorously rubbed the shampoo into her scalp. Her left hand then fell into the bath water. The girl's legs spread a little wider and then Damien heard the boy let out an audible gasp.

Damien dropped the body when the image of Sandra faded. He took a deep breath, then glanced over at his sister's body, somehow gratified that he wasn't the only one in this little alley who concealed forbidden feelings for their sibling. In Trevor's case though, his urges stemmed from the fact that while his sister enjoyed a healthy sex life, Trevor could only release his frustration with the help of online porn.

"You sad little man," he said, gazing down at the pathetic body. "You are going to die without ever experiencing the delights of pleasuring a beautiful woman." Damien then heard Elsie release a quiet moan and smiled. Perhaps Trevor may yet realise his desire before he expired. After all, his sister needed to feed as well. There wasn't much blood left inside the little man, but it would suffice until he brought her one of the larger ones.

He dragged the body over to the cardboard, then punched Trevor hard in the chest, shattering his ribs. The force of the blow helped to expel a little more blood from his neck wound. Damien scooped up some of the liquid and held his fingers over Elsie's mouth, watching the thick fluid drip onto her pale lips. As soon as he saw her tongue push through her teeth and eagerly clean the fluid from around her mouth, Damien wiped the rest down her cheeks and along her arm, then placed the limb over Trevor's chest. Her vampire essence would complete the procedure.

"Die well, Trevor, and thank me in the afterlife. You're about to make a very beautiful woman very happy." Damien retreated, watching his sister start to stir. He didn't think it would take a long time for the predator inside his sister to detect Damien's generous gift. Now that the sad virgin had quenched one of his thirsts, the boy's delectable sister could satisfy his otherone.

Damien emerged from the alleyway and smiled at the sight of the two other men slumped in the long grass. Evidently, their bodies had decided to shut down for the night and join their female companion in sleep. Well, he had plans to make sure these visitors wouldn't wake. He hurried across the road, keeping an eye on their unconscious forms, ensuring that they were indeed dead to the world.

His beautiful Sandra had not moved from her position. Damien scurried down the embankment, his lustful gaze devouring every part of her beautiful body. He stood over her, placing his feet at either side of her head, then lowered himself and placed his knees on the grass. He gently stroked her cheeks and leaned over to kiss her warm lips. The taste of greasy takeaway food combined with dope smoke made his stomach turn. He pulled back and wiped his lips.

Sandra groaned in her sleep and turned onto her side. Damien felt a little sick, not understanding where this ailment had come from. As she moved, he saw something flutter under where she had lain. He reached over and picked up a bundle of screwed up, grease-stained plain paper. He took a tentative sniff, and the foul odour of spicy food covered in garlic sauce burned his nose. "You have got to be fucking kidding me," he growled, tossing the offending object over his shoulder. The sickness he felt inside came from what this woman had for her last meal.

Damien placed his hands on her head and closed his eyes. Her sleeping mind showed Sandra and her companions receiving abuse from a group of chavs slumped outside a takeaway. They all gave back as much as they received before staggering away, giggling. Sandra's stomach begged her to ram the food into her mouth right now. Her brother and her mates were all telling her to wait until they got back to their site because the food would taste better washed down with lager. She was having none of that though. Sandra told them she needed to be satisfied right now.

The tall youth stood next to Trevor had thought her statement was just priceless and told her he'd be able to sort her out, but still, she'd have to wait until they got to the site. He was worried one of the locals might have stumbled on their hiding place and made off with all their gear.

Sandra had laughed alongside the others, knowing that before the festival was over, she would definitely be taking Nathan up on that offer. She knew he fancied her to death. Did it matter that they were both engaged? Well, not to Sandra. Granted, her Tommy was the sweetest, kindest, and most generous man she had ever met. The fact that his parents were loaded just sealed the deal in her opinion. The only downside was her hunky man wasn't the greatest lover in town, and he certainly couldn't satisfy her desires, no matter how hard he tried. Nathan's girl just adored him, and Sandra knew he would do anything for his fiancé. He would never do anything to hurt her, and despite his flirting, that included sleeping with Sandra.

He noticed the girl's inner-self begin to react to his proximity. Some dormant area of Sandra's mind had already woken, knowing that the girl was in mortal danger. It now struggled to alert the rest of her body, to warn that a predator was in her midst.

Damien watched her limbs jerked spasmodically. She would be waking at any moment, and he couldn't allow that. Her alert mind would spoil his plans. He dived back into her mind and drew back from the torrent of concocted nightmarish creations currently flooding into her dreaming psyche.

"Sandra!" he hissed, shaking her arms. "It's me, it's Nathan." Damien put his hand across her eyes. "Please, I don't want you to make a sound, the others are fast on. I want you, Sandra. I want you more than I've wanted anyone in my life." He took an audible breath. "We'd both be seriously fucked if the others catch us together."

"You sound so different," she slurred.

Damien ran his fingers along her inner thigh, grinning wildly as she reacted to his exploratory hand by closing her legs and pushing his hand as far as it would go.

"The smoke must have fucked with my voice," he said. "Don't let it concern you. I'm going to make you very happy, Sandra. Is that what you want?" He traced the outline of her groove through the material, not surprised to discover the girl wore no panties.

"I want you to keep your eyes shut tight, Sandra. We're going to play a game. No peeking though," he growled. "I mean it, one peek and that'll be the end of our playtime." He found the shape of her clitoris through the leather and pressed down hard, then leaned towards her ear. "There's a good reason why Georgia doesn't like to let me out of her sight."

Damien moved his other hand off her face. "Promise not to look?"

Sandra nodded. "Oh yeah, I'm good at keeping promises."

"We'll see about that," he said, hooking his fingers into the top of her trousers. He ginned as she moaned out loud and lifter her bottom in the air. Damien pulled the leather down her shapely legs. The flesh looked so much more delicious uncovered. He lifted her legs into the air and ran his tongue down, only stopping when he reached the top of her warm thighs.

"Please," she begged. "I need to feel you inside me."

He couldn't ignore his own lust any longer. Damien climbed off the girl and pulled down his trousers and boxers. The cold night air felt good on his solid penis. He knew it wouldn't stay cold for much longer. He fell to his knees and pulled her body hard against his.

She gasped as Damien entered her. He wrapped his fingers around her sides and settled into a slow rhythm. Grinning as she moaned loudly, he took his time to enjoy the girl.

The urge to bend down, puncture her skin, and drink was almost impossible to ignore. As he thrust into her body and the girl eagerly responded by pushing forward when Damien slammed into her, his essence demanded that he dive down and open her neck.

Damien bit back a howl when he felt her close to climax. His essence instinctively knew what she wanted from him. It took an incredible amount of stamina to ignore his urge to drain the girl, so much so, he had not realised that he had given Sandra her first climax.

He saw the confusion in her face when her eyes shot open. Damien skimmed along the surface of her mind and only found her pleasure receptors turned on to full. Despite the fact that throes of ecstasy gripped her tight, he could not allow her to cry out a word to alert the others. Damien placed his hand over her mouth, uncertain if he should have done with it and just kill her.

Sandra smiled and wrapped her arms around his neck. "I don't care who you are," she purred. "Oh my Lord, that was just incredible. Please, don't leave me?"

He'd never expected this. Damien gently pulled the woman off him and gazed down at her beautiful and flawless body. "Take off the rest of your clothes," he whispered, watching her happily comply. Just like that female vampire had enthralled him, he had enthralled Sandra.

What an astonishing gift!

He pulled her supple body into his embrace, relishing the feel of her soft flesh against his.

Damien had an obligation to fulfil though, and his conversation with his mother could not wait either. Damien needed to know what was happening, and he knew she'd be able to fill in any missing details.

"Listen to me," he hissed, pulling her away and standing up. "You need to leave this place. You need to do that right now. Forget the festival, forget your friends, and just go." He wiped away her tears. "Stop that, I know where you live, Sandra. I'll come for you. I promise."

He pushed the weeping girl away, scooped up her clothes, and ran back up the hill, where he discovered both men were still sleeping. His sister needed more food, but he couldn't take both of them. Damien chose Nathan and threw the drunken youth over his shoulder before running back into the alley.

He saw his sister before she saw him. Damien was so happy to see her awake. She spun her head at the sound of his footsteps and glared at him. She sat, huddled against the corner of the building, shivering with the cardboard wrapped around her body.

Blood, gristle, and pieces of wet flesh wrapped around her visible body and soaked into her covering. Nothing remained of the boy save for a stripped and bloodied carcass.

Damien threw the clothes towards her. "I see somebody was very hungry. You know that all that red meat is bad for you. It won't do your figure any good." He smiled at his sister, trying to be relieved to see her finally awake, but he could not get past what she had done to the boy's body. He dumped the other one on the floor.

"I brought you another present, Elsie. I didn't think the first one would fill you up. It seems that I might have been wrong?"

She snarled at him, showing Damien her new teeth. They were a lot larger than his. She jumped up. Damien felt his own essence filling his body with adrenalin, urging him to flee, to turn away and race out of the alley before it was too late. Elsie leaped forward, moving at an impossible speed. She knocked him to the floor, following him down, wrapping her fingers around his neck, and holding him in a vice-like grip. No matter how hard he struggled, Damien could not move her; his sister was far stronger than him.

"You have turned me into a fucking monster!" she screamed into his face.

Damien turned his head, feeling hot spittle blasting from her mouth. He tried one more time to shift her hand off his neck.

"Those evil bastards killed my Ben, thanks to you!" she sobbed. "They ate him, didn't they?" She looked across at the bloodied skeleton and moaned aloud. "Just like I did with him. I ought to kill you for your stupidity." She then looked over at the other body and ran her long tongue over her lips. "I ought to kill you, but I won't. I mean, you have brought me another gift."

He felt her blood lust rising, felt as though he was lying under a pylon charged with a million volts of electricity. Damien actually feared for his own life. He really had created a monster. He was like a zebra under the paws of a lioness.

"If you hadn't brought me him, Damien, I would have killed you and feasted on your dirty blood. Let me tell you right now though: if we do ever cross paths, I will kill and consume every part of your hateful body."

She stood up and glided over to the groaning boy. "I suppose I should thank you for the clothes as well. Before you enquire, yes, I do know where you got them from. Maybe I'm being too hard on you? After all, you are only a man, just an eager pawn in the service of that woman." She laughed. "You really don't know how deep she has her claws into your flesh, Damien. Even now, I can feel the hag's claws hooked into your mind. You're just another one of her pet doggies." She dropped to her knees beside the body.

"Now, get out of here before I change my mind."

He staggered back at the horrific sight of her jaw unhinging like a huge snake. Her dagger-like teeth burst through her gums, filling her mouth with an array of razor sharp, curved canines.

Damien ran out of the alley, reaching the embankment in seconds. Neither of the humans were there. All he saw was a patch of flattened grass. He made his way down the slope and threw himself down, feeling like a building-sized rack had just fallen upon his body.

Chapter Seven

Their collectors hunted in the far lands, beyond the great mountain ranges. Their quarry was the strays cast out from other clans. The Gods and Demons demanded a heavy tribute in return for their protection, so the hunters needed to fill the five large cages on the outskirts of Freya's settlement.

As a child, Freya knew it was forbidden to speak to the prisoners. Their parents explained the ones in cages were less than human, no better than the animals they slaughtered for food.

She had no reason to doubt their word. After all, the ones kept in the tribute cages did indeed act like animals—they spoke in a hard to understand guttural tongue, and rumour had it they had a fondness for the cooked flesh of children.

Freya could not remember exactly when the true purpose of why their settlement kept the tribute cages full dawned on her. Perhaps she always knew, but her immature subconscious refused to accept the horrifying truth.

There were times when she wished her childhood ignorance had never gone away. The fear and self-loathing which they all felt seeped deep into their bones. The elders in the settlement had always tried to reassure their following, asking them to remember how life was during the times before the tributes, back when the monsters took what they wanted, how they all lived in fear of losing their families during the raids.

Now, they had peace, of a sort. Now, they were able to live.

Freya wasn't the only one in the settlement who shared the unspoken belief that although the monsters would not take them, their souls would never be clean. If such an afterlife existed, then their entire clan was destined for eternal torment once their bodies ceased functioning.

The days of plenty had vanished now. A war raged between the two vampire clans, and as a consequence, the monster to whom they owed their allegiance had demanded more and more tribute.

Now, most of the tribute cages had lain empty for weeks. The few pitiful specimens currently inside cages—strangers found raiding the crops or criminals caught disobeying the Enforcer's laws—wasn't half the amount the settlement offered to their masters. Even the dullest of dwellers understood the consequences of handing over less than what was acceptable. Their master would simply fill up the quota with the dwellers' elderly, sick, or their children.

There was no other option though. Their collectors dare not stray far from the settlement's perimeter. Their status no longer held immunity. Both clans picked off anyone stupid enough to travel the empty roads.

Freya sat up in bed, pulled back the rough woollen cover, and climbed out of her warm pit. The next few hours demanded a sharp mind, clear of disturbing fripperies. Thinking like an old fishwife could only bring about uncertainty followed by disaster. Fretting about their situation would not bring about a magical change.

"Count your days well, Freya," she murmured. "Just be thankful it's unlikely you would end up in the tribune cage." Freya stood up, removed her nightdress, and laid it at the end of the bed. Her dressing could wait a few moments. The cool draft blowing in from her windows and playing across her naked body felt so divine. Freya stretched her leg muscles, bending down and running her hands along her flesh.

She glared at the fat pile of worthless skin sill in the bed and sighed quietly. Sometimes she really wished she had chosen another path for her life. Freya cupped her left breast, allowing her fingers to caress the contours. What would it be like to actually have a man who would treat her like a real woman as opposed to some object whose only purpose was to make him eject his seed?

She found comfort in the absolute fact that no matter what happened this morning, at least she would be saved from occupying their woeful amount of flesh away to their master's castle. She snatched her gown from the wooden hook behind her and quickly threw the material around her body.

They wouldn't dare to take her; she was the Enforcer's wife. The fat slug might be the one who made the law, but Freya was the one who ensured the collectors carried out their duties with diligence.

She quickly tied the belt, watching in disgust as drool slithered down the fat man's wet lips and landed upon the woven straw mat under his head. Perhaps she had better revise her sense of value. Noone was so indispensable in their master's eyes. She, as well as the other dwellers, was painfully aware that their masters only saw them as livestock. The only reason why their settlement had flourished was because one Enforcer deep in their past had taken the decision to supply the vampires with tribute.

"Nothing lasts forever," she whispered, attempting to tune out his loud snoring. As Freya bent down to pick up her sandals, the stale stench of bad beer escaped from the man's mouth. The fumes almost knocked her sideways. Her own breath stayed locked inside her mouth as she retreated towards the door that led into the compound. Her heartbeat raced like a galloping horse. The foolish man had committed the unforgivable sin of drinking the night before the arrival of their masters. They were all dead. The vampires would not take this insult lightly. Freya turned and ran for the door, not knowing what to do.

"Nothing lasts forever," she cried. "We'll all be lucky to last past this day."

Freya pulled open the door and stared up at the early morning sun, warming her face. She glared at the group of five collectors sat beside their barn. It appeared they were too engrossed in losing money in some dice game to have heard her open the door. Looking at the state of the forecourt, Freya wondered if she was the only person in the settlement who actually valued her life. Those lazy fools had not started on any of their assigned tasks.

She silently closed the door and tentatively made her way across the wet cobbles, avoiding the animal dung and puddle of mud. They had two carts full of fine sand, left over from the last visit from their masters, inside that barn. This courtyard was supposed to be clean this morning, ready for the sand to go down. It would take them more than half a day to ensure the stones were clean now. Half a day that they could have spent washing the tribute, making sure none of the filthy creatures had rolled around in their own shit.

"There isn't enough money in that cup to buy even one of you from tribute," she snarled, gaining little satisfaction at the collective gasp coming from the collectors. How these idiots were able to catch anybody out beyond the settlement was a complete mystery to her. Were they that engrossed in their silly game not to have noticed her walking towards them?

"My husband has yet to wake." She stepped back, her foot narrowly missing a pile of manure. "Perhaps he will wake before this yard is clean. Perhaps he won't. You all know you'll be joining the tribute if this task is not complete." Freya turned and hurried towards the compound, listening to them untangle their flailing limbs to try and make a start on their jobs. She knew her name would now have less value than the foul residue spread across the courtyard. They would spend the next few backbreaking hours imagining methods to either kill her or eject their worthless seed into her holes, perhaps even both. It did not matter what they thought of her as long as they completed the task before the appointed time.

She did not need to look behind to know five pairs of eyes were watching her as she opened to the door that led into the compound. It must destroy their very large self-esteem to have such a beautiful woman order them about like they were no more important than unruly children. As for worthless seed? Perhaps the opposite would be more appropriate. It was not a huge secret amongst the dwellers that the Enforcer's wife could not give the man a child.

Even from the bottom of the compound, the faint moans echoing from the tribute assaulted her ears. She examined her nails whilst walking between the dozens of cages, relieved that the collector had at least cleaned up this area. Even the sand beneath her feet was fresh. Freya reached the first occupied cage and peered through the iron bars at the young girl who had made the mistake of trying to steal from their orchards three moons ago. They had no idea where she came from and questioning her had proven worthless; nobody understood a word she said. Normally, they did not give away females, no matter where they came from or whether they had transgressed their laws. A good healthy female of child bearing age could provide the settlement with more children, a commodity they desperately needed, But their healer had proven that, like Freya, this poor girl's insides were not designed to grow new life.

She watched the girl sleep, wondering if she even knew of her fate. If they weren't living in such frantic times, Freya would have allowed her to leave the settlement. The similarity to her first experience within this very same cage after the healer had declared Freya a burden to the settlement was too great to ignore.

"I do wish you had chosen another settlement to raid, child," she whispered, holding the bars. The girl stirred. Freya saw the five men—the other captives—further down the compound rise and approach their bars.

"Your time with us will soon be over. I do not know what the master will do with you. Perhaps you may survive unchanged. I know they do keep some humans as servants. If you prove your worth, that may still be your fate."

There would be little chance of that happening. This girl, like the rest of them in here, would end up divided into rough cuts of meat, either to feed their soldiers or to use as spare parts for the Clan's dwindling stock of beast fighters.

"If I had been born with your dull looks, child, my life might have gone down another path." Her beauty had singled her out from the rest of the settlement's children long before she had reached the age to wed. Only her overprotective father and wise words from her mother had allowed Freya to have any kind of innocent childhood. "I wish my body had not filled out." She looked down at her large breasts, remembering how almost every man in the settlement had attempted to bed her. Many had succeeded. It hadn't taken long before the Enforcer had noticed her promiscuity. His concern stemmed from the fact that even after so many men had used her, Freya was not with child.

She sighed. "Perhaps not." Freya turned away from the cage, knowing full well that if it had not been for the enforcer taking a liking to her, at least a lusting after her young, firm body, she would not be where she stood now.

Freya jumped at the sudden sound of a quiet sob coming from the girl.

"Please, don't leave," she whispered.

Freya spun around and grabbed the bars. "You ... you can talk?" she stammered.

The girl nodded. "Please help me, Freya. I don't want them to eat me. I'll do anything. I really am sorry for stealing your food." Tears streamed down her cheeks. "It had been days since I last ate. My settlement threw me out with the rubbish."

She stared into the girl's eyes, trying to find any untruth in her words. All she heard was quiet desperation. The other cages were very quiet, and she knew they could all hear the exchange of words. Freya also knew that despite what her feelings told her, there could be no possibility of her releasing the child. Even her status would not protect Freya from the wrath of the dwellers. Freya closed her eyes and suppressed a sob. She could not walk away and leave the girl in there; her conscience would not allow it.

"Listen to me," she whispered. "Take this key, go lie back down, and wait until the others have lost interest. If they see you unlocking the door, they will raise the alarm."

Freya turned around and gasped in surprise at the sight of the five collectors stood at the end of the compound, with her husband stood behind them. Instinctively, she backed towards the cage, watching them approach. The looks upon their grim faces told her everything she needed to know.

"Did I not tell you!" giggled one of the collectors. "She is planning to let them all out. Just look at the male tribute. She has already been inside their cages. Your wife never leaves them alone."

Her husband pushed past the men and strolled between the rows of cages, his eyes not leaving hers. "Should I even be surprised, Freya?" He ran up to her, raised his arm, and slapped her left cheek. The force slammed her body into the cage.

"It is all lies!" she cried out, feeling hot blood drip from her split lips. "Those wolves do not care about the future of our settlement. As soon as the masters arrive, they will flee into the wilderness."

"Now you really are allowing your lying tongue to vomit fiction. The master would have stripped our settlement weeks ago if it wasn't for them bringing in much needed tribute." The large man pressed his face against the bars. "Little girl, I have a present for you." He took out a green apple from within his deep pockets. He turned and smiled at Freya. "The dice were kind to me, last night."

Freya tore her eyes away from his stare and saw the girl reach towards the offered prize. "No," she whispered.

Her husband pushed her away from the cage.

When she tried to get up, she found the collectors holding her down. Freya watched the girl slowly close the gap between her and the nodding man. His hand snapped forward, and his fingers managed to grab the girl's hair. The small key fell from her fingers and clattered onto the dirty floor when the enforcer slammed her hand into the bars.

"Looks like I owe you an apology," he said, smiling at the collectors. "Freya, I have enjoyed our time together, but the safety of the settlement must come before my needs. The First Father himself is coming to inspect the tribute tonight. Perhaps your addition will persuade him not to strip the settlement bare."

Freya looked down at the broken child, watching thick grey liquid seep from her broken skull. "You are an evil man," she spat. "I hope the First Father eats out your black heart."

The enforcer chuckled and moved away from the gate. He stooped down and picked up the key. "I think the only thing he will be eating out is you, my lustful but unfaithful wife." He unlocked the door. "Amulius is going to be most happy with my tribute."

***

The sudden movement jerked Darlene awake. She shook her head, watching that pivotal moment from her past life fade like old smoke. She took in a lungful of warm night air and gazed into the First Father's crimson eyes. "That was so vivid," she murmured. "It felt as though I was actually reliving the event."

He shrugged his great shoulders. "The time before my first bite has started to unfold. These memories built up your inner core, they helped to govern how you lived your many lives after I had to leave you, Freya."

She smiled and ran her nail down his cheek. "Call me Darlene now. It's the name I prefer." It did feel strange to hear her old name fall from his lips. She realised now that the name just didn't belong to her anymore. "You still haven't told me why you slept for so long, Amulius."

107

"It was not my intention to …" The great vampire blinked, then slowly ran his thick tongue over his teeth, before chuckling. "Okay, I shall call you by that name if it pleases you. Darlene, I did not intend to sleep for all the countless sunups. Like the bear, our clan would only hibernate until our food supply had time to replenish. It would have taken just a few human generations for the beasts to refill the land."

Darlene leaned back and watched an aircraft pass overhead, the light blinking regularly across the night sky. She turned her head and gazed at the back of her house, wondering if her true husband knew just how the humans had filled the land. Evidence of their work lie everywhere. She wasn't sure if this ancient creature realised just what marvels his prey had conceived of in the eons he had slept. She feared he wouldn't adapt and would underestimate them.

It wasn't just the vampire who craved violence. Darlene closed her eyes, completely aware that she now considered herself a fellow vampire, a separate species to the human. She would have to help her husband to adapt. One fact did stand out: their former meals would not be happy for their masters to try and impose authority.

"I ish that, like that bear, my sleep was peaceful, Darlene," he whispered. "My enemy could not afford to allow me to wake first. He took the extreme measure of invading my home. He and his surviving filthy clan had the impertinence to fall into my own sleeping pit."

"I don't understand. He had you. Why did he not put an end to you right there?"

Amulius shook his head. "The time to fight had passed us by. Our only concern was to protect our bodies before the long sleep took us. Darlene, the mystics had activated the cycle. All vampires were to hibernate. There could be no exceptions. We were down to our last few. Why do I need to explain this, Darlene? You were there."

She remembered wandering through blasted landscapes, the air thick with the stench of sour vampire blood and torn flesh. The scavengers were many, everyone fighting for the pitiful remains of what little human meat they could find buried under the mountains of inedible, infected undead flesh.

It took Darlene many weeks to actually find another living human survivor. "There was very little of anything left once the vampires had gone to sleep."

He shrugged. "Enough were left alive to allow the beasts to recover and breed. We weren't foolish enough to completely destroy our favourite food source. If we killed them all, how would we ever awaken? Scattered amongst the beasts were others like you, Darlene, who carried my mark. I was not the only one who did this; my enemy had employed the same tactic."

She looked at him sharply, unsure of what this meant. "I thought I was the only one, Amulius. Now you announce that you have other wives?"

"Do you not know anything? Once we sleep, the only substance that will wake us from our slumber is the blood of a human that carries the Clan's mark. I spent all those years locked in a mental struggle with my enemy, each one trying to lure our respective thralls over to the well. My enemy believed if he slept beside me, his influence would be stronger. It appears he was correct."

The great vampire rose and pulled Darlene off the ground. "It matters not," he growled, wrapping his thick arms around her waist. "The past is the past. We live for the moment, and right now, this Clan needs new blood."

Darlene nodded, smiling at him. She sensed Amulius trying to gain access to her secret thoughts, just a tentative brush, but it was there, looking for some tiny crack so he could gain full entry. "Make love to me, my beautiful husband," she begged, brushing her hand over his crotch. There was only one part of her body she would allow Amulius to enter.

His probe recoiled like a startled snail shrinking into its shell. Not that he had any hope of creaking into her mind. Paul was right; her mental powers were greater than his. Her husband had not told her everything. How did he wake? She felt him stiffen beneath her expert fingers. Darlene chuckled when a tiny groan escaped his mouth. Perhaps, she shouldn't be so harsh. After all, she still hadn't explained about her two children, that she wasn't as infertile as she first believed. She wasn't sure how the vampire would react to this stunning revelation.

"As much as I want you, my immediate concerns are more pressing." He took her hand away and kissed it. "Food is abundant." He flared his nostrils. "I can sense those filthy things amongst the herd, Darlene, but they have taken very little food." The First Father frowned. "This does not make any sense. It was against their whole ideal. Why do they not swarm?"

She took his hands. "Look around you, my husband. The humans have not changed that much since our time, only it's other humans who have protected them from harm. Don't compare these peaceful beasts to the cows in the fields. Their guardians will bite back, and their weapons make the Swarmer flesh dragons look like drugged rabbits."

He exhaled impatiently. "Darlene, I am aware of how they have taken the materials around them and moulded it to suit their purpose."

"Then why doesn't it make sense to you?" she snapped. "If those things did follow their primal instincts and swarm, the authorities would have this town under a lockdown within an hour. The army would come in with helicopters and tanks and soldiers, carrying very big guns. They wouldn't stand a chance."

"It does not make sense to me, Darlene, because I have never credited their First Father with a brain built for thinking ahead."

Darlene kept her mouth shut. She didn't think it wise to remind him that, apart from her, he was the only survivor. "If food is abundant, then why are we in my back garden, looking up at the stars? You've already told me that even though they haven't tried to convert the whole town in one night, they have at least made some of the locals into their own kind."

An alien emotion briefly passed across the First Father's face before his scowl returned. Darlene blinked, not completely certain she had seen that look of hesitance etched upon his face. He stormed over to the back door, scooped something off the floor, and returned to her location.

"What does this say?" he demanded, thrusting a torn piece of paper into her hands.

Darlene uncrumpled it and looked in confusion at a full-page advert for some protein supplement to add to milk. "Amulius, I don't understand. It's just an advertisement. They're trying to sell something that's supposed to build up your muscles. Why do you look so distressed?"

"And why do you even ask me that question, Darlene? Have you any concept of our lineage? I am the last of the Deathgazers. I can trace my blood back to the first vampire. I am pure. I am undiluted." He dropped to the ground and drew his legs up. "All I see around me are uncountable hordes of mongrel humans." He reached over and snatched the paper from her hands. "Nothing is what it seems here. You tell me this human has taken some kind of potion to make him look like a prince? How am I supposed to recruit an army of vampires, when the food hides inside false bodies?"

"Welcome to the future, my husband. I do feel your pain. Such vast expanses of food and you have no idea where to start?"

He shook his head and exhaled loudly. "We live for such a long time, Darlene. I cannot allow myself to choose the wrong specimens for fear that somewhere in the far future, my poor decisions will turn against me."

She picked him up off the floor and kissed him. "Amulius, if you don't recruit tonight, you won't have a future." Darlene dragged him over to the back door. "Come on; let me be your guide." Her own blood began to pleasantly boil as she looked at the smiling hunk holding the tub of protein powder against his toned chest and giggled quietly before she screwed up the paper and tossed it into the garden. Darlene knew exactly where to take her husband.

Darlene pulled him across her lawn, looked to her left, and spotted one of her neighbours leaning out of the window and openly staring at the pair as they scaled the high wooden fence separating her property from a stretch of derelict land. It wouldn't surprise Darlene if the nosy bitch had taken a few pictures on her phone as well. She landed in the knee-high weeds and turned around, watching the neighbour close the bedroom window. She decided there and then that the woman would be getting a visit from her later on that night.

"What amuses you?"

She shrugged and took hold of his hand. "Oh, nothing," she replied, grinning up at his confused features. "I think it's just taking more time than I thought to adjust to what I have become." Darlene led him through the rubbish strewn ground, listening to him emit the occasional growl, followed by a sigh. "Are you okay?"

He shook his head. "I do not enjoy this place, Darlene. It is too crowded. My observations have shown the beasts to be more like vermin. Their filth is everywhere. They remind me of Swarmers too much." He squeezed her hand tight. "I fear their foulness will infect me when I feed."

The white glow from the streetlights reflected from his wan face. Darlene jerked to a halt, spun Amulius, and slammed his back into the fence overlooking the back of the shops in the town's main shopping parade. "Wait, are you telling me that you have not tasted since awakening?"

The vampire took his time to nod. "I tracked down the remaining thrall and sipped from her, but I have yet to properly feed. I have not found a beast that does not disgust me, Darlene. I would rather die than to allow their foul blood to contaminate me."

Darlene took a step back to look at him, was he serious? "Is it that important to you? I thought that blood was just blood."

"Blood is the life, Darlene, it is also death. My death would last another thousand years if I willingly took inferior blood." He squeezed his hands tight. "Take me to where you are leading me, my wife. Perhaps I will find what I seek there, though I doubt it."

The blood Darlene had taken from Paul still flowed through her, and she couldn't understand his reluctance to feed.

After spending such a long time cooped up inside a well without feeding, he should have rampaged through the town by now, she thought. *If I was in his place, I wouldn't have hesitated. Damn the consequences.*

Darlene nodded to herself, deciding he would drop this melancholy feeling once he saw where he was taking him.

She ran over to the fence and jumped up, climbing over the barbed wire running along the top with ease. Darlene loved how her body responded to her desires now. She felt more alive than she had at any time throughout all of her previous lives. She ran along the top of the brick wall, leaped into the corner of a carpark, and giggled at the sight of Amulius struggling to keep up. He managed to pull his bulk onto the wall, then jumped down, falling into the side of a red sports car. The grin slipped off her face. "Are you all right?"

"Perhaps I have been too hard on myself," he whispered. "Perhaps I should have fed."

She lifted him up, threw his arm over her shoulder, and dragged the groaning vampire towards the large glass building at the front of the carpark.

"Where are you taking me, Darlene?"

"What is wrong with you, Amulius? I just don't understand why you're allowing your body to perish." Darlene had no trouble carrying the vampire over to the entrance of the building and leaning him against the wall. She was getting very concerned over the speed of his deterioration. Had his body mass shrunk in the last few minutes? Was that even possible?

"I've already explained," he slurred.

Darlene carried him through the double doors, blinking at the harsh white light blasting away their shadows. Amulius hissed and covered his eyes. She looked over at the checking-in desk and at the two large men behind the counter who were deep in conversation over food nutrition. Perhaps her husband wasn't alone after all with the obsession of keeping toxins out of the body.

She sat Amulius down upon a plastic chair, groaning in annoyance as he slid onto the floor.

"I'm sorry, miss," announced a young twenty-something, dark haired man. He glanced over at his older colleague, who sighed dramatically. "But this is a member's only club." The man leaned over the glass counter. "And I don't recognise either of you."

"It doesn't matter," she said, smiling at the other man. His wavy blonde hair hid a defined face, and she judged him to be in his early thirties. He certainly knew how to take care of that gorgeous body. Darlene approached the desk, looking at them one by one, deciding which one to choose. She leaned to one side and saw the gym behind them wasn't terribly full, but guessed there was enough flesh in there to keep her husband happy for quite some time.

"Seriously, miss," said the dark-haired man. "I really must insist that you leave."

As far as she was concerned, his speech had just sealed his fate. "What if we wanted to join up?" she asked, grinning as some of his bluster vanish when he saw her large teeth. Darlene whipped out her arm and wrapped her fingers around his throat. Before the other employee had time to react, she lifted the struggling man off his feet, pulled him over the top, and threw him hard. His body slammed into the concrete wall beside the front doors and slid to the floor in a boneless heap. Darlene didn't need to check the body to know the impudent fool had said his last words.

She grabbed the other man by the arm and pulled him towards her. "Don't struggle so much," she whispered. "You don't want to end up like your buddy." Darlene cracked his head into the counter when his struggles became troublesome. The blow knocked most of the fight out of his body. She gazed in desire at the pulse vein running across his neck. She couldn't stop herself from opening her mouth and sinking her fangs into his flesh.

Her husband's quiet groan pushed through her own desire, reminding her of what she needed to do. Darlene pulled the man over to where her husband lay and rested the young man's head on the vampire's chest, then pushed two fingers into his wounds, hooked them, and yanked them back out. The flesh ripped open, and a torrent of warm blood spurted over Amulius's cheeks.

The sudden change in the vampire's posture startled even her. Amulius lunged forward, his gums split open, and huge pointed teeth filled his mouth. She sighed with relief when he tore through the side of the man's throat and guzzled down the blood gushing from the wound. Darlene looked down at the lifeless lump of flesh beside her feet and wished she hadn't been so violent.

"It is like a forgotten nectar," said Amulius, rising to his feet. He stooped down, picked up the still bleeding body, and dumped it on top of the counter. "Perhaps I should have listened to you earlier," Amulius said, wiping his mouth. He laid the body's arms by its side and chuckled. "Oh, what delights this bright world has to offer!"

"Are you all right?"

He rushed over to Darlene and threw his arms around her. "I have never felt better." The vampire looked over her shoulder. "That was a waste though."

"Amulius, will you tell me what's happened to you? I thought you were about to die a few seconds ago."

"It is the blood, my wife. The stuff flowing through his veins is so rich, so unlike the watery stuff I used to feed upon back before the great sleep. The cows really have gotten fat." He pulled her over to the door that led to the main weight room. "Come, I need more." Amulius opened the door and glanced back at the man he'd left on the top. "It will take his body a few minutes to change, enough time for us to finish this."

He ran into the room, and Darlene gasped at how fast he moved. The vampire crossed the space between the door and the first treadmill in a blink of an eye, diving onto a young blonde woman who hadn't even noticed him until it was too late. He pulled her to the floor and bit into the side of her neck, then he was up, in search of his next victim.

Darlene saw that the dozen or so people in this room had only just started to realise something was seriously wrong. When Amulius allowed his third victim to scream out, the remaining people stopped their activities and ran en masse towards the door. She targeted a huge six-foot, middle-aged man, waited for him to get close enough, then leapt on him. Darlene ran her fingers through his grey crew-cut hair and then bit into his neck, rolling off him as he dropped to the floor. A young woman just a couple of years younger than herself was running towards Darlene, and she grabbed her loose top as she passed and threw her at the panicking crowd trying to all get through the door at the same time.

The flying body took down all but one man who had succeeding in squeezing through the tight bodies. Darlene flew after him, pushing away the other dazed men and women. She ran through the open door and dived onto his back. Her sudden weight caused him to stumble. She wasted no time in sinking her teeth into his flesh. This time though, Darlene drank deep, enjoying the taste of his blood as it filled her mouth.

"You need to watch this, my wife."

She stood up and walked over to Amulius as he finished biting the last human.

He walked back into the lobby and gently placed his hand upon the chest of the man lying on the counter. "We have just made seven others in our shape, Darlene. Each of these seven new vampires has within them the potential to end your life. We have to ensure that does not happen."

Amulius opened the jaws of the motionless man, then held his wrist over his mouth and used one of his pointed fingernails to cut a deep line through the flesh, a few inches from the palm. Several drops of deep red blood fell into the man's mouth before the wound closed up.

"Listen to me," snarled Amulius. "You are the First Son of the Deathgazer Clan. The vampires sleeping in this room are your children. Protect them, keep them safe, and ensure they obey me at all times. Their misdemeanours are your misdemeanours. Keep them under control, and you will be rewarded. Displease me, and your children will feast upon your flesh."

He spun around, laughed, then grabbed her wrist. "We now have our first children, Darlene." The vampire pulled her into his embrace and ran his long fingers up her inner thigh. "Now, while the First Son is tutoring the others, we should find them some meat. They will be very hungry when they awaken."

She growled in annoyance. "No, all that can wait, Amulius. I need you to give me *your* meat. I can't wait any longer."

"Yes, you can my wife, and you will." He threw his head back and laughed. "But only for a moment." He grabbed her shoulders and dug his nails into her flesh. "Can you not sense the blood, Darlene? One of our enemies is right outside. There is a Swarmer in our midst." Amulius ran over to the door. "Our children will have vampire blood for their first meal!"

Darlene ran and followed Amulius out of the door, then stopped dead in her tracks, gazing in utter shock at the sight of her only daughter sitting on the bonnet of a Land Rover.

Elsie looked up at Darlene, not the least bit surprised to see her mother here. She slid off the bonnet of the vehicle and walked up to Amulius while keeping her gaze fixed on her mother. "I blame you for my condition. My whole fucking life has been torn apart and it's your fault." She stopped before the great vampire and looked up and down his thick body. "So, I see my mother has a lover?" Elsie unfastened her blouse and allowed it to fall to the floor, then threw her arms around Amulius.

Darlene screamed and ran forward, then found herself crashing into the side of the building when Amulius lashed out with his powerful arm.

"You can wait until I am finished with her," he snarled.

Chapter Eight

The scene in front of him just didn't make an ounce of sense to Cade. If his mouth dropped any further towards the floor, he'd be scooping up the discarded cigarette butts littering the pavement. The bunch of giggling teenage girls leaning against the window of the takeaway hadn't noticed Cade standing behind the parked silver estate car. Their gazes were all staring through the window at a small group of teenage boys who were arguing with the Asian guy behind the counter.

"It all looks so normal," he whispered.

Cade looked behind him at Katy peering around the corner of the travel agent's shop. She shrugged.

"Did you expect to find dozens more dried up bodies scattered across the road?" she asked when she joined him behind the car, keeping her head below the roof. "Cade, come on, what do we do now?"

He listened to the girls' harsh laughter, watched them tap on the glass. Cade always tried to keep his distance from this type of crowd. His appearance always brought out the worst in all of them. He sneaked a glance at Katy, realising she would have fit right in with that lot currently giving the poor shop worker a hard time. Even so, Cade still felt it was his duty to go warn them, to beg those kids to go and lose themselves in a large crowd.

"My agenda hasn't altered, Katy. I'm going to find those evil fuckers and end their existence. They killed my mother. I can't allow them to take another life."

She turned away from watching the others through the car window. "That's great, it really is, Cade. The only question is how? We have no idea where they are now."

He shrugged. "I know I don't have all the answers. I guess we keep walking through the town until my birthmark starts to itch." Even to his ears, that sounded lame.

"Are you sure that's a good idea, Cade? I mean, it didn't itch when you walked into your house."

Was this girl even paying attention to him? He'd already explained the difference between the two clans. The image of his mate, Damien, suddenly filled his thoughts. Oh hell, in all the turbulence, Cade had forgotten all about him and his sister. They had the same mark, the same brand as him. He dropped to the floor and dug out his phone.

"What are you doing?"

"Ringing up a mate," he answered, pulling up Damien's number and holding the phone to his ear. Damien's aunt lived a few miles outside of town; Cade reckoned they should be safe out there. He sighed when the phone dropped onto Damien's voicemail. He pushed the phone back into his pocket without leaving a message. It might be a good idea to make their way over there. Cade looked at the girl beside him, he'd be better company than this chav.

Katy slid her fingers into his and squeezed.

Cade felt the guilt of dismissing the girl crawl through his system. God, he could be such a twat. This chav had saved his life, for crying out loud. "Come on, let's get moving." He stood up and walked around the car, then stopped dead when Cade saw she had not moved an inch. "What are you doing?"

"I can't go out there!" she hissed. "Those girls know me."

It took Cade a couple of seconds to understand her meaning. He could not believe he was hearing this. He marched up to her, resisting the urge to grab the front of Katy's blouse and shake some sense into the girl. "Are you having a bloody laugh here?" he growled. "After all that we've been through, you're still concerned about your social standing?"

"I'm sorry; I didn't mean it to sound like that. I …"

Cade spun around and marched away from her, crossing the road and heading towards a taxi rank. Her words had cut him deep. He honestly thought there was something special between them. Hell, he should have known better. Despite everything they had been through tonight, deep down, Katy would never change from being a shallow, idiotic, and selfish little girl. The chances were if their paths had not met, Katy would be with those other morons outside that kebab shop tonight.

"Please don't leave me here!"

He had every intention of doing exactly that. He should have stuck to his own kind. It shouldn't take him long to get up to Damien's aunt's place. If the taxis were still running, that is.

Just before he reached the taxi rank, Cade turned around and saw Katy approaching the other girls. He sighed, wondering how long it would take her to point him out, after telling them all some stupid lie about him following her there or something. Cade forced back the hot tears of betrayal. He was such an idiot for going with her in the first place. He should have known better.

"Fuck them all," he said. "You don't need them; you certainly don't need her." He leaned against the lamppost and closed his eyes, gasping in shock when the bestial image of his mother filled his vision. Cade shook his head and groaned when his arm started to itch again. "Oh no," he said. The shadows across the road from the takeaway grew darker, and he watched two uniformed figures step out from behind a large van. They were the men taken from that police car earlier. Cade didn't need his irritating birthmark to supply him with that information. Cade could tell they were vampires just by the way they moved. Each one appeared to waver like a ghost across that road.

He saw that the girls outside the shop had already spotted them and were now banging on the glass. Cade thought they must have already guessed what they were until he saw them all spin around and wave at the approaching vampires, smiling and giggling. Even Katy joined in. Could she not see through their masquerade?

He jumped a mile when he heard the noise of a car engine approach. The car stopped beside him and the driver wound down the window.

"Where do you want to go, buddy?"

He shook his head and raced around the front of the taxi. "Get yourself home as fast as you can," he said urgently, to the middle-aged man staring back at him. "Bundle your family inside your car and just get the fuck out of town!" Cade turned and ran back over the road, watching the three figures get closer to the girls.

"Don't just stand there, Katy!" he screamed. "Get them all inside. Can't you see what they are?"

Her face changed to horror when the three vampires crouched and hissed at Cade. He watched her finally get his message and push the complaining girls into the shop. The three vampires changed direction when the shop door slammed shut. They now ran towards Cade.

"What the fuck is going on here?"

Cade turned around and yelped when the taxi driver grabbed him in a bear hug.

"I know your game, sonny. What the fuck have you been up to? Stealing cars, I bet." The man looked over Cade's shoulder. "Probably something worse, judging by the looks of those three coppers."

"Will you get off me, you idiot!" he screamed. The imagined pain coming from those three sets of razor-sharp teeth cutting into his neck gave him the energy he so craved. "I'm so sorry," he said. "You should have listened." Cade brought his knee up hard, feeling it slam into the testicles of the taxi driver, who released his grip and fell to the floor, groaning in agony.

Cade jumped over the man and easily dodged the approaching vampires, guessing the man on the floor had distracted them, and he was no longer their main target. He felt like the biggest coward on the planet for playing such a fucking dirty trick on the man, but what else could he have done? It wasn't his fault the taxi driver didn't listen.

Cade reached the takeaway and banged on the window, seeing all their faces pressed against the glass. They were all staring in disbelief at the sight of the policemen ripping into the poor taxi driver.

The shop worker raced over to the door. Cade swallowed his frustration and shame, still not believing he'd done that just to save his own worthless hide. Of course they weren't going to believe his tale about needing to leave town. Who did he think he was kidding?

The door opened, and he almost fell back outside when Katy ran into his arms.

"Oh my fucking God, Cade." She sobbed. "I'm so sorry. I really didn't mean any of what I said."

Cade held her tight against his body, feeling her rapid heartbeat against his ribs. He watched a thin youth, sporting a blonde razor-cut and dressed in full denim, take one more look outside before he glared at Cade.

"Are you going to tell me who the fuck you are, what is going on, and why are you touching up my mate's girlfriend?"

"Shut the fuck up, Darren!" Katy yelled. "You wouldn't understand, not even if I drew it out in crayon for you."

The shop worker bolted the door and ran over to the phone. Cade listened to him shout across at his fellow workers in the kitchen. He had no idea what was being said, but judging from the panic in all their voices, it wasn't good.

The shop worker glanced out of the window and then stared at Cade again. "Real police don't do that," he said. He ran back over to the counter, ducked under it, and ran through the kitchen.

Cade hurried over to the one whom Katy had called Darren and grabbed the front of his jacket. "Now you listen to me, knobhead. Those things out there will eat you." He pushed him over to the opening that led into the kitchen. "Your Asian friends have already made a run for it. I suggest you and your little pals do the same."

"They're coming over here!" said a young dark haired girl. "What are we going to do now?"

Darren took the panicking girl's hand and pulled her into the kitchen. "Do what he says, you clown!"

Cade watched them all disappear into the next room, then turned and saw the vampires stop right outside the door and try the handle. He winked at them and showed them a single finger, laughing as they all roared back at him.

"Shouldn't we be following the others?"

He chuckled and nodded. "Why? It's not like they'll come in here now, is it!" He pointed up at the huge plastic menu hung above their heads. He then pulled her into the kitchen and walked over to an aluminium container half full of brown powder. Cade dipped his hand into it and crumbled the stuff between his fingers. "Just look at their faces, Katy. I bet they all know garlic when they see it." He watched them all turn and disappear into the night. "I thought so. I know of a couple of coppers that frequent the Hellraiser nightclub on the other side of town. They once told me that most of the station coppers live out of takeaway boxes, on and off duty."

Katy ran past him and peered into the next room. "The others have gone."

"I just hope that, unlike that taxi driver, they do the wise thing and get the fuck out of the town."

Cade spotted a large cleaver hung on the metal wall, wiped the garlic off his hands, then walked over and lifted it off the wall. He picked a tomato out of a Tupperware dish, placed it on the chopping board in front of him, and slammed the cleaver down, watching the razor sharp blade slice the fruit cleanly in half.

"You can't be serious, Cade."

"Of course I am," he said, grinning at the girl. "We need to tool up."

"Yeah, but, are you honestly going to tell me that you could bury that blade into somebody's neck?" She frowned. "Tomatoes don't bleed, Cade."

He shrugged, then tucked the cleaver into his belt and walked up to Katy. "I'm so sorry," he said.

She sighed. "No, it's me who should be apologising, sweetheart. I acted like a complete arsehole." Katy brushed her fingers through his long hair. "I don't always think before I open my gob, Cade." She looked over at the kitchen doorway. "I know that none of my so-called mates would have risked their neck to come back to save me. That includes my now ex-boyfriend."

Cade kissed her gently. "You wouldn't be saying that if you had heard my thoughts after I'd left you."

She giggled. "I bet you called me a right load of shitty names. It doesn't matter though. I was still in the wrong." Katy smiled. "Do you feel good about helping that lot get away?"

Thanks to his actions, the people in this shop had not suffered the same fate as the taxi driver. Maybe if he saved more, the crushing burden of guilt for allowing that man to lose his life would ease? Cade wasn't that naïve, but he did know that he wasn't directly responsible for his death, just as he wouldn't have been able to save his mum.

Katy suddenly leaned forward and kissed him. "Don't blame yourself, hun?"

He pulled her back. "How did you know what I was thinking about?"

"The shadow passing across your face was a bit of a giveaway, Cade. I mean what I say though, there's nothing that you could have done."

He sighed heavily. "I guess so."

"No guessing so!" she snapped. "You need to stop this right now. Look, those things are not going to stop, just like we aren't going to stop trying to destroy them. More people will die, Cade, no matter how hard we try. If you don't nip this angst in the bud right now, it'll consume you."

"Don't you think that I know this?"

She nodded, "Of course you do. I never thought otherwise. It still doesn't stop you from thinking that you could have saved your mum, you know, like if you hadn't listened to me, for example? Cade, I haven't stopped thinking about it either."

He pulled the girl back into his arms. "Oh fuck, I'm sorry."

"Don't be; just listen to me for a minute. Even if you had ran home before that vampire had got there, then what? I mean, do you honestly think she would have listened to you? And don't give me that crap about she might have known something, because you didn't. I reckon that this strain—this curse—has been passed through your family for generations, Cade. It only activated in you because you went near those buildings."

He shrugged. "I still might have been able to get her out of the house."

"Okay, so maybe she had believed a crazy tale about vampires being real, Cade. How do you think he found her in the first place? It's not like a thousand-year-old vampire would have looked her up on Facebook, is it?"

"So, you're saying there's nothing I could have done?"

Katy nodded. "If you had been with her, Cade, you would be dead as well. It's that simple." She swept her hand across the empty kitchen. "And, if you had died, then who would have saved all these people in here?"

Cade released her, hurried over to the shop front window, and pressed his face against the cold glass. He gazed out into the dark street and allowed her words to sink in. He hadn't thought of it in that way, he had been too busy allowing the guilt to eat into his conscience like strong acid.

"It will never go away, Cade," she said, embracing his back. "That's normal, believe me. I know these things."

"You do?"

"Yes, and if we survive this night, maybe I might work up the courage to tell you about it." Katy gently tapped on the glass. "Right now though, we do have a job to finish. Those policemen are still out there, along with those fuckers who followed us back into town." She shuddered. "I don't want to think how many more of the townsfolk could be changed."

"Yeah, you're right. Okay, let's get this done," he replied grabbing the door handle. "It's weird, I can't see any of them out there. Do you think they could have gone after the others?"

"No, that much I do know."

Cade glanced back at her. "What makes you so sure?"

"It's silent out there, that's what. Have you heard anyone screaming? Both Tessa and Carol have a good set of lungs in their bodies. Believe me, Cade. If any of those vampire coppers were on their tails, half the town would have heard their bellows by now."

Cade started to nod, then stopped when he saw her face change to utter horror. The girl staggered away from the window. Cade spun around just in time to see the three vampires running at full speed towards the shop. He turned and threw himself over Katy's body, managing to pull the cleaver out of his belt before the window exploded inwards and filled the floor with shards of glass.

He rolled off the girl and pushed her towards the kitchen, hoping she'd be able to get to the other door before they caught her. One of them jumped over his prone body. Before he had time to shout out a warning, another one of them stamped down on his wrist. Cade screamed out in agony, catching sight of one of them kicking the weapon to the opposite end of the shop.

The two vampires dropped to the floor and placed their knees on Cade's limbs, pinning him to the floor. He glared into the eyes of the closest one, seeing specks of red liquid tainting both of his eyes. It took him just seconds to realise that he knew this copper.

Cade had seen him a few times in the centre of town, usually asking the local crowd of skateboarders to stop playing around the pedestrian zone outside the shopping mall. The youths thought his requests were hilarious, ignoring the man's calm demeanour. They only obeyed the request when the copper's partner reluctantly left the comforting warmth of the patrol car to provide back up.

"So, you fancy yourself as a hero, do you?"

His partner smacked the other vampire hard in the shoulder. "What are you doing, Frank? Stop it with the conversations and bite the bastard. Can't you sense it?"

Cade watched the other vampire shake his head.

"He belongs to the other clan."

Cade struggled, trying to toss the two vampires off his body. He caught his breath at the sudden sound of Katy's scream blasting out from the kitchen. He'd lost her. That other one must have killed her. "Fuck you!" Cade snarled. He spat into Frank's eyes, then leaned forward and head-butted the vampire in the forehead.

Frank jerked back, his flailing arms catching his partner. Cade bucked his body, and the movement gave him just enough leeway to shuffle out from under the pair. He jumped to his feet, his heart soaring at the sight of Katy still alive. Her condition would not stay like that for long; the remaining vampire's face was just inches from her neck.

He launched himself at the vampire and crashed into his back. The momentum carried the pair of them over to the ingredient table. Cade saw his chance and thrust the vampire's head into the tub of garlic powder.

And found himself thrown back into Katy.

He looked in astonishment at the incredible sight of the now headless vampire falling to the floor. His head had simply detonated, spreading a thin layer of blood, brains, and tiny pieces of splintered skull over the back wall.

He heard the crunch of glass and looked up to see the other two vampires racing out of the shop. The dull ache in his wrist brought him back to earth. Cade coughed, then stood up and helped Katy to her feet. "Are you okay, sweetheart? He didn't bite you, did he?"

She slowly shook her head. "No, I managed to keep him off me." Katy strode up to the body, bent over, and patted him down. "Shit," she muttered. "I kinda hoped that he'd be carrying a gun."

The congealing scarlet mess from the vampire's head dropped from the ceiling, covering everything in gore. Cade waited until most of the stuff had peeled off before he tentatively leaned across and grabbed the container. There wasn't much of the powder left. "We still need to get the other two," he said. "Somehow, I don't think they'll be quite as arrogant after seeing what happened to their buddy."

"Did you see their eyes?" she asked.

Cade nodded, trying to rub some life into his wrist; it didn't hurt as much now. Luckily, his body recuperated quicker than anyone else he knew. He looked at his birthmark, finally understanding the reason for that mystery. "You know what? I think it's a gradual process for them. Like growing up or something. Their eyes weren't fully crimson, and they certainly weren't as strong as the others we encountered." She ran over and picked up his cleaver. "I think you might be able to use this after all."

Cade took the weapon from the girl and stared at the body.

"What's wrong?"

"Clue me up on what can kill a vampire, Katy. You said you've seen most of the movies, just go through the basics for me."

"What's to tell? I thought everyone knew what kills them. You know, stake through the heart, sunlight, cutting off their head."

"And garlic?"

She shrugged. "That depends on the movie, I suppose."

"But we do know that it does work. Just look around you, sweetheart."

"Cade, until today, I thought vampires were just all made up, like the fucking tooth fairy and Santa Claus. Watching my dad's movies doesn't make me an expert on the subject. I'm sorry."

He chuckled. "You've done pretty well so far." Cade held the cleaver up to the light, watching the rays reflect off the metal. "Did a cleaver put down any vampire in these movies, Katy?"

She looked at the floor and shook her head. "Not one that size, Cade. It's great for tomatoes, but I'm not sure it'll be effective against them."

"Yeah, that's what I thought. Size isn't everything, you know." Cade leaned over the body and wiped one side of the blade over the ragged hole.

"That's just gross."

Cade flipped the cleaver and repeated the procedure to the other side, then picked up the container and emptied the last of the garlic powder over both sides of the weapon. "There, now we're ready. Let's just see how brave these bastards really are."

Katy grabbed the door handle and glanced back at him before pushing open the door. As Cade stepped outside, the distant sound of screaming reached his ears. Katy moaned quietly and looked back at him. He could clearly see her terror. He felt it as well. The realization of their dire situation was beginning to sink in. Cade looked down at his bloodied cleaver coated in garlic powder and felt like the world's biggest idiot.

What the hell possessed him to believe that he actually might stand a chance against these monsters?

Katy tapped him on the shoulder, and he turned to see the taxi driver staggering towards them. He looked drunk and certainly didn't seem to be that much of a threat. That thought died when the man caught their scent. The taxi driver shivered and tensed up. Cade watched in horror as the man shot forward, coming towards them like a bullet fired from a gun. His gums burst open, and huge teeth, shaped like ivory tusks, grew from the wounds.

He pushed the girl behind him and raised the cleaver, hoping to God that the stuff on the blade would have the same effect on him as well. He then blinked rapidly as a large blur collided into the demonic taxi driver and knocked the man to the ground. The shape roared and then plunged a sharpened metal pole into the taxi driver's open mouth and through to the tarmac under his head.

"Hello there, Cade."

Cade took his eyes off the abomination and saw the dazzling image of a gorgeous woman standing above the mess, holding a long, silver, pointed pole in her slender arms. "Elsie? Is that really you?"

"Listen to me, both of you. This is your one warning. The First Father is most displeased, If he even suspected I was here, he would likely kill me as well."

She shifted, and Cade gasped when there were suddenly only a few inches separating them. She lifted the cleaver out of his hands, chuckled, then ran her long tongue over the surface.

"Such trinkets will bring down the degenerate Swarmers, but your toys are useless against us, Cade. The First Father had laid title to this town. You need to go, get out of here while you still can." She brushed her cold hand down Cade's cheek. "There will be no quarter given to them. The Deathgazer clan will wipe the filthy Swarmers from the land."

Cade blinked again and found himself standing in the middle of the road. Katy wrapped her arms around his waist. He could see no sign of his best mate's sister.

"What are we going to do?"

Cade had no answer for her.

Chapter Nine

It upset Jalim to witness so much meat go to waste. He picked up his blade, held the severed head between his knees, and scored a circle above both ears. These tools were so fine, it amazed him these knives were so readily available. This world was rich in everything. "Except for vampires," he said, giggling. He licked the blood from the knife, set it back down, then pushed three fingers under the cut skin and tugged it off, revealing a shiny bloodstained skull.

"What are you doing?"

Jalim wiped the blood from the top of the skull and rapped his knuckles against the bone. He then looked up at his companion, annoyed that he had been so engrossed in his task, he had failed to hear Dylar enter the room. "You were told to keep our new friends company."

The other vampire shrugged while pushing the flap of skin around with his foot. "They have not woken." He frowned. "Forgive me, Jalim, but I am not confident they will wake. This all seems wrong."

Jalim swatted his foot away. "Do not allow those thoughts to enter your head." In truth, Jalim had his doubts as well. He had infected many of the beasts back before the sleep. Swarmers were required not to leave the beasts pure. Denying the Deathgazers their food was an effective method of killing them. Although, beasts bitten by anyone other than the First Father just turned into undead ghouls, fit for nothing other than battle fodder.

Jalim clearly heard his companion's thought. The other vampire did not think Jalim's idea would work. He could not chastise Dylar anymore than he could persuade him the sun would never rise again. The only way Jalim could turn his companion into a believer was by proof.

He placed the head on the floor, held it by one ear, and picked up a small hammer. "This is how I used to activate my Flesh Dragons. I injected my own unique powders, dissolved into an alcohol solution, directly into the head muscle of a captured human." He smashed the hammer down on the skull, grinning at the sight of the large crack running across the exposed bone. "It takes a certain skill and many years of practice to do that, Dylar." He carefully picked away the splinters and used the tips of his fingers to pull the skull apart.

"It is not supposed to make a difference how you extract the beast's head muscle, but I believe that it will lose some of its potency if you do not handle the delicate organ with care."

"Did you keep any of your powders?"

"Yes, Dylar, because that is the one thing I simply had to drop into my pocket before we had to sleep for a thousand years."

Jalim stood up and held out the one-half of the bone holding the muscle and carefully walked over to the brick arch that led into the next underground chamber. Their five recruits lay exactly where he had left them, on his hastily built beds of salvaged wooden doors lying on piles of bricks. He could have left them where he and Dylar had dropped them after finding the beasts huddled around a burning metal drum, but like his fastidious routine with the skull, Jalim had to give this procedure ceremony.

"Will this work?"

He glared at the huge idiot peering over his shoulder. "It would not work if I was feeding your head muscle to the recruits, Dylar. Still your annoying, flapping lips before I hurt you."

It pleased Jalim to see Dylar shrink away. It also pleased him to see the eyes of two of his recruits flicker under their lids. It might have been impetuous to believe they had smelled the arrival of the muscle. More likely, the ghouls were simply waking from the effects of the bites.

"They will not be ghouls," he muttered, nearing the closest man. Jalim placed the opened skull beside the man's head, intently watching for any signs of movement. He leaned closer and grinned as his first recruit opened his eyes. His expectation sank when he saw just a few crimson flecks floating in his pupils, the usual indication that they had created the lowest of the low, just another worthless ghoul.

"What can you see, Jalim? Has it worked? Did we do it?"

He ground his teeth together and tuned out Dylar's irritating noise. He had not yet given up hope. Jalim forced the ghoul's jaw open, then, with his other hand, he picked up the half skull and tipped it, watching the grey and crimson sludge drip into the open mouth. Almost as soon as he stopped pouring, Jalim saw the recruit's pupils darken. It was as though he had poured the fluid directly into its eyes.

"I can't remember the lines!" he snapped. Jalim ran over to the other vampire, frantically searching through his memories to when his First Father ordained him the First Son. "Hold this and do not tip it." Jalim stared into Dylar's deep crimson eyes, chuckling at the ease with which he found the words that Desmonus had first said over Dylar's prone body. "Thank you," he said running back to the moaning recruit.

"Listen to my words," he said. "I make you the First Son of the Dragonshine Clan. The other vampires sleeping with you are your children. You must protect them, and ensure that they obey me at all times. Their misdemeanours are your misdemeanours. Keep them under control, and you will taste flesh daily. Displease me, and your children will sharpen their teeth on your bones."

He watched his new First Son run his tongue over the slight bulges of his growing canines, feeling a sense of nostalgic pride, remembering his first time, thousands of years ago. Jalim rushed to Dylar and took the skull out of the other vampire's hands, then ran over to the next recruit.

Jalim performed the same procedure with the other recruit before handing the skull back to Dylar, who had shadowed him. "Have you been watching my motions?"

Dylar nodded. "Are you going to let me do the others?" The vampire caught his breath. "Oh, I'll never forget this honour."

Jalim backed away, shaking his head and wondering how long it would take the young vampire to cease behaving like a stupid puppy. He looked over at his new First Son and felt a genuine sense of kinship with his new vampire and a genuine sense of astonishment that his idea had actually worked.

The vampire raised his chest off the board, blinked a few times, then stared directly at Jalim. "I should hate you for what you have turned me into. Yet, I only feel love and the desire to please."

He watched his First Son climb off the board.

"Tend to your children," he said, nodding in approval as the vampire obeyed without hesitation. "Focus on your duties, my First Son. Remember your previous life but do not desire it."

The new vampire stopped. He spun around and burst out laughing. "Are you having a fucking laugh, son?" He stretched out his arms, spread his fingers and swivelled the arm around in a tight circle. "Well, bugger me. There's no pain, none at all. Until you sank your teeth into my throat, I had no future." He sniffed. "Well, maybe I had a future where I'd probably die this winter, alone and hungry with the rats chewing on my old bones like an ice lolly."

Jalim's First Son took the skull from Dylar and crouched beside the remaining recruit while Dylar hurried back to stand at Jalim's side.

"This is so exciting. May I ask you just one question, Jalim? Why are we called the Dragonshine Clan?"

"Is that not obvious? We were very lucky here. I still do not understand why my experiment has worked. I know the Swarmer clan has been wrestling with this dilemma for many thousands of years. Although I know not of any record of another vampire using a head muscle to fix them, I am sure it must have been used sometime in the past. I am a skilled alchemist, Dylar. The Clan used my talents to create a vast array of terrifying creations." He sighed, remembering his first experiments, all those years ago. "The Flesh Dragons were my best work, and I intend to improve on the design." Jalim laughed at the sight of the other vampire's startled face. "What, you thought I would stop? My new breed of dragon will stamp those foul clans into bloodied pulp."

Jalim turned away and watched his new First Son tend to his vampires. In his haste to comfort them, the First Son had kicked the skull, spilling the last of the head muscle across the floor. Jalim vaguely wondered if the other vampire even cared that his worn boots had flattened what remained of the dead vagrant into the damp stone.

He turned back and noticed his colleague's eyes fixed upon that broken skull. "Does something vex you?"

Dylar took his eyes off the crushed bone and hung his head. "Yes, I fear we took them too easily," he murmured. "They all saw us approach. I scanned them and saw, through their glazed eyes, two monsters. They did not care; they did not run. Even when we dived on their filthy bodies, none of them put up any struggle."

"Do I have to explain their behaviour one more time?" he hissed. "To a man, they were all drunk on whatever foul substance passes for draft in this new age. Also, they were all broken men who had lost their clan. Their reactions were normal. Do not let this matter concern you."

He expected his comforting words to calm down the fool, to stop him dwelling on this quandary, yet he sensed the vampire becoming more agitated as each second passed. It made no sense. Where did this sudden apprehension come from?

"I cannot sense them, Jalim. All their thoughts are veiled to me. It is like trying to read that wall. They are new-born. My First Son used his mind to help my journey. We all shared our thoughts and the elders sent their own passive images to all of us new-borns." He grabbed Jalim's shoulders. "This place is too strange, too hard to understand. Just look at your new vampires, Jalim." He walked up to the nearest one and lifted his arm. "Have you felt the quality of this cloth? Even in this condition, the weave is finer than anything we could have worn before we slept."

Jalim watched the young vampire draw in a rapid breath before running past him, heading for the large hole that the pair of them had knocked through so they could get inside these two chambers.

Once again, Dylar took on the features of some terrified rabbit, but this time, Jalim could not understand the reason.

"He had a bottle in his hands before I killed him. We need to find out what was inside." The vampire climbed through the hole.

"Why are you acting like this?" Jalim shouted. He received no reply. He turned to watch his new clan; they were now all awake and sat in the far corner of the chamber, quietly taking amongst themselves. He would allow them to rest for the remainder of the night before he took them on their first hunt when the sun next dipped below the hills. Jalim looked over at his First Son and attempted to read his mind, expecting to sense a jumble of chaotic thoughts. He frowned. Dylar was correct, there was just nothing there. He tried to read the others and received the same result.

Jalim spun around and hurried after his companion. It pained him to admit that he had been wrong to believe his colleague would sever his clan connection so easily. Swarmer blood ran through Dylar's veins, and he suspected nothing would change that fact. He glanced back at his new clan and saw them all gazing at him. He could not read any of their expressions.

It did not matter, they were his new clan, this was a new world, the rules were bound to be different. He would learn to understand why their thoughts were shut away. Jalim clambered through the hole in the wall and caught sight of the back of the vampire. As he cleared the top of the steps, he expected Dylar to run forward and head for the main doors. Instead, he turned towards the cooking area of this abandoned building.

He needed to reach a decision on how to deal with the other vampire, preferably, before the sun did rise. At this critical moment, his new clan demanded a strong cohesion. He could not afford to have Dylar amongst them if his loyalty was divided; it would break up their bond.

Jalim reached the top of the steps and stopped, listening to Dylar's frantic activities in the next room. Whatever decision he arrived at, Jalim did not believe the young vampire would flee back to the Swarmer Clan. He headed over to the rotten wooden doorframe, wondering just how powerful his new clan could be if he fed them on Dylar's rich blood.

"I have found it!" announced the young vampire, running over to Jalim, holding a clear bottle out in front of him. "It is a noxious potion, Jalim. This vile potion must be ..."

The vampire's words died on his lips and Dylar jerked to a halt. He silently cursed his own stupidity for not covering up his thoughts. This could be difficult. What Dylar lost in intellect, he made up in brute strength.

Dylar held the bottle up to his face before he let it go. "How can such a well-crafted object be so fragile?" he murmured, staring at the glittering shards of broken glass lying by his feet. "I was ready to accept you as my First Father, Jalim." Dylar lifted his eyes. "Perhaps, even ... I even hoped that I would be your First Son?" He advanced a couple more paces.

Jalim resisted the urge to flee, even as the young vampire's mouth yawned wide and his teeth grew longer, pushing up through his gums.

"I know that it is in our nature to deceive, to scheme." The vampire lunged forward, closing the gap between them. He grabbed Jalim's shoulders and thrust his long nails deep into his hard flesh. "It is also in our nature to betray. We do enjoy that one, Jalim. We all have the ability to protect our fragile egos by detecting these traitorous thoughts in the minds of our colleagues." He shrugged. "Well, to some degree anyway."

Dylar leaned close to Jalim's ear. "Your obsession to become a First Father has clouded your judgment. I was trying to help you, Jalim, to show you the error of your ways." He suddenly pushed Jalim back, nodding as the vampire crashed into the wall. "I will not end your life. For a time, I saw you as my friend. The only one who showed me any worth since our wakening."

He backed away, keeping his bright crimson eye fixed on Jalim.

The ten deep puncture wounds caused him little discomfort, his only hurt originated from the dawning realization of how badly he had misjudged the young vampire. Not that he would ever apologise for his blunder, his pride would not allow that.

"I am not short on intellect, Jalim. Perhaps I am a little naïve in the ways of vampires, but that is to be expected, I am not that long changed. I do know that I have been too trusting."

"Did you snatch that thought from my mind?"

Dylar nodded. "Perhaps I misled you regarding my ability? With the exception of the First Father, I had no problem in taking thoughts from any mind, including those supposedly hidden away. At least, that was until you changed those six men."

He leaped onto the worktable and clambered across until he reached a large broken window in the middle of the wall. "Despite your recent treatment of me, I still feel that I owe you two pieces of advice, even if, deep down, I know my words carry very little weight."

Dylar pushed the last few shards of glass out of the window frame.

"Your new clan does not need you, Jalim. They do not need anyone. Please, trust them even less than you trusted me." He grabbed the window frame.

"Dylar, I do believe you said two pieces of advice?"

He climbed through the window, turned and gave him a single tight smile. "The Swarmer clan has found us. Every one of our colleagues are now around the side of this house, standing in amongst the weed infested garden, getting ready to enter."

Jalim heard him drop and raced over to the window, leaned out, and watched the young vampire race through the garden before scaling a high wall and disappearing into the night.

Was Dylar lying to him? Was he just trying to leave Jalim feeling somehow inferior before abandoning his new clan?

Jalim filled his lungs with dusty air. It did not matter. Dylar's pathetic attempt to unsettle him would not work. "May we never meet again," he growled, turning away from the window. His only regret was that his new-born clan would not be enjoying their first taste of sweet vampire blood tonight. Maybe he should alter his plans and allow them to hunt tonight. "It was the brains that did it." He chuckled. "Of course it was."

That was the reason why they could not read their thoughts. His extra supplement must have acted as a screen. "Yes, I'll allow them to taste flesh before I let them sleep." That made sense. If they dined on uncontaminated flesh, the food should flush out the chemicals flowing through their bodies. "Then I will be able to read them, and all will be well."

Jalim hurried through the house, eager to issue his new orders to the newborns. He knew Dylar's comment about the Swarmers standing outside the house was just a hastily concocted lie, but it did not stop him from worrying that the vampire would eventually lead them to his roost.

"Let them come," he growled. Not that he believed his old clan would seek him out, at least not tonight. There were not enough hours of darkness left for them to risk such a mission. "I am the First Father now. Let them seek me out." Jalim nodded, satisfied with himself that all was now well. He reached the stone steps, looked towards the front door, and dared them to enter his domain. After a few moments, he smiled, then made his way back down the stairs.

Jalim climbed through the hole and blinked in astonishment. None of his new vampires were in the first chamber. He slowly looked around the room and noticed that the mashed head muscle had gone too; only small pieces of skull remained, scattered across the floor.

He ran through the archway and discovered no sign of them. This made no sense. He knew none of them had left the chambers, they could not have gotten past him. What concerned Jalim more was that he had told them not to move.

"Newborn vampires do not have the capability for independent thought." This did not bode well. He recalled Dylar's ominous words and wondered if he should have listened to him. "Where are they?" he asked himself.

They had been in this chamber, Jalim saw the evidence next to his boots. The new-borns had feasted upon the headless corpse before making their escape. It took a moment for his brain to comprehend that the now desiccated corpse was not the only anomaly in the chamber. Jalim spotted one of the doors lying on the floor at the rear of the chamber. He walked over, noticing rotten splinters of wood forming a trail over to the dark green door.

He shook his head, not believing their low level of mentality. Jalim slid his fingers under one of the edges and lifted it up, grinning at the sight of the uncovered drain. It must have taken significant strength to break through the thick metal bars sealed into the stone.

"And I gave those ungrateful worms that strength," he muttered. He could see why they had to find something to cover up the mess: they had bent the bars out of shape. Jalim leaned over the hole and leered down, but his night sensitive eyes could not detect movement down there. "Why did you not drop the body over the hole?" he whispered, dropping to his knees.

Jalim lowered his legs over the hole and grabbed hold of one of the broken bars before pushing the rest of his body through the gap. His feet dangled a couple of feet above a fast flowing stream of black water. He spun his head, and his ears caught the sound of a few rats scurrying through the sewer system, but he could not detect any sound that might come from his missing clan. Jalim looked up and squinted, sure that he could hear the sound of footsteps above him.

"Dylar, perhaps?" He released the bar and dropped into the freezing water, glad the level only came up to his ankles. He waded over to the edge and jumped onto the stone ledge, trying to see evidence of their passing.

"Had a feeling that you'd try to follow us down here."

Before Jalim had time to locate the disembodied voice, multiple pairs of arms snapped out of the darkness and wrapped their long hands over both his wrists. He grunted and struggled but stopped all his movements when he spotted a faint human-shaped mass stepping out from a deep-set brick archway on the other side of the sewer tunnel and a pair of dark blue eyes speckled with flecks of bright red glared back at him.

His First Son left the alcove, jumped into the black water, and climbed up the side of the banking. The figure approached Jalim, then ran a single filthy fingernail down the side of Jalim's cheek. "You don't half look surprised to see us, buddy. You thought we'd just fucked off, didn't ya! Me and the lads spent a few years down here, you red-eyed freak. We know all the good spots to bed down, and we can move real quiet too."

He leaned in a little closer, then suddenly burst out laughing. "Oh my, ain't that a fucking pisser! First of all, yer mate does a runner, and then you find that your precious clan have all turned on you and about to get real nasty like."

Jalim gazed at him. "I should have listened to him. I should have just changed one of you. I should have not been so optimistic."

The tramp giggled. "You sure don't half speak funny." He sighed. "Now, don't get the wrong idea about us here. It's not that we ain't thankful for these new gifts. I mean, I can't remember the last time that I could move like this, at least not without feeling like all me bones were gonna split. As for this night seeing malarkey, that's gonna come in handy, that I can tell you!"

"Don't forget the mind reading bit, that's a good un," interrupted one of the tramps gripping his wrist.

Jalim quickly scanned him and still found that he could not read his thoughts. That did concern him. There were many new things he had learned tonight. Jalim should not have been so impatient. He, of all vampires, knew the importance of that virtue

The ex-First Son scowled. "Henry, what have I told you about flapping those lips?"

He reached into his coat inside pocket and pulled out a slim metal stick. It reminded Jalim of a broken spoon handle. He watched, astonished, as the tramp pulled out a blade from within the handle. He marvelled at the implement, the beasts had invented so many ingenious devices. Jalim needed to learn more.

"Thing is, we were all pretty wasted when you and yer big fat mate jumped us. I think you've already guessed that we sorta spent most of our time in that condition. Hell, why the fuck not? It's not like we had anything else to live for." The ghoul pressed the blade against Jalim's cheek and drew it down to the corner of his mouth. "Thanks to what you two did to us, it appears that we all have a different addiction now."

The burning hunger he now sensed from the rest of the ghouls around him ignited his own desire to drink. He forced his body to relax while watching this foul animal use the blade to collect Jalim's blood before he swung his head back and opened his mouth. The ghoul visibly shivered and moaned out loud when Jalim's blood splashed onto his thick tongue.

"Oh, oh that sure does taste so fine," he blurted, staring at Jalim with shining eyes. "I can't tell you what a shock it is to actually taste something. My taste buds were pretty much wiped out years ago."

Should Jalim feel bitter resentment or even disappointment at his current situation? He could not blame these filthy ghouls. These things were the lowest of the low. Their insatiable desire to feed on any living flesh knew no bounds. The ghouls had no cohesion to any clan. Every vampire also knew their duty to put these things down upon sight.

The other ghouls shuffled further to the sides and stretched him farther out while the remaining ghoul lifted the sharp blade and pushed the point into Jalim's flesh, just below his right eye. "The others just wanted to attack you as soon as they saw your body drop into the water. It took some serious persuading to stop 'em from ripping you into little bits."

"You are very generous," Jalim replied with a grin. He opened his mouth, making a point to ensure the ghoul saw his large teeth. It did please him to see the filthy creature take an involuntary step back."

"Are we doomed to spend our lives in darkness now that you've bitten us? See, I can feel the weight of the sun already, even though there's another hour before it emerges." He slashed the blade down again, opening up another long slit in Jalim's flesh. "We're going to make you last until the sun sinks again. Why not? It's not like we have anything else to do."

The ghoul paused. "Why are you smiling?" he asked, frowning. "Have you any idea how much pain we are going to put you through?"

"You talk and talk when you should just cut and cut." Jalim thrust his legs forward, slamming his foot between the ghoul's legs. The force knocked him back into the water. Jalim growled, then pulled both his arms in, scattering the remaining creatures. He grabbed the nearest one, opened his mouth, and ripped out a chunk of its pale flesh from the side of his neck. He lifted the groaning ghoul above his head, laughing as the ghoul's hot blood soaked his head and dripped down his face. He threw the corpse into three of the things who were advancing towards him, hissing and baring their fangs.

Jalim reached into the water and dragged out the wet ghoul. "There is so much to learn about this new and exciting world, my friend." He wrapped his fingers around the ghoul's throat and lifted the struggling creature off his feet. "I do enjoy sinking my teeth into an enigma. The ones that scream are my favourite." Jalim punched his rigid fingers into the ghoul's guts, his sharp nails easily puncturing the flesh. "Even now, I can feel your mind opening up to me as I feel my way around the inside of your ribcage." He wrapped his fingers around the ghoul's intestines, squeezed tight, and pulled the offal out of his abdomen. "There," he gasped, feeling the walls of the creature's mind finally collapse. Jalim pushed his way in, mentally grinning when he found exactly what he was seeking. He dropped the corpse into the water and watched it float away in the current.

Jalim opened his eyes and saw the remaining ghouls lying in an untidy heap just under the hole that led into the chambers. The reason for their quiet demise stood behind the pile of bodies. "Hello," he said, nodding at Dylar. "So, you came back?"

The young vampire shook his head. "I never left. Why would I leave you, Jalim? You are all that I have left."

"You told me the Swarmers were outside."

"Yes, just like I told you I could not read the minds of these things. I lied about that as well. They were always going to betray you. I saw that as soon as I scanned their thoughts." He shrugged. "I needed you to see that I am all you have left as well, Jalim. You are proud and stubborn. This appeared to be my only way to prove that."

"Do you want to see where these tunnels lead, Dylar?" He held out his arm, nodding in approval as the young vampire hurried over to take the peace offering. "You are my First Son. I will not allow the Dragonshine Clan to be just me and you, my friend." He looked down in disgust at the dead ghouls. "Perhaps we cannot turn the beast into our kind, Dylar. It matters not, we shall create them instead."

Chapter Ten

He pulled his hand back, gritting his teeth and trying not to shriek out in agony. Damien wrapped his shaking hand around his wrist and brought the back of his other hand up to his face, moaning in anger at the deep burns running from his wrist all the way down each finger. The pain began to subside, but the damage was in no hurry to heal.

"You have got to be fucking kidding me," Damien moaned, squinting in pain as he saw the dawn slowly eat away the shadows. "Just what am I going to do now?" Those burning rays has almost cooked him alive; they certainly made his hand look like he'd just dipped the flesh in strong acid. He knew if he hadn't dived under this pickup truck, a stinking black puddle of slime steaming in the morning sun would have been the only thing left of his body.

Just one shadow remained beyond the safety of the truck, beyond that, though, only death awaited. His intended destination, a narrow alley, was just a few metres from this truck. He gazed at the back of his hand again, noting with relief that the deep ugly burns did not look so bad; even so, there wasn't a chance of him reaching that alley without the sun turning him into black slop.

"You were a fool to go there," he muttered. Despite her warnings, Damien had returned home, constantly on the lookout for his vengeful sister. He'd found nobody there, although he'd found plenty of evidence of struggle and plenty of blood splats. Looking back, he found it weird that the only sight that had really distressed him was the state of his bed covers. His newly enhanced senses had smelled his mother's juices on the sheets. Some fucker had laid his own mum in his bed, and it wasn't his father.

The dozens of posters he had plastered across his bedroom walls should have given him the first clue. Damien had stood there, his hand pulling the quilt over the sheets with their offensive stains while he gazed at his leather-clad beauty above his bed. The Countess Angelina adorned many House of the Unholy posters. The head of her vampire sect ruled over her mythical land with impunity. The band had even teamed up with a major American comic company to chronicle Angelina's blood-soaked life in paper and ink.

Damien probably knew more about the vampire myth than anyone else in the town. He had still fled from that house though, despite knowing that if the morning sun's rays caught him, he'd probably end up melting.

"That much is a certainty," he muttered, watching in fascination as the damaged flesh began to lose some of its rawness. His body had started to repair the injury, but the process wouldn't be instantaneous. Watching the meat heal reminded him of the minute hand on a clock face.

He tilted his head back, trying to judge the distance between his trapped body and the promise of cool shade. It appeared to only be a few dozen metres. He'd be able to cover the distance within a few seconds, but even that short space of time was too long. The sun had almost boiled hand down to the bones after just a lightning quick exposure.

His idiotic decisions had put him in this ridiculous predicament. Damien knew he shouldn't have gone and knew he should have stayed in that house when he realised the time. "You could have grabbed the sleeping bag from the cupboard and crashed on the carpet. Hell, you knew you were alone."

Even as the words left his lips, Damien knew that would have never happened. That house stank of his most bitter enemy, his rival clan. His rational mind couldn't accept this division, but Damien could not ignore his blood and these powerful new feelings that surged through his new body. Rationality didn't enter the equation anymore. "You have Swarmer blood running through your veins," he muttered.

Instead of going off on this fool's errand, why the fuck had he not tried to seek out Eleanor? After all, that's what she had told him to do. "Yeah," he sighed. "You're at the beck and call of your new mistress."

Was it the last bit of the rapidly shrinking human part of his mind refusing to bow down to the vampire's sway? If that was the case then he might as well give up right now, because it wasn't working. Hell, even thinking back to the erotic thoughts he had about Elsie made him feel like a guilty schoolboy. Fuck knows what the vampire would do to him if she found out about the girl on the embankment.

Damien suddenly snatched his foot away from the edge of the edge of the truck, whimpering as the burning sun grazed across his boot heel. "Why am I even fighting this?" he cried. "I belong to her. I'm Eleanor's property."

He whimpered again when something brushed past his feet. He leaned across and resisted the urge to break out in a fit of hysterical laughter at the sight of a black and white cat darting across the road and taking shelter under another car.

"Yeah, that's right, moggy. This is my spot and don't you forget it."

He sighed, wishing his owner could somehow find a way to recover her lost property without that hateful sun melting him like a tub of fucking ice cream. That was unlikely to happen. She and the rest of them were probably all asleep now. For some reason, Damien couldn't shake the image of them all hanging upside down from the rafters in his aunt's barn like a bunch of giant bats.

The cat lay down and fixed its bright green eyes on Damien. He guessed it just couldn't understand why a human had decided to lie in its favourite spot.

"Why the glare, you ugly cat? I don't want to be under here, you know. If I could get out from under here, I would do." The animal didn't seem impressed with Damien's apology. "Okay then, what would you do in my position?"

Damien vaguely wondered if he was finally losing his mind. He returned the animal's hostile gaze. "Not that there's such a thing as a vampire cat. At least I don't think so. Still, it probably wouldn't bother you. I bet all that thick fur would keep your little body safe."

He blinked, wondering if he really was so stupid. He looked down his body. "It's only your hands and face that you have to worry about, you fucking moron." Damien gritted his teeth and called up all his reserves of bravery, then pushed his foot very slowly out from the safety of the shade. He felt the heat immediately, and although he imagined his foot bursting into flames, the flesh beneath the fabric stayed singe free.

"Fuck me!" he gasped, bringing his leg back under the car. It might not have harmed his flesh, but the action still felt like the bravest thing he'd ever done in his life. He looked at the truck's muck-spattered undercarriage, his heart hammering in his chest. Damien wanted to burst into tears. He knew he wouldn't be able to do this, there was no chance. Even now, he could feel that huge yellow ball getting higher and higher as each second passed. Its oppressive weight made him feel like someone was placing heavy rocks on his body, one at a time.

Damien shrieked when he heard the one sound he hoped to never hear. Someone had climbed into the cab of the truck and turned the ignition. The engine roared o life. He had maybe three seconds before the vehicle moved away. That sun would turn his body into a pool of steaming goo exactly one second later. He grabbed the top of his jumper, then used his legs to shuffle down, watching the fabric move up his face until it reached his eyes.

With his vision now occluded, Damien couldn't see the metalwork above him, not that it mattered. As soon as the truck moved, if he didn't cover up the rest of his face, the sun would boil away his eyeballs anyway. Within the confined space, he managed to wriggle out of his leather jacket and pull it over his face just as the truck began to move. His terror increased to extreme levels when he felt the hot rays warm up the leather. Damien struggled to his feet, yelping when he heard a distant voice shouting. The fear of someone running over to snatch the coat off his head was just too great to contain.

He pelted across the road, not remembering where the alleyway was. Damien cleared the tarmac just before another car raced down the road. He heard its brakes screech and knew they had stopped to investigate. "If it's the police, I'm so fucked!" His body slammed into a stone wall, and he lifted the jacket just a crack and saw what looked like the entrance to the alley. He ran over to it, sensing those deadly rays lessen as he ran between the two buildings.

His eyes quickly adjusted to the gloom, and he almost smiled at his lucky escape. Damien couldn't yet break into a full smile due to the three pairs of heavy footfalls right behind him. His senses, already heightened from the adrenalin, calmly informed him that if they were here to assist, they would have shouted out by now. He stopped running and gingerly lifted up his jacket. Right by his side, he saw a boarded-up door. Under the peeling black paint were two faded letters that could be an M and an A.

Damien nodded to himself, finally working out where this alley led. He nipped into the alcove and pressed his body flat against the door. Right now, the morning sun wasn't shining down here. He guessed this alley would remain in darkness until this evening. He pulled the jacket from his head and waited.

The pursuers slowed down and stopped just before they reached where he hid. Damien didn't know who they were, but he was confident they weren't the law, given the cloud of tobacco smoke drifting into view. He grinned when the sound of a cough reached his ears.

"What the fuck was it?"

Damien leaned further back and waited to see if the owner of that voice would move into view. She sounded young, perhaps about sixteen. He grinned to himself, hoping her beauty was more appealing than her rough sounding voice.

"I don't know, probably a tramp or something. Come on, we're going to be late for work."

He listened to the footsteps recede, then peered around the corner, watching the male take the girl's hand before stepping back out into the sunlight. He didn't like how he felt right now. It seemed as though the tables had turned, and now he was the one to run and hide.

"Fuck them," he muttered. "Fuck them all."

Damien turned and examined the ancient door. This was used by the market traders many years ago, before the council built the new extension. He still remembered he and a few of his mates trying to sneak in through this door when they were kids, convinced mountains of goodies lay just beyond the door. They never did succeed. All the market traders used to stand here smoking for most of the day.

Damien found, to his surprise, that the wood easily gave away when he pushed his hard fingernails into it. "Bloody hell! I have got stronger." He noticed a few bricks lying around the door and concluded he wasn't the only one who had tried to get through. A large piece of splintered wood dropped to the floor as he thrust his nails deeper. It did seem strange that the council would leave this door unprotected. There were three padlocks down the side of the frame, but he reckoned anyone armed with a crowbar would be able to get them off.

Another piece broke off.

"It'll be bricked up on the other side," he muttered. "My luck can't hold out for that long." He crouched down, hooked his fingers under one of the loose boards, and pulled, almost shouting out at the sound of the nails pulling away. Dim yellow light shone out of the hole he'd made.

"Oh, this is just awesome," he chuckled, pushing his arm through the hole. Damien reached up and felt along the gap. His fingers closed over a bolt. Moving his fingers along, he found a large padlock, wrapped his hand around it, and pulled. The lock came off and dropped to the floor, and the door slowly slid inward.

Damien stepped inside, quietly closed the door shut, and dragged a large table across the door to keep it closed. This place should be empty; it now opened just twice a week, thanks to the new shopping mall that some private company constructed across town a few years ago.

That meant he had the place to himself. It wasn't due to re-open for a couple more days, so he'd be able to at least rest here in peace until tonight. He leaned against the wall and closed his eyes, gripping his leather tight. It took considerable willpower not to collapse onto the floor, curl up, and go to sleep right here and now. Despite his confidence that the market was empty, he still needed to check it out, just in case the place had a caretaker or janitor's office somewhere in the hall.

Finding the room occupied would be a bonus too. He ran his tongue across his lips and smiled at the thought of having one final drink before he slept through the day. He believed fate owed that much at least.

He wandered up the narrow corridor, heading towards a set of plastic curtains a few metres away. Damien yawned. Perhaps, it might be better if he just laid down here, curled up against the wall. Why bother searching for food? If there was some sort of security in the market, they were bound to spot his slumped body eventually. Damien slid down the wall, dropping his aching arms down. A tight smile played along his face when he noticed an old rusty hook screwed into the ceiling. "I ain't no bat, though," he whispered, allowing his eyelids to drop.

His body craved rest; every muscle ached. The traumatic change wrought through his system now demanded some down time to adapt, but his mind refused to comply. Damien drew in a short breath, feeling like he'd just been dropped into the ocean.

Groaning, he lifted his eyelids and gazed in confusion at the thick, translucent plastic curtains. Decades of constant use had degraded the plastic, and the scratches made it next to impossible to see what lay beyond.

"What's stopping me from sleeping?" he whispered, wondering why he was keeping his voice so low. This was just ridiculous; what the fuck did he have to fear now? He instinctively glanced at the ceiling, glad there were no skylights in this part of the market. He reminded himself to avoid those when he did enter the main area.

Something had prevented him from completely shutting down. Although his enhanced senses were still largely untested, Damien still trusted them to keep him safe. They hadn't let him down so far.

He ignored the protests from his aching body and quietly got back on his feet, not taking his eyes away from the plastic. Now that his mind was focused on imminent danger, whether it was real or imaginary, those senses he now relied on went into overdrive.

Every sight, sound, and smell was checked, everything inspected with the utmost care, unwilling to discard anything that might pose a threat. He couldn't work out what the hell was wrong with him until he took in a large breath. Damien chuckled as he caught the scent of a very familiar taint: the faint smell of slaughter. That's what hadn't allowed his senses to shut down.

Damien hadn't really noticed it, at least not on the surface. The smell of raw meat along with all the other smells floating through the market aisles had always been present every time he set foot inside.

The hot deli stall had opened up right at the top of the market a few months ago. The smell of roasting chicken used to drive him wild, although he remembered that the taste never matched the expectations. Elsie used to go crazy for the bakery located in the middle of the market. She had a real liking for fresh-baked bread.

He approached the curtains, keeping to the side. Even she, just like him, would appreciate the rich scent of fresh blood that got stronger the closer he got to the plastic barrier. He knew the single row of butcher's stalls was situated beside these curtains. That delightful smell did not come from any cow though, that much he did know.

His new vampire enhanced senses stopped him from bursting through the curtains, and he flattened himself against the wall when his ears picked up the sound of footsteps dragging something heavy over the stone floor.

Damien then felt the light touch of another mind grazing over his. He blanked his thoughts, purposely bringing up images of fog laden beaches and misty twilights, not wanting the vampire to latch onto anything specific.

"Why have you stopped, Healiod?"

The sudden appearance of such a loud noise caused Damien to start; he hadn't been expecting to hear such a thunderous voice. He saw the blurred outline of two figures right outside the curtains.

"I thought I felt someone else."

The other figure growled. "Brother, you will feel me ripping off your tiny head if you cause me to drop this body again. Healiod, you are acting like some virgin boy on his wedding night. Stop your fretting. The First Father will be busy with his new toy at least until the sun sets."

Damien didn't recognise those voices. They weren't the bastards who jumped on him and Elsie at his aunt's house. He did know they were from the same clan, his blood told him that much. They were his family now. He resisted the urge to scoff; like they'd accept a jumped-up little turd like him into their clan.

He wished he could see them. The temptation to try and read their thoughts ate into him, he so needed to learn more about these vampires. Damien believed the one who had done most the talking so far was the closest blur to the plastic curtains. He concentrated on that dark shape and decided to take the risk. He closed his eyes and remembered how easy he found it to read the minds of those idiots up in that tree.

If those vampires at the house had managed to catch him, Damien had no doubt that the fuckers would have torn off his limbs without breaking into a sweat. He had gained extra body mass, thanks to his feeding tonight, even so, those vampires must have been at this blood sucking business for centuries, they'll be old hands at this game. They'd have no problem in ripping up his body like it was made of wet tissue if he went up against them.

There was one endowment he suspected that both of those clowns lacked in sufficient quantities. He didn't have their brawn, but compared to the ones that he'd already met, he was a mental giant. He was going to bet the two in front of him were just as stupid.

Damien composed himself and focused on the moving shadows beyond the corridor. Without a pause, he found himself standing on the other side of the plastic curtains and staring at two of the largest males he had ever seen. His heart almost ceased beating when the one still holding the body suddenly swivelled his huge head and stared right at him. He got ready to run, clenching his fists and trying to remember the layout of this market, desperately thinking of any place he'd be able to hide without these huge vampires finding him. Damien let out his held breath when the vampire's eyes darted past him and focused on a fire extinguisher bolted to the tiled wall a few feet from where they stood.

The vampire then returned his gaze to his companion when he growled at him. Just looking at these two jokers, Damien knew he hadn't been wrong about them being able to pull off his arms and legs. Even the smaller vampire's heavily muscled body strained against his black leather tunic. They both looked exactly how he perceived vampires to look: built like fucking battle tanks, ugly as sin with an attitude to match. They could have stepped right out of any of his bedroom posters. In truth, they scared the shit out of him, but their appearance also gave him hope that before long, he'd be able to match their bulk. Damien just hoped that as his body filled out, he wouldn't lose his good looks.

"Am I carrying this alone, brother?" snarled the smaller vampire. "Healiod, are you listening to my words?"

Damien stared at the one named Healiod. His most prominent feature, after he got past his bulk, had to be his hair. He wore it in a tight pony tail that stretched all the way down his back. Was the vivid red his natural colour? Damien had difficulty believing such a vicious looking monster would take time to dye it. He shrugged, then again, what did he know about these individuals apart from their lust for blood? He smiled, thinking that their lust was now his lust.

The smaller vampire didn't seem share his brother's love for hair. He had none. Elaborate tattoos covered his smooth dome. Apart from their preference for black leather, Damien saw no family resemblance. Perhaps, they were just clan brothers?

"I am listening to your words, Helix, but I find no interest in them." He picked up the body's legs. "Now, if you were to explain to me why you are shaking?"

Helix vigorously shook his head. "Your eyes need replacing. I am not shaking; my body is as still as this corpse."

Healiod chuckled. "Even your head pictures are dancing, brother. I have known you for all of our tainted lives, both as human and as vampire. I know you better than you think, Helix. Perhaps even better than you know yourself. That, though, is not an idle boast, you have never been such a complicated creature."

"You know nothing about me. Just for once, stop trying to berate my senses."

"I have no clue as to what you are saying!" cried Healiod. "I say you shake, and you deny it and call me a liar. How is that an insult?"

"Your insults are in how you move when we converse, they are behind every word that falls from your mouth."

The large vampire sighed heavily. "Helix, your body quivered, that is what I saw. Tell me why?"

Damien watched the smaller vampire turn his head around the market.

"I forget your senses are not so finely tuned, my brother. It is simple, I can feel the presence of another vampire, maybe another one of our clan?"

Healiod burst out in laughter. "You are such a fool. It is the First Father you sense. Even I can feel his presence." He growled again. "Oh, what I would do to enjoy those two human females he has with him." Healiod glared at his brother. "I urge you to focus on our own task and not to allow your nomadic thoughts to stray close to his."

"It was not his I detected!" cried Helix.

The large vampire dropped the body and grabbed the front of his brother's tunic. "Listen very carefully to my words, Helix. If Desmonus discovers we have fed, not once but many times, he will punish us. If Desmonus discovers we allowed our after feasting to change into ghouls, he will gut us and order the rest of the clan to consume us. Is this how you wish to end your existence?"

Helix shook his head.

The back of Damien's head smacked into the wall, and he snapped his eyes open, immediately aware a significant amount of time had passed. His internal body clock had never been very accurate until he had changed. He didn't doubt the result. Somehow, his body had just decided to shut down on its own volition, and over four hours had passed.

"Why the fuck don't I feel any better then?" he muttered, flexing his arm, frowning at the stiffness in his muscles. He slowly got back to his feet and approached the curtains, quietly confident that, like him, the other visitors had all found hidden niches to curl up and sleep away the daylight hours.

He glanced behind him at the corner of the wall and felt the desire to return and see if he could sleep off some of this ache. "No, I can't do that, there is still so much to find out."

Damien knew he probably wouldn't get a better time to gain a little more information. From what he had found out already, he didn't think it would be that difficult to sneak into their sleeping minds.

He pushed his way through the plastic curtains, instinctively cringing at the spears of sunlight highlighting the walked-in grease and lumps of blackened chewing gum stuck to the paving slabs. He almost hissed at the hateful sight of all that daylight.

"For fuck's sake," he muttered, carefully edging his way away from the deadly rays and keeping his back pressed against the metal shutters. "I'll need some sun cream. I think factor one million should cover it." Despite his effort to make light of the subject, he knew it would take him a long time to get over the fact that he'd never feel the sun on his face again. That did suck, big time. "So, I'm banished to the dark for all eternity." Damien hurried through the butcher's quarter, intending to make his way up to the top end of the market. He figured that, like him, the other vampires would rather keep the sunlight away from their flesh, and they'd gravitate towards the old part of the market. The old Victorian building was gloomy as fuck. Not many traders operated up there now.

Damien knew of a dozen forgotten hiding places in the old quarter where a couple of sleepy vampires could catch forty winks. Not every stall had shutters, and it wouldn't take much effort to break through some of those thin wooden boards that covered the stall windows.

As he ran along the stone floor, heading away from the butcher's quarters, he found it hard to clear the mental image of two evil vampires sleeping in the middle of a floor full of soft teddy bears, probably sucking their thumbs.

It took Damien just minutes to reach the old quarter. He welcomed the gloom and the darkness, despite his earlier regrets about never feeling the sun, and as he wandered down the dark aisles, he found his urge to feel warmth quickly diminish. He stopped beside a mobile phone repair shop and slowly turned in a tight circle, keeping his ears open, trying to detect any sounds. Apart from his own slight breathing, Damien couldn't hear anything.

They couldn't have left. No way, that just isn't possible.

He calmed himself down. Those two vampires had to be hiding in here somewhere. All he had to do was to keep looking. Right now, those creatures were at their most vulnerable, and the last thing they needed was a bunch of angry villagers carrying burning torches, digging up their still bodies, and tying them to a huge stake.

Damien shook away the bizarre image and hurried through the aisles, keeping his senses attuned for signs of their presence. He couldn't feel their minds anywhere, but they couldn't have just left the place. Where else would they go?

His probing senses suddenly flew back when their tentative touch brushed against a hurricane-like force. A mind infinitely more powerful than any he'd ever encountered. He fell against a discount clothing stall, trying to push his trembling body through the wood.

This mind could only belong to their Swarmer First Father. Damien caught his breath, remembering he was *his* First Father now. This didn't make any sense to Damien. He knew the First Father was in the market, he sensed his presence ages ago, but it hadn't been much different from the other clan minds, at least not when the First Father was awake. Damien now saw the First Father's true power. Whilst sleeping, the vampire's roaming thought hunted down any suspicion. He dreaded to think how he rooted out any dissent amongst his clan. That sleeping mind was powerful, crackling with dark energy. Damien honestly believed the First Father could literally turn any other mind into a lump of thoughtless mush, if he so desired.

He dropped to the floor and shut his eyes tight when he felt that incredible mind heading towards him. He thought about the mist and fog again, trying not to cry out when the First Father's cold mind brushed over his. Damien's body broke out in tremors when he felt the mind leaving him.

Damien climbed up the front of the shop, feeling like he'd just walked through a tornado. The power in that vampire's mind really did scare him. He now saw why he couldn't find the other minds. Their own survival depended on secrecy. He took a deep breath and tried again to locate them. Now that the First Father's mind had swept the area, perhaps they would feel the coast was clear. He focused on their signatures, feeling something very cold close by. Damien grinned; he had found them. It was a weak trace, but he knew exactly where they were now. Frustration overcame him when he discovered that no matter how hard he tried, there was no way inside their thoughts. Of course not, he should have figured that out as soon as the First Father's incredibly powerful mind left him feeling as weak as a baby.

"What a delightful surprise."

Damien yelled out in shock when he felt a huge pair of hands land on his shoulders. He dropped to the floor and rolled, looking up at the sight of another vampire glaring down at him. The vampire's face suddenly changed to utter astonishment. Damien felt the vampire's mind attempt to process the fact that his food was another vampire.

There was no way he was going to hang around until this idiot's brain had shifted into first gear. Damien jumped up and raced down the aisle, listening to his pursuer's furious roar.

What the hell was he doing? Damien wanted to stop, turn, and explain to this monster that he was part of their family now. He glanced around and saw the inhuman abomination gaining on him and knew this evil bastard would not listen to any discussion. His pursuer didn't see him as family, only as a tender morsel.

"Fuck you too!" Damien snarled.

He jumped onto the wall and scaled up the brickwork, the hard tips of his fingers easily finding enough grip in the old mortar. Damien looked down at his pursuer's murderous expression and wanted to laugh. "Are you going to calm down?"

As he leaned a bit too far out, his fingers began to slip, and Damien panicked and grasped out, his fingers finding and grabbing a length of thick material attached to the ceiling. The cloth came away in his hands, and he cried out as daylight streamed through the previously blocked up skylight.

Damien let go of the cloth and tried to wrap his fingers around a thick pipe, but his fingers just refused to obey his commands. He spun his head around and watched in horror as the huge vampire below him jumped out of the path of the falling material and stepped straight into the sunlight streaming into the market. The result was cataclysmic: his whole body began to melt like a candle in the path of an acetylene torch. The dying vampire's scream slammed into Damien's mind. He felt like he'd just been hit by a speeding truck. His fingers lost their grip, and he fell, slamming into the hard concrete floor below and narrowly missing the fatal sunlight.

He turned his head away from the sight of the vampire's dissolving body, finding that he couldn't move his legs. The fall must have broken his bones. He felt no pain yet, but he knew that delight wouldn't stay suppressed for long.

Damien felt the others waking up.

Chapter Eleven

Cade couldn't remember what had jerked him awake. He listened to the incessant bird chatter, trying to work out just how that noise was supposed to be restful. Right now, he'd give his right arm for a shotgun. Cade lowered his head, wrinkling his nose as his movement caused the soft heather under him to release more sweet scent. He decided it must be the plants that brought out of his restless slumber; the smell reminded him, indirectly, of his mother's dressing table.

Cade slowly sat up and brushed pieces of plant out of his hair. He arched his back, feeling the bones crack. His muscles weren't his friend this morning, that much was certain. Cade attributed his numerous aches to yesterday's strenuous activities and not to him bedding down on an improvised bed made from heather and a piece of dry carpet that Katy found rolled up behind a wheelie bin.

He quietly chuckled to himself, remembering all those times when he and Damien had fallen into drunken slumbers at assorted house parties around the town. "I've never woken up next to such a hot girl before though," he whispered, gazing in admiration at Katy's smooth back.

His thoughts of desire paused when the girl suddenly jumped and gasped. Cade snuggled closer and ran his hand through her hair. "It's okay, sweetheart," he whispered, leaning forward to kiss her cheek. She moaned again but didn't wake up. He rested his hand on her shoulder and caressed her tense muscles. *She must be in the middle of a dream*, he thought. By the way she was twisting about and groaning, he doubted it was about fluffy clouds and unicorns.

"Baby?" He jerked her shoulder. "Come on, snap out of it."

Katy yelped, then her eyes snapped open. Her momentary confusion vanished when she saw Cade, and her face broke into a soft grin.

"Hey there, handsome. Fancy meeting you here." She reached out, grabbed his hair, and pulled him closer. "It's time you finished something." Katy pressed her soft lips against his and kissed him passionately.

He couldn't help but respond when she wrapped her naked legs around his thighs and pulled him tight against her body. "Baby?" he gasped pulling his head up. "Sweetheart, I so want you, more than anything else, but we need to figure out what to do!"

She shook her head. "Hush, it's daylight now, they'll be sleeping, and right now I can't think of anything else but the feel of you inside me." She grabbed his head. "Now you listen to me, Cade McCrae. Somehow, we are still alive. How the fuck that happened is a miracle."

He saw her eyes filling up and automatically wiped away her tears. "Everything is going to be all right, you'll see."

"No it fucking won't!" she snapped. "When the sun goes down, those things will be back." Katy grabbed his wrists. "We might not make it to see the next sun up." She stared into his eyes. "'Cos you're not going to leave, are you?"

He shook his head. "No, I can't leave. I can't run away from this, Katy. They need to be stopped."

She nodded. "Oh, baby, please, let's just get the hell out of town. I don't want to die, and I don't want anything to happen to you."

He caught a ragged breath, looking into her terror-struck eyes before rolling off her. "Sweetheart, what choice do we have? They aren't going away. It doesn't matter where we go, you can be sure that they'll find us again. These fuckers are like a plague."

Katy broke down. "But, it's not our fucking problem!"

He shook his head, sure he had heard the noise of a car engine. Cade sat up, gazed down to the bottom of the embankment, and saw over two dozen assorted vans and cars slowly winding along the previously empty lane. Cade turned away and looked into her beautiful eyes. "Baby, there is nobody else." He leaned back down and kissed her softly on the lips, then passed the girl her top. "Look at this, sweetheart."

"Oh shitting hell, I'd forgotten all about them."

Cade nodded, he had as well. How ironic was that? The annual Ichiban Metal Festival was the only event he and his fellow metal loving friends looked forward to. The rest of the town hated it. Sure, they were grateful for the vast amount of disposable income a few thousand seasoned metallers brought to the town, but none of the locals could be comfortable with so much long hair and black leather mingling with the country tweed and beige jodhpurs. The festival was the only time when Cade actually felt normal.

"Babes, we need to find a way to stop those things before the sun goes down." He pointed down at the motorcade. "Do you remember what Elsie said?"

"Yeah, something about this was their town?"

He nodded. "There are two clans here, Katy. We already know that. At first, I thought those bastards would start fighting again, right here, in this town." He watched a dark blue van at the front slow down, then turn and drive into an open field. "That's not going to happen."

"How can you be so sure, Cade?"

The other vehicles followed the van into the field. He stood up and saw that the other lane beyond this field was already packed with cars. "The Swarmers are not as strong as the Deathgazers," he said, remembering the images that flowed through his mind while he was by that ancient pit last night.

As he closed his eyes and felt his mind slipping back, the ground beneath his feet lost cohesion. Cade stumbled and fell. His eyes snapped open, and he saw that a dozen wooden houses, built in a rough circle, had replaced the cultivated English countryside. He spun around, trying not to slip again, and saw that Katy was no longer with him.

What was wrong with his body? Cade had a mild nauseous ache nibbling at the pit of his stomach, but apart from that, he felt most chilled out. He couldn't wrap his head around it, hell, his emotions should be spinning like clothes in a washing machine.

As he turned away from the ramshackle buildings, Cade discovered that he wasn't alone. There was a group of men, women, and a few children stood around a large black stone. They were motionless and mute. Curiosity got the better of him, and he stepped out of the muddy puddle, sighing when he saw the state of his trainers.

Cade approached the group, noticing that none of them seemed the least bit interested in his presence. Unlike him, the people were all dressed in similar rough woven clothing. They appeared as though they'd stepped out of the middle ages.

Beyond them, he saw a large barricade built from tree trunks encircling the area.

Where the hell was he? Cade still found it hard to understand why he felt little emotion. Unless this was just a dream? That could explain it. Perhaps this is where Katy had come to before he woke her up. It would explain why the people hadn't seen him. He walked up to the nearest one, a young woman about the same age as him. To try out his theory, he placed his hand upon her should.

He let out a yelp of surprise when the woman turned and placed her own hand on his. Cade's emotions then hit him with the intensity of a speeding truck when she turned around and he gazed into the young face of his mother.

"Thank you, Dalain," she said, giving him a tired smile. "I did not doubt you. I knew you would not shirk from your responsibilities." She pushed him forward and pressed him back against the black stone. "The elder will see what you have done this harvest eve as a sign that we are the ones for the Powers to favour."

Cade looked at the sallow faces of the assembled people, trying to make sense of her words. The rest of the people had still not spoken. Then, as if at the command of some hidden signal, they all looked up to the top of the large stone. He followed their gazes and saw, to his horror, that these savages had manacled a young girl to the surface. From here, he could see the blood pooling beside her mouth. He staggered back, pushing his way out of the circle. As he retreated, Cade saw that the blood wasn't just localized around her mouth. The poor girl was lying in a lake of her own blood. Dozens of shallow cuts crisscrossed her thin body. At first, he assumed that she was dead, then her arms twitched.

"What the fuck have you maniacs done to her!" he shouted.

The woman who looked just like his mother took his arms and led him back into the circle. She didn't seem to be the least bit bothered at his outburst.

"Get off me, you weird bitch!" he snarled.

The woman acted as if he hadn't even spoken. "Come, Dalain. They'll be arriving presently. We need to ensure you show fortitude in the face of their enemies."

Cade found his body moving of its own volition. He couldn't stop himself from leaning towards the woman and kissing her gently on the lips. He then found his body walking past the gathered people and touching their shoulders as he passed each one. He returned to the woman and gripped her hand tight.

The woman tensed. "They are arriving! I feel their lust and desire."

The others all spun around, gazed into the air, and moaned in terror before dropping to their knees.

"Remember the words of our First Father!" she shouted. "Do not run and do not make eye contact. The Flesh Dragons will go for our sacrifices, but the Swarmers will divert their trajectory if they sense you."

Cade saw several black dots in the sky, getting larger as they approached. She called them Flesh Dragons. It didn't take a great leap of deduction to realise just what was heading this way. Cade felt his own knees go weak as he started to make sense of their appearance. There were four of them. Dragons was a good description—the flying creatures were huge, and the smallest looked about the same size as a business jet. They looked like a cross between some prehistoric flying reptile and a giant bat.

A single figure sat astride each creature, and they were now close enough for Cade to make out their features. They were dressed in rags, similar to the people around him, but their clothing looked more like the wing membranes of the animals they rode. He watched them fly over their heads, circle, and then land atop the huge black slab.

The chained-up girl wasn't so quiet now. Cade tensed up and wanted to shut his ears at the heart tearing screams bellowing from her mouth.

"It'll be soon over," murmured the woman beside him.

As hard as he tried, Cade could not get this body to respond to his demands. He wanted to get this evil woman off him, slap the harpy, and try to help that poor girl. Her screams suddenly ceased as the huge creatures all dipped their long smooth necks to allow the armour-plated heads access to the girl.

Cade had to suppress the need to moan and weep when the noise of crunching and wet sounds of feeding reached his ears. He could only take solace in the fact that her end was quick and her pain was now over.

Cade felt his head turn and was a little shocked to see the woman openly weeping.

"I know they told me not to expose my sorrow. Why can I not, my husband?" she whispered. "Dalain, please don't allow them to witness my tears. I think …" She drew in a sharp breath, turned away from him, and gazed at the surface of the huge smooth, black obelisk. "Dalain remove your eyes!" she hissed. "They're ready."

Cade's eyes didn't move. He saw the ground surrounding the terrified people rumble, then several large, leather clad figures rose up. Cade sensed this body's mouth attempt to scream out as they seemingly glided forward. He gazed into their bright crimson eyes, and his blood turned to water.

The figures turned their heads simultaneously and gazed in his direction. Their jaws yawned wide, and sabre-sized canines burst through their bloodied gums. The nightmarish creatures then took their lantern eyes off Cade and looked up towards the surface of the black stone.

A bone shaking roar burst Cade's ears. His hands clapped against his ears, and he saw the others all drop to their knees, crying out in pain. At first, Cade assumed the abominations on the stone had issued that noise, but then he saw the black-clad figures surrounding them closing their huge jaws.

The things above had seen them, and despite the frantic efforts from their protesting riders, the creatures waddled to the edge of the stone and swooped towards the waiting figures. Cade watched them all remove curved, black metal blades as long as he was tall from hidden sheaths on their backs. The creatures assumed a defensive posture and, as soon as the Flesh dragons were close enough, swung their blades, cutting through the flying constructs' necks with ease.

The riders tumbled from their saddles and onto the rough ground. Most of the creatures fell upon the shrieking riders, and within seconds, the noise had ceased. The two remaining figures replaced their blades and walked over to the woman stood next to Cade.

"You have done very well, Listrulia. Thanks to your cooperation, the Swarmers have lost their advantage in this province."

The woman bowed her head. "We are but willing servants, my First Father."

The figure nodded. "You have served your tribe and your masters with due diligence, and for that, I will allow you to serve me in another purpose."

Cade felt powerful hands grip his arms as the other figure grabbed him. He saw the remaining people receive the same fate as the others took them as well.

"I don't understand!" cried the woman, "What have we done to displease you?"

"The need for flesh is paramount, Listrulia," the figure replied. "We won this battle, but the Swarmers are still eating into our lands like parasites." He nodded to the figure holding Cade. "Juan, take him to my house and see to it the others go to the rendering chapel."

Cade screamed himself awake. He opened his eyes and gazed into the eyes of Katy. "Bloody hell!" he gasped.

"I've been trying to wake you for over an hour!" she said. "What happened to you?"

He sat up and looked at the surrounding countryside. Even with the huge wooden barricade obstructing his view, Cade knew the village had been right here, in this spot. While he had been lost in another time, more vehicles had arrived. The fields below were packed.

"I don't know what happened to me," he confessed. "Somehow, I found myself back to when these vampires ruled this land." He shivered, thinking of those terrible creatures. That woman had called them Flesh Dragons. He knew they weren't an animal born; those vampires had made them.

"What did you see?"

Cade took her hand. "Baby, you don't want to know. Really, you don't. I have figured out what is going to happen though. All that lot down there will help to spread this vile plague across England."

She shook her head, "Elsie said they were going to stay here."

"The clue is in the name, Katy. Back in our distant past, the Deathgazers looked after their livestock. Believe it or not, most of the humans were happy with this arrangement. I'm guessing that arrangement went on for a long time." He shrugged. "Why not? Their vampire masters protected them and made sure their animals were well fed. Apart from the odd tribute, the humans could get on with their lives." He mentally pictured the sight of those things landing one the stone slab and the look of disbelief etched on those villagers' faces when the vampires dragged them away. It wasn't difficult to guess the purpose of the rendering chapel. "The Swarmers weren't keen with this farming idea and just took what they wanted."

Cade turned and gazed back at the town buildings at the back of the woodland. "The Swarmers had all night, and yet, they only turned a couple of people? Since when does that make sense? They know their enemy is in the vicinity. You'd think by now, every human in town would be hiding from the sun."

Katy stood up beside him. "It scares me that you know so much about them." She rammed her bare feet into her shoes. "And these blackouts fucking terrify me."

Cade shrugged again, unable to find a way to calm her fears. His visions frightened the crap out of him as well. As each hour passed, he found yet another nugget of ancient history suddenly worm its way into his mind. "Don't be, forewarned is forearmed, I suppose. It just means that we stand a better chance." Even with this new knowledge, he wasn't sure just how much of a chance they did stand. The temptation to grab the girl's hand and get the hell out of town was hard to suppress. He dared not put down odds of not seeing another dawn if they did stay in town.

"Does your phone still work?" she asked.

"I have no idea." He brought his phone out of his pocket. It felt strange in the palm of his hand. Cade slid the *on* bar across and stared at his welcome screen. After what he had been through these past few hours, gazing at the phone screen made him want to burst into tears. Everything on here now seemed so pointless. He remembered his frustration at not beating Damien's high score on their shared online games and the insults he traded with his mates on Facebook. He looked at Katy, realising that despite the fact that they both lived only a few miles apart, he had never met Katy online. Should that bother him? Cade nodded. "Yeah, it seems fine. Why do you ask?"

"This used to rule my life, you know." Katy said. "I spent more time on here than anywhere else."

Cade couldn't argue with that assessment. He suspected most of them in town were in the grip of their small block of shiny plastic.

"So, try as I might, I just cannot think of anybody who can help us out." Tears rolled down her cheeks. "Christ, this just fucking sucks." She angrily slammed her phone back into her pocket.

He took hold of Katy's hand, then pulled her up the embankment. Cade saw a park bench overlooking the park and guided her over to it. "What else did you expect?" he asked, sitting her down. "Just look at me, Katy. Just look at my appearance. I'm into all this vampire stuff, and even I have nobody I could turn to. All my mates live in the States, and yeah, they're all as geeky as me." He stared across the green, wondering how the guys would react if he did tell them about the situation over here. He then sighed deeply, knowing they'd just call him an attention seeking dork. Of course they would; hell, he'd do the same.

"Come on, honey, it's time we made tracks. We have a lot to do today." Cade pulled her up and wrapped his arms around her, "Well, that's if you still want to stay with me, sweetheart."

"Cade, surely there must be someone in town that we could tell? I know you have lots of friends who dress like you." She looked down the embankment. "We have a town full of freaks now. What about them? They won't all openly scoff at our story, will they?" Katy gasped. "Oh, I'm so sorry, I didn't mean to call you a freak. It just kinda slipped out." She ran her fingers through his hair. "You're my special guy, Cade."

Her word did sting, just a little, but he wasn't going to make a big deal of it. Hell, the group Katy hung around with called him and his mates a lot worse than that.

"I don't think any of those will be able to help, honey." The idea of asking some of the newcomers for help had crossed his mind already. It would be in their benefit. Come nightfall, if he didn't stop them, those Swarmers would be running through those fields, like wolves amongst sheep. "Just because they all dress like me, and I'm sure that more than a few of them will have all the Twilight books, and all believe to be expert in the vampire myth."

"There you go then," she replied, smiling.

He shrugged. "It's not real though, is it? At least that's what everyone else thinks. Believe me, those down there are just as close minded as everyone else, Katy. Vampires don't exist."

"We're on our own?"

It took him a moment to realise she had included herself in that sentence. "We could spend the whole day trying to convince other people to help us, Katy." He suddenly smiled. "I don't believe I've been so daft!" Cade grabbed her hand and raced across the green. "I think I've just figured a way how to stop them."

He reached the children's play area and pointed to the row of shops opposite the main gates. "There you go," he said, grinning. "There's our secret weapon!"

She shook her head. "I'm not getting you at all. I'm sorry."

Cade took her over to the gates and pointed at the gaudy, purple fronted building on the end of a block of terraces. "It's the only one in town, thank God." He smiled at the girl. "Always full of women obsessed with their appearance. The freaks love it. I thought you would be very familiar with the place."

Katy smacked him on the shoulder. "You cheeky bastard," she giggled. "My skin is naturally brown. I don't need to go to a tanning salon to get it topped up, thank you very much." She looked back at him. "I still don't get it though."

He covered his eyes with his hand, then looked up. "UV light is supposed to the one thing that can definitely kill the bastards. Come on, let's go shopping." He ran through the gates and over the empty road, not believing he hadn't thought of this before. "All we have to do then, Katy, is to find where the bastards have bedded down for the night. That shouldn't be too hard, there can't be that many places to hide in this town, can there?"

Katy burst out laughing. "Are you serious? For crying out loud, sweetheart, there were a bunch of vamps hiding in the buildings that you told me you knew like the back of your hand! Think of how many cellars there are in Welbourgh. Most of the houses are dead old. Then there's the sewers and all the abandoned houses, not to mention all the outbuildings around the farms. We could search for weeks and not find them."

Cade leaned back against the wall, "You really know how to put a downer on things." He felt his euphoria slowly leave him.

He tried to keep hold of at least one piece of his idea. "Okay, but at least we do have another weapon to use against them."

"That's if we can get inside, Cade. In case you haven't noticed, the shop is shuttered up." She walked up to a sign beside the door. "It doesn't open today, sweetheart. I'm sorry. Look, if it's any use, I have been in here before." She held up her hand. "I only came in here with my mates. Anyway, I did notice that the place was full of beds, nothing small." She walked up to him. "And nothing that came with batteries."

The sun was now over the trees. Somehow, they had already wasted a quarter of the day. He turned around, wanting to kick the crap out of the shutters. Despite what Katy said, he knew that there must be at least one portable UV lamp in there. He took out his phone, looked up at the sign, and punched in the number. "There's one way to find out," he muttered. "I bet the lady who runs the place will be able to help me." He laughed. "Oh, don't worry, I won't tell her that we're hunting vampires."

Cade turned to look at Katy and saw her gaze was somewhere else. He saw two dark blue cars parked on the opposite side of the road. He was sure they weren't there earlier. The girl shivered.

"Are you okay?"

"Just turn around, Cade. Oh hell!" She grabbed the wrist of his jacket and pulled him away from the building. "Run!"

He just managed to keep up to Katy's pace as she raced down the empty street, her burst of speed surprising the hell out of him. He thought he was fast. Cade tried to grab the back of her jacket and jerk her to a stop. He couldn't believe that after everything they had been through, she was fleeing from some idiots in cars—no way could they be that scary.

Katy glanced over her shoulder and gasped, her face full of terror. He heard the car engines start up.

Katy put on another burst of speed, then ran around the corner of a large department store. There was still nobody about.

The two cars were right behind them.

Cade followed Katy through a set of sliding doors that led into the town's bus station. Just like with the rest of the town, Cade didn't see anyone about, not even the ever present security guards were in their usual spots. This didn't feel right.

The image of all the other townspeople slumbering in dark places, hidden from the sun, wouldn't leave his mind. He shook his head; no, that was one thought he refused to entertain. It was just really early, that's all.

Katy was already at the other side of the station, peering through the glass doors that led into the bus station's carpark. She didn't appear to be too eager to leave. He spun around at the sound of car doors slamming shut. The two men must have seen them enter the bus station and were quickly making their way towards the doors. Cade leaned against a metal locker and watched them approach.

After what he had been through so far, Cade point blank refused to let a couple of goons intimidate him. They reached the entrance, and Cade now saw them in glorious detail. He inwardly groaned. He knew the pair of them. Not that it was much of a shock, their town wasn't that large, and not many folks were strangers to each other, especially ones with reputations.

They were just a couple of years older than Cade. He remembered them from school, and even back then, the bastards were born with bad bones. Adrian Lloyd and Steven Lloyd used to fancy themselves as a pair of small-town Kray twins. They used to terrorize him and his fellow metal loving pals, keeping up the persecution all the way up until the pair of losers left to join the dole queue. Cade grinned to himself and clenched his fists. That was all a few years ago, and time, plus the regular workout at the gym, had turned that geeky, thin, long-haired boy into a bloke who doesn't run from anyone, least of all two old school bullies.

They had seen him, and he enjoyed seeing their expressions change from glare to shock. He guessed they recognised him too and could see he had put on quite a bit of muscle since their last encounter. He nodded at them. He was so going to enjoy this.

Cade took one step towards them, then stopped dead. He glanced back and found, to his horror, that the other pursuers must have slipped in through the other entrance.

What scared him more than anything was that Katy was actually talking to them, and she didn't seem to be in the least bit distressed. "What the hell is going on?" The two men rushed past him, giving Cade the briefest of glances. He followed them, getting more and more confused.

He shouted out when they grabbed Katy's arms and pulled her through the sliding doors. Cade raced over and found his way blocked when the twins pulled out pistols from inside their jackets.

"You have got to be fucking kidding me," he growled.

Through the window, he watched one of the cars screech into the bus waiting area. "No way." Cade glared at the grinning men. "What, like I'm scared of you two fucking clowns?" He swung his arms up, catching their wrists. Their weapons flew out of their hands. Cade shouldered past them and raced through the doors.

He reached the car just as two more goons bundled Katy into the back seat. "Get the fuck off her!" he shouted, ducking his head and peering inside the car. A young, dark-haired man grinned back at him. Cade stood shock still, staring at the ghoul's blood-stained eyes.

"Thank you for keeping my girlfriend safe, Cade," he said. "Now fuck off."

He found two pairs of hands jerking him away from the car and binding his arms to his body.

"He's going to fucking kill us, literally, for letting you pull a stunt like that," growled Adrian. "Best we make sure it isn't possible for you to do it again."

Cade watched the car speed off and felt the barrel of a gun dig into his ribs. He turned his head and glared at the man. "Is it true that you two still suck each other's dicks?" He watched Adrian's mouth form an *O,* then snapped his head forward and butted the man between the eyes. Cade snatched the pistol out of Adrian's numb fingers and raced back through the bus station door, catching his breath when he heard the sound of the other pistol fire. He crouched down and ran towards the other entrance, holding the gun tight, wondering what the hell he was going to do now.

Chapter Twelve

Darlene realised she could pick out their scent beneath the strong smell of floor polish and hint of old sweat. She got to her feet and stretched, her fingers almost touching the storage room's low ceiling. At either side of her, squashed up against the two walls, her husband's new army of embryonic vampires slept. Darlene lowered her head, gazing down at the blond-haired, muscle-bound behemoth curled up and sleeping like a giant baby beside her feet.

He stunk. They all did. The smell coming from them reminded her of old road-kill on a boiling hot day mixed with after-shave. Darlene straightened her back, looking down at the abomination, watching him pant like an exhausted dog. It bothered Darlene that the emotion she felt for her husband's babies was repugnance. Why was that? This is what she wanted: to sit by her husband's side while their children went out and brought this town to its knees.

"Only, I'm not at his side," she growled, quietly.

Her foot strayed close to the blond man's face, and he responded by pulling his lips back and uttering a quiet growl. Darlene flinched and skipped back a step. She counted to three to regain her composure, then growled herself, feeling a little foolish and annoyed that she had allowed this moron to startle her.

Darlene pushed her foot forward until her toes were touching his cheek, daring the bastard to growl again. One more noise escaping his lips would give her the excuse she needed to rip the skin off his face. She felt almost cheated when he just whimpered and rolled over.

She crouched down and pushed her fingers through his thick hair. It felt greasy, and her action released a sour smell of old sweat. Darlene wrinkled her nose. These enhanced senses would take some getting using to.

"You dare to threaten me?" she hissed, feeling his whole body shake. The man still slept through her words, but the emerging vampire sense within him recognised the threat to his life. She grinned. That strong sense of self-preservation would not allow this baby vampire to snooze through his imminent execution.

Darlene extended her finger, gazing in fascination at her fingernail. Her nails were long and tapered to form a spike. She hadn't noticed that before. She'd never had much luck in growing her nails, the chore of housework saw to that. Darlene smiled, instinct alone told her that a bout of washing-up or vacuuming the front room would not dull these babies.

The new vampire was now fully aware of his predicament. That was made evident when she saw him clench his fists. Her husband still had a decent looking body, but it paled in comparison to this young hunk. Even so, she could not allow this upstart to think he could better her. Darlene wrapped her fingers around his wrist, marvelling at how easy it was to keep the large man subdued. His bulk was no match for her superior vampire strength.

Darlene waited long enough for him to see he was wasting his efforts before gently pressing the tip of her fingernail against his eyelid. He suddenly became stock still.

"That's so much better," she soothed. "We can be friends, or …" she paused and made sure he saw her lick her lips. "Or, I can scoop out your eyeballs and suck on them like juicy grapes."

There was no need to start munching down on this poor puppy, the fear rising from his mind was sustenance enough. This puppy had no clue what he'd done, and the fact that he was powerless to stop Darlene made her very moist. Just for that moment, she wondered if he had the equipment to satisfy her.

"Please, mistress. I don't know what I've said to upset you," he said.

Darlene gazed into his pale eyes, noticing that the whites now contained a tinge of pink. "Maybe you don't know, at least on the surface, my young friend. It doesn't stop the taint in your system seeing me as some kind of threat." She wrapped her fingers around his throat. "You have no idea how much that upsets me."

Without thinking, she took in a great lungful of air and found herself gazing at her image through the man's eyes. What he saw shocked Darlene to the core. Her furnace-fire eyes drilled into the new vampire's gaze, and she felt his terror pinning him to the spot. Gone was her smooth, flawless skin; her dark grey complexion now resembled the surface of the moon. Her blood cooled down, and Darlene saw herself shake her head. The next moment she saw the vampire's face looking back her, his expression a mixture of confusion and alarm.

She twisted her head and saw that the others were now all awake and staring at her. Only one of them had taken the step of standing up. She watched her husband's First Son take two steps towards her before stopping. He looked around, and Darlene could almost hear him trying to weigh up his very limited options.

It was difficult to keep a straight face as the vampire neared her. His face was set, looking as if he was about to try to calm down a ferocious dog. It just looked so ridiculous considering his size. He made three of her. This was a guy who used to take his body building seriously, and the vampire taint running through his system was already working on his body and bulking it out even more. The guy was already larger than the First Father, and she suspected the taint had not finished with him just yet.

Darlene heard the sound of a quiet splutter and turned back around. She had completely forgotten she was still gripping the other vampire by his throat. She was vaguely fascinated by the new noises coming from his mouth; he sounded a bit like a mouse caught in a trap. She raised him off the blue, watching the colour in his face drain. The new vampire really did look pale now.

"Please, mistress, let us discuss this."

She sighed and reluctantly released him, not surprised by the fact that she had effortlessly lifted up a well-built man with just one arm. "What is there to discuss?" she asked, turning to glare at the other man, who had stopped in the middle of the room. She didn't think he'd dare to take another step towards her for fear he would receive the same treatment. His size didn't intimidate her. Darlene had no doubt she'd be able to handle him like a ragdoll as well.

"What's to discuss?" she repeated, walking over to the vampire. It amused her to see him react to her presence by immediately forming a defensive pose. Unlike that blond-haired idiot, Darlene knew he would do anything to stop her from treating him in such a belittling way, even if his actions enraged the First Father. His only regard, right now, was for the others now under his care. The fact that this idiot saw her as just some pet for the First Father annoyed the fuck out of her. She might have claws and be more dangerous than any guard dog, but she was still on a leash. She sensed the suspicion from all of them. That and fear.

Darlene brought her feet together and flashed him what she hoped would look like a bright, disarming, and very innocent looking smile. She took great satisfaction in seeing his whole posture change. How easy it was to take advantage of her feminine wiles. His initial confusion gave her the lever she needed.

While his mind attempted to come to grips with her bizarre behaviour, Darlene jumped into his exposed mind. The illusion of time came to a standstill while she explored the corridors of the First Son's thoughts. Darlene gained immense satisfaction from the knowledge that, just like the blond-haired vampire, this one had no idea she was encroaching on his innermost secret thoughts.

Nothing was closed to Darlene's inquisitive mental caressing. He opened up like an unlocked door, showing Darlene everything he had. Before she became too deep, she had to check on one more thing. Like the blond boy, Darlene looked at herself through his eyes.

The image of a beautiful woman smiling back at the vampire shocked her rigid. Her inner monster was well and truly back in the box. What a metamorphosis. Her heart-shaped face had filled out in all the right places, defining her delicate bone structure. The only abnormality to this otherwise classic full model look was her deep crimson eyes and enlarged canines. Not that the vampire had taken much notice, her large breasts had trapped his roving eyes.

The lust he felt for the soft skin beneath her tight clothing was driving the First Son insane with desire, threatening to overtake his every other sense. He would not dare to try anything though; he wasn't that stupid. The first Father might only see her as one of his possessions, but the Head Vampire would tear off his face if the vampire tried to take advantage. The main reason, the reason that stopped him from doing anything and was his sole problem with her, was he suspected Darlene was a lot stronger than she looked.

The First Son averted his eyes, and Darlene then noticed the vampire who had mistakenly growled at her back in his original position against the wall. The look he was giving Darlene could have peeled paint off the wall. His glare was pure poison. It didn't escape her attention that his eyes had deepened in colour in the last few minutes, and she wondered if that was because of his extra bout of excitement.

Despite the First Son's desire to rip off every shred of her clothing and take her like a rutting stallion, Darlene knew he felt the same way about her as the blond vampire did. It wouldn't surprise her if all the other newborn vampires hated her with equal intensity. She fought back the hurt, tears, and irrational sense of self-loathing. She needed to discover why her presence caused such heated emotions. What had she done for them to hate her?

She had to dig a little deeper, that's all. The trigger would be somewhere inside the First Son. Darlene pulled back and grinned when a picture of the man running for the bus exploded at the front of her mind. It felt so strange to witness this newly made monster doing something as mundane as running for a departing bus. He was called Colin Rushmore, and until just a few hours ago, he was almost content with his life. His son, Steven, wasn't following in his father's footsteps and turning into a complete bastard like he did at the age of twelve, his job paid him well enough, his large circle of friends loved his sense of humour, and he knew for a fact that half of his female friends wanted to jump into his warm bed. The only thing stopping him from taking up with their numerous suggestions, serious or not, was that his warm bed already had an occupant.

The only part of his life that didn't please him anymore was his so called 'loving' wife. Colin wasn't completely sure just yet, but his guts told him the sneaky tart had more than a couple of extra friends. According to what he had heard from a couple of well-placed friends who frequented the gym, his dearest Sharon was a bit of a wild one between the sheets. That bit Colin did find hard to believe. The woman had never been an animal with him in all their fifteen years of married life.

Darlene focused on the image of him taking a photograph of the woman out of his wallet. She mentally nodded; she knew that woman all right. She thought her name sounded familiar. She'd heard of the rumours of his darling wife being a little bit naughty as well. The last Darlene saw of her was a few days ago, being very familiar with some guy in the back of a taxi outside the off license.

She pushed away Colin's worries over his wife and dug deeper until he saw Colin in the gym upstairs. His defined muscles were shined with sweat as he ran on one of the treadmills. Darlene saw Colin's training partner, the man urging him turn increase the machine's speed, was the blond man. Why did this piece of information not surprise her?

His name was Adam Davis, and Colin had known the man since school. Now that *did* surprise her. Darlene had no idea that they were both the same age. The respect Colin had for his best friend could be a problem. The First Father would not tolerate any favouritism between the First Son and his other vampires.

Darlene heard the man moan. At first, she guessed that Colin had found out she was deep inside his thoughts. That idea vanished when she saw she wasn't the first one to invade Colin Rushmore's mind.

She gazed across his mental landscape, her focus drawn to the sight of a huge crimson block of gelatinous shiny matter submerged into the surface of the man's brain. Was this her own mind translating into imagery of what this represented, or was Darlene actually seeing the physical part of the vampire sense fusing to Colin's body?

Thick red tendrils extruded from the central mass, each end finding a separate area of his flesh before drilling through the soft tissue. Against her better judgment, Darlene drifted closer to one of the tendrils, eager to learn more. The fact that what she was witnessing had already happened to her made Darlene feel a little nauseous, but she quickly put that feeling into a box.

As she drifted closer, Darlene found to her horror that she had no other choice. The pulsing crimson mass was pulling her towards it like the moon pulled the tide, and just like the vast oceans, she was helpless to stop it.

The sweet stench of wet meat engulfed her senses just before Darlene's world turned red. The hoarse male voice, ordering her to get off the floor shocked her senses back to reality. Darlene snapped open her eyes, not knowing where she was. The only thing that assaulted her nostrils now was the smell of wet hay mixed with fresh horse manure. She gazed in wonder at five faces staring at her.

Darlene had no idea what had happened. This wasn't the storage room, that much she was certain about. "Amulius, what's going on?" She stared at her husband as he looked around what appeared to be a primitive stable. He gave no indication he even heard her calling out to him.

She then noticed another person in here with them, a young teenage boy who looked about seventeen. He was huddled in the corner, gripping a large metal blade. Darlene stood up and walked between the boy and the others, noticing that none of them had even looked in her direction. "I'm still inside Colin's mind," she muttered. She leaned against a rough wooden wall, jumping when a thin horse skittered away from her. "This is way too weird."

She had no idea who any of the others were, apart from the fact that, like her, they were all vampires. Darlene looked at the only other male in the stable. He didn't seem much older than the cringing teen. His blazing sulphur eyes found the terrified boy, and the vampire yawned wide, exposing his large teeth. It took her a moment to realise this was her Husband's First Son. She remembered him now. Darlene also remembered the boy used to frighten the crap out of her.

"Juan, I should be annoyed with you," said the First Father. "As my First Son, I expect you to keep my treats under guard."

Darlene chuckled at the sullen look the vampire gave Amulius; she had been the recipient of that particular stare from both of her own kids. This scene was from before the two clans slept through the ages, that much she did understand. What bothered her was why was it inside some bloke who was born just few decades ago?

"I shall see to it the ones responsible are punished, my First Father."

Amulius pushed back the two female vampires and raced over to Juan. "No, you will take no such action, my son. It is you who is responsible. It is you who will be punished." He snapped his fingers, and the two females ran back over to the huge vampire, hissed like angry cats at the young vampire, and ran their hands over the First Father's torso.

Darlene wanted to throw up. If her husband expected her to act in such a demeaning way, then he had another thing coming. A very bad feeling began to creep into her bones. She watched the two male vampires tear into the screaming boy.

Amulius glared at his First Son. "You will not taste blood for many nights, and your wives will not be warming your bed come the sunrise."

Darlene was watching some form of training video. As stupid as it sounded, it must be the case. When the First Father said those words to Colin, he must have also implanted these memories as well.

She blinked, and the scene changed again. This time, she did recognise the building: this was where those bastards had locked her in her own cage. She wandered down the corridor, gazing through the bars. None of the cages were occupied, and this time, there were no other people in the building with her. By the looks of it, this place hadn't been used in a long time. It felt odd to be stood here after so many years, even if she was only reliving someone else's old memories.

Darlene spun around as the doors behind her crashed open. The First Father and Juan pushed through the opening, both struggling with dragging a huge man clad in thick, rough-hewn armour. The figure suddenly roared and slammed his arms back, throwing both vampires against the cages. They leaped to their feet and dived on the giant, each one clamping their teeth into his neck—the only part of him that wasn't encased in the dull armour.

Watching them hang on to this creature reminded her of watching two big cats taking down a large herbivore. They both hung on, and as each second passed, their victim slowed his movements, until his legs finally lost all strength and gave way. The vampires jumped back as he crashed into the floor.

Juan ran over and helped the First Father back onto his feet. They were both panting, dripping in sweat, and grinning. They walked back over to the fallen giant and pulled off his heavy, horned helmet, exposing the grotesque face of another vampire.

"The Swarmers are now deplete of berserkers, First Father," said Juan. "Their defeat is inevitable."

Amulius shook his head. "Do not underestimate their guile, my son. The reports from the outer villages tell of huge Swarmer constructs consuming every human in their path. I have also received tale of them using female warriors in battle."

The look that the First Son gave the other vampire would have been comical if it hadn't been so tragic.

Darlene opened her eyes and saw Amulius's new First Son staring at her. All the other newborn vampires were giving her equal attention. She looked around the storage room, allowing the events of what she witnessed to sink in.

No bloody wonder they all hated her. They didn't see her as a threat, the bastards were frightened of her. She walked over to the new First Son, watching him instinctively shrink away and she leaned closer. "I think your old pal over there, Colin, is in need of some help. I think I was a bit too rough on him." She waited until he moved out of her way before walking over to the closed door.

Darlene looked at her watch and saw that she had only been down here for a couple of minutes. That didn't seem possible, it felt like she'd been down here for hours. Behind her, the newborn vampires spoke in low voices, just beyond her range of hearing; not that it mattered, Darlene knew they were discussing her.

She sighed and grabbed the door handle. Amulius had only asked her to go check on them, to see if they were all okay while he extracted what information he could from her daughter. Back then, it seemed like a perfectly reasonable request. Even as the honey-tinged words dripped from his mouth, her previous anxiety with discovering that both her children had been vampirised evaporated. What was left of her human soul must have withered and died at the news. Not only that, her loving Damien was now in the other clan, one of the hated enemy.

Darlene had watched her beautiful daughter sidle up to her husband, her big blue eyes catching the moonlight from the window above them. Not once did she believe the First Father would do anything untoward to Elsie. It didn't even enter her mind that she had just left her beautiful young daughter with a lustful vampire without thinking of the consequences. She moved her hand away and turned around, gazing at each of the vampires, watching their lips move up until the tips of their teeth showed. Her sudden burst of anxiety must have reached every one of the monsters down here. They were all revelling in her naivety.

"Oh, don't you worry, my mistress," gurgled Colin, unable to stop himself from chuckling. "Our First Father will take good care of your loving daughter." His friend held out his hand and Colin downward slapped it. "I know you were fumbling around inside my head, Darlene, and I hope you found what you were looking for. You are no good to him anymore, my sweet. You might look young, but you're almost as old as the First Father." Colin drew himself up to his full height.

She watched in despair as the others stood up and huddled beside their First Son. All their eyes were now glowing deep red.

"See, I know that our First Father just sees you for what you are. You have given him a new sex toy, and I imagine right now he'll be getting a lot of satisfaction out of her."

The other vampires all laughed alongside Colin. Darlene knew she'd have no trouble confirming whether or not their snide remarks were true. She daren't though, not knowing how she'd react if the head vampire was doing to her daughter what he should have been doing to her. Even so, Darlene couldn't stop a single tear from rolling down her cheek.

"He sees you as some old hag, a piece of garbage to be thrown out with the rest of the rubbish." He smiled when one of the others handed him something. The vampire chuckled. "Yeah, you're pretty fucking tough for an old bird, and I reckon you could do quite a bit of damage if we were just numbered maybe two or three." He looked at his comrades. "But we ain't. There's a few of us here." He showed her what the other vampire had passed him.

Her distraught face reflected off the shining metal blade of the katana.

"I'd forgotten all about this, Darlene," he said, running the edge of the blade down the wall. "Now, I've given this some thought and I figure the only reason why he sent you down here was so we could have some fun as well."

The others murmured their assent.

Darlene grabbed the handle, jerked open the door, and ran through it. There was no way she could fight them all, despite her rage telling her they wouldn't stand a chance. The last image she saw before running from the room was the same stupid look etched on all of their faces. Those idiots actually thought she would stick around and let them fulfil all their perverted desires with her pliant body, as if Colin's harsh words had somehow knocked all the fight out of her.

As she raced along the dark corridor, heading away from the metal stairs that led back up to the ground floor, Darlene clearly heard the sound of their shoes slapping on the concrete floor. So, the bastards were giving chase? That was fine by her. With luck, they'd split up, giving her a better chance to take them out.

The noise of their pursuit got louder, and Darlene just knew the bastards hadn't split up. She slipped through a wedged-open fire door, then ran through the first unlocked door she found. She needed to increase the odds in her favour, she needed some sort of weapon.

She found herself in another storage room, identical to the last one but without the murderous vampires with their blood raised to volcano levels. There was nothing in the room at all, the shelves had been stripped. The sound of their footsteps got louder. They were bound to check this room.

Darlene spun around, intending to get out of there. She refused to be trapped. As she grabbed the door handle, a freezing cold hand slipped over her mouth.

She struggled like a fish on a hook, but her efforts had no effect; the silent adversary was too strong. Darlene felt her strength suddenly leave her as she realized the person behind her must be her husband; none of the other vampires had his strength.

"You look so beautiful," murmured a familiar voice.

She choked back a loud sob at the sound of his voice, and it took a great deal of effort just to stay on her feet. "Paul?" she gasped, spinning around. "But, I thought, well, I thought …"

He grinned back at her. "Oh wow, what a reaction! It looks as if these new bodies of ours can take a little more punishment than we thought." He gingerly felt the side of his ribs. "It still hurts like a bastard though. The pain is lessening, as long as I don't overstrain myself."

Darlene clenched her fists, feeling her long nails dig into the soft flesh. The discomfort was enough evidence to tell her that this was no dream. "I just don't get it. How on earth did you know where I was?" It took a lot of effort to get the words out.

Her voice cracked with every word she spoke. "I really am so sorry for what I do to you, Paul. Will you ever find it in your heart to forgive me?"

He softly kissed her lips while running his fingers through her hair. "Darlene, there really is nothing to forgive. As to the small matter of locating you?" he chuckled. "We are both linked, remember? Your soul just blasted a path through the darkness. I would find you, honey, even if you were on Mars."

Darlene couldn't stop grinning. "Oh my, listen to the bard. Have you just eaten a dozen romance novels?"

He frowned. "I'm sorry. Does it irritate you?"

"Of course not, silly!" she cried, flinging her arms around him. "I still can't believe that it really is you. Oh God, I'm so glad that have found me."

Paul gently removed her arms "You need to listen to me, sweetheart. We don't have a lot of time left." He looked up towards the door. "They'll be back here any moment." Paul pointed over to the far wall, "There's a grate over there, Darlene. That's my way out of here."

"Wait, you mean *our* way out?"

He kissed her again. "No, honey, if they catch me in here, those newborn vampires will kill me. I might have stood a chance if I was still in good shape. My body still needs a lot of repairs. Don't worry, I'm not going far, I promise."

Paul released her and ran over to the door. He opened it a crack and peered out. "Yeah, they're coming back." He hurried over to the grate, lifted the metal grate off, and leaned it against the wall. "I need you to put this back when I'm inside."

"No, I can't!" she replied, shaking her head. "You can't leave me here!"

"Listen to me. You will come to no harm. They will return with the First Father." He looked back at the rectangular hole in the wall. "I have heard much on my way back to you. Enough to realise that there is a good chance that me, you, and your daughter could emerge as the top players in this."

"Elsie?"

He nodded. "These ancient vampires really have no idea what they've unleashed upon this planet, Darlene. We can't go back to being human. We must accept that. It still doesn't stop us from ensuring that we put these fuckers back in the ground where they belong."

"What about Damien?"

Paul sighed. "I'm sorry, he is lost to you. Even if you wanted to take him back, your blood wouldn't let you. His blood certainly wouldn't allow it. Now, you need to listen to me, sweetheart."

Chapter Thirteen

It looked as though his fingertips had left indentations in the metal. Damien took his eyes off the stone floor thirty feet below him and ran his fingers along the girder again, trying not to chuckle when he realised they were just imperfections in the steel. He dipped his head, making sure the vampires hunting for him were still out of sight. He couldn't see any of them, but he did hear a cry of anger, followed by what sounded like a pile of boxes crashing to the floor.

Damien slowly crawled along the underside of the girder, taking his time—he had no wish to slip. The roof of the butcher's quarter was only a few feet away, and he should be safe in there until the sun went down. He didn't think the vampires would continue to trash the place looking for him. Would they? Damien inched further towards the roof, listening to the noises coming from the top end of the market. They didn't seem to be giving up looking for him so far.

He let his legs dangle when he reached the roof, sighing with relief. Damien had never been bothered much by heights, but crawling from one end of the market to the other on a roof beam was taking it a bit too far. He dropped onto the roof, went to his knees, then leaned over the edge. Would his newly enhanced body have stayed in one piece if he had slipped?

From where he lay, Damien clearly saw the patch of black slime, still bubbling under the light from the hateful sun. "How close was I to getting caught?" he whispered, suppressing a shudder. Like the plant that he was, Damien had just stood there, rooted to the spot, gazing down at the rendered down vampire. He could hear the sound of heavy footsteps yet didn't move until the last possible moment. He had already discovered that, despite his previous fears, none of his bones were broken in the fall, he'd only given his body a few more bruises to fix.

Even looking back, Damien still believed he had been fortunate to get away. He assumed they hadn't seen him sprint up the aisle, unless they had caught a glimpse of his shadow. Most likely, the vampires had heard him fleeing, he hadn't exactly run like a ninja.

Damien had jumped into the first hiding place he found, an empty stall with a huge 'to let' sign bolted to the front. He knew the place had been empty for years, and judging from the rank smell of piss coming up from the bare floorboards under his knees, Damien guessed he had also inadvertently found the market's second unofficial toilet.

He had forgotten what they had even sold in this lot. He moved his knee off the damp patch, wondering why he was even thinking about shit like that. Trivialities left his mind when he saw the Swarmer leader step out into the aisle. He had his back to Damien, but even that was enough to shock him rigid.

The guy couldn't have been much older than Damien. Well, he didn't look much older. Not only that, compared to the two great hulking monsters standing beside him, he looked like a tiny child.

Even from where he hid, Damien felt the waves of fear rolling off the two huge vampires. How the fuck had that child managed to become their leader? Those two vampires could easily eat the wimp and still have room for ice cream.

He leaned further out, trying to catch their frantic conversations, but they were too far away for him to get any of their words. Damien sighed, then tried to use his embryonic talent to scan them. It was no use; they had clamped their minds tights. He assumed it was because they knew another one of their kind was close by until he felt the leader trying to read them as well.

Suddenly, the diminutive vampire snapped his arm forward and grabbed the bald creature by the throat. Damien's jaw dropped when he saw their leader effortlessly lift the gagging vampire up until his feet left the floor. *How is that even possible?* he thought. It was like watching some schoolgirl lifting up the back of a bus with one hand.

He needed to get out of this fucking market, like, right now. His temperature began to rise, and he felt like his heart was trying to beat its way out of his ribcage. What the hell was happening to him? Damien had never been so terrified. He wasn't the only one who was acting strange. The other vampire had dropped to his knees and had his arms over his head weeping like an injured baby. His moans turned Damien's spine to jelly.

Their leader released the vampire, stepping back as he fell and landed in a boneless heap. The heart-stopping fear that coursed through Damien's body died away, leaving him sprawled out on the floorboards, shaking like a leaf and feeling like he'd just been dropped into a snowdrift whilst naked.

"I know that you are close by, my little rabbit. I can feel your little heart beating." The Swarmer First Father raised his arms up towards the ceiling. "Remove yourself from your concealment. I simply wish you to explain your deed. I might even consider allowing you to continue existing."

Damien watched him take one step forward. His arms were just millimetres from that beam of sunlight, and the other two vampires cringed back, moaning. He did consider taking the leader up on the offer. After all, these vampires were now the only family he had left. There was nowhere else to go.

Damien then remembered that this strange looking vampire currently doing deals with his life was shacked up with the female who had turned him. That wily vampire obviously had plans for him that no doubt involved him somehow getting rid of their First Father. At least, that's the impression that he received.

"I know what you are, my little rabbit. I'm guessing that you do too now. Perhaps one of my clan defied my orders, perhaps a Deathgazer turned you? It matters not; I will not take these irregularities into consideration. I just want to know how my First Son died. Are you going to show yourself? Your time is running out and so is my patience."

Damien stopped in mid motion when the First Father turned around and looked towards the empty stall. He knew he hadn't been seen, not that it mattered. The First Father's piercing eyes rooted him to the spot. He felt like he was gazing into eternity. The leader then blinked, severing the connection. Damien scuttled back behind the low partition, feeling his heartbeat increase again. That was just nightmarish. What the hell had he just seen?

The vampire's eyes had glowed like a pair of sick green headlights. Damien now saw why he didn't need to be as big as the other vampires: that thing could just suck out your soul with one evil glare. He took a deep breath, composed himself, and slowly looked around the side again. The vampire hadn't moved, but at least now Damien could actually look at the First Father without feeling like a rabbit caught by a large fox.

Damien found his mind leaving his body and heading for the First Father. While the vampire's attention was elsewhere, Damien found it ridiculously easy to slip into the First Father's thoughts.

It took Damien a moment to realise he was no longer inside the market. He rolled onto his back and gazed up at the full moon, smelled the scent of dead leaves under his naked body, and felt the cold wind blowing over his chest. He turned his head to the left, catching sight of a young brown-haired woman leaning over a crudely made wooden bridge, which crossed a shallow stream. She held her hand in the surging water, occasionally grabbing twigs as they floated past.

Deep down, Damien knew that despite how real this felt to him, his body hadn't moved from that piss-stained floor. He fought back the panic and feeling of disorientation when the body he now shared sat up and walked over to the stream. The body waved at the girl before kneeling down and gazing into the clear water.

A pair of intense green eyes stared back at him. Damien almost screamed. He was now inside the body of the Swarmer First Father. Was he reliving a moment from the vampire's past? The girl's musical giggle reached his ears. That voice sounded so familiar. His head turned.

"I knew you would enjoy this," the vampire said.

"Oh yes, Desmonus. I can't thank you enough for this privilege. The other house slaves will be so jealous."

The vampire jumped up and ran over to the girl. "Say just one word to anyone and I will hurt you." The vampire breathed in deeply, exhaled, then sat down and dangled his feet over the edge of the bridge. "Forgive me, Eleanor," he said. "It is not always possible to stop my volatile emotions from ruling my body."

Damien had difficulty believing that this vision of loveliness was the same person who bit him. Nothing about this Eleanor caught his eye. Damien knew if the vampire he was currently occupying were to turn away, he'd have difficulty placing her face.

The girl placed her arm around his shoulders. "It is I who should ask for forgiveness, my sweet protector. I spoke without thought." She kissed the back of his head. "Desmonus, whom of those tongue dancing fishwives would even listen to some lowly servant?"

The vampire looked up into her large brown eyes. "You are such a beauty, my Eleanor."

She jerked her head back, and Damien saw tears in her eyes. He wondered if this vampire was taking the piss. He wished he could access the vampire's thoughts so he could find out what this Desmonus was thinking instead of just being an invisible passenger. Damien watched the girl wipe her eyes, wondering what it was about her that made him feel so antagonistic about her appearance. Was it because he had only seen her as a beautiful vampire? Eleanor leaned over and kissed the vampire's nose. Damien did see that at least her teeth were in good shape.

"It still takes me time to believe that you do not jest with your words, Desmonus." She smiled. "Even after two years, I still wake before the dawn bells, smiling at my fortune."

Desmonus gasped when the girl leaned across and wrapped her fingers around his flaccid penis.

"If I am your shining night star, my love, then why does your rod bend so easily?"

She started to stroke him, squeezing then releasing as her momentum built up. She giggled when the vampire's hands found her large breasts.

"Do not mock me," he said, leaning forward. Desmonus ran his long tongue across her large nipples.

"Why would I mock my lover, Desmonus?" she said, sitting down on his ankles. She lowered her head and flicked her tongue over his inner thighs. "Will you ever make me like you?"

Damien felt like some pervert peeping through a window, watching a couple copulate.

"I love you, my Eleanor, not just like you." Desmonus sat up and curled his fingers through the girl's hair. "Do not stop that, my darling."

Eleanor abruptly released the vampire's raging penis and stood up. "I want you to turn me, Desmonus. I want to be like you." She stood astride him and gazed into his eyes. "You will soon find another girl to warm your cock, Desmonus. I am not a fool. I know I am not the first girl you have used."

The vampire growled and jumped to his feet. He wrapped his fingers around her wrists and pushed her over to the edge of the bridge. "You dare to issue demands?"

Damien knew the girl must be in a great deal of pain. The vampire was not gentle with his hold, yet despite this, she didn't cry out. He inwardly sighed, hoping they'd get this argument dealt with so they could get back to the sex part. The girl might not be much to look at, but from what he briefly saw, she certainly knew how to use her tongue. Damien couldn't wait to feel that tongue of hers wrapped around his anatomy. He was sure that would take place if he could find a way to appease her comrades.

"Desmonus, I love you!" she shouted. "And I suspect you love me too." She licked her lips. "You talk in your sleep, and I have heard muttering of dissent from your comrades." Eleanor looked down at his fingers. "Please, you're hurting me."

"You will tell me everything you have heard. You will do this now or I will let you go." He picked up the girl by her wrists and dangled her over the stream.

"Do what you must!" she snarled. "I will not comply."

The vampire shocked Damien by pulling her back onto the bridge and wrapping his arms around her shivering body. What sort of relationship was this? Did this girl get turned on by deliberately trying to upset this vampire? He looked at the ugly bruising he had caused on both her wrists and grimaced.

"How do you intend to explain away these marks, Eleanor? You know the house master will expect a convincing answer."

She gazed into his eyes. "I do not care anymore, Desmonus. I just want to be with you. I want to be with you forever." The girl flung her arms around the vampire's neck and hugged him tight against her body. "I know you can sense my hot blood coursing through my body, Desmonus. It would take just one nip. I know you want to. Why do you deny your yearning? "

He pulled the girl off him. "You are right, Eleanor. I do love you. It is your warmth and tenderness that drew me to you." He looked behind him.

Damien's eyes went wide at the sight of a huge fortified wooden city on the horizon. He guessed they were a good few miles from its outskirts. The place must be enormous. He had not seen anything like it in the history books. He guessed it must be as large as any modern city, maybe even bigger. Was that where these vampires used to live?

"If you were to turn, all qualities would be lost. You would no longer be the woman I fell in love with." He brushed back her hair. "You seem to have forgotten that I am only the First Son. Although I have existed for almost as long as our First Father, I do not believe I have yet gained the gift to turn you."

"It has not stopped you from experimenting, Desmonus," growled a male voice.

The vampire pushed her back and spun around to see four large figures stepping out into the clearing. For the first time since his confinement, Damien felt emotion from his vessel as a huge blast of fury rushed through his body. Damien watched their ruby red eyes blaze. The vampires lunged, and three of them grabbed Desmonus. The last vampire turned his head and pointed at the girl.

"Do not move, child. I shall deal with you soon." He walked up to Desmonus and gently ran his long fingers down the side of his face. "It pleases me to find that your prophetic talent does not always deliver. It does not please me to hear that the rumour of your dissatisfaction and subsequent clandestine rebellion was not a lie."

Desmonus spat into the vampire's face. "You are not worthy of the title of First Father. You have reduced us all to the role of ineffectual shepherds. Amulius, we are all slowly dying. We hunt the human, not farm them."

The First Father threw his head back and roared with laughter. "Was that what you were doing with that girl, Desmonus? What were you hunting for?" He clicked his fingers. "Child, come here."

Damien watched Eleanor get to her feet and slowly walk towards the group, a huge smile was fixed to her face. He wanted her to turn around and run for her life. Did the idiot not know what these things were? They were going to rip her into pieces and eat the silly bitch in front of her lover. Damien then mentally slapped himself, wondering if he had caught stupid disease. Of course they weren't going to eat her, unless this Eleanor had a twin sister who took her name.

Amulius grabbed her by the hair and pulled her towards him. "Perhaps you do have an argument worth investigating, my former First Son. I see now that select individuals, both human and vampire, have taken advantage of my benevolent reign."

He lifted Eleanor off the ground and shook her like a rag doll. Damien heard something inside the girl crack. Desmonus moaned when the First Father dropped the girl onto the grass and her head rested at an unnatural angle. Her neck was broken.

"So it begins," he announced. "We know the names of all your co-conspirators, Desmonus. Do you have anything else to say before we eat you?"

Damien felt another emotion rise through the vampire's system; strangely enough, this vampire was feeling triumph. He didn't get it. What was there to be happy about? The vampire chuckled. Judging from the expression etched upon the First Father's face, he couldn't understand Desmonus's apparent need for jollity either.

"I do have some more words to say, you feeble-minded fool. My prophetic talent has never failed me."

The trees around them shook as over a dozen vampires dropped from the branches and landed in the clearing. Damien watched in fascination as the two holding Desmonus released him and charged the intruders. The First Father stumbled back, almost falling over the girl's broken body, then turned around and ran, disappearing into the trees.

Desmonus watched for a few moments as the intruders ripped apart the two remaining vampires, smiling as the leaf litter turned scarlet, then dropped to his knees and gently lifted the dead girl up into his arms.

"This is one event I did not foresee, Eleanor," he whispered. The vampire turned to the side. "We move tonight as discussed. The First Father will return with enough bodies to end all our existences."

Damien watched two vampires lift their heads out of the open torso of one of the dead vampires. Just that image alone made him reassess everything he knew about these creatures. He had never read or seen anything about them actually consuming flesh. He'd always assumed they just drank blood.

"Let them come," said Healiod. "They are all as soft as the newborn lamb. Have we not just proved that?"

The others laughed with him.

Desmonus growled. "And you two are proving to me that your heads are full of lamb's wool. You wish to stay and fight three hundred of the First Father's soldiers?" He stood up, lifted the corpse, and held the body against his chest.

"Will you be sharing her, Desmonus?" Healiod asked. He whimpered when Desmonus bared his huge teeth and hissed. "I meant no disrespect. We all know you had feelings for the human girl. It's just that, well, she is just meat now. It would be impractical to allow her flesh to rot."

Desmonus walked over to the twelve vampires, his feet flattening pieces of the two dead vampires into the soil. "We are only thirteen. For our new clan to survive and prosper, we need to grow. My talent tells me we shall do just that." He gazed down at the girl's face. "My talent also tells me the time has now arrived to show you why you all risked your lives to join me in my quest to find our forgotten destiny. We are predators. Our ancestors lived for the glory of the hunt."

He opened his mouth and sank his teeth into the dead girl's neck. Damien groaned in ecstasy, sharing Desmonus's pleasure as her cooling blood slipped down his throat. The vampire abruptly released his grip and looked at the other vampires' astonished faces before he licked his chin dry. "I know even the First Father cannot create our kind from a corpse." He gently laid her down, then readjusted her head until the bones in her neck cracked. Desmonus chuckled at the unbelieving faces above him. "Did you not believe I had the power to create? Did you think that, like the rest of our kind, my bite would only produce ghouls?" He stood up and pointed towards the huge city beyond the tree line. "Go now. Leave me with her. You all know where to go."

Eleven of the vampires slowly backed away, their faces still displaying rapture tinged with incredulity. Only Helix remained stationary. "You are our new First Father," he said dropping to his knees and bowing his head.

Desmonus nodded. "The clan of the Swarmers will scourge this land. This land will belong to us. The Deathgazer Clan will soon be extinct." He looked across at the city. "Those pathetic creatures that defile the very name of our kind will not roll over like dogs and allow us to end them. You must remember that,

Helix. Now go, allow me to savour a moment with our first true Swarmer."

He waited for Helix to catch up with the others before he tenderly brushed his long fingernails between her breasts. "You have always been the only person in my life for whom my talent has not worked," he said. The girl's eyes flickered. "Considering the enormous task that awaits our embryonic Clan, it may have been a wiser choice to throw your corpse to my new followers and let them enjoy your flesh. I do not need complications at this crucial stage."

Damien now saw the Eleanor he remembered showing through the girl's plain looks. The transformation took just seconds. He watched her eyes open and felt the vampire groan. He, too, saw what his bite had done to the woman.

"You will be at my side forever, Eleanor."

Damien gripped the edge of the roof, lowering his head when he saw the two vampires pass below him. Neither Helix nor Healiod had thought to look up. He knew if he was in their shoes, he would have considered the possibility that their target might not have just stayed on the ground. After all, the market was huge, and he suspected those two idiots would have travelled the same routes repeatedly by now. Damien slid further back, wondering why he relived that piece of Desmonus's ancient past.

He waited until the vampires were out of earshot before he rolled onto his front, got onto his hands and knees, and slowly made his way across the roof, heading for a hole cut into the wood near the wall. Damien smiled when the dark interior of the first meat counter came into view. He knew if he still had his human eyes, all he'd see was a rectangular hole of pure black. He reached the hole, lowered his feet, and dropped down. That feeling of being a pursued rabbit vanished and left him feeling, for the first time since running from the vampires, safe.

The wall beside Damien offered him a wide array of weapons that could help him even up the odds of surviving his inevitable conflict with the three vampires who were looking for him. He walked up to the tiled wall and ran his fingers over a long-bladed knife with a serrated edge. Damien grinned and pulled it off the wall. It would do just fine. Perhaps with this acting as a deterrent, he might actually be able to explain his situation without those three bastards draining him dry.

He made his way over to the metal shutter, wondering what reaction he would receive if he rapped his fist against the metal. It wasn't too much of a stupid idea. At least in here, he could keep his back against the wall. Okay, so he was trapped, but he was in that position already until the sun dipped below the horizon.

"You could just hide here," he whispered. That idea did sound very appealing. If he waited until dark, sneaked out, and tried to hook up with Eleanor, then perhaps he might stand a better chance of surviving.

"Hiding is what the food is best at," hissed a voice.

He spun around and raised the knife, then slowly backed away. "What the hell?"

Desmonus emerged from the space between two walk-in freezers. "You, my friend, are a mystery to me. Normally, I enjoy solving these unexplained enigmas." He thrust his arms out. "Right now, though, I have enough mysteries to keep my already deluged mind busy for the next thousand years." He laughed. "I suspect all of these human achievements must have melted the tiny mind of my ex First Father. I had warned him about the perils of attempting to domesticate the human species." The vampire's green eyes glowed even brighter.

"I see you are surprised to find me in here, my little rabbit. You thought I was still out beyond this closed metal cage, still searching for you. Did you not discover my talent of prediction when you crept into my head and stole my thoughts?"

"You knew I was in there?"

The vampire shrugged. "Not at first, no. I just sensed the lightest of touches. You are very good, for an amateur."

Damien tried not to look into his blazing eyes. He weighed up his choices. Although this monster hadn't killed him, it didn't make him feel any more secure. He got the impression that the vampire was just playing with him, like a cat tormenting a mouse. The vampire would tear into him; he decided that was inevitable. He needed to rush over and push the razor-sharp blade he held in his trembling fingers deep into the vampire's heart before that moment came.

"Why do you hold your weapon aloft, my little rabbit?" Desmonus ran his tongue over his thin lips "That piece of finely crafted metal looks very heavy. Oh yes, it is so hard to keep it held up. Can you not feel the strain it is putting on your muscles? It is getting heavier and heavier."

Damien gasped as the vampire's soft words penetrated his confused mind. The weapon now felt like a huge iron girder in his hands. He couldn't help himself; he needed to drop it.

The vampire chuckled, then bent down and grabbed the bottom of the shutter and lifted it up to his waist.

Damien couldn't hold the knife any longer. He cried out and let it fall through his fingers.

"We could not be good friends when you had that sharp knife help tight in your grip. I do understand your trepidation." Desmonus kicked the blade away. "It would have been a tragedy if you slipped, my little rabbit."

Damien glanced over at the half open shutters and his heart sunk at the sight of two pairs of thick legs showing through the gap.

"I would wish to know why my First Son has been reduced to black slime. I am hoping you will be able to explain our loss."

"It was an accident," Damien replied, trying to keep the tremor out of his voice. "Your First Son chased me before I had time to explain my predicament. I didn't want him to die." He couldn't help shaking when he remembered how the vampire's flesh had melted off his bones. "Nobody should suffer like that."

The other two vampires had now pushed their bulky bodies under the gap and taken positions behind their First Father. Damien then realised just how big these vampires really were.

"I am not convinced you are able to explain your predicament, my little rabbit. I do not know what you are. You act human, and yet we both know that is no longer the case, not anymore." He leaned closer and inhaled. "I can tell you belong to me, my little rabbit. You are a Swarmer. Yet how can that be? I do not remember biting you."

There seemed little point in concealing the information. "I was staying at my aunt's with my sister when your pals attacked us. The woman bit me," he said, watching the vampire slowly gaze towards the floor.

Desmonus then chuckled. "That is a most intriguing answer. I do not doubt your words carry some element of truth." He looked to the side. "Healiod, is Eleanor your First Father?"

The huge vampire shook his head. "No, and this worm must be lying. The power to change only comes from you. She cannot create, none of us have that privilege."

Desmonus grinned. "There, you see why I find you to be such an unnecessary distraction, my little rabbit? I cannot explain your existence, and that worries me. You see, I do not like you. I have never been comfortable in the presence of a thought thief. Your type is simply not to be trusted."

The First Father took a step back and patted his companions' backs. "I believe the only solution I have is to deny you your existence. This is a new world, and the rules have altered, that much I discern. Perhaps I will meet more like you?" He shrugged. "If that happens then their fate will be the same as yours. My little rabbit now belongs to you two. Consider him a gift in reward for your loyalty."

Damien tried to run, but the two vampires lunged forward, wrapped their thick fingers around his wrists, and dragged him back.

"The rich blood from a fresh turned vampire tastes like nectar. It will even bring back those half-forgotten memories from your very first feed."

As Damien continued his hopeless attempt to break free, he caught Helix giving his companion a brief alarmed look.

"You are generous as you are wise, my First Father. You being unable to explain this worm's existence worries me. Although we are both so eager to drain this thing, I am worried that perhaps his blood might somehow be contaminated?" Healiod looked back at Helix before smiling. "Perhaps the best solution would be for the worm to meet the same fate as our now melted First Son?"

The First Father burst out laughing. "Oh yes, I would enjoy witnessing that." He pulled the shutter up over his head, then bowed. "Healiod, lead the way."

Damien tried one more time to slide his arms out from the vice-like grip. Healiod jabbed him in the side for his troubles. He cringed again when the vampire raised his hand, but this time he just pushed Damien's head down to get him under the shutter.

Even from here, he could see that shaft of hellish, white light at the end of the aisle. He needed to do something. His life was now measured in seconds.

ELEANOR! I need your help. Please tell me how to get out of this.

He sensed little chance of his pleas reaching the female vampire, but he couldn't think of any other way out of this mess. The two vampires dragged him closer to the stream of light, and he saw the other vampire's mess had now stopped bubbling. All that was left of him was a thin film of oily material splashed over the flagstone.

"Do you now wish you had stayed away?" enquired Helix.

You beg like a dog, Damien. I was wrong to think you could help me. This is the best way to end. I shall have to find another.

No! Just give me a chance.

Damien gasped and tried once more to escape. Healiod hit him again, but Damien pushed the pain away and doubled his attempt to stop these monsters from dragging him closer to the sunlight.

The First Father's paranoia and suspicion rule his life. It helps him maintain power. Feed it, Damien.

"Helix thinks you're going to make him First Son!" Damien looked at Healiod. "He's going to kill you!" Damien saw confusion etched in the vampire's expression as a result of his lie. He scanned his mind and looked back at Desmonus. "They have already fed, First Father. That's why they didn't want me. They both defied you. They laughed at your inability to probe their minds, they …"

The air was blasted from his lungs when Healiod slammed both his fists into Damien's guts.

"Still your lying tongue!" he shouted, dragging him closer to the light.

Damien couldn't do anything to stop them now. His whole body was beginning to shut down. He felt like that last blow pushed his internal organs flat against the back of his ribs. He couldn't move!

Damien gingerly opened his eyes to find the First Father standing over him.

"I suspect you are merely saying anything to stop them from ending you. Of course you are. Although you are fresh, your essence would do and say anything to stop your body from dying. If what you say is true, then point their evidence. Do not delay, or I will complete the task myself."

Damien saw the two vampires' murderous looks and resisted the urge to give them the finger. He doubted they'd understand the reference anyway. He slowly rolled onto his back, gritting his teeth at the agony flushing through his body. The First Father placed his hands on his hips and glowered. Damien pointed to the back of a stall that sold second-hand books.

Helix fell to his knees. "Please, First Father, do not punish us. The temptation to feed was simply too great to resist. The thought thief is correct; we have fed on the blood of humans, despite you giving orders to fast."

Desmonus bent down and lifted Damien to his feet. "Maybe you do have some use. If you are able to stay out of my mind, your existence might stay with you until we meet up with the others."

Chapter Fourteen

Cade jumped back onto the pavement to avoid a green delivery truck from turning his body into a red stain on the road. He leaned against the wall of the library, trying to calm himself down, and watched the vehicle disappear around the corner, no doubt heading for the outskirts of town and then off to God knows where. "As long as it's away from here," he muttered.

Since his escape from those hooligans, Cade had seen quite a few locals heading out of the town like rats deserting a sinking ship. He'd even asked a couple of people he knew by sight why the exodus. All he received in return were blank stares and replies that they were just going off for the weekend or had a sudden desire to visit friends.

Cade waited for two more cars to speed past him before daring to cross the road. He kept his eyes fixed upon his target, convinced that the building in front of him was where those bastards had taken his Katy. He suddenly stopped in the middle of the road and grinned at that thought. There was no doubt in his mind that she was his, no matter what some undead, half-human twatface thought.

He hurried across the now empty road and looked over at the entrance to the town's sports centre. Every instinct in his body told him this was the place where that deviant had taken Katy. Hell, even from here, standing outside the door, he believed he could smell their foul stench.

There was nobody around, and the building looked abandoned. He knew that, by now, the sports centre should be open, and yet, when he tried the doors, he found the place was locked up tight. Cade peered through the doors, trying to see if there was anyone around.

"It looks like the employees have all decided to go on a day trip as well." He sighed, unsure of what he was going to do now. Cade turned around and looked at the carpark. There were a few cars here, so there must be somebody in the building. The carpark belonged to the sports centre; nobody else used it.

There was one car parked in the corner that Cade did recognise. He wandered over to an ancient souped-up lime green

Ford Escort. This car was a regular sight in this carpark, but not at this time though. The car belonged to one of the martial arts sparring partners, Colin Rushmore. He looked back at the building and frowned. It didn't make any sense. Colin would never leave his beloved car here. He loved this car more than he loved his wife. "Unless he was still inside?" Cade leaned against the side of the car and considered that possibility. Although it wasn't unknown for Colin and his fellow weight training freaks to stay in their gym all day, they had never stayed all night. "Unless they had a lock in?"

He ran his hands across the roof and told himself that gyms don't do lock-ins. He stopped by the boot and crouched down to inspect the lock. "Lock-in or not, you shouldn't have left your car here, buddy." He reached into his back pocket, pulled out a small penknife, pushed the thinnest blade into the lock, and savagely twisted it to the left. Cade chuckled when the lock popped open.

The boot swung up to reveal a black carpeted space containing a green sports bag and a silver flask. Cade felt alongside the edge of the carpet until his fingers ran over a tiny metal clasp. He pushed it back, lifted up the carpet, and chuckled again at the sight of Colin's pride and joy.

"Just be thankful that it's me who found this," he said, gently lifting Colin's katana out of its hidden pocket. "I'll give you it back, my friend," he whispered, closing the boot and locking it up.

He pulled the weapon out of its sheath, marvelling at the quality; it really was a beautiful sword. "Oh dear, you poor ghouls really don't know whom you're messing with." He replaced the sword back in the sheath and strapped it to his back. For the first time since waking up, he actually felt like he could defend himself. Although he wasn't quite the master like Colin, he certainly knew how to wield a blade.

"That is where they have taken Katy. I'm sure of it," he muttered, walking back to the building. On his way through the carpark, he spotted half a brick lying close by the wheel of a Land Rover and stooped down to pick it up, knowing he now had his own key.

Three more cars sped past the sports centre, and he noticed a couple of middle-aged women pushing a shopping trolley full of bedding along the pavement. This place really was turning into a ghost town. How the hell were the authorities going to explain this mass exodus? He looked over toward the right, past the town steeple, to where the festival was due to start tonight, knowing he had found his answer. He guessed they would use them as some convenient scapegoat.

Cade knew if he didn't find a way to halt this then a few jumped up councillors banging on about disturbing the peace would be the least of their worries. He peered through the glass one last time before he took a step back and launched the brick at the window, hoping it wouldn't bounce back. The brick shattered the glass and disappeared inside.

The noise of the glass breaking made his ears hurt, and he knew the sound must have travelled through the silent air for quite a distance. He shrugged, like he could give a shit anymore. He pushed out the last pieces of glass, then pushed his way through the hole, being careful not to slice open his flesh on a couple of glass bits that he couldn't move with his fingers.

As soon as he entered the cool foyer, Cade saw he'd just walked into a whole boatload of bad news. The air stunk of death, and the walls were coated with dried blood. Even with all this gore, Cade knew this wasn't where Katy had been taken. He pulled out the katana and took another step into the foyer, grateful for the comforting weight of the weapon.

Cade tried to slow down his breathing and watched where he stood, not wanting to give away his position. He glanced back at the broken glass and slammed his hand over his mouth to stop himself from falling about in a fit of hysterical laughter. He'd made enough fucking noise to wake the dead!

Apart from his own heavy breathing, he heard nothing except the air conditioners and the humming of the vending machines beside the doors. Cade then saw the first body, at least what was left of it. The girl looked as though she had fallen into a combine harvester. He bent down, picked up a heavy coat lying on a chair, and placed it over the worst of the damage. He didn't know if he should continue. He knew these things had to be put down, but his priority lay in rescuing Katy. He was her only hope. He didn't doubt she was living on borrowed time. Cade looked up at the wall clock and saw it was just past midday, there were still plenty of hours left before the sun went down.

Cade backed away, heading towards the broken door. He felt like the world's biggest coward, but what other choice did he have? He wouldn't be able to live with himself if anything happened to her. "I'll be back for you lot," he hissed, averting his eyes from the mess on the floor. He had to come back—he owed it to that poor girl whose life those monsters had taken.

Cade yelped when he heard the sound of something crashing to the ground beyond the reception desk. He crouched and moved to the side, taking up position behind the coke machine. The interior was too dark to see anything, and he daren't yell out. A dozen different images of a group of blood-thirsty vampires cascaded through his mind. "Because that's really going to happen," he muttered, feeling the warmth of the sun on his broad back.

"Is there anyone in there?" he shouted feeling a little foolish for shouting into the dark room. Cade counted to ten, guessing that the wind blowing through the smashed door had probably knocked something down. "It's time you left."

He had already decided where to start his search for Katy. The first place he needed to go was back to her house. Hell, there *was* nowhere else to start. Apart from where she lived, he knew very little about the crowd with whom she hung. Cade certainly had no idea where her ex-boyfriend lived. Walking around the town for the next few hours hoping to spot his car sounded like a fucking ridiculous idea. "You could borrow Colin's car," he said to himself, turning around to gaze into the carpark.

"Help me!"

Cade spun back around and ran over to the front desk, not caring if any of those things were around. He knew that voice. "Where are you, buddy?" he shouted. Cade jumped onto the surface of the desk when he heard someone cry out.

"Is that you, Cade? Of fuck, it is! God, please get me the fuck out of here!"

"Are you trapped?" he shouted back.

"I just need you to help me. Please hurry up!"

Several thoughts went through his mind, pushing out the most pressing one of rushing in there to help his mate, Colin Rushmore. For a start, although that was his voice, it did not sound a bit like him. Cade detected something disturbing under that tone, as if his friend was laughing at him.

"Are you okay in there?" He almost fell off the desk when three pairs of bright scarlet lights peered out from out of the darkness. He jumped back, watching in horror as three figures crept out from the dark room. He saw Colin in front, smiling at him. His huge teeth were stained with the blood of some poor victim. Cade held the sword out in front of him, determined not to be the next one.

"That's my katana, you bastard! Give me it back!"

He didn't believe he was hearing this. The sly, oozing voice had just vanished. This monster sounded just like the guy he hung around with. Cade almost did just that. Only his lightning fast reflexes saved him from becoming another victim as the two vampires beside Colin lunged forward at incredible speed, their impossibly long arms reaching towards Cade's body. He saw the long fingernails heading towards his tender skin at the last moment and jumped back, clumsily swinging the katana across their path. The blade missed them by inches, but it did cause the three vampires to shrink back, hissing at him.

Cade growled in fury, not willing to take this crap anymore. He lifted the sword and ran towards them, gaining little satisfaction in watching the three of them retreat into the darkness. He saw their lantern-like eyes glowing from the far side of the room.

"Yeah, that's right, hide away in a dark room where the big hard Cade can't get you," he shouted. He remembered the tanning shop and decided there and then to go back there and see if he could grab a UV torch. The vampires wouldn't be able to hide from him then. "I'll be back." He suppressed a chuckle, wondering if he should have asked them if they had seen Sarah Connor. "Hey, Colin, guess what? I'm going to steal your beloved car and scrape it along the side of a building, then piss on the seats before setting it on fire."

The resulting roar of anger made Cade feel much better. As he turned, trying to banish the sickening image of his mate ripping into that girl like some ravenous jackal, he caught a tiny glimpse of something glowing just by his feet. Cade jumped back, realising exactly what it was. He cried out and thrust the blade forward, just as the concealed vampire jumped up. The sword pierced the monster's flesh.

The weapon felt good in Cade's hands. The carefully wound leather of the handle was easy to grip, despite the copious amount of sweat pouring from his palms. He pushed the sword forward, expecting to hear him cry out, but he'd been too slow. This time the vampire had moved out of his range.

"Come out and fight, you bastard!" Cade screamed into the darkness.

"Drop my sword, you twat, and we'll consider it."

Cade backed away, heading towards the doorway, swinging the katana slowly from side to side, still waiting to feel one of them jump on him from behind.

"Just look at the sexy Cade, boys. With his long dark hair, big muscles, and swinging my Katana like a fucking golf club." Colin chuckled. "I tell you what I'll do, my friend. If you stop acting like Conan the Barbarian and put my bastard katana gently on the floor, I'll see if I can convince my pals not to dine upon your pretty face."

He couldn't see anything, and judging from the vampire's mocking voice, Colin was moving around the room. Cade found the back wall and pressed himself up against it. At least now, they wouldn't be able to circle him. "I didn't come here to fight with any of you. Colin, I was only looking for my girlfriend."

"Don't you dare try to bullshit me, Cade. So you've suddenly found yourself a girlfriend over night? When the fuck did this happen? I thought you were still lusting after the barmaid at the Rose and Crown."

Colin was now to his left, probably close to the doors that led to the swimming pool. His voice had lost the deep tone. He almost sounded like the guy he used to train with every weekend.

"I did meet her last night," he replied. "As cute as a button. I don't think you know her."

"As cute as a button?" laughed Colin. "Listen to yourself. You've gone fucking soft. You'll be spouting poetry next. Come on, spill it, what's her name?"

For the first time since entering this dark room, Cade could make out a moving shape at the far side of the room, and he guessed that was where Colin was. He tried not to grin. He didn't want these things discovering that his eyes were beginning to adjust to the darkness. "She's called Katy Barnes."

"Oh, you have got to be shitting me! You've been screwing that tasty piece? Hell, if her ex finds out, he'll try to stick my Katana right up your fucking arse."

"Slimy looking bloke with short, blond, close cropped hair?"

"Yeah, Alvin Black. He's a right little hooligan. He lives near the park in one of the big houses. His parents are fucking loaded …"

Cade didn't bother to listen to any more, he knew exactly where he needed to go now. He edged along the wall, smiling while trying to find the other two vampire shapes. Apart from Colin, who he noticed was now closing in, he saw no other shapes. "One more step, Col, and I swear, I'll gut you."

Colin giggled, but he did stop moving. Cade reached the doorway and ran back into the foyer. He cried out at the sight of the other two vampires leaping over the desk and running towards him and caught the blurred shape of Colin lunging for him from out of the darkness. He dropped to the floor and rolled to the left, bringing the Katana up and swinging it around. He heard the quiet gasp of one of them as he felt the metal slice into flesh.

Cade jumped to his feet and spun around as one of them leaped towards him. He brought the sword up, then chopped it across. The vampire's head dropped onto the carpet as the razor-sharp edge sliced through the flesh like a hot knife through a block of butter. Colin yelled an incoherent curse and slipped back into the darkness, but the other one charged Cade.

The vampire then stopped dead and jumped back, chuckling when Cade blindly swung the Katana.

"You missed me, you little shit," he snarled. The vampire jerked his head over to the dark room and looked back at Cade. "Oh, you're in for it now, buddy. Can you hear that? The First Father is coming. How fast can you run?"

Cade found that he couldn't even move his feet. He looked over and saw Colin emerge from the dark room accompanied by another figure. Cade's body refuse to obey his frantic commands to get the hell out of there. He watched the huge vampire stop beside the desk and pick up the head that had rolled against the base of the potted plant.

"So, you are back, my son. I see your mate is not with you? That is a shame. I would enjoy meeting that one again." He pushed his fingers deep into the bloodied stump. "Your bothersome action has reduced my number by one." He tilted his head to one side, then wrapped his fingers through Colin's hair and pulled him back. "You are my First Son. Your irresponsible act had resulted in the death of a precious commodity."

"Please!" gasped Colin. "What else could I do? He had a sword, and believe me, that guy knows how to use it."

Cade tore his eyes away from his struggling ex-friend and concentrated all his energy into trying to move his feet. From the corner of his eyes, he saw the First Father push Colin onto the floor.

"You have one more chance" growled the huge vampire. "Give me the correct answer and I shall not throw you to what remains of my clan." He released Colin and pointed to Cade. "What do we do with him?"

The aching muscles down the inside of Cade's leg felt like they were about to snap like taught elastic, but he persevered, feeding on the pain, allowing it to flow through him, using it to fuel his anger. His efforts rewarded him when his left foot moved back a single inch. Despite the agony he was suffering and feeling as though he had just completed a marathon, Cade tried to move it further back, ignoring the beads of hot sweat dripping down the side of his head. From the corner of his eye, he noticed the two remaining vampires inch forward and swung the katana in a wide arc.

"You change him, First Father. We need to replace the vampire he beheaded, and he would be an excellent soldier."

Cade slipped his foot back a couple more inches. The triumph for completing such a Herculean task drained away when he saw the huge vampire look away from Colin and glare at him. The expression on the vampire's face darkened when he saw that Cade had managed to move his leg back. Cade redoubled his efforts as both Colin and the First Father advanced.

"It makes me almost proud to watch you attempt to flee, my son," growled the First Father. "The fact that you have moved at all proves to me that you indeed have some Deathgazer blood flowing through your veins." He suddenly bent down, picked up one of the crouching vampires, and threw the body at Cade.

Cade fell back, and his paralysis broke as the shrieking vampire crashed into his chest. By sheer will alone, he managed to keep the Katana in his hand, knowing that if the sword fell, he would have no chance of surviving. The remaining vampires rushed him, and he screamed when Colin dropped to his knees and landed on his ankles.

"Hush, you big baby," Colin said, laughing. "What happened to no pain, no gain?"

Cade yelped as the other vampire fell onto his sword arm, pinning it to the carpet. The First Father stood above him, smiling down at Cade's groaning face.

"It is only after the bite when my Clan vampires realise their good fortune. It will be the same for you, my son. I feel your hatred and deep fear, and although I find your curse unpleasant, I am willing to forgive your transgressions. It is just the way of things."

Cade refused to concede to his fate. He took his eyes off the huge vampire and swung his other arm around his trapped body, formed his fingers into a point, and jabbed them into the eye of the vampire crushing his other arm. The monster wasn't prepared for the attack, and he shrieked and fell back. Cade swallowed the urge to vomit at the sight of the wet, grey jelly covering his fingernails and swung the katana down. Colin jumped back to avoid the deadly blade.

Cade ran between the First Father's legs, heading for the safety of the sun. He screamed out when he felt one of them grab his foot. He saw only one way out of this. He threw the sword towards the door, sighing in relief when the handle punched through an unbroken pane of frosted glass and let a new stream of sunlight penetrate the gloomy foyer. Cade felt them release his leg as they all cried out in fear and retreated into the darkness. He got back to his feet and hobbled over to the door, not bothering to look back.

"Fuck you," he shouted, feeling tears of pain and stupidity flow down his cheeks. He reached the door and groaned in relief as the bright sunlight warmed the top of his head. "I'll be coming back for all of you." Cade turned his head, glaring at the red lantern eyes visible in the gloom. "You diseased abominations are living on borrowed time!"

Cade picked up the katana and hobbled over to Colin's pride and joy. He drew the tip along the side of the car, grinning savagely at the thick line of shining silver left behind from the katana's blade. He sat on the bonnet and admired his handiwork. It was a childish act, but it gave him a little satisfaction. He rolled up his trousers and grimaced at the ugly, thick, blue bruise wrapped around his ankle. No bones were broken, but he knew his walking would be severely impaired until the bruising faded. Even with his phenomenal metabolism, it would still take a while to feel halfway decent again. Those bastards had really worked him over.

He took out his phone. "You have got to be joking." A full hour had gone. It felt like only a few minutes since he'd decided to enter the sports centre. Still, at least now he had some idea where to look for Katy.

Cade rolled down his trouser leg, then slowly placed both feet back on the ground while keeping his weight on the side of the car. Between the sports centre and the edge of the park where that bastard lived was about a couple of miles worth of urban urea to traverse. Cade reckoned it was less than a mile if he used the shortcuts, but there was no chance of that with his damaged leg.

He took a deep breath and let go of the side of the car, sighing with relief when he didn't crash onto the floor. Cade took a couple of experimental steps away from Colin's pride and joy, nodding to himself. His body was already hard at work repairing the damage; the pain wasn't so bad now.

As he limped across the tarmac, heading for the road, Cade tried to ignore the dull ache wrapped around his anklebone. "Just take it easy, my son. You'll soon be as right as rain," he muttered to himself as he crossed the road. "Take the weight off your feet, drink plenty of fluids, and rest up for a couple of days." Cade silently told his overprotective imaginary nurse to fuck off

He walked past a row of shops, all still closed, and ducked into a passageway that led to the town's main high street. His imaginary nurse must have taken the subtle hint as he could no longer hear the voice whispering to him. "You do know who that voice belonged to buddy," he said. A sudden onrush of built up emotion flooded through his body. He slid down the damp wall and pressed the palms of his hands hard against his eyes. Of course, he knew who that voice belonged to.

"I murdered my own mother!" he yelled as the tears seep past his hands. Cade pressed his head against the wall, feeling the stone cut into the back of his head. He kept the pressure on, wallowing in the pain, feeling his blood dribble down his neck as the stone broke his skin.

"Fuck you all," he growled. "I don't want to do this anymore. I want to go home." He suddenly caught his breath at the sound of a distant scream. Cade snapped open his eyes and stood up, looking back where he came from. From where he stood, Cade saw two young men run past the entrance to the passageway. They were both carrying rucksacks. The mass exodus was still going on. Nobody would stop to see who had just screamed out; they all had their own agendas to fulfil. "Nobody cares about my pain either. Who's going to help me?"

Cade took a deep breath and wanted to slap himself stupid when the image of Katy floated to the front of his mind. "Oh hell," he said, wiping his eyes. What was he playing at? She had helped him. If it wasn't for her, he wouldn't have stood a chance last night. He hurried down the rest of the passageway, squinting in the bright sunlight when he emerged out on the pavement. Cade crossed over the road, heading towards another passageway that would take him to the far side of the park.

Katy needed him. As long as he kept that thought prominent, he'd be able to keep his grief from overwhelming him again. He'd mourn for his loss once all these evil bastards were dead.

Cade looked up, surprised to see a young dark-haired man gazing at him. As soon as Cade matched his gaze, the stranger turned his head and carried on walking the other way. There weren't many people left in the high street, and none were shopping. They all looked like they were in a hurry to get away. Deep down, they all must know how little time was left for them. He had no idea how they knew or why he felt nothing.

Cade walked past a discount store, moving to the side when a young woman suddenly stopped dead in his path. She glanced up, muttered an apology, and walked around him. He stopped and turned to watch her progress. Should he have found it strange that the woman hadn't said anything about his clothing? Cade reached behind him and ran his fingers down the katana's scabbard, wondering when it became perfectly acceptable for some longhaired, muscle-bound young man to run around town with a huge sword on his back.

He ducked into the next passageway, glad to be away from those people. There might have been only a dozen or so, but he still felt incredibly claustrophobic. Cade ran through the open bin bags, suddenly realising he and Katy had used this very passageway to get away from the vampires last night. He skirted past the body of a young man, not daring to stop, and picked up a little speed, suddenly feeling like several pairs of eyes were watching him as he ran past the old entrance to the market.

Cade ran out of there, darted over the empty street, leaped over the low stone wall, and scrambled up the steep grass slope. It felt good to be back in the park. His smile faded when he heard another cry from the other side of the park. He was certain he knew who it belonged to. Heart racing, he sped along the narrow path, listening as the familiar voice cried out again.

"Get off her," he yelled when he saw the two men dragging the screaming and yelling Katy across the road next to the park. They both stopped and stared when Cade reached the main gates. He watched them pull out guns. He knew he wasn't invincible, but at that moment, he just didn't care. He pulled out the Katana and charged them, roaring like an enraged animal.

They both faltered, and their postures changed again when Katy swung out with her free arm and hit one of them in the back of the neck. They took one last look at Cade before releasing the girl and running back towards the house.

Cade almost fell back into the park wall when Katy flew into his arms, hugging him and kissing his face.

"I can't believe it's you!" she cried. "You came back for me. Oh, Cade, you have no idea how happy I am to see you."

He gently pulled the girl off him and pushed her against the wall when he saw the same two figures coming out of the house with another person. Cade pressed his finger to his lips and ran back over the road, keeping low. The two men had placed a thick grey blanket over the other person's head and were leading him over to their car. Cade had no intention of allowing any of them to leave.

The men reached the car just seconds before he did. Cade jumped onto the bonnet and swung the katana in a low sweeping arc, slicing into one of the men's upper arm, then jumped down and violently pushed the screaming man back. The other man took one look at the bloodied sword and released his grip on the man under the blanket. Cade pointed the blade at the shaking man.

"Go on, I dare you. Pull that gun on me again."

The man shook his head, turned, and ran in the opposite direction.

"What the fuck is happening here?" asked a muffled voice. "Andy, Steven, where've you gone?"

Cade took one step closer to the man and gently grabbed the edge of the blanket. "You're all alone now, fuckface," Cade growled. He pulled the blanket off the man and jumped back as the flesh covering the ghoul's head blistered and burst into flame. He turned around and walked back towards Katy, trying to ignore the stench of burning meat.

Cade wiped the blood off the blade and pushed the katana back into the scabbard. The injured man looked down at the small fire and backed away. Once he had reached the back of the car, he turned and ran down the street, still holding his arm.

Cade looked into Katy's horrified eyes. "Now we know what sunlight does to them. I reckon you were right about UV lights doing the same to them. I think we had better go shopping." Cade glanced at his phone. "We only have a few hours left, sweetheart. Do you feel up to it?"

Katy burst into tears, ran across the road, and wrapped her arms around his body. "Oh god, Cade. Please, let's just forget about all of this. I want you to take me away from this nightmare. I can't stand it any longer!"

Chapter Fifteen

Jalim dropped to the floor, held his breath, and scurried across the beige tiles, desperate to get away. He slid under a desk and flattened himself against the far wall. After making sure they hadn't observed his movements, Jalim pushed his thin body through a hole in the wall beside a metal filing cabinet. He slowly manoeuvred his body in the confined space so he could stand up and then finally breathed out.

Warm, musty air filled his lungs as he took in a much needed breath. He didn't care about the faint smell of old damp wood. The rot was infinitely more desirable than the overpowering sickly sweet stench rolling off that woman. It had taken Jalim a few moments to realise that she had optioned to hose down her ample body in that foul chemical. At first, he honestly believed the humans had spotted him and were emitting some sort of defence mechanism.

He decided to keep that piece of knowledge to himself when Dylar returned. He felt enough of a fool already without his companion believing he had the brains of a senile horse.

He watched her, and even from in here, Jalim could sense the extreme stress coming from the other human. When he originally found this hole, he already knew there were two humans close by. He initially assumed they would be on the opposite side of the wall and made provisions to dispose of them as soon as he broke through the thin plaster. He realised his miscalculation when he pushed through the hole and saw the large window on the wall opposite to where he had come through. He saw a large female and a teenage boy engaged in an intense discussion and subtly adjusted his original plans. It looked as though he would be able to set out his intentions after all.

Jalim didn't think the woman's noxious smell was the main reason for the boy's obvious distress, although he guessed that her smelling as though she had bathed in the noxious chemicals did have a part to play in his discomfort. It appeared to Jalim that this woman was the boy's leader.

The woman could be his mother for all he cared, and Jalim cared not one bit. He had no interest in trying to unravel the mysteries of the humans' intricate social structures. All he needed right now was for the aching pain at the front of his head to clear. Jalim turned around, leaned against the lattice of thin wooden strips and damp plaster, and attempted to tune out their irritating bleating.

He could not afford to allow this unexpected bounty to slip through his fingers because he could not operate properly. When the time came to move, Jalim would just have to hold his nose. He grinned at the image of him forging into battle whilst holding his nose.

Jalim then saw a faint spray of plaster dust drift down in front of his eyes. He turned his head to watch his large companion squeeze his body through the narrow crevice between the old brick wall and the newer partition.

Dylar cocked his head and wrinkled his nose in disgust. He inched his way closer. "Do I smell roses, Jalim?" he whispered. Dylar pushed his hand under his nose. "That is revolting. What is this place? Are the humans brewing vats of scented oil?"

Jalim ignored his question. The young vampire would discover the source presently. "Report. How many humans are left within these below ground rooms?"

Dylar took his eyes away from the hole in the wall and grinned at Jalim. "I sensed two females and one male. I do not know why they are in here. Their volatile emotions confused me. They were all terrified but did not know why they felt so disturbed." He pulled his leather tunic up to cover his nose. "Perhaps they too are disgusted by that vile smell."

Jalim pulled him away from the hole. "Learn to read the signs, my friend. The smell currently stinging our nostrils emanates from a female who is in a room beyond that hole."

"It is a scented oil then? I do not understand why it is so strong. Before I was changed, a few of the young pretty girls adorned their firm bodies with extracts made from crushed flower petals."

"The woman is neither firm nor very pretty," Jalim replied, grinning. "Do not concern yourself with this matter, Dylar. Tell me, did you find the exits?"

Dylar nodded. "Yes, I discovered two doors that, judging from the breeze, led up to the surface. I ..." Dylar sighed. "One of the humans saw me. I had to kill him to stop him from giving away our presence."

Jalim shrugged. "It was a risk, and one I expected. Do not let it concern you."

Dylar sighed again. "I fear it does though, Jalim. It could be the reason why they are acting so scared. You gave instructions not to upset their minds, that the chemicals released would taint your experiment." He stopped. "Jalim, will you tell me what you have planned?" He licked his lips. "You are not going to attempt to change them again, are you?"

"Calm your fears, my friend. That is not my intention. Also, your action with the human who saw you is not why they act like a flock of sheep sensing a pack of wolves close by."

"Then why, Jalim?"

He smiled. "I have just told you, Dylar. It has been a long time since our kind has stalked these lands. Time has a tendency to scrape away the past, burying it beneath layers of half-forgotten memories. But, the human is a versatile animal, Dylar, built with a very good sense of self preservation. Unlike the sheep, their mind will preserve a racial instinct if that instinct is essential for the survival of their species."

"They remember us?" asked Dylar. "How is that even possible?"

"You, like myself, were once human. Look at how the vampire essence has shaped us. No other animal is adaptable enough to survive a transfusion with the stuff that makes us what we are, Dylar. You will never see vampire wolves or, for that matter, vampire sheep."

Dylar chuckled to himself." I have never even considered such thoughts of vampire animals, Jalim. You truly are blessed with a diverse imagination."

Jalim blinked, trying to work out whether the young vampire had just insulted him. Judging from the admiration spread across Dylar's thin face, Jalim decided to take his words as a compliment. "It is just a matter of being aware of your surroundings and being observant, Dylar. The facts are there for all to see, it is just a case of knowing how to read them." He reached out, wrapped his fingers around the vampire's arm and gently pulled him down to the hole in the wall. "Observation is such a powerful gift. The two humans do not appear to be in the grip of terror. They are not wandering about, getting ready to flee. Why is that?"

Dylar shrugged. "Judging from the way they argue, I guess their hate takes precedence?"

"Exactly! The urge to escape is a thought that does not originate from their waking mind. If those two humans had not occupied their mental energy with the strong desire to kill each other, they would be acting like the ones you witnessed earlier. You see, it is our re-emergence that has caused the humans to act like hunted deer."

Dylar frowned." I have to apologise for my next words, my new First Father. That does not make sense to me. Before I was changed, I lived close to the one of the Deathgazers' outer fortifications. Our settlement prospered under the Deathgazers. We were settled and happy. The Clan war changed all that, but our settlement never acted like frightened animals."

"You and your immediate family were fortunate to be born into one of the rare times when peace dominated the lands." Jalim turned back and gazed through the hole, noting that, finally, the humans were no longer at each other's throats. They now sat at opposite sides of the room with their backs turned to each other. Although they both were now quiet, the waves of hate coming from them were almost tangible. Jalim smiled to himself. If the female could provoke such a violent reaction as a human, just what extreme effect would the woman achieve once Jalim had finished playing with her? "Dylar, you have been told I was a Deathgazer before I became part of the Swarmer Clan."

Dylar nodded. "Yes, you were part of the group that broke away with our ex-First Father. My First Son never grew tired of regaling the newly changed with your tales of struggle and eventual dominance over the Deathgazers."

This time, there was no mistaking the awe in Dylar's words. Jalim had heard a few of the First Sons impressing the newly changed with their exaggerated stories. It did feel a little strange to find himself becoming part of a spoken legend. Jalim grinned, eager to see how his companion would react to his next few words. "Before I was a Deathgazer, I was the First Son in the Bonegrinder Clan, and before that, I helped to form the BloodSpray Clan."

"Just how old are you?"

"That is irrelevant," replied Jalim, waving the question away. "You are correct that under the Deathgazers, the humans did enjoy a few hundred years of peace. They were given time to play and to breed. Before that though, there were many clans, all fighting each other and plundering the human populations for meat and for more recruits. It was fortunate, at least for the humans, that the Deathgazers came out triumphant."

"And so the cycle begins again then, Jalim?"

He nodded, and his thoughts turned to the immediate future. The two clans would now be following their own agendas. Jalim knew Desmonus better than he knew himself. The First Father had already seen the changes the humans had wrought across the land and altered his plans accordingly, opting to wait. He was unsure how Amulius would react though. The Deathgazer First Father would make it a priority to recruit, that much was obvious. Jalim saw that plan fraught with many complications. These modern humans would be difficult to control, especially such a large amount at one time. To all the vampires just woken, the ancient past seemed just days ago. It would take them all time to adapt to this new world. Jalim applauded the Swarmer First Father for not acting like a ravenous fox in a hencoop; even so, the First Father would come up against the same problem when he did spread his wings.

"This cycle, Dylar, will end in wars that would make the Swarmer-Deathgazer conflict look like a fight between two drunken fishwives. That is my prediction, although, I am unsure of when this will happen. It could take weeks, or it could take years."

The young vampire gazed at him with a mixture of horror and glee. "I am confused, Jalim."

"Do you not believe that my words ring true?"

Dylar shook his head. "I do not doubt that. My confusion stems from your age. It is common knowledge that any vampire living beyond a certain age is able to change humans without creating foul ghouls. You must be the oldest vampire in the land. Why does this talent elude you?"

It took Jalim a great deal of restraint not to burst out laughing. "Oh, my young friend, and you tell me that you have never considered thought beyond the straight path? First, allow me to ask you one question. If our ex-First Father believed that I did have the gift, would he have allowed me to leave?"

Dylar shook his head. "No, of course not. Desmonus would have killed you and fed your parts to the rest of the clan." He shuddered. "I would have shared your fate as well. I do not think he would have allowed me to leave alone."

"He believed my power to create his undead war machines stemmed from the rare spices and powders I had collected over the centuries, aided by the hundreds of scrolls stored within the vaults under the Swarmer settlement, all lost when we had to sleep."

"That is what I believed as well."

"My power, the main source, comes from me, Dylar. The scrolls and the powders were there as a diversion. You are the only one in over ten thousand years who knows of my secret." He nodded to himself, then pushed his body through the hole in the wall and helped Dylar through. "Listen to these next words, my friend," he whispered. "The Dragonshine Clan will rule this land. It is our destiny. Unlike the other Clans, our soldiers will have just one desire, and that is to serve the Clan. Now, are you ready?"

Dylar grinned. "I am ready and eager, My First Father."

Jalim ran to the door that separated the two rooms and, suppressing the urge to rush through, opted to politely knock twice. "We need to go!" he shouted, injecting apprehension into the tone to make himself sound convincing. "The others have left. We need to leave!"

He heard the frantic scraping of a chair and stared at Dylar, pointing to the other door. "The boy will leave first. No bites, just hold him," he hissed. Jalim stood back when the door flew open. As he predicted, the teenage boy ran out and straight into the waiting arms of the young vampire.

"What, who are you people?" he cried.

Jalim peered through the window, satisfied that the woman had not moved, then walked up to the struggling human. He exhaled in pleasure at the sight of the human voiding himself. It was good to feel heart-stopping terror from a human once more. This one, unlike the others he had encountered tonight, had the full use of all his senses and had already noticed Jalim's extended canines. "I think you have just answered your own question there, my pretty little boy." He wrapped his long arms around the boy's wrist and pulled him close, then dragged him over to the door, pulled it open, and threw him back inside.

"Should you not lock it?" Dylar asked.

"Do you think they will come out?" He watched the woman's hard face melt at the sight of the horror-struck boy pointing at the window with a shaking arm. Jalim felt like waving. "Dylar, do you think you are able to bring three of the other humans to this location without harming them?"

His companion nodded. "If they have not escaped, then the task will be simple. What about the remaining human, do we leave him be?"

"I have accounted for the remaining human, my friend. Now go. I have to prepare, and although I have trusted you more than I have trusted any other vampire, there are some procedures that must remain known only to me."

Dylar nodded, turned, and rushed through the door, leaving Jalim alone with the two snivelling humans. He knew they were both watching his every movement from the room and stayed motionless, listening to them moving heavy objects around. He didn't need to turn to know they were trying to block the entrance, trying to keep him from entering. He counted very slowly to ten, then walked over to the outer door and opened it, trying to see if he could hear his companion. He had been largely correct about the main source of his power, but he had still needed the powders and the scrolls to fine-tune his experiments. It had been many generations since he had performed this procedure without his aids.

Jalim smiled as the recollection brought back an ancient memory from when he was still a young vampire, not long turned. Even then, Jalim knew he was not like the rest of his clan.

The huge crevice in the ice sheet stretched for miles in both directions. Jalim watched the First Father of the Skullcracker Clan glare at the two enemy Clans on the other side of the crevice. The two rival clans returned the huge vampire's glower, each expression from the twenty-one vampires twisted into the look of pure poison. Even though Jalim was at the back of the group, he still could not stop his body from shivering.

If his Skullcracker Clan had not discovered these weapons forged from a time when the land was green, then each one of his companions would now be on their travois, ready to be taken to their camps for skinning and eating. Jalim ran his fingers down the fine metal of his own weapon, caressing the fine impressions made in this strange material. Although the temperature was now cold enough to freeze a human's blood, Jalim still had no problem operating this magnificent device.

He noticed the two cooperating clans were ready to leave and could not help but breathe a sigh of relief. Even though they had managed to decimate their clan and claim the bodies of most of the fallen, Jalim was still glad to see them leave. He hoped his First Father would retreat from this territory and lead what remained of their clan to somewhere safer, to a land rival clans had not claimed.

From where he stood, Jalim could see his human mother and father, their frozen naked bodies lying below the corpses of three Skullcrackers. He glanced over at his First Father, wondering what was going through his mind. Did he believe now that it had been a mistake to venture into the unknown land? Thanks to his decision, their clan had lost every one of their human tribe. Their chances of surviving were now very slim. How many humans would agree to live under the protection of a clan that could not offer it? His sombre thoughts stayed locked in his head. Jalim was not long turned. To openly display such disagreement would not bode well.

"We may as well have joined the corpses. What chance do we have now?"

Jalim could not believe those words had come from their First Son. He looked around the surviving Clan members, shocked at the others nodding their heads in agreement.

"Do your inner thoughts agree with your neutral expression, Jalim?"

Jalim jerked his head towards the First Father, feeling his mouth go dry'. He wiped the frost from his lips and looked at the others. They all now stared at him, each vampire keeping their thoughts locked shut. Even the First Son stood like the corpse of a long tusk frozen in the tundra.

"You are my First Father," he muttered. "I am merely a lowly vampire. It is not my place to question your decisions."

The huge vampire pulled down his fur-lined hood and walked between the remaining clan members until he reached Jalim. It took considerable self-control not to cringe when the First Father placed his bear-like hand on Jalim's shoulder.

"It is possible my actions have destroyed our clan, Jalim. We number just six, and we only have left what we carry. Our food has gone, and we cannot even use our client tribe."

Jalim thought very carefully before opening his mouth. He had no idea why the First Father was talking to him like an equal. It felt wrong. "The Sabre-Tooth Clan was ready to move against us. We could not withstand another raid. Their client tribe had already taken our supplies for the dry season. The only reason they did not attempt to wipe us out was because we had these." He instinctively counted the bolts, sighing when he found he only had three left in the chamber. Once they were gone, the weapon would be good only as a club. "We had to leave the valley."

The First Father stroked his chin. "So, you believe the Clan's First Son is wrong to disagree?"

Jalim inwardly moaned. Right now, he wished their enemies had killed him. It would be better to have them cut off his skin for tanning than to be in this position. What was he to do? "You made the only decision available, my First Father. Your desire was the survival of the Clan. We are few in number now, but it is still preferable to the Sabre-Tooth clan flavouring their meals with our bones."

The First Father laughed.

Jalim smiled, glad he had used the correct words. The smile fell from his face when the First Father turned and grabbed his First Son by the neck and lifted him up.

"Badan, you have failed me for the last time."

The First Father squeezed his huge fingers tight. Jalim cringed at the sound of the First Son's neck bones crushing together. He watched in fascination as the First Father dragged Badan's now limp body to the crevice and dropped it down.

"You are now my First Son, Jalim," he said, turning his head. "What is your first decision?"

Jalim walked through the clan vampires, watching them take a step back as he passed them. He peered down the crevice, surprised that he could still see Badan's corpse; the crevice was not so deep after all. "My first decision would be to retrieve that body, my First Father. We have no food, and his corpse will help to sustain our weakened bodies until we find more supplies." He looked across the desolate white landscape, seeing nothing but ice and snow. Their situation was desperate. Even with the unexpected food bounty, it would take a miracle to stop the clan from going extinct.

"The role suits you, my new First Son." He looked over at the remaining vampires. "Do you agree to follow Jalim's requests as long as they do not clash with mine?" They all nodded. "That is good. Now, Jalim, would you be kind enough to retrieve that body? I am going to help the others construct a shelter. The sun will soon rise, and I do not want to burn."

Jalim fell to his knees and slowly lowered his body down until his fingers hung from a jagged, rocky outcropping. He listened to the First Father directing the others in the task of digging out somewhere to sleep while the sun laid claim to the land. Jalim released his hands and dropped the last few feet.

He wandered over to the body and lifted the torso up, watching the head flop about. It was a huge shame to do this. This vampire had taught Jalim almost everything there was to know about their kind, perhaps a little too well. It was the First Son's teachings that had helped him to make the decision regarding the disposal of the body. Jalim moved the body to the edge of the crevice and jerked to a halt when he saw something move under the vampire's thigh.

He stared in astonishment as a pure white furred mammal ran back into a hole in the rock. His astonishment deepened when he saw that the animal had taken a large bite out of the dead vampire's cold flesh. In all the time he had lived, Jalim had never heard of any creature that could eat the flesh of a changed human. Their meat was supposed to be toxic to every living animal. Jalim got down on his hands and knees and looked down the hole. The animal was right there, staring back up at him.

"Just what are you then, my little friend?" He had no idea what it was, nor did he really care. He knew warm blood ran through its veins and the meat was his for the taking. Jalim plunged his hand down the hole, gritting his teeth in surprise when the strange animal bit him. He felt the animal's teeth scrape across his finger bone.

Whatever it was, Jalim knew the beast had no fear of him, and if he allowed it, the animal could snip off his finger. He tightened his hand, grinning at the sound of the creature's tiny yelps. Finally, it went limp in his hand, and Jalim pulled his fingers free of the hole, bringing his prize close to his face.

"You are an enigma." He opened his jaw wide, pushed the animal in, and snapped his jaw shut, biting the animal in half. He crunched through muscle, sinew, bone, and fur, moaning in ecstasy as the bloodied mush slid down his dry throat. This was the only food that had passed his lips since draining the last few drops of blood from the veins of their last human eight sun-ups ago. Jalim rammed the rest of the animal into his mouth, eager to finish his unexpected meal before the others came back to see why he was taking so long.

Jalim chuckled to himself, opened his eyes, and stared into the empty corridor. It had been such a long time since he had given any thought to his early days. Even now, he had no idea of what kind of animal he had foolishly consumed. He knew he had never seen another one like it in all the millenniums of existence after the time of the great freeze. Eating that tiny beast had to be the reason why he was so different from every other vampire he had known. Just like that long forgotten animal, Jalim was a unique individual.

He slowly turned around. It did not surprise him to find his two humans had pushed a piece of furniture against the window. He could sense both of them, flat against the wall, staring at the barricaded door, waiting for him the push his way through. Like that strange animal that bit into his fingers, these two animals had armed themselves with whatever was available.

Jalim heard slow but heavy footsteps and walked over to the door that led into the other room. All the pieces were now in place. It was time to go to work. He so enjoyed the next bit. The fact that his apprentice would be watching with wide-open, astonished eyes, only served to increase his excitement.

Dylar had brought the three humans, as Jalim had asked. All three were dazed. He watched the young vampire drop them in a heap beside Jalim's feet. Blood dripped from the back of the blond male's head. The matted hair reminded him of a bird's nest.

"He resisted. I might have hit him too hard, Jalim. He is still breathing, although I am not sure of the damage I caused."

"It does not matter," Jalim replied. In truth, he had expected a small degree of damage to the humans. Whether they lived or died would not impede the procedure. It was just more enjoyable to watch if they were living and aware of their predicament. Jalim chuckled, "Dylar, you are about to witness a feat no other vampire has ever experienced. Pick up the humans and follow me."

Jalim charged the door, and the thin wood splintered when he crashed into it. The two humans' sudden screaming blasted his ears, and the sound of their terror made him want to cry out in joy. He pushed away the heavy metal cabinet they had slid against the door and stormed into the room, heading for the woman. He knew Dylar's presence would stop the teenage boy from trying to escape.

The woman's incoherent pleas made him grin even more. He felt the change rushing through his system. His cavernous mouth opened wide, and he cried out as a double row of canine teeth burst through his gums, the bloodied flesh peeling back like rolled down sock.

He lunged forward and sank those hidden teeth into her thick neck. The woman's shrieks cut short when he punched his fist into her stomach. Jalim stayed still, stroking the woman's thick brown hair, waiting for the venom to take effect. Once he heard the familiar gasp, he pulled his teeth from her flesh and gently laid her on the floor.

Jalim hurriedly back away, pushing Dylar out of the room. He looked at the teenage boy and winked. "She'll need you to care for her now," he said, laughing. He pulled the bookcase away from the window— He wanted to make sure Dylar saw all of this—then jumped over the dumped bodies and pulled the metal cabinet back, hoping the woman would not attempt to move it out of the way and the offered meat would satisfy her first urge to feed.

"I don't understand any of this," Dylar said.

"Be quiet!" Jalim snapped. He dragged the vampire over to the window and smiled at the sight of the other two females stirring. By the looks of it, the male would not be waking. It was a shame but not too much of a disappointment. The teenage boy was trying to wake the big woman. His earlier thought of hate had completely vanished. Jalim admired how the human could alter his perception of another human in such a short space of time.

Dylar took an involuntary step back, and Jalim's arm snapped out and pulled the young vampire forward again. Jalim shivered himself, even out here, where he knew he would be safe. The malevolence coming from his first creation scared the life out of him. The teenage boy suddenly jumped away, his eyes like saucers as the woman reared up, growling like an enraged wolf. She turned her head, her growl turning to an ear-piercing screech at the sight of the flesh around her arms expanding like pink balloons.

The three humans were now by the cabinet, desperately trying to pull it to the side, as if they had forgotten the two vampires were still out there. The woman's transformation was proceeding faster than any of his other subjects. Jalim hoped it was because of the woman's size and the fact that she had fed well through her life. Her flesh was now beginning to harden. Until her first shedding, she would stay that shape and size. He could not stop himself from grinning. This Flesh Dragon was already beautiful, the embryonic creature already an impressive size. He watched her dagger-like teeth push through her elongated jaw. From where he stood, Jalim could not see the screaming humans; they were still trying to drag the cabinet away from the doorway.

"Dylar, witness this, my friend." He swapped places and held onto the cabinet, watching the awe appear in his companion's face. He heard all three humans suddenly shriek out, the pressure on the cabinet ceased, and then the only audible noises were the wet sounds of tearing flesh.

"I have never seen anything so wonderful in my life, Jalim."

He joined Dylar at the window, watching his creation gorge on the offered meat. She really was a magnificent creature. The black scales now covering her naked body glistened under the artificial light. There was enough meat in there to help her insides expand into the large body. Once she had gorged, she should sleep for a few days to allow her transformation to finish. It would give Jalim enough time to start his own preparations.

"What do we do about the remaining human, Jalim?"

His Flesh Dragon dragged one of the females over to the corner. She bit into the back of the woman's neck before returning to the bloodied pool of gore on the middle of the room.

"Look at that, Dylar. Did you see what she has just done? That woman still lives. Our Flesh Dragon has disabled her to ensure she cannot escape. Look, now she eats the dead flesh, knowing her last meal will scream when she eats her."

He slapped his hands on Dylar's shoulders. "My friend, the other clans can do whatever they desire and will do. They will scheme and plot, make allegiances with other clans, and even humans. While the clans fight amongst themselves, we shall bide our time and create more of these beautiful creatures. When the time is ripe, my friend, we shall wipe this land free of every other clan." He took a deep breath. "The Dragonshine Clan will reign supreme!"

Jalim released Dylar and hurried over to the door. "While she feeds, my friend, I suggest that we do the same?" He opened the door and allowed Dylar through, then took one last look at the window and let out a single contented sigh.

Chapter Sixteen

Darlene ran over to the grill and pushed her fingers through the gaps. She struggled to hold back tears of frustration when she found he really had gone. Paul promised her that he'd stay with her, that he wouldn't let anything to happen. Darlene pulled her fingers out and brushed the tips down her dress.

"Come on, girl," she muttered under her breath. "You're acting like a pop star obsessed teen. He's young enough to be your son, for crying out loud." She knew all this, hell she'd said it to herself often enough. Even so, it still didn't stop her from feeling like he'd just ripped out most of her heart when he did finally leave her. He had just hissed that the others were making their way back and disappeared.

Darlene leaned against the wall, covering the grill with her legs. Her Paul hadn't been wrong about them coming back. The bastards weren't stopping and checking anywhere else, they knew where she was hiding. There was little point in wondering how the heck he had been able to sense their presence way before she had. She had learned from her very short time being in this state that they all had one talent.

They would be here any moment! She gasped as the cacophony of violent imagery escaping from the minds of the approaching vampires flooded her already harassed mind. It took a considerable amount of endurance to ignore their crass and lustful ideas of what they intended to do to her.

"Fuck you all," she snarled.

Darlene forced every scrap of air from her lungs, thought of Paul stroking the back of her legs through the grill, then took a deep breath and smiled.

She wanted those bastards to see her smile as soon as they stormed through that door. Their excitement was reaching fever pitch and so were their fantasies. Their ludicrous ideas of what they thought they were going to do to her body became more comic strip the closer they got to the door.

Darlene suppressed their escaping thoughts and focussed on the words Paul had left her to recite. She saw the handle turn and felt like she was watching the action in slow motion. This felt so stupid. The bastards were actually waiting for her to gasp or yelp at the fact that the big hard vampires had been clever enough to work out where she was hiding.

The vampires had dampened their disgusting thoughts now. She watched the door open just a crack and felt a huge wave of confusion tinged with disappointment flow from them. She paused; there was one vampire with the others, standing at the back. The shadowy mind had not joined in their ridiculous fantasies.

Darlene struggled to keep the smile fixed when she heard Amulius tell them to stand aside. The door swung inwards, and the First Father took one step over the threshold, then stopped, placing his hands on his hips. What remained of his new clan crowded behind him; the glee in their eyes made her want to hurl. It sickened her to see the same expression displayed on each vampire. Both her kids used to look like that every time they had grassed on each other.

"What lies have vomited from their foul mouths, my husband?" she said, sweetly. It felt so odd to emulate his speech pattern, but it did help to calm the turbulent emotions threatening to break through her thin shell.

"I asked you to perform one simple task." He growled.

Her smile faltered. She saw his naked rage building up and suddenly wished she'd ignored Paul's gentle request and just got the fuck out of here. The other vampires slowly backed away, their own expressions changing to alarm and anxiety. His bright red eyes blazed with the power of the sun. Darlene stood transfixed like a rabbit caught in a hunter's lamp. She felt like the vampire was stripping away her outer most thoughts, layer-by-layer, eager to pull out the reason for her disobedience.

Darlene slammed her hands against her ears and shut her eyes. "Get out of my fucking mind!" she screamed. She heard something heavy hit the floor and snapped open her eyes to see Amulius slowly sitting up. Had she just done that? Darlene glared at the other vampires; they got the message and stayed motionless. She ran to Amulius and helped him back onto his feet. It took a moment for his shaken mind to focus.

"Listen to me, my husband," she said. "Ignore my spat with the others, just for a moment. The others know where we are hiding." She looked over at the just-turned vampires, noticing

Elsie was missing and one of the new recruits was absent. "Wait, where's the other one?"

"Oh, he lost his head," replied Colin, chuckling.

The vampire's laughter abruptly stopped when the First Father spun his head to face him. Darlene was amused to see what little blood left in Colin's face drain away and his arrogance quickly follow suit. It worried her how quickly Amulius had recovered.

"You are all to leave us. Bring Elsie to me. You must do this task now." The vampire scowled at Colin when he didn't move. "Do not make me repeat my words!" he thundered.

The vampires jumped, turned as one, and ran down the corridor. Darlene could feel their profound disappointment that the First Father hadn't given permission to allow them to defile her.

As soon as the others were out of sight, the First Father slumped against the wall and breathed deeply. Darlene couldn't believe the change: he'd gone from a huge monster to looking like a tired old man in a matter of seconds.

"They openly defy me, Darlene," he said slowly, twisting his head to face her. "I am beginning to doubt my judgment, my queen. They told me of their treatment, and I allow them to live." He hung his head. "I am no longer fit to be a First Father."

Darlene's brain went into meltdown at the sight of this creature whom she thought she loved just a few hours ago dissolve into a puddle of pity. She dropped to her knees and ran her fingers through his thick hair, then gently lifted his head and gazed into his eyes. It was difficult to tell, but she was sure his fire had dimmed.

"Give them time to adjust, Amulius. You've thrown these guys into a world unknown to them. Think back to the last time you recruited. Compare them to the ones you bit tonight. The guys who work out in the gym honestly believed they are better than the average Joe. I'm serious here, they are gym freaks. They don't respond well to orders." She felt like such an idiot; it should have been obvious they would act in this way. Amulius had injected all of them with the equivalent of a dinosaur dose of steroids and teenage hormones. No wonder they were climbing the walls and wanting to fuck anything with a skirt.

"Listen to yourself, Darlene." He covered her hand with his and squeezed it gently. "You still defend them, even after their disrespectful behaviour."

Darlene hadn't realised she had done it until he mentioned it. "I'm just too forgiving." It didn't come as much of a shock to her that she'd already forgiven Amulius as well. Even so, now Darlene didn't know how to handle this situation. What was she going to do with Paul?

"You all live like corralled horses. It is no wonder that you do not behave as you should. My enemy has, for once, not swarmed and attempted to change every human in his sight."

Darlene suddenly remembered why Paul had begged her to stay and opened her mouth. She had to tell him.

The First Father clamped his hand over her lips. "Hush, I know what your words will be. I know of this because I sense others in this settlement who dream the deep dream. If Desmonus had swarmed, there would be hundreds more hiding under this settlement, waiting for the sun to finish her slow journey across the sky."

He struggled to his feet. "No, it will take me too long to adjust to this world, my darling wife. I also suspect Desmonus will soon discover, to his horror, that the ones he changes will not behave as he desires."

Darlene looked back into the storage room, wondering if Paul was still there. "What are you trying to say?"

He placed his hands on his shoulders. "The Swarmers will leave this settlement. That, I am sure of."

She felt his powerful fingers dig into her shoulders. He spun her around, slid his hands down her side, and rested them on the top of her firm thighs. "Darlene, I think perhaps we should follow the Swarmers plan and leave this settlement too. We can travel to a land far away from here."

Paul's words flooded back, so did the image of his tender eyes and soft kiss while trying to calm her down and plead with her to follow this plan through. "There are four Swarmers just minutes from the sport centre, holed up in the market." She looked at his confused face and realized he didn't have a clue what she was talking about. "Four of our enemies are hiding in another building in this settlement, Amulius. There is a tunnel that will take us straight to them." He remained still, staring at her, not saying a word. "Aren't you even listening to me?" she snarled. "We could end this right now."

He shook his head. "We would be sending our untrained, ill-disciplined rabble to their deaths. The Swarmers are seasoned warriors; just one of them would devastate them. No, I admire your enthusiasm, but it is too risky."

Darlene grabbed his crotch. "Have you lost your balls? I overheard them; they will strike as soon as it gets light."

"They will attack us?"

She finally saw a flash of life in his dull eyes. "They don't have a clue that we're here. They don't care about us anyway; we are just small fry to them. There's over a thousand strangers camping out in the fields around our town, it's them who they're going to go for. Their First Father will have his own army by this time tomorrow." She took his hands. "You know that then, he'll go after us. He'll have no choice, we're his enemy."

"We spent almost two hundred years locked in conflict, my lovely wife. We fought over diminishing supplies, over food and lands. Our war spiralled out of control. It almost destroyed us, it almost made you extinct. In the end, the few scattered tribes of humans took to hiding in places unknown to us, and we were starving to death." He stroked the side of her face. "He will not go after us. We are, as you said, small fry now."

"I can't believe you've just said that, Amulius. You must know, deep down, that they'll hunt us all down. We both know how they operate. In a month's time, there'll be thousands of Swarmer vampires, every one of them hunting us down! You might want to commit suicide, but I don't!"

They both turned as the other vampires walked towards them. Darlene glared at her daughter. She clamped her mouth and clenched her fists, trying hard to control the whirlpool of extreme emotions flooding her body. None of the others had noticed the pain she was going through. Amulius's new clan was too busy staring in utter lust at her beautiful daughter. Darlene watched her glide through the slavering vampires. She approached her mother and stopped in front of her.

"It's so good to see you," she said. The girl looked at the First Father. "I heard your argument in the corridor, and yes, you're right. Those muscle-bound, brain-dead dipshits wouldn't last five minutes with those Swarmers."

It took Darlene considerable restraint not to sink her teeth into the little bitch's pretty neck. How dare she stand there, looking as sweet as a new-born baby, pretending everything was hunky dory? She blanked her and focused on her main problem, intending to deal with her at a later date.

Paul had told Darlene she needed to ensure the clan stayed together, and that meant she had to stay with them. He'd said if the Deathgazers didn't stop the Swarmers, then the vampire plague would spread like wildfire. She had looked into his horrified face, not understanding his dread at the prospect of the vampires running amok throughout the land. Even after she gently reminded him that they were now vampires too, his alarm still remained.

She watched the First Father wander over to his new clan, conversing in low tones. He looked like a Shepherd trying to calm a flock of sheep. Darlene now understood Paul's fear. The vampires were quite content with their lot. She now saw the First Father's reasoning. There were so many humans now, the Swarmers would forget his clan; the impossible job of keeping the Swarmer's own clan in order would take up their First Father's time.

"Perhaps, there is a solution to this quandary?" he asked, gazing at Darlene. "While I am certain the Swarmers would butcher my new clan with ease, they would not stand a chance against my two beautiful vampire women."

Elsie placed her hands on Darlene's shoulders, leaned forward and kissed her on the cheek. **Mum, lose the stress. I didn't let the randy old bastard anywhere near me. Nod and tell him that's a wonderful idea, mum. If not, he'll kill us right now!**

She gazed at the First Father, digesting her daughter's thoughts. Did she believe her? Before Amulius had his wicked way with her, she'd have discounted her words as pure jealousy, just her daughter trying to drive a wedge between them; she had always been the more devious of her kids. Darlene watched the First Father's expression; he was still waiting for her to reply. The one thing she did notice was the *old man* had gone away. She sighed again, of course he had, that persona vanished as soon as he got his fingers inside her panties.

"Only if you're sure, Amulius," she replied. "Are you not coming with us?"

He shook his head. "Go wait over there," he said to the male vampires. Amulius waited until they were out of sight before he turned his head. "Your strength, my beautiful wife, almost surpassed mine. Elsie has already proven herself in battle. You will triumph, of that, I am sure."

Elsie dragged her mother into the storage room. Darlene watched the First Father turn and make his way to the others. "Just what the fuck is going on, Elsie?" she hissed. Darlene watched her pull off the cover. "Wait, how did you know about that?"

"The same way I knew that your not so secret boyfriend, Paul, had told you what to say," she replied. "Now come on, we need to get out of here before he realizes he's been had."

Elsie dropped to her knees and pushed her head into the gap, followed by the rest of her body. Darlene hurried after her daughter, completely confused by the turn of events. As she pushed her way through into the damp, dark brick tunnel behind the wall, she couldn't shake the feeling that she was being manipulated, or at least pushed around like a pawn in a giant game of chess.

Her daughter helped her to her feet, then bent down and replaced the grate.

"I have no idea why I did that. It's not like they don't know where we went. Come on, mum, we had better put some distance between us and them." Elsie chuckled. "It really is good to see you again, mum."

Darlene shrugged off her daughter's hand. "I'm not going anywhere until you tell me what is going on." She saw her daughter's happy smile fall off her face.

"Mum, if we hadn't moved right there and then, he would have ripped into you and torn your body into tiny pieces while his dogs slaughtered me. He only allowed us to leave because he actually believed your bullshit story. As far as he's concerned, he's better off without us."

Darlene shook her head, unwilling to believe that.

"Sorry mum, but it's true. I know you're strong, and I know you have a powerful mind." The girl paused and ran her tongue over her lips. "I got mine from you, mum. I was also boosted up.

Damien changed, then he bit me as well." She laughed shakily. "If he knew just how powerful I was, he would have never let me leave. He'd have killed me on the spot. Well, at least he would have tried."

She watched her daughter leap across the narrow channel that ran through the middle of the tunnels. A small rat scuttled between Elsie's legs, scampered up the grime encrusted wall, and disappeared into a hole a few feet above their heads. They both saw the animal, and Elsie, like her, didn't even blink. They used to be terrified of rats and mice. Had her daughter's ability to manipulate people around her improved since her change? Darlene tried to see into Elsie's mind but just received static for her troubles.

"Mum, that's very rude," said Elsie, turning around. "I wouldn't look inside you unless you gave me permission." She put her arms around Darlene's waist. "He knows that he can't control us, mum. Do you remember Mr. Anderson's dog?"

She nodded. "Of course I do. That miserable old thing wouldn't let anybody in the garden. It really hated anybody in a uniform. Oh, and kids, the dog couldn't stand kids."

"Damien used to deliver the old man's newspaper there. He used to have to just launch it over the fence 'cos the dog just went batshit as soon as Damien got close to the property. Well, one morning he did just that, and for once, the dog didn't come out and try to kill him through the wooden slats. It turned out that the dog had decided he'd had enough of not being able to kill any passing pedestrian and decided to attack his owner instead. It didn't kill the old man, but he was in hospital for a few months after the attack. That old dog is just like the First Father, mum. I have seen inside his head. All that crap about wanting to take you away from all of this was just fantasy. He certainly isn't prepared to just sit on the fence and watch the Swarmers take over the planet."

"So, what do we do now?" Darlene asked. When she looked at her daughter, she saw the image of a queen sliding along a giant chessboard. Darlene was now just a pawn in this bizarre game, and she no longer felt in control of anything anymore.

"Well, I think it's safe to assume that we're no longer part of Amulius's little gang. Even so, I still think we ought to follow the original plan to take out those bloody Swarmers. It makes perfect sense to get rid of the highest danger first." Elsie glanced over her shoulder. "We can deal with that old perverted bastard another night. I don't think he's going anywhere."

Elsie slid her fingers up the damp bricks, stopping just below the small hole. The rat poked out its nose and gave the vampire's finger a tentative sniff before fleeing back inside the hole. "Did you see that, mum? Our flesh and blood is toxic to every other creature. The First Father even told me that the flies won't even lay their eggs in our corpses. The only creature capable of digesting our bodies is another vampire." She chuckled. "I can't believe that, mum. I used to be terrified of the little bastards." Elsie tapped the bricks. "I think the Swarmers are a bit like rats, you know. If we don't stop them, they'll be everywhere."

"Honey, tell me about your brother, tell me what happened."

She shook her head. "I can't, mum. Look, all that matters now is that he's just like one of them, he's a dirty Swarmer."

"I won't accept that, Elsie. He's your brother, for crying out loud. We need to save him."

Elsie didn't say a word. She didn't need to; Darlene felt the anger flowing through the girl's body. It was like standing under a power line.

"I know he's a Swarmer, but so were you, honey. Maybe, if we found Damien, we could—"

"No mum!" Elsie shouted. "His fate is sealed."

"But he's your brother!" she persisted. "If we both bit him, passed on our own blood, well, it could work."

"He killed my Ben!" she cried. "The bastard dragged him out of my arms and threw his body at that pack of dirty Swarmers!" She choked back her sobbing. "I heard them rip him apart, and all Damien did was laugh. I'm going to kill that bastard with my own hands." She growled.

The girl spun around and marched away, leaving Darlene shaking like a leaf.

"I can't kill my own son," she whispered.

"You daughter is right, Darlene. He has to die."

She spun around, gasping at the sight of Paul appearing from behind a brick column. He pressed a finger to his lips.

"Calm yourself, sweetheart. I don't want Elsie to know I'm here. I know how hard this is to accept, but you need to believe me. Damien is no longer your son." He looked over at the departing vampire. "Just like she is no longer your daughter. He's a strong one, he could even make First Father. That means he'll spread his dirty Swarmer blood far and wide. He has to die." He ducked back behind the column. "Catch up with her," he whispered. "I'll meet you at the end of this tunnel."

She turned around and saw her daughter staring at her. "Even rats look after their young, Elsie."

"Not all the time. When they're threatened, they'll eat them. Look mum, I seriously doubt that he'll be with that lot anyway. More than likely, he'll have found his own little secluded spot to rest until the sun goes down. He might have even left town by now."

Darlene bit back a reply about him never straying too far from home and followed Elsie through the dark brick tunnels. She hoped her daughter was right. Deep down, Darlene knew Paul and Elsie were right about Damien, and her blood would no doubt compel her to lunge for him anyway. There was no other way.

"Oh, well would you look at that," muttered Elsie. "I did wonder when your absent boyfriend was going to make an appearance."

Darlene watched Paul climb out from a small tunnel a few feet off the ground and drop down, landing in the shallow stream of dark water. She noticed that his movements were a lot more fluid now. It might have been a trick of the dim light, but she was sure he'd also filled out a little bit since she last saw him.

"Elsie, I'm guessing you knew about me and Paul before we all changed?"

She nodded. "Yeah, I've known for a couple of months now, mum. Oh, don't worry, I didn't tell anyone."

Darlene didn't know whether to cry or to laugh out loud. "Wait, how the hell did you find out? I made sure that we were very careful."

"It was just the little things, mum. Call it a female's intuition. Like the faint smell of aftershave in the room. I'm good with smells, and I know what dad and Damien wear. There was also the shining expression in your eyes when I got back from college. Although, I think the biggest clue was when I found his necklace in my bed. The one with his name engraved in the back of it."

"Hello there, Elsie," said Paul, when he reached them. "Who'd have thought we would be meeting up like this?" He looked past them. "To be honest, I am surprised to see just you two. I expected to be hiding away as the Deathgazer Clan marched past me, ready to fuck up the Swarmers."

Elsie smiled back at him. "Well, the plans have been altered. There's just the pair of us here. Oh, and you, I suppose. That is, if you have the balls to go up against the other vampires."

He stared at Elsie for a few second before he nodded. "There's no other choice, is there?" Paul looked at Darlene. "Okay, I'm ready."

Elsie climbed up the metal ladder bolted to the wall and used one hand to twist the handle on the cover. "Don't you worry your pretty little head, Paul. We'll protect you from those nasty vampires." She chuckled before pushing up the cover and climbing out of the tunnel.

Darlene looked and Paul and smiled. "She means well, and she's right, we will protect you, hun. I will anyway." She gently pushed him over to the ladder. "Go on, up you go." She waited for him to clear the tunnel before following him up.

As she emerged into the market, the first thing she noticed was that darkness had already fallen. The second thing was that she was alone. Darlene frantically spun around and saw her companions racing down one of the aisles, heading for the main entrance. She chased after them.

It took her just seconds to realize they weren't alone. Directly in front of them was the largest vampire she had ever seen—he towered even above Amulius. He was dressed head to foot in ancient black leather, but his most distinguishing feature was his long mane of jet black hair. The vampire ran to the entrance and burst through the window.

Darlene joined the others and watched the vampire join his colleagues. They all turned and laughed at them before disappearing into the night. She sighed, looked down at the stone floor, and spotted something very familiar. Darlene stooped and scooped up a small silver bracelet. "Oh fuck," she cried, recognizing the present she had given Damien two Christmases ago.

Chapter Seventeen

The sight of the clear night sky, filled with stars and a heavy moon, made Damien want to run through the deserted town laughing and screaming at the top of his lungs. He had never felt this good. It was the best high he'd ever had.

"This is your first true night, my new First Son. Savour this moment. The sun is now your enemy, but no matter, for the moon and her daughters will guide your senses to your forthcoming kills."

Damien watched the brothers bow their heads and quietly recite a prayer. The sight of them praying caused him to pause; he hadn't expected them to do that. Was this the closest these animals got to having a religion?

"Damien, why do you stare?" The Swarmer First Father walked up to him and placed his hands at either side of Damien's head. "If the name of the noon and her daughters is invoked, it is wise to follow the actions of your fellow Clan members," he whispered. Desmonus glanced at the brothers. "Their last First Son was also their priest. It is wise to remember that although it is in their blood to obey, you could be presented with unwanted tribulations if they think you mock their faith."

Desmonus suddenly released Damien's shoulders and jumped away from him, then cocked his head to one side.

"First Father!" cried Helix. "What has he done to you?"

It didn't escape Damien's attention that those two clowns were glaring at him with accusing eyes, automatically thinking he was to blame for the vampire's odd behaviour.

"This settlement is too quiet," he replied. "I hear only our voices."

Helix shrugged his great shoulders. "Is that not how the settlement should be at this late hour? They sleep in their beds, or hide from us, dreaming and hoping they will wake in the morning unchanged."

"I predict many will not tonight, my brother," added Healiod. "Especially the firm young maidens."

The brothers chuckled.

"Cease your lustful ramblings!" snapped the First Father. "I have already explained our situation to you twice now. Is it so difficult to adjust your thinking? Look at the buildings around us. Do they resemble crude wooden shacks to you? Perhaps it is time to block up the holes in your heads to stop your wits from leaking out."

Damien suppressed a chuckle. He loved the way these guys spoke. He wondered how long it would take them to adapt and start to talk like him. Looking at these two brain-dead clowns, he guessed it would never happen.

"Do you not remember how this land looked when we emerged from our long sleep, Helix? Even you asked me if we had woken on the moon. Remember how the lights on the ground were like running through all the moon's daughters?"

The town wasn't completely dark, the streetlights were on, but there wasn't a single shop was open. Metal shutters covered every shop window. "This isn't right," he muttered. "Some of the shops ought to still be open, it isn't that late. The pubs and the takeaway should definitely be open right now."

"Damien, I regret some of the words you utter are unfamiliar, but your meaning is quite clear." The First Father leaned against the side of a green Ford Focus and stared at him. "I did not expect this to happen so quickly. The thought had taken up residence, but I believed that time truly had scrubbed away our legacy." He scowled. "I fear the humans have fled this settlement."

The brothers looked at Desmonus and then at each other. "Our legacy?" Helix asked. "You mean they remembered us? This should not surprise me; we used the humans as food and slaves for many generations. Our tales would have been passed from mouth to mouth for many generations after."

"That is not what I mean. This is their inner minds taking control of their brains and telling them what should be done. I do not think they were even aware of their actions."

"It's a racial memory," murmured Damien. "I've read about things like this before." He looked up and down the empty street. "Never on this scale though. You guys must have really scared the shit out the humans in your time to make such an impression."

Helix ignored him and marched over to the First Father. "If they have all gone, then how will we expand the clan? Without fresh bodies, the Deathgazers will destroy us for good."

Desmonus moved off the car and stood behind Helix. "Follow this road, my son. Can you not see that collection of tiny lights peering out from above the rooftops? I see you can, Helix. There are huge crowds of humans all bunched together in some fields beyond this settlement. There is enough meat there to last us for a long time."

Helix eagerly nodded. "Oh, yes, I see that now."

Damien heard the noise of technicians starting to test out the sound system and giggled quietly to himself when he saw the other vampires' reactions. He guessed they had yet to experience a metal festival.

"First Father, the riddle is solved. The people from the settlement are over there. My guess is they are trying to work out what that dreadful noise is."

"It sounds like a thousand fox cubs, all caught in wire snares, all screaming out for their mothers," his brother said.

The First Father gazed at Damien. "Is he correct?"

Damien grinned. "Healiod is right about the bands, but right now, their skivvies are just tuning up all the equipment. As for what Helix said? No way, the townsfolk stay well away from the festival, mostly they spend their time bitching about the noise and what effect it'll have on the house prices or some shit like that." He turned around and slammed the palm of his hand against the steel shutter. "It doesn't stop them from keeping the shops open until midnight, trying to skim off as much money as possible from the visitors."

"It does not matter then about the humans all running from their homes," said Helix. "Our food has not gone anywhere!"

"You truly are an idiot," snarled Desmonus. "This, I did not predict. It made sense to believe the Deathgazers would act in their own pre-determined method of putting down their roots, changing a few of the humans, then attempting to milk the rest like big fat cows. Conflict is now inevitable; we fight for the same resource."

The brothers laughed. "We are still many, and he is just one," said Helix. He looked at Damien. "We have already started to build and expand."

"We waste time," the First Father said. "If there is to be a fight, then we should join up with the others. I want to see the rest of my Swarmer Clan. I am also eager to see Eleanor." He looked at Damien. "I believe she has some explaining to do."

Damien conjured up the image of him sitting down to eat a huge plate of chocolate ice cream, covered in stale vomit and horse manure, just to stop his mind from dwelling upon Eleanor's perfect breasts.

"Once our clan is complete, we can begin our work." He grinned at the brothers. "While I am aware you two did not obey by rule of abstinence the previous night, you still were able to reign in your natural desire to swarm. Tonight, all your lusts, crazes, and desires will be sated. If Amulius is there, remember, he is only one vampire, he cannot fight all of us." Desmonus then walked over to Damien. "Now, my new First Son, perhaps it is time to discover why Eleanor took it upon herself to play the role of First Father?"

The First Father lunged at him, and Damien's quick reactions were no match for Desmonus's lightning fast movements. He felt the vampire's canines sink into the flesh on the side of his neck before his whole body locked up. Damien was helpless, he couldn't move a single muscle. He wasn't even able to blink.

His eyes lost focus, and the view of the pavement and the First Father's dirty black boots dissolved into one blurred mess. The sensations of sight, sound, and feeling left him. The only experience left to Damien was thought, and the First Father was delving into that like a fat worm eating through black soil. He was powerless.

The vampire's dominant probe stripped away every barrier, exposing all of Damien's innermost thoughts.

Blazing white light exploded behind Damien's eyes, and he saw the image of his mother, followed by his father, and then Elsie. The First Father was bleeding out every shred of knowledge from his mind, soaking it in like a dry sponge plunged into water. The kaleidoscope of faces stopped when he was shown a full-frontal view of Eleanor. The image wasn't from his mind. Damien had never seen her like this before.

He couldn't stop the sensation of arousal when the image turned her head and winked. The low light illuminated the vampire's well-proportioned body hiding behind very thin sheets of green and purple gauze. He groaned in pleasure as she walked up to him, took hold of his wrist and placed his hand over her full breast.

Damien hooked his fingers behind the material and tugged it down, exposing the full beauty of her creamy white flesh. She released his wrist and dragged her fingernails down his chest. He lowered his head and watched her hand stop at his waistband. She then got down on her knees and unfastened his trousers, freeing his erect penis.

He watched her grip his shaft hard, lift the organ up, then slowly run her cold tongue along the underside until she reached the head. Eleanor giggled and pushed his full length into her mouth. She held him tight with her powerful lips, then slid him slowly out, stopping when she reached his head.

The pleasure circuits in his brain blew when the woman somehow wrapped her long tongue around the tip and gently squeezed and caressing the sensitive flesh.

She suddenly released him and stood up. "He knows now, Damien," she whispered. "I should have realized he would peel you like an onion. Worry not, my lover; this particular transplanted memory is hidden away. We will bide our time. It is one thing we have on our side." She wrapped her arms around his naked body and pulled him tight against her. "I must go; he is close to ending this. I will play my part, Damien, worry not."

Damien cried out in shock when the world reverted to its former state of absolute blackness before his senses abruptly returned to him. He screamed when he looked down and saw the town hundreds of feet below his body, rapidly reaching up to embrace him as he plummeted through the night sky. Damien shut his eyes, anticipating his body smashing into the hard floor any second.

The eye-watering stench of rotten meat combined with a sickly sweet smell of fermenting fruit suddenly filled his nostrils. Damien snapped open his eyes and found his body lying on the pavement, slumped against the metal shutter, the memories of his last few minutes quickly fading away. He saw the two brothers grinning down at him, then saw the First Father crouching beside him.

Desmonus leaned closer until his mouth was a whisper away from Damien's ear. "Even now, I feel your mind desperately trying to hold on to your recent memories, yet, no matter how hard you want to hold them, they slip away like smoke from a dying fire. No matter, I have what I need. The aroma still lingers, does it not?"

Damien nodded, unable to clear his nose.

"The thick crust of Eleanor's alluring perfume is not often breached. She strives to maintain the reflection of the sweet young virginal maiden, Damien. Once you do break through, the reality is that Eleanor is just an ancient, disease-ridden, living corpse." He stroked Damien's ear. "You are but a puppy dog for her, a plaything, a child's toy, my young rabbit. You are not her first, Damien."

The first Father pulled him off the floor and leaned him against the metal shutters. "This world will give my devious little woman a medley of new playthings. You will not be the last embryonic vampire to fall for her silly games either."

"First Father, can we chew on his bones now? It is more than he deserves for the trouble his presence has caused."

Damien looked into Healiod's blazing eyes. He knew that he wouldn't have stood much of a chance if just one of them went for him, let alone two. Damien felt like he'd just been run over by a truck. What the fuck had just happened to him? He felt great just a few moments ago.

Even if he was outmatched, Damien wasn't going to allow these bastards rip into him, not without a fight. Even if the odds were insurmountable. He clenched his fist tight. As soon as that vampire leaned closer, Damien intended to push his fingers into Healiod's throat. Even as his brother and the First Father ripped into his flesh, he would, at least, have the satisfaction of taking one of them with him.

He then remembered that Desmonus could have killed him at any time. Unless they were just playing with him? Damien just wanted to go to sleep, he was confused and very tired.

"Damien is still your First Son, Healiod." Desmonus turned around and grinned at the brothers. "You might find your First Son to be a worthy adversary. Perhaps you two should reserve your scorn and open ridicule?" He looked back at Damien. "Do you think it would be wise to see him lose his temper?"

Helix just sighed, "My First Father, I am just a lowly vampire, your word games confuse me. I look at this pathetic creature. I see not a great vampire, just some wasteful human who was unfortunate to meet your wife. I mean no offence, First Father, but his presence makes my stomach churn."

"And you feel the same?"

Healiod nodded. "Yes, my First Father, more so than Helix."

Desmonus stepped back and winked at Damien. "Then if either of you are able to defeat this little rabbit, you can claim title to First Son. Damien, these two clan members enjoy throwing their opponents to the ground, standing on their backs, and then twisting off their heads. It is advisable not to allow either of them to get you into that position."

He watched the two brothers separate and step to either side of him. Damien knew escape was not an option. He glanced at the First Father, waiting for him to tell his gorillas to back off. This had to be another stupid test, surely, it must be, the bastard even winked at him.

Healiod growled and lunged for him. Damien managed to duck just in time and rolled to the side. He heard the huge vampire crash into the metal shutters and quickly turned to see him spin around. Damien saw the huge dent in the metal—it looked like the shop had just been ram-raided. He twisted his body, crying out when Healiod's brother swept his legs out, catching his ankle. He stumbled but managed to thrust his hand down to stop his body from hitting the floor.

From the corner of his eye, Damien saw Healiod running towards him. These bastards were slow, but he knew it was only a matter of time before one of them got hold of him and threw his body onto the pavement.

The First Father laughed. "He is like an eel. You two really are lumbering idiots. Cooperate, and he will be yours."

Damien glared at the First Father, he clenched both his fists, he'd had enough of this bullshit. "Fuck the lot of you," he growled. "I just about had enough of your crap!" He turned and ran at Helix, pulling back his arm. He screamed out in fury and rammed his fist into the vampire's nose. The result of his sudden assault halted him as his pile-driver blow shattered and flattened the vampire's nose. The vampire flew backwards and crashed into the side of the green car.

Damien looked at his blood-stained fist and then at Helix lying against the car, moaning quietly. Healiod ran past Damien and helped Helix onto his feet.

"At this moment, Damien, I suspect that concern for the well-being of Helix is not on your mind," chuckled the First Father. "He will recover though. The damage is superficial, his body repairs the damage even as we speak. Healiod, your head has not so many holes as your foolish brother. Did it not occur even to you that I would not give the First Son position to some pale blooded lamb?"

He marched over to the two vampires and clamped his hands on their shoulders. "Healiod, did you believe that whilst sleeping, Eleanor somehow attained the gifts given only to a First Father?"

The large vampire shrugged. "I know not what I thought. It is easier to accept the evidence before my eyes than to try and unlock the mystery. I am sorry, my First Father, even as a human, I did not dwell on issues too complicated."

"There is no mystery, Healiod. It is just improbable. Your new First Son has diluted Deathgazer blood running through his veins." He growled. "I see even this revelation just skates over your befuddled mind. Think back to before we went to sleep. Do you remember a human female called Maisen?"

Healiod slowly nodded. "Yes, I remember her. She had thick, long black hair and intense blue eyes. I also remember her breasts were very large. She was one of the girls you chose to pass on our bloodline."

"Well, it was her descendant whom we feasted upon in the hole. It was her sweet flesh that reactivated the Swarmer Clan."

Healiod burst out laughing. "Are you saying our new First Son is nothing more than some forgotten waking meal?" He chuckled to himself then frowned. "Do you think Eleanor would have known how her bite would affect the human?"

"It is unlikely. Did you know this mutation could cause a change in humans? I did not know of this. Our race has not slept like this since the time of the great freeze. I do not think there is any vampire so long lived who would have being able to foresee this outcome."

"What about Jalim? He was from before the time of the freeze."

Desmonus spat on the floor. "He was a senile old fool," he snapped. "That demented wizard had problems remembering his own name on most days. Do not utter his name in my presence ever again. Eleanor saw an opportunity to make mischief and seized upon it, as she is wont to do."

The First Father approached Damien. "Now, it is time to finish your initiation into the Swarmer clan." He held out his hands, palm up. "Clasp my wrists, then close your eyes."

Damien followed his instructions, trying not to wince when the First Father's fingernails dug into his skin. Before Damien shut his eyes, he saw both brothers spin around.

"First Father!" shouted Healiod. "The other clan members approach."

Desmonus nodded and smiled. Damien knew the First Father must have been aware they were already on their way to join them, it was written all over the vampire's face. He waited for Desmonus to turn around before trying to catch a glimpse of Eleanor. He saw the female vampire immediately. He couldn't miss Eleanor, she simply shined compared to the thugs dressed in filthy rags who shambled behind her.

There were no sweaty palms, no raised temperature, nor was there any sign his heart was about to make a run for it. Damien felt nothing for her; he didn't even find the woman all that attractive. He sighed and turned his attention back to the First Father, wondering what he ever saw in the woman.

Desmonus's face was an emotionless mask. "It is recommended that you do not allow your cock to grow whilst you are in her presence, my First Son."

He shrugged. "Don't worry about that. She really isn't my type, buddy."

"Eleanor is everyone's type. Just look at how the others act around her. They follow her like puppy dogs."

Damien did see it; the other males in the clan all had their brains in neutral around her. "There's no worries with me, Desmonus. I'm not in the habit of stealing another bloke's girlfriend."

"That is reassuring to hear," he replied. Desmonus turned around and faced the four new vampires. "I trust you were able to find somewhere to sleep in the new world while the hateful sun completed its journey through the sky."

Damien saw how the faces of those three male vampires changed from shock and bloodlust to just shock as Healiod walked amongst them, whispering into their ears. It was difficult to judge Eleanor's reaction; she didn't seem to be all that surprised to see him still living.

He tried not to cringe when he remembered how he acted in the market and guessed that he did kind of come across as some kind of love-sick puppy when he reached out to her.

It pleases me to see you are still around, Damien.

He glanced at the woman and nodded once. He should have told the First Father about their mental contact. If what Desmonus said about her was true, and he had no reason to doubt him, then her familiarity could lead to complications. The woman was still staring at him; she made him feel uncomfortable. There was something at the back of his mind, like a large fly bouncing around the inside of his skull. Damien gave her one last glance, shuddering when Eleanor gave him a sly wink.

Healiod returned to tending his brother and nodded to Damien as he passed him. Would they believe Healiod's whispered words, or would he have to prove himself once more? Damien was happy to do just that if any of them did try their luck.

Desmonus turned back around. "Damien," he whispered. "Look at them. They cannot believe a weak-blooded specimen such as yourself is now their First Son. They will not believe Healiod's words, and they will not fully accept my decision. I do not blame them; their vampire essence is the true instigator in this scenario. You will have to prove your worth again."

Damien couldn't care less what the others thought about him. If they still believed he was that same terrified youth from last night, then they'd see the error of their thinking.

He gritted his teeth again when the First Father grabbed his wrists once more and dug long fingernails into his flesh.

"Oh, I am hurting myself, as I know that my rough handling of your delicate body causes you distress," he mocked. "Worry not. My bite will soon drive out the last of your humanity."

Damien didn't like the sound of that.

"You were a mongrel. You have never been a pure human. How could you be like the rest of the herd when you have blood tainted from my Clan enemy running through your veins? If I was a First Father who could not adapt to a new situation, Damien, I would have killed you, and then I would have killed

Eleanor for attempting to undermine my position by upsetting the balance."

Desmonus chuckled and dug his fingers deeper into Damien's flesh. "I can adapt well. I see a challenge and turn it around and make it an opportunity. I have just finished off your change. Did I mention that you are about to die? Perhaps my Clan strain will revive you, perhaps not." He shrugged. "If that does happen, then one of the others will be very eager to step over your corpse and become my second in command."

The vampire's boasting voice began to lower in volume before finally fading away. Damien felt his lungs contract. The movement was involuntary, and he had no control as every scrap of air escaped from his mouth. He stared, fascinated, as the breath solidified directly in front of his face. It looked like a cloud of pale yellow candy floss suspended a few feet from the ground. He tore his eyes away from the occurrence and looked at the others, intending to ask if they had a clue what had just happened. He doubted that any of them would answer as they, too, like his breath, had frozen in mid pose.

"Okay, so this is so fucking weird." They weren't even blinking. He looked down, thankful that at least he could move his body. Damien lifted his hand, then extended his index finger. "Just what did that clown pump into my neck? I feel like I've had my drink spiked with LSD."

He prodded the cloud, yelling in shock and pain. He felt like he'd just touched the metal plate of a hot iron. "You bastard!" he snarled. "I bet you know what's happening to me," said Damien, glaring at the First Father's frozen stare. The cloud then contracted and faded away

"Okay, playtime is over, guys. I would like this to end now." Damien groaned, feeling a sudden sharp, stabbing pain in the base of his stomach. The pain spread up throughout his chest, filling him with thousands of needles, all pushing into his soft flesh. He fell to his knees, clutching his guts tight, then jerked his head up and filled his lungs. The needles-like pain vanished as the air he took in chilled his body down to freezing. He blinked slowly, watching the other vampires slowly start to shift.

Damian stared into the First Father's eyes, watching the vampire's glare change in slow motion to his big grin. He groaned and found himself close to falling when real time reasserted itself.

Desmonus rushed forward and caught Damien, putting him back onto his unsteady feet.

"Welcome to our Clan," Desmonus said. "It seems your spirit was able to fight off the clutches of the moon and her daughters." The First Father pressed the fingernail of his index finger into Damien's bicep.

Damien watched and grinned as bright scarlet blood ran down his bare arm. The First Father had managed to push his nail and the tip of his finger into the wound before he pulled it back out. There was no pain. "Am I dead, First Father?"

Desmonus licked Damien's blood off his finger, then shook his head. "No, the dead do not bleed, nor do they speak. We exist in the void between." He grabbed Damien's shoulders and turned him to face the gathered vampires. "This is your new First Son of the Swarmer Clan. You are now his children. He will protect you, keep you safe, and ensure you obey me at all times. Your misdemeanours are his misdemeanours. This is your first and only warning. He will punish any dissent with impunity." He pointed to Helix's face. "Helix took the assumption that the First Son's slight build was a sign of weakness. I suggest you do not repeat his mistake."

The new arrivals gave Damien the briefest of acknowledgment before something else caught their attention. They turned as one, lifting their noses into the air. He had no idea what sort of game they were playing, nor did he really care.

Damien looked at the crater the First Father had dug into his bicep, noticing the blood had already stopped flowing and now looked a bit like a miniature pool of red water. He smiled to himself, finding the tips of his canines were notably larger.

There was no doubting it now; he was one of them. Damien was a Swarmer vampire and … He suddenly caught the scent of something wondrous. His blood heated up like boiling water rushing through his veins. The Clan now looked at him, their bright shining red eyes waiting for him to give the order.

"They are yours to command," the First Father whispered. He lifted his own head. "There are three of them, and they travel towards the fields. The humans are not from this town. One is a female, she is young." He spun his head around. "Give the order, you fool! Your clan needs feeding. I need quick and quiet deaths, without alerting the main herd."

Damien nodded. "Eleanor, take Helix and head north."

"Have you lost your mind?" she cried. "They go west. I will not allow you to cut me out of the hunt."

"For fuck's sake, you stupid tart!" Damien growled. He charged up to Eleanor and viciously shoved her, watching with amusement as the other new arrivals jumped back when she crashed into the brick wall between two shuttered shops. "I'm not cutting anyone out of the hunt. They'll take a left and cut through the side of the park. It's dark. There's no way on this planet that any lass will go through there at this time. There's a large gate that will take your prey straight into the largest field. Eleanor, get to that before them and they'll just fall into your arms."

He looked at the others. "It's my town, remember? I know the ground. Now go hunt them down." He smiled at the sight of Helix picking her off the floor. She slapped away his arms before fleeing into the night. The other Clan members stayed together and raced down the street.

The First Father quietly laughed. "You will make a fine addition to the clan. Once we have fed on their blood, we shall endeavour to complete tonight's task. Now, I believe you should join Eleanor and Helix. I suspect it will be them who claim the prize. I give the female to you, Damien. You are now a full vampire. Your body has lost all its natural heat. If you do not feed, you will begin to feel the insides of every bone in your body turn to ice, the cold will spread through you until you die the true death. Only human blood will halt the atrophy."

He nodded and spun around.

"Then go, feed from her or fuck her, I care not. Just ensure she stays dead once your needs are sated."

His ears only caught the last sentence. Damien raced after the two vampires, determined to catch up with them before they caught those three humans. Desmonus was right. Even now, as he ran, the coldness was beginning to spread. He shivered, then shook his head. "Stop it, you dickhead," he muttered. "The bastard was winding you up."

Damien leaped over a low wall, then ran across a carpark and into the deserted bus station. He was right about them needing to head towards the gate, he just didn't bother telling them there was a quicker route there. He ran out of one of the departure bays and saw two human shapes already at the top of the hill. "That's impossible!" he gasped, when his vampire senses told him that the two Clan members were almost at the gate. Damien put on a burst of speed, groaning when he caught sight of the humans as well.

He ran up the embankment and stopped dead when he saw that Eleanor must have doubled back and lain in wait for the humans. She already had the girl. Damien watched the vampire press the girl's head into her chest, muffling her screaming.

"She's mine!" growled Damien. He saw Helix running after the remaining humans. "The First Father promised her to me. Give me the girl right now."

Eleanor growled back at him. "You're just as bad as the others, Damien. I've invested a lot of my time into you. I know none of my words will make sense to you. The First Father has been inside your head and thrown a few levers and pressed plenty of switches. I expected that. What I did not expect was this!" she screamed. Eleanor placed her hands at either side of the girl's head and viscously twisted.

Damien clearly heard the girl's neck snap. The vampire threw her at him. He looked down and gazed into the face of his Sandra. He glared at Eleanor. "What the fuck did you have to do that for?"

"Because she had what I wanted. Now, the harlot is dead. Now she is just a vessel to be drained."

He fell to his knees and lifted her loose head. "I told you to leave here. Why didn't you listen to me?"

"After all these uncountable years, it still amazes me that it does not matter whether you are human or vampire. If you are a male, then you think only with your cock." She walked up to him. "Do not waste her blood, Damien. Her heart is still but it will not impede your feeding." She crouched beside him. "There are only two outcomes for you, Damien. By the time this night ends, either the First Father will tear you apart for betraying the Clan, or …" she smiled, stood up, and started to walk away. "Or, you and I will rule the Swarmers together."

Chapter Eighteen

He needed to move, not too much, just a couple of inches would do it. But Cade dared not even move his eyes, let alone move his backside. The spare battery in his back pocket would just have to dig into his flesh for a little longer. He desperately wanted to reassure Katy. He could feel her shivers through his own shirt.

The three figures had not moved. If it hadn't been for his built-in early warning system, Cade feared they both would have tripped right over them. He ordered his heartbeat to slow down when he realized just how close they'd come to getting ripped apart like wrapping paper on a Christmas present.

The spare battery felt like it was now trying to dig out a huge chunk of flesh, and he also felt his hand going numb. That did worry him; his torch was in that hand. If it fell to the floor, chances were the bloody thing would break. Cade risked a single, slow glance down to his hand. He didn't even know if the torch would work. Oh, the UV light worked fine, but for some stupid, unexplained reason, Cade still believed that it wouldn't have any effect on a vampire.

"Oh no, please, God!" Katy whispered. "They must have seen us." She started to shuffle back down the embankment. "We need to get out of here, Cade."

He reached down and wrapped his fingers around her wrist. "We need to stay. You know what's behind us. This is the only way out of here." Cade looked away from Katy and focused on the three vampires in the distance. They had moved, but he didn't think they were heading in this direction.

Katy had stopped struggling. It felt like he now held a rag doll. He gently brought her back up and rolled over, grateful when the battery stopped its journey into his body. Cade held the girl tight against him and brushed his lips against hers, thanking the gods when she responded and kissed him back. "Hun, we're going to be okay. I promise I'll let nothing happen to you."

He watched a ghost of a smile play over her lips before her apprehensive expression forced it away. He took solace in the fact that at least she wasn't as traumatized now as she was just after they had left the park. He hoped.

The three vampires raced across the dark field at an incredible speed, looking like a movie on fast forward. How did he hope to compete against creatures that could do that? They reached the gate that led into the next field and perched on the top, balancing like giant crows. Cade took a deep breath. This was it. If he didn't move now, he knew those nightmares would have won. The field that those things were looking into was crammed with dozens of tents. The festival goers wouldn't stand a chance once the vampires started to work their way through them.

"I can't just stay and watch this," he whispered. "They'll slaughter all of them. Either that or make even more just like them." He slowly sat up and rested the torch on the ground, base up. Cade pushed the button forward, lifted up the torch a couple of inches, and gazed at the grass under the beam, bathed in violet light.

He saw them drop into the field and groaned. It was now or never. He turned off the torch and scrambled to his feet. "Sweetheart, you don't have to come with me. You should be safe here."

Katy stifled a cry. She looked behind her before getting onto her hands and knees.

Cade helped her up. "Stay close to me, hun." He passed her the torch. "At the first sign of them, shine the light in their faces."

Even if the light didn't burn them like the sun, the brightness could give them enough time to get away.

Cade took Katy's hand. "We'll get through this, I promise." He pulled her across the dark field, heading towards the gate. It took him considerable effort not to break down into hysterical tears. How the hell could they get away from creatures that moved faster than any other animal on the planet?

Katy squeezed his hand. He looked back at her and saw another smile on her face. Cade squeezed back.

"You know the torch will work, Cade," she said quietly after catching her breath. "It'll be like a flamethrower to them." She suddenly put on a burst of speed and pulled him towards the gate. "Come on, we have to get into that field before they spot us." She reached the gate just before him and started to climb over. "Look, if they see us in the field, they'll just think that we're a couple of outsiders, we'll stand a better chance of staying ahead of them."

Cade nodded and followed her over the gate, not bothering to mention that no festival goer in their right mind would wear the style of clothing that Katy had opted to wear. She stood out like a sore thumb. Still, with luck, the vampires wouldn't spot that. He followed her over to the first tent, stopping dead when he saw the guide rope at the last minute. He crouched down and scanned the field, suddenly realizing he had lost sight of them. Cade glanced at Katy, intending to tell her to be ready with that torch, when he saw a huge shadow right behind them.

He reached out trying to grab her arm, but it was too late. Another hand took Katy's arm and dragged her screaming body away from him. She dropped the torch. Cade dived for it, fumbling with the button, trying to turn it on.

"No, don't do it!"

Cade fell back and looked up into Katy's imploring eyes. She reached down and snatched the torch out of his numb hands. The large man behind her rested his hands on her shoulders. Cade looked up into his blazing red eyes and paused. His instinct told him to kill the fucker, to slide the sword from his back and plunge it into the vampire's face, and yet Cade saw something he'd never seen before. This vampire was acting, well, human.

"Please, Cade. Don't hurt him. Paul's my stepbrother."

He watched the huge vampire gently wrap his hands around her waist. It shocked him to see how relaxed she was now. This monster was her stepbrother? It made him realize just how little he knew about the girl. He stayed on the ground, not daring to move. Unlike Katy, he hadn't forgotten about the two other vampires. He didn't know where they were, but they couldn't be that far away, his senses were still screaming at him.

"That's a big weapon you have there," whispered a female voice right by his ear.

Cade stifled a scream when he twisted his head and found himself face to face staring into the blazing eyes of a beautiful blonde. He swallowed hard, sensing the last member of their trio on the other side of his shivering body. He felt like a gazelle surrounded by lions.

"I always told Damien that you looked like the strong silent type," said the girl. She ran her freezing fingers down his arm.

"God, I used to fancy the arse off you, Cade." She stood up and pulled him onto his feet. "I still do."

"Elsie?" He gazed at the teen girl, having enormous difficulty comparing this deadly creature to the girl who used to give him puppy eyes when she thought he wasn't looking. Cade slowly turned and looked at the remaining vampire in the trio, not all that shocked to find Elsie's mum looking back at him. He flinched when Elsie stroked his arm again.

"You need to relax, Cade. We're not going to eat you," Elsie's mum said, chuckling. "Believe it or not, we all want the same thing."

"If I do sense that you're about to use your katana on any of us though, Cade ..."

He saw Elsie move at impossible speed. Before he had time to even blink, the blonde vampire's hand was resting on Katy's throat.

"Well, I think you can guess the outcome," she finished.

Paul knocked her hand away. "Will you leave her alone, Elsie?" The vampire bent towards Katy's head and whispered into her ear, dropped his arms, then walked over to Elsie's mum and embraced her.

That knocked Cade for six. He assumed the male would be shacked up with Elsie. He stared at the blonde vampire.

"So, what do we all want?" Cade asked. The fact that he managed to speak without his voice cracking amazed him. Just standing so close to these monsters made his flesh creep.

Katy grabbed his hand, then wrapped her arms around his back. He saw that her shivers had returned.

Paul picked up the torch, looked at Cade, he then passed it to Elsie. "Before you ask, yes, the torch will work." He looked at the other two vampires before returning his attention back to Cade. "I've seen you around town, and according to Elsie, you seem like a decent enough guy." He looked over at Katy. "And you're a vast improvement over her last boyfriend." He grinned. "No offence, lass."

Cade nodded. "Great, now I'm feeling all warm and cosy."

"Pandora is well and truly out of the box, buddy. No matter what we do now, the vampire plague is going to spread across the planet. We can, however, attempt to slow it down."

Cade looked at these three vampires, still trying to work out what they were playing at. "Yeah, that much I have worked out. But, unless you haven't figured this bit out, you three are vampires. Or has that detail slipped your mind?"

"We can't help what we are, Cade," Darlene said.

"They're closing in," Elsie hissed.

Her mother nodded. "Look, Cade, we're running out of time here. We all know that we've changed. Just as I suspect deep down you know that you have a taint of our blood running through your veins." She caught her breath and looked nervously at her daughter. "I can sense them too. Shit, they're all here." Darlene ran over to Cade and grabbed his shoulders. "Listen, if you want to help, then you can start by getting that big sword out and using it." She closed her eyes for a moment. "Oh wow!" She chuckled darkly. "I see you have already tussled with Amulius's new Deathgazer Clan. Are you ready for round two?" She pointed to the end of the field. "They're over there, all ready to engage with the Swarmers."

Cade looked at her in utter bewilderment. "Seriously, are you having a fucking laugh here?" He should have known this was coming. These jokers just planned to use him as battle fodder, as a diversion. "Look, Elsie's mum. I was lucky to get out of that gym alive. Those fuckers will eat me and Katy for their supper."

"No, they won't," said Elsie. "They're not as fast or as strong as us. Also, I'm staying with you." She snatched the torch out of Katy's hand and flicked it on, pointing the beam at the floor. Elsie took a deep breath, then swept the light across her ankle.

Cade's jaw dropped. He watched in amazement as the flesh on her leg bubbled up like grilled cheese. Elsie turned off the light and gave the torch back to Katy before limping over to the gate and slumping against it.

"See, it's isn't all doom and gloom, Cade."

"Are you all right?" Darlene ran over and crouched beside her daughter. "What the bloody hell did you have to do that for, you silly girl?" Darlene glanced up at Cade. "You don't have to prove yourself to anyone."

Elsie sighed. "Give it a rest, mum," she replied, grinning. "I'll be okay in a few minutes. It really isn't as bad as it looks." She used the gate to get back to her feet and limped over to Cade. "You've not only survived the last day and night, you've also taken on our kind and beat them." She smiled at Katy. "This one's a keeper, lass." Elsie glanced down at her leg. "Fuck, that really did hurt. I wasn't prepared for that. Listen to me, Cade. You're not an idiot. The chances of all of us coming out of this unscathed are pretty slim. At least we do have a chance. If we sit back, we'll all be dead or …" She licked her lips. "Or, we'll be changed."

Cade reached back and took out his katana. The handle moulded into his fist. It felt good to hold it again. He knew he was caught between a rock and a hard place here. No matter how sincere they sounded, there was no way he could trust them. "So, let's assume that the impossible does happen and we slay the 'other' monsters. What happens then? Do we all live happy ever after?" He left the question hanging.

"We'll cross that bridge when, if, we get to it," snapped Darlene. "Look, we need to go, right now!" she kissed Elsie on the cheek. "Take care, honey."

Cade found himself suddenly alone with Katy and the monster trapped inside the shell of the gorgeous blonde teen. He looked over to where Darlene had pointed, trying to see if he could get a fix on them. It was useless; the vampire standing next to him frazzled his radar.

"So, you still think I'm a monster?"

"Get out of my mind, Elsie," he growled.

The vampire chuckled. "I wasn't in your mind, Cade. That's the whole point. You broadcast that one on all frequencies. Okay, I get it. You're not happy about me being here. Just try to get over it, you big ape." She looked at Katy. "That goes for you as well. Both of you should be thinking happy thoughts," She pointed at the tent beside them. "Shelia has just finished off the last of David's cans of Carlsberg. She's a bit pissed with him because he didn't go into the town to pick up some more. She's seriously thinking of letting the idiot snore himself to death and see if there's any action going on. Those thoughts and similar ones are what the other vampires will be picking up. Does this sink in, or do I have to write it down?"

"I'm not a complete idiot," Cade snapped. He lifted his leg over the tent's guide rope, trying to remember which bands were due to play here tomorrow, and walked a little closer to where Darlene had pointed.

"There's three of them hiding behind that portaloo." Elsie suddenly streaked past him and ducked down behind the large orange tent just in front of them. "Fuck, they know we're here!"

Cade's adrenalin-fuelled body shifted into overdrive when Katy screamed. He spun around, and her voice abruptly ceased as two huge bodies slammed into her, knocking her into the side of the tent. Cade ran forward and punched the tip of his katana into the first shadow, grinning with glee as the body stopped moving.

Elsie dived on the remaining vampire. Cade watched in horror as her teeth split open her gums before she lunged her face forwards and bit into the side of the other vampire's neck. She growled, then jerked her head back, spraying herself and the tent with his thick blood.

She pulled him off Katy. "Sort out the other one!" she shouted.

Cade tore his eyes off the grisly scene, and spun around. The vampire wasn't dead. He ran and tried to grab the handle of his sword, but the vampire shifted his body, then pulled out Cade's Katana and threw it to the floor.

The vampire growled at Cade, "My turn, you shit." The vampire swept Cade's legs, knocking him onto the ground. "My first bite," he said, crawling onto Cade's legs.

He couldn't even get off the floor, the fall had knocked all the air out of him. The vampire was now pulling himself up past his knees, And Cade smelled the odour of congealed blood on the vampire's breath. He frantically brushed his hands across the cool grass, trying to find anything he could use to stop this abomination from getting any closer.

"No you don't!" snarled Katy.

Cade looked up and shrieked when he saw the vampire literally turn into a small inferno when Katy shown her torch straight at his body. He flung himself back and used both legs to boot the now smouldering ruin away from him.

"So much for the 'big hard man' image," Elsie said, giggling. She helped Cade back onto his feet. "Now I can see how you've managed to stay alive, Cade. I should have guessed that your female back-up must have done all your donkey work." Elsie stooped and picked up his katana. "Can you at least try to keep this in your hands? Without it, you're just a cocktail sausage without a stick to the other vampires."

Cade meekly took his sword from her hands, then smiled sweetly, making sure that the vampire 'heard' exactly what he thought of her mocking tone. He saw her mouth opening and tuned out her voice, not wishing to hear anymore of her taking the piss.

As soon as he relegated her annoying voice to background noise, Cade found he now knew exactly where the remaining Deathgazer Clan were hiding.

"Katy!" he hissed. "Give me the torch." When she didn't immediately respond, he snatched it out of her fingers, turned on the beam, and shone it away from the portaloos, towards an old campervan.

"What are you doing?" shouted Elsie. "You're going in the wrong sodding direction!"

He ignored her shouts. Cade trusted his senses more than her feelings. They hadn't let him down so far. The purple light picked out the logo of a heavy metal band sprayed onto the side of the van. "Oh, that's ironic," he muttered. "That's Damien's favourite band." He dropped to the ground and shone the torch under the van, smiling when he saw three pairs of boots on the other side.

"Come on out, Colin, if you think that you're hard enough!" Cade shouted. He stood up, keeping his fingers firmly wrapped around the sword handle, and almost jumped out of his skin when he heard the sound of shattering glass. The van door on the other side slid back. Cade didn't know what to do; he hadn't expected them to do that. Were they going to try and drive off?"

He turned around to see his companions running towards him.

"Look out!" screamed Elsie.

Before he had time to turn back around, a huge object crashed into him. The torch flew out of his fingers, and Cade saw the light beam spear through the dark sky, the violet beam twirling like a Catherine wheel before the torch crashed into the ground. The light suddenly extinguished, and Cade feared the impact had broken it.

Cade had remembered Elsie's warning and had not relinquished his grip on the Katana. He screamed and swung the blade into the shapeless mound pressed up against his body, but the blade just harmlessly bounced off the surface.

His confused senses finally reasserted themselves, and Cade saw just what had ran into him. He dropped down and rolled to the side before jumping back onto his feet. He jerked his head over at his mysterious attacker, just catching sight of the vampire pulling the heavy carpet that he'd thrown over his head and body.

"You sneaky bastard," Cade whispered. He slid to the left as the vampire turned the other direction and swung the katana, grunting in satisfaction as the sharp blade sliced into the back of the vampire's neck. Cade pulled the blade out of the wound, then swung again, slicing through the rest of the neck.

He spun around and saw Elsie jump on to Colin's back. She bit him, then leaped away when his thick arm reached for her. Despite the fact that he was three times her size, he was clearly outmatched at every turn. Cade saw the damage Elsie had inflicted when Colin slowly turned. It amazed him that the vampire could even stand. She had ripped out half of Colin's throat. Ragged strips of bloodied flesh hung down, brushing his shoulder like scarlet fabric.

Colin suddenly lunged forward, and Elsie jumped back. The vampire stumbled and crashed into the ground. Elsie dropped to her knees and sank her teeth into the other side of Colin's neck.

Cade turned away, sickened, and suddenly felt his heart in his throat when he realized that Katy was nowhere in sight. Cade ran to Elsie and jumped over Colin's prone body. He spun around. "Katy!" he screamed. "Where the fuck is she, Elsie?"

The vampire looked up. Cade tried not to flinch when she growled at him. He tightened his grip on the Katana handle, resisting the urge to slam the weapon tip down on the back of her neck.

Cade looked around the dark campsite, trying to see anyone at all. He groaned in despair when he saw a crowd of people congregating at the edge of the field. Their panicked voices hit him like a blast of hot air. Cade knew what that signified: the other Clan had arrived.

"Calm your feelings."

He growled and spun around, glaring at Elsie's face, just millimetres from his. "You're the one who lost her, you cold bitch!" he snarled.

She wrapped her fingers around both his arms. "If I so desired, Cade, I could squeeze my hands tight. Within moments, my fingers would press through your skin and meat until the only thing stopping me from forming a fist would be your bones." She closed her eyes. "Cade, it's your rollercoaster emotion that's your enemy. If I hadn't taken out Colin, that big fucker would be chomping on you right now. There's just the First Father left now, Cade."

She released his arms and nodded over to the approaching crowd. They were running straight towards them, screaming like banshees. Elsie pulled him into her embrace and turned around as the crowd ran past them, heading for the next field. He then felt the vampire spin him back around.

"They would have trampled you under their feet, Cade." She said, grabbing his wrist and pulling him away from the two vampire bodies. "Come on, I know where she is now."

She dragged him around the flattened tents, only stopping when they reached an old Ford Cortina. Cade saw Katy's body sprawled out on the car bonnet and ran over to her, weeping. "He's killed her. Oh god, the bastard has killed my Katy."

"Amulius wouldn't have done something so crude," Elsie said, when she caught up to him. She hurried around to the other side of the car, gently put her hands on the side of Katy's head, and slowly turned her still face. "I think your life just got very complicated, Cade."

Cade looked in horror at the two small puncture marks in the side of Katy's neck. He threw back his head and howled.

Chapter Nineteen

Darlene threw the Swarmer corpse down beside the young man sill convulsing on the grass. She wiped the dead vampire's blood from her mouth and dropped to her knees. "I'm so sorry," she whispered, looking down at the side of the young man's neck. The Swarmer had certainly done a number on the kid. The front of his black t-shirt was soaked with his blood. She straddled the boy, wrapped her fingers in his long black hair, and lifted up his head. Through her tear-blurred vision, Darlene watched him open his eyes and hiss at her. He must have sensed what Darlene was about to do, as his bucking movements increased in ferocity.

She slammed his head down, bursting into huge sobs when she heard the back of his skull crack open. Darlene wanted someone to do the same to her. "You're at peace now," she mumbled. Darlene tore her eyes from the boy's accusing eyes and looked around the campsite. This was no campsite any more, it now resembled the aftermath of a battlefield. Paul ran over to her and lifted Darlene off the boy's body. She saw that he'd already dispatched three Swarmer victims. He didn't seem to be affected as badly as her.

Paul wiped away her tears and gently kissed her. "Darlene, you're wrong, this is breaking my heart into little pieces. I'm just not letting the grief consume me."

"You read my mind?"

He shook his head. "I didn't have to." Paul looked down at the corpse beside her. "If you hadn't ended his life, he would have gone back home, killed his whole family and his friends."

"Paul, I'm sorry. This is tearing me apart!" She followed his gaze down to the dead Swarmer. Judging from his ragged attire, Darlene guessed she had just taken out one of the original vampires. Paul's body suddenly shuddered. "Are you okay?" she asked.

"None of this makes sense," he uttered, looking back at her. "He's not the First Father, Darlene, he's just some minor vampire. How was he able to change the boy?" He stiffened and pointed his shaking arm towards a long-haired youth, dressed only in a black t-shit. "Oh shit!"

Paul released her and raced after the youth. Darlene now saw just how fast he was going. He'd been changed and was already running down his first victim, a young blonde girl who couldn't have been much older than fourteen. Darlene saw Paul reach the boy. He pushed the newborn vampire down, wrapped his hands around his neck, and squeezed them together.

She looked in dismay as two huge vampires grabbed the blonde girl as she raced away from Paul and dragged her struggling body into a large tent. Another Swarmer ran past her. He turned around, growled, then dived onto a blond boy. Within seconds, the Swarmer was streaking away, leaving his victim on the ground, shaking.

Darlene couldn't move her legs; she found her body frozen to the ground. Her mind simply could not take in the overpowering sounds of shrieks and helpless screaming mixed with the hoarse growls of the newborn vampires emerging from their incredibly fast change in order to hunt down and change even more humans.

The blonde girl ran out of the tent, and Darlene found her paralysis broken when the girl ran toward her. Darlene saw that the girl's eyes were already beginning to acquire their scarlet taint. She swept her arm out, effectively clothes-lining the girl when she tried to run past her.

The two Swarmer vampires ran out of the tent and walked over to her. She lifted her foot, said a silent prayer for the girl on the ground who was thrashing as though demonically possessed, then slammed her foot into the side of her face. Darlene wanted to throw up when her shoe caved in the girl's skull.

"I can smell the stench of our enemy in your blood, you foul witch," growled the larger vampire. "If we did not have our set tasks, we would both enjoy filling your holes."

Darlene clenched her fists and glared at the vampire beside him. He had yet to speak. She felt the wave of lust coming off the pair of them; these disgusting creatures would like nothing better than to abuse her.

She saw Paul just a few steps away from the bald vampire and saw the hate in his eyes. Yet he radiated no thoughts at all, it was like he was a ghost. Darlene clenched her fists tight, feeling her nails break the skin. The sensation of her freezing blood rolling down her flesh helped her focus on the two Swarmers instead of Paul's imminent attack.

Darlene glared at the vampire beside the bald one. He still had yet to speak, but there was no need. She heard the vampire's disgusting thoughts. His mind continued its implausible scenario of him pushing his huge member inside her while the other one muffled her screams of agony.

"Is that the best you can come up with, you sad little man?" Darlene asked with a smile. She saw silent rage replace the vampire's sudden shock. "Maybe that would have terrified the thick whores from your time, you medieval tosser. Your childish fantasy does nothing for me though." Paul was ready to lunge. Darlene lifted her hand in the air and wiggled her pinkie. "Not when I know that you're both hung like mice."

The vampires roared. Paul wrapped his arms around the bald vampire's neck and dragged him back. When the other one spun around, Darlene jumped and crashed into him, and they both went sprawling onto the ground. Darlene wasted no time. She crawled onto the vampire's back and sank her teeth into the side of his neck. She jerked her head away, gagging on the foul stench as a fountain of dark red blood exploded from the vampire's wounds. She choked back the revulsion and bit into the other side of his neck.

She climbed off his back and spat out some of the dead vampire's vile fluid. "Why are we even bothering?" she cried, watching Paul end the other one's foul life. "We stand no chance of stopping the Swarmers from spreading."

Paul hurried over and grabbed her shoulders. "We put an end to the source, honey. We exterminated the vile bastards that slept for so long. You're right that we can't stop it. The plague was inevitable a soon as they climbed out of that pit."

A quiet moan escaped her lips as she looked around her. They were the only ones moving now in this field. Darlene knew they weren't alone, about half the tents were still occupied, their sleepers having no clue that their drunken binges had undoubtedly saved them from changing into monsters. The newborn vampires and the survivors continued their struggle in the next field.

"Honey, look at me and you. Especially you, Darlene. You've had this stuff inside you for centuries. We're not acting like they are."

"We did though."

He slowly nodded. "Yeah, you're right." He took her hand. "And the stuff running through our veins is pure Deathgazer. These kids only have diluted Swarmer filth in their systems. Don't get me wrong, this contagion is going to be bad, but it won't be the end of the world. The authorities will eventually see what's going on, and they'll stop it." Paul pulled her through towards the field. "If we don't put down the ones that caused this, we really will be facing Armageddon."

Darlene knew he was right and tried to get a grip on her out of control feelings. "What's wrong with me, Paul? I'm a vampire for crying out loud. I'm supposed to find all this blood, death, and gore exciting!" They stopped by the dry stone wall that separated the two fields. Just like in this field, there were very few in number left now. Both the survivors and the new Swarmers were running away.

Paul shrugged his shoulders. "Honey, I'm not sure. Perhaps me and you are just different? Maybe we are the start of a new clan? Only time will tell, Darlene."

"All you will be seeing is the death of your woman before you join her corpse." Amulius stood up from behind a small tent. He looked at the pair of them before wiping the back of his hand across his mouth. "This is a most interesting development, is it not? I am like I was from waking into this new place. My initial plans, tattered like a Swarmer's cloak." He moved like lightning.

Darlene jumped back, but it was too late for Paul, the First Father had already caught him in his deadly grip. Amulius lifted him up by his throat, then threw the vampire behind him. Paul landed in an untidy heap and didn't move.

"Do not worry, my traitorous woman, he is not yet dead. It is so surprising that he has survived for so long. The essence within him is most tenacious." Darlene's own scream was choked back when he moved again impossibly quick and put both his hands around her neck. "He will not die until I have dealt with you." The First Father looked back at Paul. "I want to find out why that young vampire was able to evade my senses. It will be a useful talent to possess." Amulius gazed into her eyes. "He wakes. Goodbye, my sweet Darlene."

Darlene kicked out with her left foot, striking him in the ankle. The vampire grunted but didn't loosen his grip. Amulius moved his head a little closer, opened his huge jaws. Darlene looked into that cavernous mouth and hoped he wouldn't make the pain last. He then shook he head, slowly closed his mouth, and started to squeeze his fingers.

Darlene felt her vision fade as the vampire applied more pressure. She heard a voice but could not make out the words, the noise of waves crashing against the inside of her head drowned out every other sound.

Her world went grey. There was no pain. Darlene's senses just vanished as the greyness enveloped everything, only the sound of those waves reverberating around her skull held sway now. The sound increased in volume, until the noise was unbearable. Darlene's senses flooded back, bringing an agonizing fury from deep within her body. She snapped open her eyes, seeing that her entrance back from the dead visibly shocked the First Father. She knew his iron-like fingers had crushed her neck, and yet she had not died.

"This is not possible!"

Darlene lifted her arms, pressed them against her chest, then snapped them forward. Amulius suddenly released his grip, and he staggered back and fell over the low stone wall. Her fingers went up to her neck. She ran the tips of her fingers along the deep grooves the First Father had left in her throat, feeling the flesh beneath her fingers expand and fill out. She tried to speak and found the task utterly impossible right now. Instead, Darlene ran to the wall and looked over, expecting to see the First Father still lying there, but he had disappeared.

She leaped over the wall and ran to Paul's still form, knelt on the grass, pressed his head against her chest. Despite the First Father's boasting, Darlene knew he had really hurt Paul. She brushed her hand down his chest, and he moaned when she touched the broken bones ripping though his flesh under the fabric.

Paul looked up into her eyes. "I'm not sure I'll be able to mend again," he whispered, running his tongue over his cracked lips. "All my bones are broken again, Darlene. I'm so sorry, but this time, I really am going to die." Paul exhaled and slowly turned his head. "You're still here, so I'm guessing you put down the First Father. I hope you made him suffer."

Darlene wanted to tell him that he was going to be all right, there was no way she would allow him to leave her, not again. She brushed his hair to the side, then bent down and kissed the top of his head. Darlene tried to move his face back, but he wouldn't shift. She followed his gaze and saw the remaining Swarmer Clan heading in their direction. She choked back a gasp at the sight of her son next to the Swarmer First Father. He looked so different now; Damien was twice his original size.

Paul looked into her face and offered her a single sad smile. "I'm sorry it didn't work out for us, Darlene. Well, at least now we'll die in each other's arms." The vampire closed his eyes.

They hadn't spotted them yet, that much, she did know. Their vampire senses were far inferior to her own. Darlene grabbed the bottom of the tent by Paul's feet and slowly pulled it over their bodies. She closed her eyes, found an opening in her son's mind, and dived inside.

Chapter Twenty

Damien felt something like a cold breeze rush through the inside of his skull. He looked sharply at Eleanor, wondering if the nosy bitch was trying to poke inside his head again. He dismissed the notion as ridiculous. There was no way she'd be able to see his thoughts without him knowing.

"There he is!" Desmonus cried, pointing towards the horizon. "Just look at the dirty coward flee from the battle. It is the only virtue he has left. You can run all you want, my friend. You cannot hide from me. I shall find you, Amulius, and I shall end your miserable life."

"This world is a big place, Desmonus." Damien studied the First Father, watching the man play with his fingernails. His exterior showed a vampire that had succeeded in making sure his plans were fruitful. Below that, though, Damien sensed a great anxiety, as if he was waiting for something else to happen.

The First Father laughed out loud. "You still think like a human, Damien. Our timeline is not measured in days like those pitiful specimens. The Deathgazer Clan will become extinct, that is an absolute conclusion. Time is irrelevant."

"He'll just find another set of humans to restart his Clan."

Desmonus shrugged. "I do not doubt that, Damien. Even so, just like his last attempt, his next effort will also end in failure. His blood, as well as his ideas, belong in the past. This new world belongs to us, to the Swarmers. Thanks to you, Damien, our clan will purge this new land of all that stands in our way." The First Father closed his eyes and smiled contentedly.

Damien rubbed the side of his neck. The multiple bite marks had long since healed, but the humiliation still remained. Just before they had reached the campsite, the First Father had ordered him to lie down. Desmonus had then sat on Damien's chest and told the rest of the Clan to each take blood from his neck. He remembered the brothers taking great enjoyment in ensuring their bites were very painful.

He achieved a great thrill in the knowledge that neither Eleanor nor the First Father knew they were the only original vampires left in the Swarmer Clan. This fact made him very happy. By drinking from him, Damien had become linked to each and every one of them. The only vampire he still could not read was Eleanor, and that was because Desmonus forbade her to drink from him.

Damien now knew that the dozens of new Swarmer vampires the former Clan members had made would listen to him and him alone. He had his own army. Was this why the First Father was so edgy beneath his triumphant exterior? Had he realized that he'd bitten off more than he could chew? He pushed the thought away. He had enough to think about without looking for devious schemes within even more devious schemes. If he wasn't careful, he'd end up just like the bitch standing beside him.

He still needed to sort her out for what she did to him with Sandra. It wasn't fair. Why did he never have any luck with females in his life? The only one who hadn't fucked him over was his mum, and he didn't think it would be too long before that happened. Damien could sense her close by. Bumping into his mum was one meeting he was not looking forward to. How the fuck would he be able to cope, knowing full well she had Deathgazer blood running through her veins? He would have to kill her, there would be no other choice.

Damien felt the female take a step closer. She waited for Desmonus to turn back around. The First Father's eyes continued to follow Amulius's progress as he made his way across the dark fields, heading for the forest. Damien looked at the woman, trying to work out what she was playing at. He shook his head. Damien had no idea what she was doing now. He blanked the bitch and watched the shadow disappear into the trees. Why had his mum not gone with the Deathgazer First Father? He could still feel her presence. There was no obvious sign of her, and Damien wanted it to stay that way.

"We should find the others," Desmonus said. "Their absence is beginning to worry me."

Eleanor laughed. "Why should it, my First Father? You know where they will be. Each and every one of your Clan will be inside one of these little fabric shelters with some young female. Human or changed. Perhaps in Helix's case, even dead." She chuckled. "Allow them a few more moments of pleasure, Desmonus. We both know their responses will be sharper after they are sated."

"It is one answer." Desmonus wandered over to a flattened tent, stopped, and gazed at the fabric for a few seconds. "Eleanor, I sense a great anticipation coming from you. At first, I just thought it was just my suspicious nature coupled with your tendency to construct elaborate games."

Damien couldn't explain why, but he felt a great deal of relief when the First Father moved away from that ruined tent.

"You are playing another game." Desmonus looked directly at Damien. "Yes, I can see that now. He is your unknowing game piece." He chuckled. "That is very clever. I applaud you for your ingenuity."

Damien took a single step away from the female. Something was happening here. He could feel both their emotions rising past the danger point. They were both staring at him as well. For the first time since bumping into these insane bastards, he actually wished the other Clan vampires were still alive.

The First Father suddenly ran over to him. "You mean that they are not?" He wrapped his fingers around Damien's shirt collar and threw him down onto the ground. Desmonus straddled Damien and grabbed the sides of his head. "Where is my clan!" he screamed.

"Leave him alone! If it wasn't for him, you wouldn't have a new army." Eleanor stopped her advance when the First Father extended his forefinger and held it directly above Damien's eye.

"It is wise to stay still, my devious little fox. I shall deal with you once I have extracted the required information from his head. Although I have been inside once, I shall take a more forceful approach on this occasion."

Damien didn't need to read the First Father's mind to realize that he meant his words. "All right!" he screamed. "Yeah, all your original Clan are dead! The Deathgazers slaughtered the bastards. You know what else? I'm glad of it too." Damien shut his eyes; he had just one chance left. The newborns would save him, they had to. Their only purpose was to obey his commands. Just like his was to obey the First Father's word. Well, fuck Desmonus; he had no intention of losing an eye and probably half his brain just because the First Father had lost some of his vampires. "If you hurt me, you loony fucker, what's left of your Clan will tear you apart!"

"You are but a blind lamb, cast into a wolves' den, Damien. Even Eleanor would not try to turn the clan against their First Father. You see, I am the clan. I am their trunk. They are just leaves hanging from a branch."

Feed his paranoia. Give the bastard what he really wants.

He managed to catch Eleanor's eye, trying to work out exactly what she was trying to say to him. Damien was way too stressed out to think clearly. "I don't know what you want!" he yelled.

Desmonus leaned a bit further down. "I want you to tell me why my clan is now dead, and I want you to tell me what you are planning with the she-wolf." He pressed his finger hard against Damien's eyeball. "Time for talk is over."

Tell him the Deathgazers are in this field! Do it now. I can't afford to lose you, my son.

Mum!

"There are Deathgazers hiding in this field." He pointed at Eleanor. "She's the one who's betrayed you, First Father. She told them to kill your Clan."

The First Father slowly climbed off his body and dragged Damien onto his feet. "You are worse than she is. Your lies become more ridiculous the longer I allow you to exist." He threw him at the woman. "Do you see how quickly this one would betray you? You have ripped off more meat than you can chew, my devious wife."

Damien found himself back on the ground when Eleanor pushed him away from her. Eleanor walked straight past him and wrapped her arms around the First Father's waist. She then leaned forward and kissed Desmonus.

Tell them that you're not lying about the Deathgazer Clan hiding, Damien. You only have one chance at this.

"If I'm lying, First Father, then explain where the others are." He leaned onto his elbow. "You can't explain it because they are all dead. The Deathgazers killed them all, just as they are about to kill you two."

Get them to move ten steps back, Damien.

He grinned at them. "I am your First Son, Desmonus. Despite everything, I still believe in the clan, I still believe in you." Damien slowly got to his feet. "I'm supposed to get you to move ten paces back, First Father. By then, you'll be in striking range of the enemy clan. At least, that's what they ordered me to do."

The First Father released Eleanor. "Just kill him, I tire of his games. We have work to complete."

The female vampire ran over to Damien. He watched her jaw elongate like a snake about to swallow a rat. He staggered back, listening to the First Father chuckle behind her advancing form. His amusement suddenly ceased when the ground below his feet erupted. Eleanor spun around and gasped.

"It is a Flesh Dragon. Oh, moon and daughters, not here."

Damian watched open mouthed as some monstrous creature of nightmare equipped with claws the size of daggers burst out of the black soil. Those black claws pushed through the First Father's writhing body and dragged the shrieking vampire back under the Earth.

"Just what the fucking hell was that?" Damien screamed, not too sure he hadn't imagined it. He looked at the disturbed soil, swimming in blood, and knew his eyes hadn't deceived him.

"I was ready to share it all with you, Damien!" screamed Eleanor. "All I will be sharing with you now are my teeth."

She ran forwards, then her body suddenly stopped a couple of feet from him. Damien watched her eyes dim before she fell to the floor. He looked at the man standing in her place, the tip of his sword dripping in red.

"Fuck me! Cade?"

The man nodded, then raised his katana. "It's best that you don't sound so relieved to see me, my old friend. You're next."

"Leave him be, Cade."

Damien looked up to see his mother limping towards them. He glanced at Cade, then at his mum. "So where do we go from here?"

Epilogue

The house seemed so empty without the kids and Darlene. Geoff picked his way around the broken furniture, avoiding the blood stains covering the carpet and the bed. He filled his nostrils with the rank air.

"This is not what I need right now."

He wandered over to the broken window, watching the sun peek through the trees on the horizon.

Dawn had revealed the true horror of last night's violence, mayhem, and slaughter in glorious colour. What survivors that were left now simply wandered aimlessly along the town's roads and pavements. To Geoff, they looked like they had just lived through a World War Two air raid.

He had yet to check on the town's annual visitors. Even from here, though, he could see two columns of black smoke spiralling into the sky. It didn't take a genius to work out that they had been hit pretty badly as well.

Geoff took his mobile phone from his back pocket and speed-dialled a number he had prayed he would never need to ring. The receiver on the other end was picked up immediately.

"They're out," he said. "Both clans, probably." He sniffed again. "Deathgazers definitely. Activate the lockdown, Brother General. Containment is now a level one priority. Scramble the missionaries and arm them. I'll contact you again once more information is available."

He pushed his phone back into his back pocket and walked over to the wardrobe. He had received no word from any of the other operatives in town, so he had to assume they were either dead or changed, which, he knew, meant the same thing anyway. Geoff opened the doors, noting exactly which dress was missing. He turned and walked back over to the bed and slumped down, putting his head in his hands. Despite his training and despite him knowing this might happen, he still couldn't stop the hot tears from rolling down his cheeks.

To continue in
Woven in Blood – The Hidden Order